SKY
WAVES

P9-BJA-470

Praise for Michelle Butler Hallett

“skill and confidence ... economy and power”

– *Books in Canada*

"a rich and demanding read ... Butler Hallett seems often to be creating from a subliminal place, riding on intuition, unencumbered by the counsel of editors."

– *The Globe and Mail*

“draws from all of her influences to create a genre that is truly her own.”

– *The Calgary Herald*

"her characters speak from the margins of society, or of their own sanity ... her writing is succinct and taut, her topics both universal and so offbeat as to be genuinely original, and her manner spare and unsparing.”

– *The Telegram*

"Sanity, madness, torture in the name of science – *Double-blind* is wonderfully original while chillingly based in history. It really shook us up. Through the chronically self-deceived mind of the narrator, the novel delves into profound questions of ethics in a morally ambiguous world, and comes up with tragically ironic answers. The writing is incredibly layered, with metaphor and symbol perfectly balanced against the hard neutrality of scientific language."

– *Sunburst Award Jury*

a novel / a drew

Michelle Butler Hallett

St. John's, Newfoundland and Labrador
2008

Canada Council for the Arts
Conseil des Arts du Canada

Canada

We gratefully acknowledge the financial support of the Canada Council for the Arts, the Government of Canada through the Book Publishing Industry Development Program (BPIDP), and the Government of Newfoundland and Labrador through the Department of Tourism, Culture and Recreation for our publishing program.

Cover Design by Paddy Moore
Layout by Joanne Snook-Hann
Printed on acid-free paper

Published by
KILLICK PRESS
an imprint of CREATIVE BOOK PUBLISHING
a Transcontinental Inc. associated company
P.O. Box 8660, Stn. A
St. John's, Newfoundland and Labrador A1B 3T7

Printed in Canada by:
TRANSCONTINENTAL INC.

Library and Archives Canada Cataloguing in Publication

Hallett, Michelle Butler, 1971-
Sky Waves / Michelle Butler Hallett.

ISBN 978-1-897174-33-3

I. Title.

PS8615.A3925S59 2008 C813'.6 C2008-904389-8

“The carrier waves which are sent out by a radio station may be divided into two categories: first, the ground waves, and second, the sky waves. During the daytime the sky waves have no effect upon the coverage of the station because they travel upward and are lost, but at night these sky waves play a very important part because they go up and hit the Kennelly-Heaviside layer and are reflected back to the earth. ... It is this reflected sky wave that causes fading, inasmuch as the fading area exists where the ground wave of the station interferes with the reflected sky wave of the same station. Despite the faults and unreliability of the sky wave, a very large proportion of the radio audience depends upon sky-wave reception for its evening programs.”

—Waldo Abbot and Richard L. Rider,
Handbook of Broadcasting:
The Fundamentals of Radio and Television, (1937) 1957.

drew n.

1. In ‘knitting’ a fish-net, a certain number of meshes formed in a row. … ninety-eight meshes in a drew.

—*Dictionary of Newfoundland English*,
edited by G.M. Story, W.J. Kirwin and J.D.A. Widdowson.

“i’ve been crying all of my life
but here, entwined in sinew and fire”

—Hey Rosetta!, “open arms.”

“And I was so afraid
I have travelled so far
Blaming the horizon
And shouting at the stars
Oh I was so afraid
But I’ve come so far
Oh I was so afraid
But I’ve come so far.”

—Amelia Curran, “Scattered and Small.”

STATIONS

SPARK

1. SNOTTY VAR
in which Nichole Wright explains herself.

May 14, 2008

My uncle crashed his Tiger Moth.

Great-uncle, really, if you're going to get particular, and yes, all Robert Wright's duty, defiance, anger and hope fell out of the sky seventeen years before my birth. Yes, *that* Robert Wright, the one who started VOIC Radio. Money's involved. Social standing, too. And dogs. Like Atlas in that tiny photo, a saddled Newfoundland with my father at four astride his back, fat little legs kicking the dog in the ribs, Robert standing to one side, hand out in case his nephew fell, peering at the photographer, smiling, worried. I thought the dog had been a bear. Two hundred and seventy pounds, Atlas weighed, huge even for his breed, seven feet two inches nose to tail. The saddle fit.

The dog at the crash site, Artemis, stood almost as high as Atlas, the story goes. Big enough for a lost girl to ride out of the woods. No saddle. No celebration. Because my uncle crashed his plane looking for that girl. Some people tell me the missing one was a blind boy lost near Windsor Lake, or a toddler who'd wandered into a quick fog on Topsail Beach, or an adolescent madgirl who, all glassy-eyed with her own voices and visions, chased something no one else saw into the woods. That last one would make the best song or the longest book, so it can't be what really happened, but Robert did take up his plane for all sorts of lost ones.

Turns out my great-uncle sought a girl called Rose Fahey, a Catholic, who lived in Riordan's Back, on the other side of the inlet from the mostly Methodist Port au Mal, where my crowd of Wrights came from. You'll find Port au Mal and Riordan's Back on the map not too far from Harbour Grace. God, Port au Mal ... the dead walked the earth out there on Sundays, while the living kept themselves inside, except the children, who got shoved and booted out to play in all kinds of weather for the sake of fresh air – stink of it: diesel, guano, fish guts, salt. The Sunday attractions in Port au Mal didn't help: stacked lobster pots, moored trawlers, drawn lace curtains and two services, morning and evening, in that airless clapboard church. Once, accidentally visiting an elderly great-aunt in 1978, I attended evening service. I say accidentally visiting because Dad had taken me out to Port au Mal to look at a small piece of land already willed to me by my grandfather, William Wright. Not that I expected that vicious badger ever to die. Gibraltar would crumble, seas rise, sun explode, and my grandfather would persistently stand where once he stood – at the edge of the water, burning alder in a holed oil drum, rubbish piled on either side – hunched. Land. Well, Dad looked at the land while I studied the hard froth on a balsam fir: snotty var. Then, with a twig, I pricked turpentine cysts on a spruce. Really, I think Dad just got me out of the house so Mom could get some sleep after being up all night with me and my fire dreams, and my throwing up. My grandfather had intended to divide the land between all of his grandsons, then, if anything remained, among the granddaughters, but I, being the only infant to slip the crib death snare, won the jackpot.

So. The ancestral home. Port au Mal, 1978, a good century removed in culture and accent from that throbbing metropolis St. John's, where we got American television, Canadian television, CBC radio and BBC radio, as well as VOIC and VROM; Port au Mal, sliced out of time and dropped at random, like a boulder by a glacier. That sounds like St. John's, too. Regardless, Dad's car broke down. A dozen or more gulls circled overhead, quiet. Dad scowled at the coming fog, until he took my hand and we slipped and stumbled over lichen and rocks to an old house Dad thought he recognized from a photograph, or at least remembered being told he should recognize it. The thin and wrinkled lady opening the door stood just an inch over me – and me only seven years old. Her green eyes, her heavy brow, splotched hands – well, thinks I, there I stand in a century, because she had to be at least a hundred and twelve, and because she ported the same forehead and eyes as every other birthed-Wright. She recognized Dad, called him William's Stephen, and Dad called her Aunt Ellen. She listened to his story of the car, of it being Sunday with no chance of a tow, of needing to get me back into town, school tomorrow. Aunt Ellen nodded, then told Dad she did not have a telephone. She smelled funny – kerosene. Fog became drizzle, so my hair got wet in no time. Aunt Ellen said something about neighbours having a telephone, but it would be a bit of a walk and then a bit of a wait. Perhaps Dad would like Aunt Ellen to look after me while he straightened out transport? Perhaps Aunt Ellen could take me out to evening service?

Dad said yes. Dizzy, I held Aunt Ellen's hand. She smoothed her soft fingers over my cuticles, informed me that young ladies do not bite their nails, and walked very quickly to the clapboard church. We passed quiet front yards where dogs ate their dinner but watched us all the same.

Aunt Ellen wore a dress, stockings, black high-heeled shoes, and a plastic headscarf. Her coat, like her dress, fell at mid-calf. Long dark hairs grew at the edges of her mouth, and long white hairs curled up under her chin. Her eyebrows bushed out thick and black, just like mine would without regular attack by tweezers and wax. Relief there, plucking out chin bristles or brow hairs; I tweezed something daily. But Ellen's thick lips – red, almost winey, no feathering or bleeding of lipstick – lovely. I never learned how to do that, always end up with a smudged and murdered mouth. My hand felt grimy in hers, and my sneakers whopped, undone.

The fog hid the gravestones. Aunt Ellen opened the low church door to evening service.

Evening service. Mostly men. Mostly older. Not one candle, and certainly no electric lights. Evening service meant the intellectual rigour and moral reckoning of prevenient grace, corporeal resurrection, general damnation and the undeniable if inconvenient end of the world, originally scheduled for March 24, 1974 but still coming to the faithful and damned alike. Darkness of interiors. Minister in the dusk, faceless, just robe and words, so gentle, so soft, far beyond the need to compel or convince, self-evident truth of God's grace and displeasure, my brethren, sins of the fathers visited upon the children's children …

That's where I started to cry. Bad dreams and Mom scrubbing vomit out of my blue shag carpet and my new bedspread with the daisies on it, asking me, as she retched herself, if I'd digested a single bite the last few days or just saved it up for the middle of the night; Dad probably lost in the fog and after falling in; diesel and fish guts and this little old lady with her beautiful mouth, and now sins heaped on grandchildren when I'd never wanted the land, didn't even know why anyone cared about a stretch of rock and grass and the remains of a hearth ... Aunt Ellen patted my hand. Men fingered their eyes. Sin omnipresent, my brethren, grace a mystery: only endure. I whispered to Aunt Ellen I might be sick, and the waves of kerosene off her nearly did it. She stood up, took my hand again, and held me in check when I tried to run. Outside, fog had retreated, maybe a mile offshore, and some evening light remained. Aunt Ellen's soft little hand held me fast. Dad nowhere. Within the fog, just this side of the fire rocks, a small iceberg glowed, dully. Physics of it, something to do with refracted light, melting and evaporation, with the ice itself feeding and becoming the fog. Berg bits floated on waves as seagulls would, except the ice decayed. Breaking and beautiful. Only endure.

A terrible day.

Robert crashed in the late afternoon of July 12, 1954, skewed eyesight useful; even his father, old Captain Tobias Wright, had finally to admit his myopic and colour-blind son found things lost within the black and green smudge of spruce and fir.

Once he found this lost girl, Robert shot a flare. Then the engine cut. Sounded. Cut again. And he just dropped. Already flying low, Robert and his little Tiger Moth called *Newsbird*, canvas and balsa wood painted RAF yellow, succumbed to an angle of descent – and to trees. Witnesses cringed, waited for fire. The lost girl emerged from the woods on the back of Artemis. Hardened turpentine ooze, pus white against bark, had attracted the girl, and she'd stopped, burst cysts on another tree and then dropped the twigs into the sudden pond at her feet. Deep ponds opened up like sores in those woods, Dad told me – very easy to fall in and be lost. Perhaps snotty var saved her.

So. Evening of July 12, 1954. A lost child, aged eleven, emerged. Robert Wright, aged fifty-three, pioneer of radio communication in Newfoundland, died. Thomas Wright, Robert's son, struggled with his grief and with VOIC. Newfoundland and Labrador had five years before voted Responsible. And the fog made it too dull to see.

Am I getting through to you?

I need – you see, this is why I am requesting an arts grant of $7,500.00, so I may take the next six months away from my job as copywriter at VOIC Radio. A detailed budget is attached.

With thanks for your consideration,

Nichole Laika Wright.

Because I must write this book.

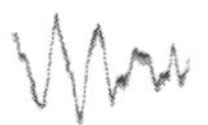

2. CQ 1
in which Robert Wright discovers himself.

1919-1934

Bzht.

Distress. In a small Marconi station in Komatik, Labrador, Robert waited for signals of distress. Spark-gap transmission. Glass jars charged by a big motor generator – storage battery. One cylinder and a flywheel – engine. The flywheel spun hard enough to merit a governor; no need for constant ignition. Spin spin spin ... The engine charged the battery. The battery powered the large spark coil. Robert Wright plucked dots and dashes from the random air and extracted meaning – when he received anything, that is. Howls and whistles in his ears as he logged the utter lack of distress signals, thanking God as he knew he should, yet regretting the boredom. Robert Wright glanced up at a map of Labrador and found himself and the Canadian Marconi Company, the head of a pin, a dot: Komatik, 1919. A few Esquimaux, a few Moravians, one clapboard church, three houses and the Marconi station. What had Cartier said? The land God gave Cain.

Captain Tobias Wright had scowled when Robert told him. —You're going to Komatik? Labrador, dear God, nothing but nuisance birds and deceptive sky. Wireless? Depraved, that is, depraved luxury even to send distress calls, let alone have them received and passed on. How can you trust what you can't see, Robert, you who can't be telling your colours and myopic as a stump? What the hell good is it for you to receive a distress call and then relay all the way down to Fogo when there were no vessels near enough to help?

Considering such encouragement while pretending to read – hating his father – Robert decided Tobias would be proud of a lightning scar down his body. Meanwhile, Melville's devious-cruising *Rachel* found another orphan.

Jane tried to hide her sadness. Then she smiled as though indulging someone and stitched at new woollen underwear for Robert.

Robert could not look at Jane while she handled the garment.

William, who at eleven should have had more sense, tapped Robert's arm. —Shall you see Esquimeaux?

—Of course.

Their mother Hope, who kept the store and the domestic peace, tallied the books. —Tell me again, Robert dear, how spark works. Tell us about Marconi receiving the three dots on Signal Hill.

Ellen, the youngest, coughed. Robert picked her up off the cold floor and cringed, waiting for the Captain's warning complaints: *Don't get so close to her. Avoid her exhalations, for the love of God. She's got a bad cold.* Complicity: *a cold, some bad cold, will she ever be rid of that cold?* Ellen suffered consumption. Once, Robert had been stunned enough to think that tuberculosis marked only the poor and the dirty, the families with streels for mothers. For the wealthy and powerful Wrights, lords of

Port au Mal, tuberculosis in the family seemed about as likely as a detached moon rolling near the well. So, nothing wrong. Ellen must simply be kept warm, fed the best, coddled and disciplined at the same time, schooled at home by Jane who had declined a posting at the school in Ellsworth Bight to teach her sister, but still, nothing wrong.

Now Ellen smiled at the older brother she adored, whose bare temples she now stroked, teasing him. —Your brain's too big for your skull, so it's pushing all the hair out.

Robert hugged her too hard, felt her ribs, her rapid pulse.

Parting gift from his mother: an Ingersoll pocket watch. —It's a Radiolite, Robert dear.

Robert cradled the watch in his right palm. The candle, burnt low, offered little light, but the watch took it regardless. Creamy white numbers, modern and squared, separate second-hand measuring out a minute at a time on the bottom instead of a six, all against a black face. The numbers, hands and brand name glowed greenish-white in the dark, like a captured ribbon of the northern lights. Beautiful, expensive, eerie.

—Mother, I hardly know what to say.

Hope closed her son's fingers over the watch. —Don't tell your father.

Mail to Komatik depended on ice floes and coastal boats. The occasional company of the other wireless operators – collegial enough, two men from Toronto, one from Montreal, all three terrified by strange sky and dark rocks and monstrously tall scarce trees in the protection of the southern bays. Robert did not fear the land, sky or trees. He feared the water, yes, but also something bigger, harsher: the sound of wind tormenting the Moravian church, the noise of utter loneliness.

Robert's heavy spectacles slid down his nose as he pointed at the pin on the map marking Komatik. *Here I be* – no, Mr. Francis would correct that – *here I am, firstborn son of a prosperous family in a prosperous outport, old enough to go to sea but too young to have gone to war.* Younger men had woven extra years, lied and gone to Europe, but Robert's surname imprisoned him. Who would risk Captain Wright's anger by ferrying Robert to St. John's to enlist? Who would dare carry off the eldest son of Hope Jackman Wright, the inlet's main merchant? Robert thought he'd be useful in communications. Tobias reminded Robert of his eyes: *Half-blind fool like you? Give up on it now, because you'll never be a man.* Neither one spoke of Robert joining up after that, just as neither man spoke of Ellen's true illness, or of William's long discussions with the rough and unmarried George Simms.

Robert lined up three spare pins and stuck them in the bottom of the map. Marconi's three dots from Poldhu on December 12, 1901, did not penetrate the aether to wander or decay; that signal bounced off the atmosphere to be heard in St. John's. Marconi heard the Morse code S – if Marconi received the signal at all, if his desire and faith did not create those dots as young men going to war created their years. Plucking out Morse code over static, hiss, whistles and noise like some blizzard of aether – tricky, Robert would agree, even difficult. But if someone received the signal, then the signal existed as surely as rocks. Forces other than human must modulate radio waves – mangle them, obscure them, boot them to another place or time, to another receiver ... Poldhu's signal to anyone who might hear, Cape Cod, St. John's, Komatik, Cape Race, Fogo, Cape Breton: *CQ, calling all stations.* Seek you. Morse code carried on simulated and clumsy continuous waves generated by spark transmitters, bursts of information, the radio wave itself sounding like a spark: *bzht*, and then the information; *bzht,* like a warning, a clearing of the throat; *bzht* and information. The expertise: men not only patient enough to tune but smart enough to recognize sulphate corruption on plates; men steady enough to listen, quick enough to act.

Shifting sandbars at Sable Island, massive and fragile towers at Cape Breton. Learning the trick to soap the back of his neck and thereby feel clean even after a day of heavy gear, grease and spark. Glace Bay nearly home, nearly right. Attending socials and suffering examination by mothers, usually dismissed for his bad eyesight but tolerated for his clean nails and exquisite courtesy. Helping to set the reception of the Ottawa time check at Camperdown. Communicating with ships at sea. Sparky, Spark, the Marconi Man, the Wireless Man, Robert Jackman Wright, respected not for his surname, for being merely his father's son, but for what he could do, respected for who he'd become.

Boston in 1930, teaching now for RCA, paid very well and courting Miss Etta Cleary. Then encountering, in a new class, a face and body language familiar before its owner opened his mouth – Newfoundlander, from Riordan's Back, about ten years younger than Robert: Richard Fahey. Robert took care not to comment on voice that morning, took care not to speak to Richard Fahey at all – mustn't risk favouritism. Fahey persisted, smiling, offering news of Riordan's Back and Port au Mal, of the rest of Conception Bay. Once Fahey passed, despite Robert having been particularly hard on him, the friendship began. Richard stood for Robert when he married Etta, and Richard promised to watch after Etta and the children in 1932 when Robert returned to Newfoundland, tasked by a St.

John's merchant named Canning to build a transmitter so he might advertise his store, Port of Call, to anyone in range with a wireless set.

Some frenzied genius seized Robert then. Fruition: years of learning, years of patience, and now, time to create. Sleep decayed, fell away. At four in the morning, he'd sit up in bed and sketch plans for his independent radio station.

Despite Robert Wright showing what several commissioners called *moral enterprise*, his ideas and vigour displeased the Commission, for this particular show of moral enterprise could not yet be taxed. So necessary paperwork got delayed, got lost. Weeks piled up. So did snow. One January morning, 1934, in the hearing of many on Duckworth Street, Robert briskly informed Commissioners Gulliver and Grant-Mainwaring that they understood nothing of business and radio because they hadn't got the sense God gave a louse. After this burst of information, a quiet decision infected the Commission: whatever plea, request or proposal that came to the Commission with the remotest attachment to Robert Wright would be delayed or denied. Grant-Mainwaring disagreed, but communications did not fall into his portfolio, and the fog and the rocks and the utter contrariness of Newfoundlanders tired him. One glimmer of success in a man, and his fellows hauled him back down. How they turned on one another. Just as his wife seemed to turn on these people with her clipped common sense; yet she brought candy whenever they travelled outside St. John's: *For the children, dear, they have nothing.* She gave it sensibly, first calculating numbers, then rationing it equally to bony, dull-eyed youngsters, more than once explaining they should eat the gift. Grant-Mainwaring could not quite articulate why the candy, or even Newfoundland, irked him so, and he did not try to explain it to his wife.

Robert Wright's transmitter for Canning's Port of Call worked beautifully – startling, really, raw twentieth-century technology coalescing in the fingers of a man in nineteenth-century dress. Robert Wright's voice – beautiful, too, his accent now a curious blend of throaty Boston, broguing St. John's, glottal Port au Mal, and hard-palated BBC. Etta's letters diminished; Robert hardly noticed, and the sky clouded and cleared, released rain and snow; the townies bought wireless sets, and the Commission's radio station made its broadcasts, but Robert's repeated proposals to the Commission of Government for his own station?

—We gave up the right to vote for shoddy mistreatment?

Commissioner Lee, one of the three Englishman, corrected Robert.

—You people aren't fit for the vote. We're doing what's best for you.

Protesting murmurs from the three Newfoundland Commissioners, and from Grant-Mainwaring. Robert slapped his fourth complete proposal down on the Commissioners' table and strode out of the room, jaw so tense his molars ached for days. Gulliver, a Newfoundlander, picked up the proposal and glanced at the title page – *Plans for a Private Radio Station of 10,000 Watts, Capable of Reaching the Southern Portion of Conception Bay* – before throwing it on the fire. Grant-Mainwaring's spectacles reflected the flames as he scowled, taking care not to remember which Commissioner had just done that and smirking just a bit when he realized a man as stubborn as Robert Wright possessed many copies of that proposal, and he'd likely typed them all himself, two-fingered pecking in poor light.

More Water Street stores got radio licenses and broadcast music and their own advertisements. Robert lost a great deal of sleep and wrote Richard Fahey a great many letters.

William, visiting his older brother, shook his head. —Got a scowl on you that looks like it's carved into rock, got black sacks round your eyes, and you're losing your hair.

Robert ignored him – or perhaps didn't hear him – and spoke beautifully and at some length about radio improving the lot of Newfoundlanders, about the need to connect the rest of the world, about communication; William interrupted.

—Our gold.

Robert looked up.

William smiled. —My share of the Wright family gold coins. Turned twenty-five and got my share.

Suddenly very tired, Robert shook his head.

—Robert, you need to finance your own station somehow. No one's going to give you a transmitter.

—I'll bloody well build that myself.

—Out of what? Spruce boughs and sailcloth?

Robert studied his brother. They looked enough alike to be thought twins by strangers. —How is Ellen?

—You tell me. The San is here in St. John's.

—I've been busy.

William wrote to Ellen regularly and read of her boredom and misery – but no sense telling Robert that. —Take my share of the gold. Those coins have got to be worth a small fortune by now.

—William, I cannot take your gold.

—You're not taking it. I'm giving it to you.

—Those coins have been in the family since – since God knows when, divided amongst the sons –

—Until we've got sons fighting over the one remaining coin? A stunned tradition. Here.

William placed a small black velvet bag on the table before Robert.

—That's my share. George Simms been after those coins for years, offered me thousands. I wouldn't sell. Be like selling my birthright. Giving it is different. You take those coins, and you go see George Simms. And you know what else I say, Robert? Fuck the Commission of Government.

Simms, a fat and pale barrister living in St. John's these days, recognized the coins' value and paid well. Simms smiled hard enough to crinkle his eyes. —Small price to own pieces of the Wrights.

Robert ignored him.

Richard Fahey wired more scarce cash and his solemn oaths of business partnership from Boston. Together Wright and Fahey would change Newfoundland, plough it up, truly serve an illiterate populace crying for guidance. God, the educational possibilities of radio alone! Robert finally slept, quite unwillingly, suddenly unable to get out of bed for seven days. He kept dreaming of the coins, of the shocking weight of forgotten treasures. European gold coins hauled across the Atlantic in 17-something by ancestor Jeremiah Wright. Obtained, how? Wright even his real name?

Sudden letters, same post, three from Richard Fahey, two from Etta, 1936 – four years? Four bloody years since he'd left his family to build a radio station, since Etta stopped saying *I love you*? Cool with him on his last visit about sixteen months ago, all nag, *Robert, look at me, are you listening?* Richard as good as his word, good as gold, sailing with Etta and the youngsters from Boston. Soon, on the foggy waterfront, Robert welcomed his oldest son, Thomas, so tall now, a great big boy of five, welcomed his daughter Marie, four, struck by her toddling after Thomas with steady determination, and welcomed Etta, thin and sickly, a six-month baby girl in her arms –

Etta met his gaze, dared him a moment to ask, flushed dark red.

Quick math. Sixteen months. Yes. Yet she'd not written a word of another child ...

One did not speak of such things. One did not even think of them. Could not be. Etta his wife, the baby *his* daughter, despite Etta's face deformed by quickly exposed guilt...

Robert shook Richard's hand, thanked him for seeing his family safely home, and then turned away, plagued by his father's voice: *You'll never be a man, Robert.*

His wife. His daughter. Carry on, for the love of God.

Robert checked the time, first catching the reflection of his face in the back of his pocket watch. Tired, so very tired ... delighted at the weight on his arms as Thomas pulled at him, and he knelt down to smooth the children's hair when he really wanted to embrace them. Thomas stood very straight, the baby fussed, and Marie questioned Thomas, over and over, pointing to Robert.

—Who dat? Who dat? Who dat?

3. AN OBITUARY
in which journalist Rose Fahey neither explains nor discovers the late Jack Best.

Globe and Mail, April 9, 1994.

Building the Boat: A Study of John Edward Best, Prime Minister of Newfoundland and Labrador.

The Republic of Newfoundland and Labrador has lost its main architect. John Edward Best, fondly known as Jack, died in the Estuary Rest Home on March 24, 1994. A lawyer, Jack Best came to political prominence in the mid-1940s when the question of Newfoundland and Labrador's future was hardest to answer. Best campaigned for a return to Responsible Government versus confederation with Canada, and the decision in March of 1949 demonstrated the split of opinion: Newfoundland and Labrador elected not to join Canada by 51 percent.

This split dogged Best throughout his career. The opposition party retained a robust number of seats in each election, and Best won his own seat by narrow margins. Twice, in 1955 and 1966, the opposition pushed for and got referendums on joining Canada. In 1955, the population voted 54 to 46 to remain a republic. In 1966, the vote was 55 to 45. Public opinion on the expense and inconvenience of referendums was reported in minute detail by VOIC Radio, the republic's major radio network. This worked to prevent further serious questions of statehood.

Best entered immediately into economic partnerships with several American and European firms, arranging for development of mines, hydroelectricity and pulp and paper. Social changes after 1949 in Newfoundland and Labrador were rapid. Best promised to electrify the island by 1951 and Labrador by 1952. Most homes were electrified by 1953, with some notable exceptions in rural Labrador. In 1955, the government removed education from the control of the churches, a move which caused much upset and nearly cost Best and his party the next election. Best insisted that money saved from duplication of education services could then be invested in the cottage hospital system.

A particular challenge facing Best's government was distance. Many people on the island lived in scattered and isolated outports or on tiny islands offshore, to say nothing of Labrador. Unexpected investments in telecommunications went some way to solving these problems, with a favourite exaggeration being that many small outports had radios, telephones, televisions and even computers before they had a paved road.

After successfully developing hydroelectricity at Menihek and Hubbard Falls in Labrador, on the Exploits and Humber Rivers in Newfoundland, and then experimenting with wind power in Wreckhouse, Best's government brought to Newfoundland and Labrador a new prosperity. Discoveries of nickel and, later, oil and uranium, as well as the sale of hydroelectricity to Ontario and the state of New York, kept the republic economically self-sufficient.

Despite a wide vision, Best was thought by some to be narrow-minded, as he tolerated no dissent within his party after losing his first motion in 1949. His catch-phrase, "There's the right way, the wrong way, and the Best way" was often parodied in comedy routines. Best fired thirteen cabinet ministers between 1956 and 1975, breeding the likelihood of unimaginative yes-men rising to the heights of political power. Political historian Clancy Morrow explored this problem in his 1981 biography of Best, *Best Man for the Job*. The resulting stagnation led to dissatisfaction within younger party members, with three of the most promising crossing the floor within one week. In an interview broadcast on VOIC Radio in 1982, Best claimed that generational alienation was part of his long-term plan: "I'll force the spark and passion in the younger generation by pissing them off, if I have to. We've gone soft."

Another troublesome feature of Best's rule was his intimate involvement with Newfoundland and Labrador's broadcasters. Best was a longtime friend of Robert Jackman Wright, who started and controlled VOIC Radio until his unexpected death in 1954. When VOIC Radio passed to Wright's son, Thomas, Best soon placed the younger Wright on various advisory committees and eventually on the Board of Directors of BRATNL, the

Broadcast Regulators Association in Telecommunications of Newfoundland and Labrador. No other media-owner ever served on the BRATNL Board, and while no wrong-doing was ever proven or even formally proposed, suspicion remained about the potential despotism of information when the country's major radio network was so closely tied to the government.

Best governed Newfoundland and Labrador without interruption from 1949 to 1975. In 1962, scandal rocked the government. Backbencher Lorne Goodyear was caught in the background of a VONB-TV live *vox pops* soliciting a prostitute. Far worse for Best was the embezzlement of government funds, and subsequent flight to Argentina, by Minister of Resources Gerald Canning, followed by the revelations of Nazi wartime activities of electrical engineer Johann Haldorf.

In 1975, aged 74, Best suffered a mild stroke. Six weeks later, having recovered his power of speech, he announced his retirement. An election shortly followed, handily won by the former opposition. That party is still in power today.

In retirement, Jack Best remained a vibrant figure, often touring schools. Grade five students in Newfoundland and Labrador are required to memorize what has become known as the "Mess of Pottage" speech that Best made during the Debates in 1948 and 1949. Best often judged impromptu recitations of this speech, a task he is rumoured to have disliked. In the late 1970s and early 1980s, Best lobbied for international aid in patrolling the republic's declared two hundred mile limit on the fishing grounds of the Grand Banks. Canada and the United States rebuffed Best, but Portugal did offer to come to aid in exchange for certain privileges within the limit.

The point became moot in 1992, when, despite decades of economic diversification, Newfoundland and Labrador was devastated by the long-warned collapse of the northern cod stocks. At Republic Building on February 14, 1992, Newfoundland and Labrador fisheries minister Doug Kelsey was preparing to make the announcement by television to a group of angry fishers locked outside. It was estimated over five hundred men and women gathered on the lawns and roads around Republic Building. Jack Best, fearing a riot, and, he later said in a lighter moment, not looking forward to picking Kelsey out of the Bubble in St. John's Harbour, stood on the sidewalk in front of Republic Building and addressed the crowd. Shortly afterward, mounted police were able to disperse the crowd without use of force.

On the Republic Building steps that day, however, Mr. Best suffered the first in a calamitous series of major strokes which soon rendered him an invalid in the Estuary Home. He regained his speech twice more but was unable to walk or feed himself.

Jack Best's wife Colleen died in 1942, and their one child, a daughter, died in 1940. In 1951, in a move highly unusual for the time, Best adopted an infant girl whom he called Calliope, and raised her with the help of his older sisters. Jack Best is survived by daughter Calliope Best, and granddaughter Claire Furey, recently shortlisted for a Republic Emerging Artist Award for her untitled mural featuring a man's arm under a seal pelt reaching for a bowl.

Columnist Rose Fahey was born in Riordan's Back, Newfoundland, and lives in Toronto.

4. CONTINUITY 1
in which VOIC Radio explains independent broadcasting.

TEST CENTRE 1:23

Logged to play at 4:59a and 11:59p M-F, 4:59a S & S.
Run dates: June 1, 1967-TFN

INSTRUCTIONS: Cart off three copies, one for control room, one for production, one for the safe.

VOIC Radio is a proud broadcaster in the Republic of Newfoundland and Labrador. The VOIC Radio Network covers the island, with stations and repeaters from St. John's to Port aux Basques, to Baie Verte and St. Anthony, the Southern Shore and the Burin Peninsula. VOIC blankets Newfoundland! Since 1936, VOIC has brought you the news before anyone else. International, national and local: VOIC Radio is there. The VOIC Radio Network is proud of the role it has played in the development of Newfoundland and Labrador, from broadcasting the referendum debates of 1948 and 1949, to its penetrating journalistic coverage of the news of this moment. VOIC is committed to Newfoundland and Labrador. VOIC is committed to you. For that reason, 570 VOIC in St. John's has installed generator backup. In the event of a power failure, VOIC will remain on the air, because you depend on it. In the event of a power failure in an outside network station, said station will switch automatically to 570 VOIC St. John's. Great expense? No. Great investment, investment in the people of Newfoundland and Labrador. And 570 VOIC is the only broadcaster, radio or television, in Newfoundland and Labrador to have installed such a rigorous fail-safe. Even when all else is dark, VOIC is there, still a leading light. As a responsible broadcaster, the VOIC Radio Network adheres to the rules and regulations of the Broadcast Regulators Association in Telecommunications of Newfoundland and Labrador and to BRATNL's high standards of integrity in news delivery, commentary, musical selection, advertising material, and live audience call-in. Should you at any time have a concern with something you have heard on any station of the VOIC Radio network, your first step should be to contact that station. If, after contacting the station and receiving a written reply as spelled out in BRATNL regulations paragraph five subsection twenty-seven, you continue to feel your concerns are not sufficiently addressed, please direct your comments to BRATNL, PO Box 8570, St. John's. VOIC. Connect to the whole world on VOIC.

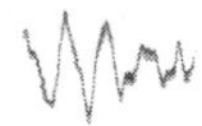

5. SILVERN VOICES 1
in which VOIC *Free Line* host Neal O'Dea speaks in the voice of a common man.

August 28, 1965, and September 14, 1984

Angry and sick, salt spray drying on his face, Neal O'Dea patiently explained to visiting American Calvin Bryson that he owed his nausea to stings, not the swell. Neal had never vomited out on the water, until today – twice now. Two hornets had stung Neal's hand as he'd cast off lines on the wharf – the insects stunned by cool air, aggressive – this on a beautiful Saturday eaten out by unpaid work for VOIC when he'd already punched his regular week on the air hosting the *Free Line* call-in show. Trapped on board Thomas Wright's bright yellow motor yacht *Newsvoice* and expected to entertain Bryson ... no, not seasick, but, in his father's vernacular, *poisoned.*

Bryson owned BrightSun Engineering, the major partner with the government in Newfoundland and Labrador's hydroelectricity grid. Bryson also owned a goodly part of Thomas Wright's desire. Thomas Wright owned the VOIC radio network, and he hoped Bryson would invest in the network's expansion. So Thomas had ordered Neal duly to impress the American: *You sound smart, Neal. You talk to him.* Disgusted with Thomas, and himself, Neal had agreed, adding he'd planned to visit his father that Saturday, so perhaps Mr. Wright could drop him off in Riordan's Back?

Feeling quite runty at five foot three next to the six-foot Bryson, Neal almost didn't hear Bryson's question.

—Which one is Riordan's Back?

Newsvoice had entered a deep and narrow inlet of Conception Bay. Neal opened his eyes and pointed; the hornet-sting rash had spread up his forearm. —Over there. Port au Mal's on the other side. Mr. Wright's family is from Port au Mal.

—Is it true that one community is Catholic and the other Protestant?

Neal smiled. —Oh, yes.

—And you. Thirty-six and a broadcaster. Never wanted to be a fisherman?

—Father had me out a few seasons, but he really wanted me to know something else. I did the elocution course at the Normal School and went off to Canada.

—University of Toronto, Mr. Wright tells me. Just like that?

Just like nothing. —Worked for campus maintenance. I audited a fair bit, but you don't get any credit for that. My brother John likes to say I'm the most educated man in Newfoundland, but I can't prove it. Worked the mines a while, Ontario, Quebec, New Brunswick. Came back for Labrador, then went down in St. Lawrence after fluorspar, then back to Ontario. Shaft-sinking when I got out of it. Good money. Nearly drowned once. Nowhere near the ocean. Hanging on to a ten-foot rock two thousand feet under, drowning nonetheless, apologizing to my father. Synge would have loved it. Riders to the shaft.

Missing much of this – wind, context – Bryson squinted. —I studied anthropology myself. Are these stages?

Neal felt hot shame. Just a moment of it, a shard, but shame, undeniably. Rickety houses, perched on thin sticks, lacking only one goodly push to collapse them clacking into the sea. No insulated bungalows here, no cul-de-sacs and front lawns, no carports. Riddle fences, outbuildings, backkitchens, all to an unaccustomed eye sprawling but in fact organized by kin, convenience and good use of old materials. Tied to the stages, neglected dories bobbed. In a few weeks, or maybe tomorrow, schooners under sail would return from the northeast shore and the Labrador where men prosecuted the fishery and still said *prosecuted* – phantoms, old photographs, shedding sepia with each movement. Schooners under sail, yes, but Bob Jackman in Port au Mal had bought a trawler, and the fish plants paid by volume. Neal frowned. *Nineteen sixty bloody five.*

A rag of stench on the wind from the plant farther up the bay at Little Cut Head – Bryson did his best not to sneer; behind him, Thomas Wright complained, his loathing of fish guts clear. Neal's stung hand burned hard. Mines: holes in darkness for asbestos, uranium, gold, fluorspar, more than nets, for the love of Christ, more than fish. Ripping a living then, the way an angry child would rip pages from a book, ripping it out of the water, out of the rock, split, gut and dry, pry, comb and pack, cod strangely blue under water, Blue John strangely beautiful and sudden in dull rock, rip it out, truck it off, sleep in camps more like prisons. All this moneyed brutality while Neal's father Ange kept a root cellar and mended nets by hand. Then Neal recalled feeling mortified at U of T when he referred to a Bach fiddle partita – mortified then, furious now, mostly with himself.

Bryson pointed to land, to the black wires drooping slightly between poles. —It's all in place. Electricity. Telephones. Most people have a radio. Television's not far behind. Gold mine. A society like yours has an easier time adapting to new media.

Neal's accent clotted up in anger. It did that, precisely at moments he did not wish it. —A society like mine? Backwards, you mean?

Bryson winced. —No, no. I mean pre- …

—Pre-literate?

—Pre-industrial. No. What I'm trying to say – Mr. O'Dea, please, a pre-industrial society like yours has not forgotten its milieu of oral culture, has not pried itself –

Neal hoisted himself onto the wharf. The engine idled; Bryson's voice carried now.

—Listen to me. Your society already understands how small the world is. Connections. Wires and names, shared piers and outbuildings – is that what they're called? You people understand that if one man takes a leak in the well, we all suffer.

Not caring that Thomas Wright stared hot corrupting death at him, Neal strode away from the dock. Bryson's voice thinned back into the thrum of the yacht's engine, and the wind changed, carrying fog.

The garbage I put up with for Thomas Wright. Come Monday morning, I'll be hauled apart.

People like mine.

Neal walked towards his father's house, sports jacket, chinos, acrylic sweater and white Keds as incongruous in Riordan's Back as a palm tree.

Yet he walked like his father, bent slightly at the small of the back as though fighting a headwind.

Ange O'Dea, who occasionally still needed to explain that *Ange* rhymed with *flange*, not *range*, had unofficially retired from fishing. His sons Neal and John, and even young Fabian, wealthy and often thoughtless up in Canada, pooled sufficient money to keep him off the water and took turns paying his utility bills. So now Ange spent his days cutting wood, picking berries, and looking after maintenance at the district schools. And baking delicious bread. Neal had no idea when or where his father had learned to bake, but the old man's bread won prizes at the church fair each summer.

Ange stood waiting for Neal in the kitchen, at the back of the house. Suddenly, everything smelled right: tar paper, spruce splits, birch smoke, baked bread and that metallic scent, almost like salt water or spilled blood but muskier, that came off Ange himself. Ange nodded to his son, to the one he'd dreamt for years would drown, and finished spreading margarine over the tops of the loaves. Neal nodded back, helped himself to the teapot.

Ange carefully folded the wax paper. —Take some berries over to Jeannie Hicks in a minute. What are you staring at?

—Your beard.

—Shaving's a nuisance.

Neal hid his smile behind the envelopes he now pretended to study. His father's white hair had gotten a bit long, too. Perhaps Jeannie Hicks liked long hair and a beard.

Between the light bill and the phone bill lay a small envelope from Mrs. Matthew Sexton in Sudbury, Ontario. Neal recognized his sister's handwriting immediately. —Father, you've got a letter from Liz.

Neal heard himself: so professional, radio smooth, much more so than with Calvin Bryson. *Yes now, talking to Father like that.* Modulating his voice into something more believable, Neal read Liz's letter out loud three times, a litany of her children's school grades and shoe sizes, troubles and accomplishments.

Ange smiled. —Her boy now, he takes after you, getting into fights and punching above his weight. And that daughter of hers will be tormenting the boys soon, if she's anything like her mother. I wish … she sounds right proper and far away on the phone. Bread's cooled off by now. You take one of the buckets of berries, and we'll go to Jeannie's.

Outside, surprised at the blue and purple of the rocks – all grey at a distance – Neal asked Ange if Jeannie still feared her radio.

—Don't you laugh. Come twenty years, the youngsters'll have something you're scared of.

—She's only scared because she doesn't understand it.

Sunlight glared hard through the fog, making it painful, despite dullness, to see. Ange pointed at hidden spruce. —So foggy today the birds are walking.

—Just like waves on the ocean. Already there. Radio just harnesses waves and loads them with information, like stuffing a bottle with a message.

—Don't go spilling the berries. Took me all day to pick them.

As the O'Deas walked the shore to Jeannie's house, electric lights flicked on to shine through window after window; in the living room of the grand new Fahey house, a television glowed. Neal called Jeannie Hicks *Aunt Jeannie* – not for blood but respect. Adults other than Neal's parents had all been *Uncle* or *Aunt,* except for the wealthy Wrights in Port au Mal – Captain, Missus, Mister and Miss there.

Ange knocked on Jeannie's back door but did not wait for an answer before opening.

—Nothing is after changing, Neal. When the weather's not civil, women light the lamps. Jeannie? Need you to do me a favour. I'm after picking too many berries, so you got to take some.

Jeannie bustled out of the kitchen, wiping her hands on her apron.

—Angel O'Dea, you're too good to me. Neal, come over to the wall 'til I check your shoulders.

Neal did not hesitate. He kept still while Aunt Jeannie got on a stool and measured the width of his back and the length of his arms, pencilling his boundaries on the wall. Once she got down, she fingered his acrylic sweater. —What in God's name is that? Store-bought, I suppose?

—A gift, Aunt Jeannie.

—Seagulls could knit better. Catch your death in a store-bought. Thought you had more sense.

Neal decided he would not pass this judgement onto Liz, who had sent him the sweater last Christmas; she'd bought it at The Bay. —But Aunt Jeannie –

Ange interrupted, loudly. —Neal's going to fix your radio.

Jeannie glanced round before confessing to Neal. —The voices aren't right. Come in and out, like travelling ghosts. Not that I believe in ghosts. I want to listen to you on VOIC in the mornings, Neal, but I can't find you.

She pointed to a Grundig MusicBoy squatting, somehow malevolently, on the table closest to the window, between an aloe vera and a cherry tomato plant. Neal bent over the radio, thinking of his father's

Hallicrafter Sky Buddy, of the two large knobs and how his younger brother John had wanted to suckle them. Jeannie had enabled a shortwave receiver, not AM. Neal flicked the switch: static in waves, then a distant language, young woman counting.

—Ein, zwei, drei. Ein, zwei, drei.

Jeannie darted back to the kitchen. —See? Voices.

A test signal, the woman's voice pleasant enough, but the steady counting, clearly live from the variations in tone and the sigh at one point, unsettled Neal.

—Ein, zwei, drei.

Ange didn't like it, either. —Turn that off.

Neal enabled AM. Hidden within the noise all the way down to 570 VOIC: ship-to-shore. *—Southbound Two, Southbound Two, this is* Rhonda Grey*, do you read? Over.*

A dim reply from the station Southbound Two. *Rhonda Grey* gave her distance, but particulars got lost in static.

Then: *—This is* Rhonda Grey. *John Dunne has a message for his wife, Anne, in Bangor. Can you relay? Over.*

The signal faded.

Neal continued to VOIC – The Beatles, "Help." —Found it, Aunt Jeannie. Keep the radio like this, and you'll get VOIC.

She nodded, pleased. Then she handed a can of heavy cream to Ange. —Give that a shake so we can have it with the berries. Neal, I'll have you a proper sweater come Christmas. Dark blue. Bring out your eyes.

Neal asked for that sweater the evening he died, after Ange had fed him soup.

6. CULTURE SHOCK 1
in which Gabriel Furey comes of age.

September 2, 1968

Gabriel Furey caught his reflection in the cab's rear-view mirror, and obscuring the view of St. John's behind him. *Head shaved for sacrifice, b'y. Look like I just escaped something.*

The cabbie smiled. —Spruce Court, is it, there by Bond Street?

—How'd ya know?

—You're not the first St. Raphael's boy I've driven there, and I dare say you won't be the last.

Some sort of excitement – fear? – pricked Gabriel's stomach. Free. Eighteen. Out on his own. Done with St. Raphael's Home for Boys. Buzzcut and shave only as old as the daylight, one final mark of Raphael upon him. Mouth open, eyes big, scared as a landed fish.

The cabbie stopped at a red light. —Those little apartments in Spruce Court are all right. Nothing to write home about, but good enough for starting out. Bit of privacy for a change.

Gabriel took care to deepen his voice. —Be all right once I get settled.

—Just stay away from the bars 'til your hair grows out. Anyone can spot you for eighteen with that St. Rape's job. All you're missing is a burning seal on your forehead. Listen, now. There's a superette down your way, open 'til three in the morning. Sell ya stale bread on the cheap.

They drove some more, Gabriel studying the mist. The wipers thwupped.

—Spruce Court, my son.

Gabriel leaned forward. —How much?

—I charges the Church.

Gabriel tried not to watch the cab drive off. Rucksack cutting his shoulder, two keys poking his leg, fraying his pocket – big one for the outside door, little one must be the apartment door ... stink of wax, piss, beer, smoke, sweat, cabbage. The white floor glared. Three floors up. Cheap wooden doors painted primary and secondary colours – Gabriel's key fit the yellow door. A neighbour behind a blue door coughed in harsh futility. Another neighbour played a radio: VOIC, loud and tinny.

Corner apartment – bedsit, really. Kitchenette, fridge and stove. Rustpocked chrome table. One chair, vinyl backpad knifed open. Lights so bright. Bugs in the bathroom, earwigs and carpenters, once-white tub nearly as dark as the latter.

But a toilet with a lid. And no other toilet in the room.

Gabriel Furey had fifty dollars. Brother Michael Stephens leaning forward, desk gone dark and dented, fifty-dollar bill pinched between thumb and forefinger and offered forth like water with berries in it. Gabriel imagined cold metal in his hands, imagined calluses warming, fingers curling – *Copper pipe to the temple. Can't look him in the eye.* Brother Stephens with that one piece of money as though Gabriel must perform one last act to merit blessing. *Now then, Mr. Furey. Your first two months' rent are paid. Take this money and get some groceries. Should tide you over until you get a job.*

Fifty dollars.

Stay away from the bars until your hair grows out.

Brightly lit but losing to the fog, the superette stocked more than Gabriel could imagine ever needing: bread, Spaghetti-Os, toilet paper, Comet powder, sliced bologna, chocolate milk, margarine, peanut butter, and India Ale, the one with the Newfoundland dog on the box, the bottles brown like Gabriel's eyes – that had to count for something.

The woman behind the counter, maybe thirty-five but looking fifty, bulged over her polyester pants as she stared at *Coronation Street* on the small black and white television while tallying Gabriel's purchase. Then, seeing Gabriel's haircut, she took a breath as if to ask him a question, but she let it go.

Spaghetti-Os. Cook. Do I need a match? Electric, electric.

Back to the superette for a can opener and a pot. *Coronation Street* had not progressed.

Gabriel dumped the wet pasta into the pot and then wished he hadn't. He squinted at the can, the instructions like a cipher in moveable type: Heat on wol. Rits foten.

Wol?

He tried again. Hear on low. Stir foten.

Stir, right, got that much. Hear on low – heat? Foten. The fuck –

Stir often.

Fled. Gone without comprehension.

Another neighbour turned on another radio, and the staticky treble racket carried, pierced: *Connect to the whole world on VOIC! VOIC top news. This VOIC Noonday Gun Newscast is a presentation of Kelloway's Old Fashioned General Store. Kelloway's, in the former Mahon's Building on Water Street. Kelloway's, just what you needed.*

Once more, Gabriel tackled the label.

Stir. Fine. I'll stir ya.

In a stiff and dark drawer, Gabriel found a plastic spoon and a bottle opener.

—Well, that decides that.

Two and a half beers in, the smoke started – Spaghetti-Os bubbling and burnt, freedom charred to the pot.

—Fucking stink.

Gabriel knocked over his open bottle of India when the Spaghetti-Os scalded his mouth. He knew he'd dream of ravens and crows that night. Striges, too. Old dread chilled him.

Then he cried.

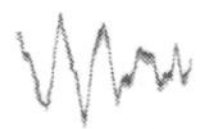

7. THREE DOTS 1
in which Christopher Francis keeps a promise.

December 12, 1901

Just a few minutes after the birth of Robert Jackman Wright back in Port au Mal, Christopher Francis, grateful for his wool jersey, wiped sleet from his face and walked into Mahon's General Store on Water Street, St. John's. A travelling teacher, normally visiting communities up and down Conception Bay, Christopher had come into town on an errand for Mrs. Hope Wright, who needed a letter delivered to her brother on Cochrane Street, a simple errand. Truth told, however, Christopher had come into town for books.

Dark wood and white lettering, barrels of pork, copper pots hanging from the ceiling, fabrics, raisins, tea and coffee, ladies' garments, finally, the books. Surely Mahon's bookshelves were the best part of St. John's. Christopher's fingers brushing the pages of locked and until now, distant treasures: Dickens, Miss Austen, and ah, really? *Typee* and *Moby-Dick.*

A voice murmured at Christopher's shoulder. —'Heaven have mercy on us all – Presbyterians and pagans alike – for we are all somehow dreadfully cracked about the head, and sadly need mending.'

Cost, but my savings. Books so heavy.

Mr. Mahon tried again, a little louder. —Fine day for a good book and a pot of tea.

Christopher looked up. Instead of struggling not to knock off people's hats, he stood struggling not to spend most of his money on books in Mahon's General Store.

Mr. Mahon grinned. He knew the look. —I said, fine day for a good book and a pot of tea. Fine day for a duck, too. Don't know if this fog and rain will let up. Better than the snow, I suppose. You're a reader?

—Teacher. But I have not got much time to read.

Mr. Mahon tapped *Great Expectations* and *Moby-Dick.* —These two will keep you going all winter, if you can afford the lamplight.

—Lamplight, yes.

Mr. Mahon glanced over his shoulder, as though expecting his wife to screech a command. —I got a quiet store here, and nothing now would please me more if you bought those books and sat there to read one. I'll even make you the pot of tea. No charge. For the tea.

—I … thank you. Thank you very much.

Mr. Mahon shrugged. —'Tis all I want to do today myself. It would be the next best thing to watch someone else. That fellow there, Ishmael, teacher like you. Before he went whaling.

Christopher stared down at the book covers. Imported. So expensive.

Mr. Mahon kept talking, gently. —Can't live without books. Named my three sons Kipling, Stevenson and Conan Doyle.

Board free, but new clothes ...

—And Dickens, Dickens now, Magwitch and Estella –

Token donations to families for lamplight. He must have lamplight. But books …

—The most amazing wedding cake …

Christopher could bear no more. —I'll take them. But I cannot stay.

Mr. Mahon's face fell. —You're going?

—I must. Please wrap them well.

—*Great Expectations* and *Moby-Dick*, excellent choices. Are you sure you've not got time for that tea? Not even a cup? Very well, sir.

Ten minutes later, Christopher Francis, spectacles blurred by the freezing drizzle, stood at the bottom of Cochrane Street. Cold air scraped his face, and the books tugged his arm. Yet he'd promised Mrs. Wright he'd visit her brother, Peter Jackman, and give him a letter. So much easier to say Peter Jackman had not been at home, to lose the letter in a gust of wind, let it soak to illegibility in a dirty puddle, to deny the old wound. For shame, that Christopher Francis, grown man and teacher, still gritted his teeth at the thought of Peter Jackman. Christopher tasted seaweed and beach rocks, grass and soil: *nancy boy*. The appalling taunt, untrue but no less humiliating, Peter Jackman and George Simms catching him from behind, knocking him down, two stocky boys atop a bony one, pushing his face to the ground: *nanceeee b'y* whispered in his captive ears, hissed and spittled, and only Peter Jackman, George Simms and Christopher Francis knew of it.

Time. Time gone since then, since boys' foolishness. Standing at the bottom of Cochrane Street, hungry, suddenly hoping Jackman would offer him dinner, Christopher glanced at foggy Signal Hill and hoped tomorrow's newspapers might report on the Italian count's progress – though why Marconi needed a kite to receive a signal from Poldhu … yes, the letter, sister to brother, he must deliver it. Asked a favour. Simply what one does. Christopher turned away from Signal Hill and struggled up Cochrane Street to Jackman's room.

8. DEBATE IN THE HOUSE
in which Callie Best stands up to her father and introduces further problems.

October 10, 1970

In the same kitchen where she'd started flowers from seeds for Brownies, finished tedious homework and eaten many suppers alone, Callie Best now accepted the cup of tea from her father, recognizing it as an opening salvo. Before he could follow with words, she catapulted simple truth. —I'm not asking for your blessing, Dad.

Jack stood in front of the window over the sink. Black sky interrupted by stars, but the stars fled, it seemed, as more and more streetlights went up. —My blessing isn't the issue. Getting married is. Remember that ancient rite, Callie? Did your man Mr. Furey ever hear of it?

—Gabriel wants nothing more to do with the Church.

—And he wants nothing to do with a proper job, either. He turned down that position I got him at the Holyrood Sub-station. There's good money in hydro-electricity.

—Fine pile of painting and sculpture he'll get done stuck between turbines, steam, knobs and ducts.

—Or BRATNL. They always need office clerks.

—Gabriel's dyslexic. I don't think –

—You can't just move in with a man and set up house because you're too addled with lust to think straight. Like some demented call girl.

Early wound. —Dad! I love him.

—Your mascara's running. Take my hanky. You don't need that paint around our eyes, Callie, you're already beautiful.

—I choose to wear mascara.

—Remember the time you came home with your hair cut in bangs, just after I told you not to? Beautiful brown hair you had, all one length and down to your waist, off your forehead …

—Beautiful because you chose it.

—Calliope Ann Best, if you knew what I put up with in the House today … please, don't test my patience any further.

—I love him.

—He's a handsome young fellow, no doubt.

—*Love* him, Dad. Would sacrifice for him. Do you understand me?

—But no daughter of mine, indeed, no Newfoundland girl who holds herself and her family in any esteem whatsoever, will live in sin.

—I am not your old-time toothless electorate. Nor am I some orphan in a diaper. I will not stand here and be told how to think.

She stood three inches taller than Jack. She had been sitting at the kitchen table, but now she got to her feet and put her hands on her hips. She spoke coldly. Jack didn't recognize her.

—Twenty years old, Dad. Age of majority even on this demented navel-gazing treacherous bog of an island!

—Callie!

—I love that man. And I am going to live with him.

Jack steadied himself against the counter and nearly knocked over the teapot. His adopted daughter sounded like his father – how? Five foot six, willowy, hair past her shoulders and still in those thick bangs he disliked, all the way down to her lashes. Now her blue eyes burned within circles of ruined ink. Like he'd struck her. Which he'd never done. Lectures and silence had always kept Callie in line. So now Jack Best retreated behind the mask he wore when Listening Respectfully to the Honourable Member; he sneaked into silence.

—Did you hear me? I am going to live with him.

Jack said nothing.

Callie glared round the kitchen, her favourite place in the house, struggling not to run to the small pantry off the servants' staircase and cry. Then Callie squirmed, jeans and bra too snug. *Already?*

Jack said nothing.

Already. Yeah. Maybe if I threw up on him. —I don't know why I'm arguing with the leader of a republic who calls himself a Prime Minister.

—Prime Minister means first among equals.

Got ya. —But Prime Ministers report to royalty. Who do you report to?

Jack's neck hairs stiffened as his cheeks flushed. —History.

Callie rolled her eyes and put on her coat. Her untouched tea remained on the table. —History, right. Precisely what Gabriel wants to break away from. Start fresh.

She walked out, slammed the door.

No one had ever walked out on Jack Best.

Beyond any pretence of patience now, Jack shouted at the kitchen window, reasonably sure Callie would hear him. —And what in the name of Jesus is his problem with history?

9. MYOPIA SKY 1
in which a dead body barges in on Robert Wright.

September 7, 1913

Dire Sunday boredom.

Robert squinted from a back window, one overlooking the shore, but still could not see, could not decipher. Black mound moving: Casseiopia, the Wrights' Newfoundland dog. She'd barked, one deep rumble – a bad sign. Then she'd run into the water, very intent, out where the shelf fell away, and dove. Surfaced, something dull yellow in her mouth. She dropped it, barked again.

Tobias Wright grunted, rustled his newspaper. —Robert, what is the matter with that dog?

Robert nearly answered that whatever addled Cassiopeia could hardly be his fault, but instead Jane coughed.

Tobias turned a page. —Give it up, Jane.

She took a steadying breath, held it. Her rib cage jerked; several coughs broke free.

Hope put down the Bible. —Jane. Your father asked you not to cough.

—Yes, Mother. I am sorry, Father.

Still hidden by print, Tobias grunted again.

William sniffed. Hope clicked her tongue. Jane swallowed her own saliva desperately, trying to fend off another coughing fit. Tobias shook the newspaper sharply, briefly revealing his face: indistinct flesh, dark pits for eyes, black hole for a mouth. Like anyone else's. Robert stooped when he walked, watching the ground for obstacles. Reading made him ill, small type on flat books drawing him bent so that his neck and shoulders often got sore, so that his head hurt. Smart enough, both Mr. Francis and the travelling nurse agreed, just weak-eyed.

William dabbed at his nose with a hanky. Robert stared out the window, seeking the dark blur of Casseiopia.

Gone under?

Silence.

Casseiopia reared on her hind legs and shoved her front paws against the window, barking once more. Robert screamed and knocked over a lamp. William yelled, Tobias cursed, Hope called on God, Jane coughed so hard her lips went blue, and Ellen, the baby, who'd slept maybe three hours of the last twenty-nine, bawled. The room, darkened by that huge dog blocking the daylight, contracted, so that siblings tripped in one another trying to escape. William helped Jane to her bedroom; Robert darted outside. Tobias threw down his newspaper, snarled at his wife to go quiet the infant, and strode to the back window.

The dog leaned there still, a good four inches taller than Tobias. He stared up at her, at her strands of drool and dark eyes. She barked once more.

—Get down!

No one played or worked by the low shore. Not like near the rock called the Devil's Couch on the high shore. Down on the low shore, currents snatched.

Yellow. Under the water.

The sea sparkled as sunshine fought with fog.

Yellow, rough shape of a man.

—Don't be getting wet.

Accent and grammar almost foreign – religion, class. Young man's voice speaking past the wood separating Port au Mal from Riordan's Back at this deep end of the inlet. Robert knew the sound even though he could not see the face: Angel O'Dea, about his age, from Riordan's Back, carrying a dead rabbit. Robert scowled. Ange's voice had dropped so smoothly, while Robert's shook like slob ice.

—Snares. Didn't be seeing I'd come this far over. How are you, Robert?

Grown men addressed Robert as *Master Wright*. How dare Angel O'Dea –

Casseiopia barked again. Five times in one day, from a dog who might go a year without a sound.

Ange laid the rabbit on some beach rocks. —Something's in the water.

—Yellow. Right there. It shifted. Bide here.

—For the love and honour of God, don't be so foolish.

—How dare you talk so on a Sunday, Angel?

—'Tis Ange, not Angel, as well you know. Or are you so blind that you can't see sense? I know you can't be telling your colours.

—I take no guff from the likes of you.

—You're after forgetting that I am not bounden and owed to your family. You be no captain to me, so you can step out of your father's boots right quick.

—You shall bide here, Ange, while I go for help.

—No good can come of me staying here when I can't be seeing what you're after seeing. Think, b'y. Don Mallory, gone missing in June. Be nice if his missus got something to bury. Might stop those dreams some of the women get, their man lost and tangled up in the seaweed worse than the woods and trying to come home. My mother dreamt that for years.

Tide rattled the beach rocks. Robert said nothing.

—So keep an eye to it, Robert. I'll be getting your father.

—See that you do.

Ange climbed up to the Wright house. —Keep an eye.

Robert stood on the shore with Casseiopia. Foam broke on the low rocks that created it. The yellow shape retreated a few inches.

—Wait.

The yellow shape shifted half a foot now, turned, released a wad of fatback – no, a bloated hand.

—Wait!

Robert ran into the water, hand outstretched for the drowned man's sleeve, and tripped. Pressure roared in his ears, and a current took him. And the corpse. For it had been a man, but which man Robert could never say. He surfaced, swam back towards shore, meaning to get the corpse by the shoulders, but his numb fingers slipped off the oilskins. *Must be green,* Robert told himself, *must be green oilskins, everyone says I call yellow green.* Beneath him, the corpse bobbed, and Robert reached for the shoulders again, but then he'd slipped under water, tumbling, struggling like Jane earlier not to breathe. So cold. Wool sweater a weight. Touch of that white hand, but the sense of peace that's supposed to come of drowning, where – ah. Oxygen deprivation, Christopher Francis had taught him. The airless brain collapses, higher functions cease, the lungs suck in water. Dire peace.

Peace.

Teeth.

Casseiopia at his neck, biting through his shirt and sweater, dragging Robert's face towards the surface, sunlight and fog, pressure and the violence of drawing breath. Two shapes on the low shore, man and boy, indifferent current, cold. Robert twisted against Casseiopia, because if he could be free of the dog, he might get warm under yellow.

Casseiopia heaved Robert ashore.

Tobias, knees clacking on beach rocks, screamed at the sky. Then he took Robert in his arms, still shouting, some of it coherent. —My son. Not taking this one. Mine!

Ange peeled seaweed from Robert's face.

When Hope asked Tobias what happened as they both stripped their son, Tobias sneered. —Half-blind fool fell in.

Ange, crossing the threshold to the Wrights' grand house for the first time, smelled boiled vegetables, just like in his mother's house. —No, sir, he did not.

Jane stumbled with a load of blankets, shocked to see Robert naked. Skin so white, hair so black – when had hair grown *there*? Jane looked instead to the fair O'Dea boy. Had he just dared to contradict Tobias Wright?

Tobias busked Robert hard enough to bruise. —Did you speak to me, O'Dea?

—I said, he did not fall in, Captain Wright.

Robert's teeth rattled, and he moaned.

—Robert saw a body, Captain.

—Robert can't see past the end of his nose. Have you never heard of myopia?

Darkness on the floor; Robert collapsed. His mother quickly covered him, and his father carried him to the daybed. Someone held hot tea to his mouth; he drank, then spoke, looking at Ange.

—Why did I have to see the body?

—'Twas coming ashore.

Tobias scowled. —You saw no body.

More tea. —Why did I have to see him if I couldn't save him?

Ellen screeched, knees drawn up to her belly. Jane soothed her, coughing, while Hope tucked another blanket round Robert. William took Casseiopia outside.

Tobias pointed at Ange. —Mallory?

—I didn't be seeing, Captain.

Brief peace.

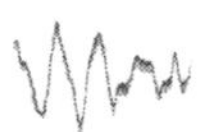

10. EXCERPT WITHOUT REMUNERATION
in which Nichole Wright exposes herself, oh, so craftily.

New from Hangashore Printing! A searing upcoming novel named Once I Stood by young new talent Cassandra Vocum, who is not yet twenty!

As Carla Furlong leaned against the statue of the Virgin Mary on the school grounds, she looked at me quizzically. "Describe it again."

"It's like winking out, like your memory's a star gone behind a cloud, and then you sort of come to in daylight, and you're really not sure how you got there."

Carla said, quietly, with conspiratorial weight, "Does it happen a lot?"

"Not as much as it used to," I hissed. "Or like being blind after your picture's taken, when you can't see after the flash has gone off."

"Nancy," opined Carla with heavy knowledge, "that's not normal."

I wanted to go home so I could roll up my sleeves and cut my arms. I muttered, "I hate getting my picture taken. But I must."

Turn the page for another fall title on Hangashore Printing's list for autumn 1991!

11. SLEEP ARCHITECTURE 1
in which a feverish Claire Furey
discovers herself in the former VOIC studios on Chapel Street, premises which also happen to be her home.

Dec. 12, 1978

Claire threw off sheets and blanket to immediate chill. Driven: no sleep, edges here tipping past existence to a new plane, not so much abyss as rock facings, scraped and worn and descending far past salt water, rock and water each scouring the other, foam the proof. Her sleeveless summer nightdress, when had she gotten into it? Yesterday morning, panties and undershirt – pretending to wear the season's most stylish one-piece swimsuit, strutting, promising herself only another year, or maybe five, before she could wear a stunning two-piece underwear bikini like her mother: Callie, all those curves, lace on her panties, frayed bra gone yellow at the underarms … just not today. No need to call out. The silence of the house – no vacuum hum, no washer thrash, no cooking-pot clang – told Claire her mother had gone out. Maybe that's why the softwood floor dipped, or had the pine gone to sap?

Downstairs then. Where VOIC used to be. Gabriel said their Chapel Street house should be a heritage site. Maybe they could even be live-in caretakers.

Callie's voice once, sharp and ragged, like old steel wool forced to scrub one more pot, as she lifted chips from the deep fryer and shook her head the same firm way she shook the basket. —Living with tourists and placards? Bit tricky, don't you think, Gabriel? People marching around at all hours.

Gabriel still ruminated on the idea some Sundays, once he'd leaned back from his plate of dinner, demolished long before it got cold. —The old control board sat right there, where the chesterfield is now. And they'd smoke and read the news and have preachers in here on Sundays.

A few times Gabriel even played Radio with Claire, spinning his records while she introduced the songs and gave news and weather reports. But she had to wait for Gabriel, because she mustn't touch the record player. —Too precious, Claire my ducky. Needle scratches the vinyl just once, and the whole thing is ruint.

Playing a record often meant a fight with Callie: —Where'd you get the money to pay for that?

Gabriel would sit back on the chesterfield, carefully cross his feet on the coffee table and light a cigarette, daring Callie to deny him the pleasure of a bit of April Wine, KISS, Eagles or Johnny Cash. *Just you dare.* Music helped him draw, he said.

Even then, Callie might stab. —Radio's free, Gabe. Food you got to pay for.

Claire quietly sided with Gabriel. You had control over your records – way better.

Claire sneaked into the living room. The house had gone up shortly after the Great Fire in 1892, in that great hurry to build shelter before snow. Original softwood floors, layers of varnish and layers of dirt, knots, whorls, blackstained questions. Crevices and cold, the latter seeping through Claire's hands and knees. Then she smelled smoke, steel, and sweat. She looked up: eight men in old-fashioned suits, short and thin like people in pictures from before 1949. Crooked and missing teeth. Oiled hair. A round-keyed typewriter and a pile of file cards. Old microphone. Ashtray. Gentle scratch of a pencil on paper. A man with thick black hair, not oiled, and heavy spectacles he needed to push up his nose, sitting down in front of the mic, tapping his cigarette in the ashtray, taking a breath to speak ...

—Claire, my ducky, what are you doing out of bed?

Gabriel. Dad. Resenting the interruption, the need to ask, concerned nonetheless.

Claire shivered – summer nightdress, fever. —I'm not alone?

—I'm here. Your mother and I aren't going to leave you by yourself when you're sick.

Gently kissing her forehead, Gabriel picked her up and put her on the chesterfield, right where he'd been sitting, took off his sweater and tugged it down over her. —Stick your arms through, there you go. For God's sake, Claire, waves of heat coming off you.

Bitter powder of chewable Aspirin, sweet acid of Tang. Late afternoon, sometime after four; Claire couldn't focus on the minute hand. Gabriel turned over the record. Then he took the afghan and tucked it round Claire's legs.

—Stomach hurts.

—I know, ducky. This'll take your mind off it.

Gabriel leaned behind the record player and took out a sketch pad. Not a kid's newsprint doodle pad from the shelf next to the bubblegum machine in the discount store, but a real artist's sketch pad, just like Gabriel used himself.

—Supposed to be for Christmas. Your mother'll have a canary when she finds out I gave it to you.

The late afternoon light stained and shadowed the living room blue, and Claire pretended surrender to the tide, to swim from chesterfield to kitchen, record player to fireplace – chimney blocked and sealed years before. Underwater, untroubled, sculpins and conners accepting her, fronds of seaweed flowing on currents like a drowned woman's hair, a woman who'd sunk far, far through the bottom, and her Dad so big and warm beside her ...

—Take a 2B pencil, ducky. Soft lead. Draw big, now. Fill the page.

Her fever broke near the end of side two. Neither Gabriel nor Claire noticed the silence. The light thinned. Callie came in with groceries, asking them both if they wanted to go blind, flicking on lamps. Claire resented the interruption. Callie placed her palm on Claire's forehead, then glanced at the sketchbook.

Gabriel and Claire both tensed, waiting for Callie to get angry.

Instead, sighing first, Callie stroked her daughter's hair. —That's really good, honey. You get that from your father.

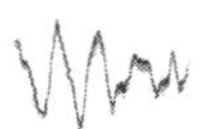

12. ANY RESEMBLANCE IS PURELY COINCIDENTAL
in which Claire Furey convinces Nichole Wright to get her picture taken.

September 9, 1983

—Nichole, you look really good in those colours.

—Nobody looks good in a uniform.

Claire leaned against a statue of the Virgin in the St. Brigid's Academy yard. This particular statue, Virgin West, stood larger than her sister, Virgin North. A third Virgin stood in the main entrance, right hand raised not in blessing but in question, as though Mary wanted to ask a passerby for directions. —At least we get to wear pantyhose. Elementary girls are stuck in knee socks.

—You didn't answer my question.

—I just told you. The time I had the flu and Dad gave me the sketch pad. Memory in patches, right? Is that what you mean?

—But when you're not feverish. Ever wink out then? You don't even know it 'til you wink back in, and suddenly you're dizzy and –

—Like Tracy? Petit mal?

Nichole sighed. Her green eyes seemed to shrink, retreat under her forehead.

Claire ignored the urge to run inside as the first bell rang. Junior Form girls at St. Brigid's simply did not hurry to class. —Nicks, you look so angry.

—Sometimes I don't know how I got here.

The second bell rang.

Claire picked up her book bag. —Come on, it's picture day. I got new lip gloss you can try.

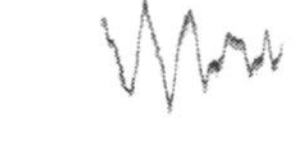

13. CONTINUITY 2
commercial break

READ DATES:	Dec. 12, 1936 until further notice
CLIENT:	PORT OF CALL
SPONSORSHIP:	* Quarter to Eight News, Monday, Wednesday, Friday * Noonday Gun News, Tuesday and Thursday * Political Perspective, five o'clock, Monday to Friday
SELLER:	Robert Wright

WRITER: RW

READER: RW

It is a tradition in St. John's to expect the finer things, a tradition some of us may question. But when the finer things are not just expected but easily found, then one knows the tradition is sound. You will bask in this tradition at Port of Call on Water Street, where Mr. Harold Canning himself is ready to assist you. Port of Call imports the finest from England, from tea to the china cups you serve it in. For the tradition of finer things, visit Port of Call, owned by Mr. Harold Canning. Port of Call, Water Street. Make it your next port of call.

14. DIOGENES SYNDROME 1
in which William Wright, at the end of a riot, decides that readiness is all.

April 6, 1932

Marry a wealthy girl. Gather it all together. Expectations resumed – damn Father for losing the fleet. Credit and desperation of fishermen, hauling us down with them, us, the Wrights of Port au Mal. Damn Father to Hell. Robert took all the blessings of being a Wright son – damn him, too. Love him regardless. So does Ellen, never mind the fact he ignores her.

Even Robert subject to Father's will, in the end: no university for the Wright sons, no, sir, learn by doing. Correspondence courses. I become a law clerk. Maddens Father no end, but I say to him, 'And which of us banked money last year, you on the water or me in an office?' Like I sneaked out under his gaze. Stuck in Labrador then with Gerald Canning. More correspondence, more book-learning, until I'm hardly a lawyer, hardly a doctor, hardly a teacher but some scraps of all three – more than most men and certainly enough to get by. Scant readiness.

Father calm over cabbage on Sundays, says to me 'Do not be thinking yourself smart and able as Robert.' Mr. Simms always spoke to me properly, with respect. Sometimes we wrestled. Mostly we discussed philosophy, the necessities of intellect and leadership. But not once would

Mr. Simms accompany me to evening service, I say, not once, no, for he says 'Lies and foolishness, William, worse than Catholicism. God gave man intelligence with which to haul himself out of the muck. Never let anyone beat you back down. With that intelligence comes duty. Explore mysteries with me, William. Far beyond the Masons. Pain and deprivation will reduce your weakness and shove you into the white light of knowledge. The same white light as is forecast by your evening service's End of Things? Evening service will drive you mad. Let me guide you to the white light. Ignore the moaning.'

Ignore the racket last night? Moans and mutters and shouts – ten thousand people descended on Colonial Building. Not one shred of courtesy among them, not fit for elected government. Don't deserve it. How can starving men lob rocks, I ask you? Me and Canning then, right quick to get Squires out of there. Ten thousand rioters, ready to turn on their own Prime Minister. Never saw the like. Squires forced to call an election, then. You'd think our precious common man had learned after the four separate governments of 1923 and 24.

Stink coming off that crowd, the mood, like some dark electricity ... I wonder now, looking back on it, if such emotions might someday be strapped and harnessed to automated typewriters, like player pianos, or to government telephony equipment – convert mob anger to some sort of calming signal, amplify and broadcast it back to its very source, for the mob's own good. I've asked Simms about such possibilities, but he reminded me I need pain and deprivation before I can expect knowledge. Accept the violation of riot. Be more than Captain Wright's second son, not-Robert, even at the End of Things. Readiness is all. Gather. Marrying a wealthy girl helps.

15. MISE EN SCENE
in which Nichole Wright exposes herself, artlessly.

May 15, 2008

Hard.

1978, I think.

Boxes of slides. Nature shots. Beauty of nakedness. Posing before a young spruce, uglier than the nearby fir, unsymmetrical. Pleasing. To me.

—Under the wild cherry tree, and then you may have ice cream.

But no, I'd stay at the spruce. Didn't. Happen. Small plane snarled in the sky.

—No more today.

How could I remember that? Too young. Spruce, fir, cherry? But the date? My age? Flat. Seven? Remember? Couldn't. Happen. Because he loves me. Endure.

—Can I look at the pictures of the Newfoundland dogs now?

16. STEAM, PUNK
in which Jack Best and Gabriel Furey discuss marriage and electricity.

December 11, 1970

Cameras flashed and rolled as Johann Haldorf guided the Prime Minister through the facilities. —Hubbard Falls is the second-largest underground power station in the world. Harnessing the somewhat frightening power potential of the water gives a man a good feeling. What had simply poured off the mountain and risen skywards in steam and great waste is now diked, dammed and directed. The Best Reservoir is, by far, the largest body of fresh water in the republic.

Jack knew all of this, knew nearly as much about the Hubbard Falls project as Haldorf himself, but he needed now to report to history. And public relations. Best and Haldorf, both men in their sixties, must also show the younger generation how progress worked. Pointing to the map on the wall showing the reservoir, Jack nodded. —How large then, Mr. Haldorf?

—The spillway is larger than Ireland.

Reflected winter daylight, captured with an ingenious and expensive arrangement of solar panels and mirrors, poured in the Gothic-arched windows. Three of the windows had been made with stained glass, one in tribute to Jack Best, one in recognition of HydroForce Labrador Corporation, and one in various shards of pink, white and green. The remaining window glass, tinted shades of amber and gold, lent the light unusual warmth. Haldorf believed in the healing power of sunshine, especially in winter; tasks on the upper two floors of the power station had become coveted work assignments.

Haldorf pointed to massive pipes, painted royal blue and numbered in gold.

—Power is frightening, yes, but I see no reason it should not be beautiful. I have deliberately hearkened back to a more graceful time in my designs, taking the early twentieth-century hydro stations in Wisconsin and Washington State as my inspiration. You will notice the old-fashioned numbers. However, the turbines and machinery, beneath this civilized coat, are strong enough to power New York State. Just think a moment of the industry there, the manufacturing, the people, and their thirst for electricity. Think of the revenue! Fossil fuels will see their day end soon. Hydro is honourably clean. Ugliness of modern design – I tire of it, as do we all in this new decade. One cannot even call it 'modern.' Just exhausted.

Jack nodded, uncertain, as Haldorf's eyes closed. Cameras flashed.

Haldorf woke up. —Along this corridor, we have one of our top construction teams.

Jack shook hands with sixteen men, including Gabriel Furey. Then one of the reporters called for a film re-load break, after which Jack shook hands with the last four men again. Gabriel laughed the second time shaking Jack's hand, until he saw Jack's eyes.

Once the dignitaries had left, Gabriel's foreman punched him on the arm.

—Where do you get off laughing at Jack Best?

—How come we got no Eskimos working here?

—We're not gonna have any Fureys working here if you keep that up.

—We're in the middle of fucking Labrador. Where are the Eskimos?

—Up in the Arctic with the penguins and the polar bears, I s'pose. Not like we can have Eskimos and Naskapi Indians and whatever the fuck else they got up here at this. They can't even speak English. All they does is hunt. Mind you, I wouldn't say no to a feed of caribou.

Gabriel tried to read the map. The Best Reservoir measured two thousand square miles of new flooding. A small piece of Labrador, unless you happened to live, hunt and bury your dead on that ground.

The floor telephone rang, and the foreman answered it.

Two thousand square miles? That can't be right.

—Furey.

—Is that really two thousand –

—Report to Haldorf's office.

—Why?

—Will you fucking do as you're told? Just this once?

So Gabriel reported to the quiet office. He'd done so only once before, on his first day; Haldorf liked to meet all the workers personally, shake their hands, pass them a large piece of iron ore he kept on his desk so they might feel its weight. Haldorf had been well-dressed and spoke with the faintest German accent, enunciation crisp, and his vocabulary rivalled that of most dictionaries. Gabriel had felt stupid many times in his life, but never stupider than in that well-lit, degree-lined office, meeting the genius who had electrified the republic, and who could lob that heavy piece of iron ore from hand to hand like a tennis ball. Immigrant, too, worked his way up from nothing, the story went. Gabriel took a breath, knocked, and stepped inside.

Behind Haldorf's desk sat Jack Best, leafing through a big black photo album.

Gabriel took another breath. *What's the fucking protocol for this, now?* —Mr. Prime Minister.

Jack turned a page. —You could have washed your hands first.

Gabriel glanced down at his fingers. Grease, oil, the odd cut and scab. —Busy workin', b'y.

—Good money up here?

—You tell me, Mr. Prime Minister. You got me the job.

Jack looked up from photos of the Reservoir. —Believe me, Gabriel, if we had a hydro plant up in Nain, I'd get you a job up there.

—Keep me up there, you mean. Look, if you want to know if I'm willing to marry Callie now, the answer is yes. I've had enough of your little Siberia. Just get me the hell back to St. John's.

—You'd turn your back on all this money? Good opportunities up here for a man who's willing to work, Mr. Furey.

Jack said *Mr. Furey* as though insulting a member of the Loyal Opposition in parliamentary language.

Gabriel scowled. —I'm asking your permission to marry your daughter, Mr. Best. Isn't that what you wanted?

—Can't hear you over the turbines.

—I am asking your permission to marry your daughter. Will ya stop taking my measure like I'm a chunk of meat and answer me?

—Too late for that. You need to sit down?

—I can stand. Whaddya mean, too late?

—She's pregnant.

—What?

Pale, Jack nodded. —So you didn't know. She said you didn't, but I wasn't sure. About three months along. Showing. By the time we get the wedding arranged, she'll be out like a balloon. Be too much fuss made. Can't have that.

Gabriel tried to recall if he'd ever heard Jack Best speak in such short sentences before.

—Jack, I love her.

Jack stared hard.

Gabriel stared back. —Not good enough because I'm a St. Raphael's boy? When she came to you through The Anchorage? At least my parents had been married. Were Callie's? Tell the truth, now.

—Want the truth? You're not good enough for *me*, Mr. Furey. Lazy, shiftless, drunk half the time, can't keep a job, hiding in the house and farting around with paints and clay like you're in kindergarten while Callie goes out and works –

—Her idea. She wanted –

—Callie deserves better than you! And by God, I'll make sure she gets it. As long as I live, you will not marry my daughter.

Gabriel felt his moustache bristling out, but he kept his voice steady. —Sure, I already got her broke in.

The piece of iron ore missed Gabriel's forehead by maybe half an inch, breaking through the frosted glass pane in the door instead.

Gabriel looked from the jagged glass to the Prime Minister. *No point holding back now.* —Tell you something else. No other fella's been near her. That baby is mine. And I don't care what you think, because I will do right by Callie. Fucking guarantee you that.

—I could get you fired in a heartbeat.

—And back on the next plane to St. John's? I'd like nothing better.

—On the next plane back to the dole, you mean.

—Already got money put away. Not like there's anything to spend it on up here.

Fists clenched, jaw tense, Jack spoke slowly, quietly. —God damn you.

—Too late for that. Mind the glass on your way out there, Mr. Prime Minister.

Walks some fast for a short fellah. Gabriel smoothed his hand over his moustache, rocked back on his heels, clicked his tongue. *How do I get in these things?* The photo album Jack had been looking at still lay open on Haldorf's desk, colours garish: sky and water a harsh blue, soil dull brown and studded with thin grey and white rocks. Gabriel walked behind the desk, sudden ideas for paintings of the Best Reservoir kicking within his head. *What kind of rocks are they? Reservoir, yes, miles of trees drowned beneath, old river bank ... Holy Mary, Mother of God.*

Not rocks. Exposed human bones.

Footsteps, crunched glass. —*Vas is das?*

Johann Haldorf stared through his new window at the moustached grease-monkey from Team 4 standing behind his desk. Then he glanced down at the broken glass and the iron ore.

—My doing, Johann.

Jack Best's voice, shaking.

—You broke my window?

—My discussion with young Mr. Furey in there got a bit heated.

—Furey broke my window.

—No. I did. I'll repair it myself.

Haldorf raised his eyebrows. —I have workers for that. And your helicopter is due to leave, yes? That one Furey can fix it. Unless there is something else I should do with him.

Gabriel gently replaced the photo album.

—Just keep all this to yourself, Johann. Personal matter.

Haldorf looked at Gabriel with confused new respect.

Then Jack cleared his throat. —Give him a raise.

One of Jack's assistants ran up. —Mr. Prime Minister, there you are. Your helicopter's ready. And you have a meeting at the Menihek Dam this afternoon.

Jack surrendered to his schedule and strode off with his assistant to a chant of names, titles and statistics from the Menihek Dam.

Haldorf stepped delicately over broken glass and came into his office.

—Would you kindly fetch a broom and dustpan please, Mr. Furey?

—Yes, sir.

Kneeling to sweep the glass, Gabriel tried to understand precisely how the Prime Minister had made him feel not only stupid this time, but dirty – tainted, like he'd just stood before Brother Stephens with his fifty dollar bill.

No sense in feeling like this. I won this time.

Didn't I?

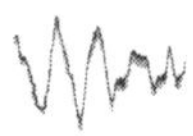

17. AN AFTERNOON'S PLEASANT DISCOURSE
in which Ange O'Dea minds his place and does not take tea with a member of the Commission of Government.

September 24, 1934

—Is any man there?

Voice of a diplomat. Specifically, the voice of an English diplomat, nearly seventy, seasoned with the Raj and assigned in his career's twilight to a troublesome failed dominion's Commission of Government. A voice of strained pleasantness, of irritated fear and overwork.

Ange O'Dea could not answer. An English Commissioner, hidden by light and a doorway, asking the likes of Ange O'Dea if he was there. *Mother of God, if he knew I was named for a lost Portuguese.*

The lost Portuguese – Sicilian, really, but there'd been no common language to explain that – had been wrecked not far from Riordan's Back in 1901. Vessels often went off course near Port au Mal and Riordan's Back. High rocks infested the waters, and various forces complicated navigation. A visiting Englishman explained it once: iron ore, magnetic fields, strong currents, deviations. Physics irrelevant, blackflies crawled in the ears, eyes and nose of the unfortunate Sicilian two mornings after his wreck. He comforted himself by reciting tales of Saint Anthony. Sometimes, he walked.

Ange's mother, Sarah O'Dea, widowed and expecting, watched him collapse. First his shoulders slumped. His left eye twitched. His right knee gave way, and suddenly his arse hit the ground. Confused, apologetic, he looked up at Sarah as a boy might to a mother.

Sarah shook her head. —I can't be lifting you.

But she knelt to help him stand.

Leaning on the pregnant woman, the sailor walked slowly into Sarah's house and said *Maria* when he saw a small picture of the Virgin Mary that Sarah O'Dea had torn from a sodden book that washed ashore about a year before, on her wedding day. Fearing it sacrilegious to nail the picture to the wall, Sarah had pasted it up with spruce sap. The sailor touched the picture; Sarah gave him spruce tea and a shawl. Then she pointed to her chest. —Mrs. O'Dea. Mrs. O'Dea.

The sailor coughed. Sarah winced. Coughs signalled danger. The sailor's noise: not consumption's wet hack, thank God, more a shallow wheeze – water on the lungs.

The sailor fell again, dead faint this time, falling against Sarah O'Dea and knocking her down. She twisted out from under him, careful of his head that it did not hit the floor, made the fire hotter, then swayed and waddled over rocks and worn ground for help.

The sailor remained insensible for the next three days – no impediment to the men gathering round him each night for several hours to discuss the day's catch. A twine knife caught the fading light and refracted it onto the sailor's face as one man mended a net, counting the ninety-eight meshes in the first drew. Then the sailor woke up to the bony face of a young man, rimless spectacles sliding down his nose: Christopher Francis, the travelling teacher.

Christopher smiled and held a spoonful of spruce tea to the sailor's mouth.

—Angelo Stellisario.

Christopher smiled. —Is that your name?

—Angelo Stellisario.

—Portuguese?

—Sicilia. Isola. Isola? Terra Nova?

And with that, Angelo fell back to sleep.

When he woke again, well enough to stand, he found Sarah O'Dea asleep in a chair by his bed. No no no, she should not be caring for him, not in her condition. He thought to rouse her from the chair and put her to bed, but stopped before this gesture might be fatally misconstrued.

Soup cooked at the hearth: potatoes, cabbage, cod heads. He found bowls in the kitchen, then served up two bowls of soup, leaving hers on the hearthstones a few moments to cool. He drank his own quickly, hungry as he'd ever been. The potato crumbled on his tongue, the cabbage wrapped round his teeth, and the cod heads, at once gelatinous and crisp, mashed against his palate. Glancing round the main room at the hearth, the table and chairs, the torn paper picture of the Virgin, Angelo smiled and blew a kiss at the ceiling. Then he took Sarah O'Dea her soup.

Over the next week, Angelo – no one could pronounce his surname except Christopher Francis – made himself useful to Sarah O'Dea, completing housework she could not, travelling Sunday morning with the Legges to Harbour Grace for Mass – those words he knew – and eventually working the stages. Angelo Stellisario proved himself an able splitter, and the night Sarah's pains began, it was Angelo who went to Mary Legge for help.

Hard labour – first baby, big head. Mary Legge expected a day or so's work. She did not banish Angelo from the house, instead tasking him by points and gestures to keep water boiling. Dozing at the hearth, Angelo wondered if they'd need to split Mrs. O'Dea, wondered when to decide to save the child even if it meant killing the mother. Then he heard his name, sharp.

—Angelo. Water.

Sarah O'Dea screamed, called on the Mother of God and screamed again, and Angelo did his best not to look, but: woman, blood, head, baby.

Mary Legge smiled. —A boy, a boy.

Angelo parrotted her. —A-bye, a-bye.

But the baby did not cry. The baby did not open his eyes. He could only be roused with a shout and a slap. He nuzzled at the breast, suck weak. Mary Legge hid her concern from Sara, and Sara hid hers from Mary. Angelo saw it all.

Then he asked if he might see the baby, and Mary and Sarah understood.

Touching the boy on the cheek, Angelo smiled, weary and still sick. Feeling a cough coming, he turned his head and then left the room. At the hearth, he said a long prayer, uncertain where the prayer led, but he said it anyway.

In the morning, the baby cried. An odd cry, not one of pain or hunger or even wetness—more surprise and a good lungful of air. An announcement, a proclamation: *I exist.* Tears on her face, Mary took the baby in her arms to the hearth, surprised Angelo had not answered this joyful noise. The fire burnt hot. Angelo sat still, his eyes nearly shut, as though he'd fallen asleep surveying his work. His chest did not rise.

—Is any man there? Come in if you're there.

Ange O'Dea raised his chin and crossed the threshold to the Commissioner.

Tall, bald and bespectacled, Commissioner Michael Grant-Mainwaring studied his visitor as he'd study a depressing report – resigned scrutiny. The people of Newfoundland had been left on their own far too long, unguided, subject to vagaries of climate and fish. Charlatans, one of them their own prime minister, had stolen food from many tables. This same prime minister had fled to another island, this one tropical. Taxes and duties, a grab for money to service a monstrous debt, were baroque in their desperate complexity; Canadian banks were sick of bailing out this difficult and demanding older colony which then continually insulted the Dominion of Canada by dictating conditions of confederation – high astounding terms of union – or by refusing confederation altogether; and England, tired and somewhat ashamed, needing to save face, suspended elected government in Newfoundland and informed the people they needed a rest from democracy. Now this Commission need only pry Newfoundland from the mess of generations. Friends and colleagues had warned Grant-Mainwaring he'd only last a year; no one lasted longer than two years in Newfoundland. He'd feared the truth of this warning after hearing that, in the absence of a central archive for government records, vital papers were simply, almost routinely, secreted in various pigeonholes, desks and safes throughout St. John's.

Frustrated, Grant-Mainwaring turned to the Newfoundlanders themselves. To complete his task, he must first understand his task, understand Newfoundland life.

He'd heard many stories of the bone-lazy, docile and dependent outport Newfoundlander, but surely … rations, dole, cold and hard stunting hunger ... and he'd wondered, buttering his toast in the dining room of the Hotel Newfoundland, just how easily one might show what the ladies and merchants called *moral enterprise* as one slowly starved to death. Pot Cove and the children – their swollen bellies mocking satiety – quiet as Mrs. Grant-Mainwaring's offered candy fell to the ground.

Irksome. Most irksome.

But, on with the interviews.

Grant-Mainwaring stood and came round his desk to shake his visitor's hand. Surprised, Ange hesitated to return his hand but then thrust it out quickly. Grant-Mainwaring's long fingers and warm hand took Ange's hand in a firm shake; Ange's short fingers, cracked skin and broken nails returned a grasp so strong Grant-Mainwaring nearly frowned. He'd not yet acclimatized himself to the hands of fishermen.

Grant-Mainwaring gestured to a chair before his desk. —Please, sit down.

Ange sat. A fire burned behind Grant-Mainwaring's desk, and while draught rattled the windows, the wall stood free of cracks and holes. The leather padding on the back of the ornate chair made Ange feel misplaced, and he sat up very straight.

—Thank you, sir, for consenting to see me.

Grant-Mainwaring raised his eyebrows very slightly. *Consenting? Where has he learned a word like that?* —Not at all. It is one of the reasons I am here.

Ange bit the inside of his bottom lip. The phrase Christopher Francis had convinced him to use seemed to annoy Grant-Mainwaring. —So you see a lot of men?

—I do. I wish to understand how it is.

—How what is?

—Life here. Particularly in the outports. The people here in St. John's –

—Oh, they don't know nothing.

—Quite. What I mean is, the people of St. John's, some of them, have told me stories of the outports which I think are precisely that.

Ange wished Christopher Francis could translate – not the Commissioner's words, but his meanings. —Precisely what?

—Stories. For example, does your wife lie in bed all day until one o'clock because she has nothing to do?

—The hell she does.

—I thought not.

—But there are streels who do that.

—Streels?

—I 'low you call them sluts in England. We got a few streels in Riordan's Back, a few more over in Port au Mal there across the bay. Streels, you know. You just said. Women who don't do tap round the house, let everything go slew.

Grant-Mainwaring wrote something down. —One *e* or two?

—Sir?

—Did you say you came from Riordan's Back?

Ange brightened. —Yes, sir. You been there?

Grant-Mainwaring opened a desk drawer and took out a rolled chart of Newfoundland. —You have no roads. Please, show me where it is.

Ange studied the drawing a while.

Grant-Mainwaring found some tact. —So, how did you get here from Riordan's Back?

—Sailed. Then took the train.

—And the rest you whistled?

—You don't be whistling on the water. Invites the devil.

—You sailed here to see me?

Ange glanced down at his boots, toes hard bent, seams chinked. They still leaked.

—Heard you were listening.

Grant-Mainwaring glanced at his appointment book. —It is why I'm here, Mr. Morrisey.

—My name is Ange O'Dea.

—Ange O'Dea.

—Yes, sir.

Grant-Mainwaring drew his finger across his schedule and made a mental note to reprimand his clerk – again. —Mr. O'Dea. I had an appointment with one Mr. Morrisey –

Dear God, I needed an appointment? Ange glanced over his shoulder, expecting eviction. He clutched his hat, hating it, studied his boots, hating them. —Please, sir. I stole no man's time. Didn't know about appointments.

Grant-Mainwaring let his heavy spectacles slide down his nose, giving him a reason to remove them and not to see the man in the chair.

Ange O'Dea had lost his words. Ange O'Dea never lost his words. The young Ranger acting as dole officer and his Means Test – that had been endured and finally beaten by a steady patter and tumble of wit that got the Ranger laughing, then apologizing for the unpleasant formalities of the Test, finally dismissing it altogether. *Mr O'Dea, you wouldn't lie to Satan to save your soul. Here.* The dole – six cents a day. Insufficiency – the very reason Ange O'Dea sat in Commissioner Grant-Mainwaring's office, mesmerized by all this furniture inherited from previous administrations, all this furniture paid for by cheating the likes of Ange O'Dea in the first place. Insufficiency – right where Ange O'Dea planted his arse.

Ange cleared his throat. —Can I still tell you?

—Tell me what?

—How it is.

—Please do.

—Put your spectacles back on, sir.

Grant-Mainwaring did so.

Ange smiled. —I'll tell you, now. I have a wife and two sons, Neal and John. Hoping to have an Edward soon, but barring that, there's always Elizabeth.

Ange paused for a chuckle, but Grant-Mainwaring did not grant one.

Tough haul, this one. —We got enough beds to go round, not like some houses where everyone sleeps round the stove. And my missus, like I said, she keeps up with the work. Not a bit of the streel in my wife.

Ange paused again, looking at the window; outside, a horse clopped by.

Grant-Mainwaring tapped a finger on his desk. —Is there something else?

—Rotten lines.

—I beg your pardon?

—Rotten lines, sir. Nets and traps. Piled and useless. Picked up a killick this morning. Collapsed in my grasp. The lath, I mean.

Grant-Mainwaring made another note.

Never mind your pen and ink. —The killick collapsed. The water is barren. Lobsters, maybe. But even the conners and sculpins are gone. No one to buy the fish, anyways.

Grant-Mainwaring scratched out several more words.

Devil take you, look at me. —What I mean to say – 'tis not enough.

—Your dole officer can –

—You are not listening!

Grant-Mainwaring dropped his pen.

Ange stood up, voice steady. —With all due respect to your station and your coming all this way to Newfoundland, you are not listening. The dole is not enough. Not enough for me, for my family, for my neighbours, for any one of the God damned families dependent on it.

Grant-Mainwaring knew the statistics. One quarter of the population, maybe one third doled. Hungry, likely starving.

Ange laid his hat on the chair. —I'd like to see your missus make a few pounds of flour last a week.

—My wife does not make bread.

Ange nodded, not in mockery, but in some kind of understanding.

—Mr. O'Dea, your ... your words have been quite informative. Quite. Is there anything you wish to add?

—I hates to be asking, sir, but I got to be when I know proud men with thin sons. When will you fix the dole?

Fix the dole? Heal a wound left by generations of corrosive cheating and graft? Grant-Mainwaring swallowed, stood. —Mr. O'Dea, I do not mean to be rude, but I have another appointment.

Ange could smell toast and tea. Real tea. He recalled the taste of spruce buds in hot water.

—Please, Mr. O'Dea, understand this: I intend to ease your burden. I am working as fast as I can.

—I believe you, sir. Thank you.

And Ange turned and left, forgetting his hat. By the time Grant-Mainwaring found it, Angel O'Dea had long gone. Grant-Mainwaring's head fuzzed up with hunger – he'd refused that afternoon to take tea.

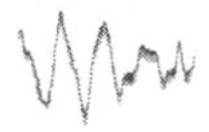

18. QUEEN'S ENGLISH 1
in which Almayer Foxe escapes to a former colony.

April 1975

Fugitive heart beating hard, Almayer Foxe – no, not his real name, just the name on his passport – smiled once more at the woman seated next to him on the plane. —I shall be working for VONB-TV, as a news anchorman.

—Nice accent like yours, I'm not surprised. I never heard an English accent growing up, unless it was a bit from the BBC that VOIC was after playing. Some long way for you to come to work, though.

—There is so much more to life than London, I feel, and – the old fool was quite mistaken.

—Wha'?

Once, when you were pretty, oh my gentle peasant, you were just pretty enough to draw the eye, despite that long jaw. Now, two children and a dull marriage later, you're faded up and thirty. Old bruises on your arms. Pretty enough for me.

—The old fool who told me that the prettiest girls lived in Singapore and the ugliest girls in Newfoundland.

She blushed but did not lower her eyes.

How she wants me, just a little caressing. Starving for it. Very like training a puppy.

—I do apologize. What must you think of me? I just noticed your wedding band. I assure you, I meant no impropriety –

—All my fault. I shouldn't even be wearing this. Trial separation. Do you know where you're staying in St. John's?

—Yes, but I hardly know my way around.

—I can show you a few things, if you like.

—You're very kind. Do I understand you people also have a Peter Pan statue, much like ours in Kensington Park?

—In Bowring Park. Haven't been there in years. You want to meet there?

—Tomorrow morning at ten?

Mine. Too easy. But mine.

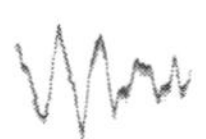

19. GEOGRAPHICAL CURE 1
in which Robert Wright defies his father.

July 13, 1947

The best part of his scandalous flight: defying calendar and clock. Sunday evening, and Robert Jackman Wright, who most certainly knew better, flew noisily over Port au Mal and Riordan's Back in his new Tiger Moth. War surplus from Gander, one of two made available for civilian purchase. The other Tiger Moth would languish years in a garage, catch fire, and then in the 1980s be slowly restored until becoming a museum piece in 1995 – but never fly, never fly. Robert's Tiger Moth received loving attention. Each individual part respected and known. Washed down after each flight. Hours of adjustments in silence. Brief escapes from the leaden responsibilities of radio, where only the signal escaped to fly.

VOIC broadcast the word of God on Sundays – good and proper and certainly expected. Mandated, too, in the lengthy Clause Twenty-six of VOIC's broadcast contract with the Commission of Government. Sunday's multi-denominational religious programming ran from seven in the morning until ten at night. Anglicans and Pentecostals before lunch, two and half hours each, chunky time slots those churches paid extra for. Noon to one, news and recorded hymns. Then the free paths to God, free to the churches at least, an hour at a time: Methodist, Catholic, Presbyterian. More Anglican. Salvation Army Band Hymn Sing. Another half-hour for Catholicism. United Church of Canada – an odd bunch in Robert's view, a little too easy on sin. More Salvation Army music. Finally, the Port au Mal Methodist evening service from the week before. Each Monday morning, the minister mailed the text of his sermon to Robert at VOIC; each following Sunday evening, Robert read last week's sermon over the air. The Social Services clause said nothing of who must sacrifice their Sabbath to ensure Sunday broadcasts. Robert, Thomas and Richard tithed their Sundays to VOIC.

So this Sunday's freedom, ever more precious for its rarity. Uninterrupted blue sky. Time, finally, *time*. Taking off from Torbay, flying out over Conception Bay, hymned organ-drone and sermon phrases echoing in his head, climb higher, higher, so close to escape, nearly loose of eye-strings and damnation and the nagging questions of corporeal resurrection after the end of all things in 1974 – well, Robert didn't think a prediction of the end could be so accurate, but the end would come, and readiness was all – how did corporeal resurrection work if one still lived when the end came? Did one actually die, or would God skip that step for efficiency? Pretty sure he'd just committed blasphemy, Robert studied the altitude and fuel gauges through badly scratched goggles strapped over his delicate spectacles – if he ever crashed, two layers of glass might blind him. Eyestrings break in death. He sang, not that he could hear himself over the Tiger Moth's engine.

—Foul, I to the fountain fly ...

Then he stopped.

Because he didn't need to sing "Rock of Ages." No obligation. Perhaps even no damnation. Perhaps, just perhaps, grace for all.

At the moment, for Robert: just flight.

Below Robert, the congregation departed evening service at the clapboard church in Port au Mal. Tobias Wright, who had not spoken for a fortnight, craned his neck back and studied the bright yellow underside of the Tiger Moth until he got too dizzy to stand. The nerve, the gall, to be flying and making a racket like that on a Sunday, the shame cutting deeper – Robert, who'd never be a man, flying ... Falling now, Tobias aimed to lie on his back and study the cloudless sky for warning, or even a message – just some scrap of meaning, despite predestination ... The Tiger Moth growled. Everyone else smiled and waved.

Not yet aware the Captain had splayed himself on the rocks, Robert grinned, and turned the plane in a gentle arc. *Newsbird*, a good name. A fine name. Imagine, smiling like this on a Sunday evening. Freedom – or at least meaning and a sharp sense of being alive in this defiance. Robert Jackman Wright, aged forty-five, who'd stood up to Commissioners and investors, judges, doctors, ministers and priests, now finally defying his tyrannous father. Now, finally, not working for someone else's version of God.

Laughing, Robert glanced below – some excitement, some old codger on his back, his companions jumping and waving, trying to draw Robert down. Nowhere to land in Port au Mal – nearest airfield was Harbour Grace, and then the need to catch a ride on a boat ... the men below now, waving, turmoiled flesh – his father on the rocks. How the hell to get to him? Presuming he wanted to. Likely Tobias shammed a fall just to attract community awe back to himself – hard to see from that height some days, but this clear evening and cloudless sky ... *Such evil in my heart? Ignore my father prone on the earth? Isaiah chapter 57, verse 20: But the wicked are like the troubled sea, when it cannot rest, whose waters cast up mire and dirt* – and from his father's grounded dark mouth, mire and dirt: *Robert, you're a defiant, myopic, useless and near-wicked God-borne fool. Plucking words from the air. My son, you need this lesson learnt, that in this world the forces you cannot see are the forces that you must fear. Heed me, Robert, heed your father.*

Updraft. Tailwind. Brisk westerly.

Robert veered off, flew back to St. John's.

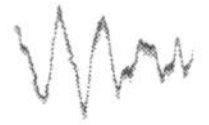

20. "DID EVER A WOMAN, SINCE THE CREATION OF THE WORLD, INTERRUPT A MAN WITH SUCH A SILLY QUESTION?"

in which Jane and Robert Wright wash up against shadows of the Great War.

November 8, 1917

—Why not?

—Because women are simply not permitted to vote, Jane. Accept it. You must have better things to worry about.

Jane Wright rolled her eyes at Robert and roughly tucked her scraggly black hair behind her ears. Her head had been shaved during whooping cough the year before, when she'd dreamt Robert had gone off to war despite being underage. He'd not have been the first. And Britain had called a second time, just having squandered most of the Newfoundland Regiment at the Somme. —But there's suffrage.

Robert Wright, back a while from wireless work on the Northern Peninsula and then travels to St. John's and Boston, looked very strong as he sat in Captain Wright's chair and hid behind an English newspaper. The fragility of his heavy new spectacles bothered him: how could he be any use on a schooner with pieces of expensive glass balanced on his nose? What kind of a man, besides Mr. Francis, needed glass to see? But the clarity. Robert could *see* Jane, see the dark green of her eyes, not just shadowy pits in her face; he could see the contents of each glass jar in his mother's store; he could decipher this newspaper's horrors without smudging his nose with ink. Beautiful clarity, lending him power. Not power over other people, no – his father's province, that – but power over his own God-given weakness. A token of the prevenient grace the minister kept preaching?

For years, Captain Wright had mocked Robert's severe myopia, impatience exploding whenever the boy tripped. Mrs. Wright had sighed when Robert held books close to his face to read them, even then sometimes defeated by small print. In May 1917, an oculist in St. John's pronounced Robert's defect shattering and far beyond the reach of medical science. Merely tired of hopelessness while her husband noisily submitted to it, Mrs. Wright counted out several paper bills and ordered Robert and the Captain to take the largest schooner in the Wright fleet and sail to Boston – to obtain gear for the shop, of course, and some new-fangled candy. Robert believed this, at first, until Tobias asked him over supper how the young man might earn the respect of fishermen now, what with his weak eyes and coddled voyage to Boston for spectacles? A mustered crew, a rough voyage, all for the Captain's son?

But – clarity.

Learning to focus without dizziness, learning not to squint. Salt spray and fog obscured the lenses, but they might be cleaned. Gratitude when the spectacles slid down his nose and exposed his old blurry world atop his new one. Carefully positioning the spectacles, unknowingly stretching his mouth downwards in a parody of arrogance as he did so, Robert tasked himself to catch up. Much-loved mathematics without the headaches, quick progress to spherical trigonometry and navigation, to physics and the grace of radio waves ... seeing sculpins lurking at the wharf poles as he climbed up the stage, or individual trees instead of one dark smudge, or Christopher Francis looking up sadly from a letter Mrs. Furneax had asked him to read to her amongst all the people gathered in the Wrights' store.

Such responsibility.

To escape, Robert decided to tease his sister. —Oh, yes, we must suffer the suffragettes. The vote, indeed. This is the foolishness that comes of you wearing bloomers. I am shocked Father allows it.

Jane almost answered that aloud. *Father has no say in the matter. He ignores me and my bloomers and my daring to read, just as he ignores anything he prefers not to face. I will not be ignored!* Instead, she tore away Robert's newspaper.

Quick anger lit Robert's face, but his smile soon returned. —Really, Jane, you must become informed about matters before you can expect to be allowed to vote.

—I am informed.

—By tardy newsprint.

Robert ducked as though to dodge a blow, laughing.

She held up the newspaper and picked an article at random. —*British Empire forces take Passchendaele with valour and* – oh, Robert.

She threw the paper to the hearth.

Robert studied his sister then as though she were someone else – a woman, yes, but also being with emotion and intellect, another actual person, just as complex as himself.

Crying, Jane ran from the front room.

Robert picked up the newspaper with smudged fingers. Boys he'd gone to school with in St John's were dead: John Hussey, Millar Freeman, Harry Martin, Jim Court. Robert's older cousins Ken and Tom Jackman had gone over; Ken was still alive, so far as anyone knew, but Tom was listed as missing. Albert Furneaux, who had been in St. John's when the first call came, had just returned to Port au Mal, wounded at Beaumont Hamel, invalided to England and then discharged, *Medically Unfit*.

Jane had gone to see Albert Furneaux, whom she'd adored and hoped to marry – there'd been talk of promises and betrothal. Mr. Francis accompanied Jane on her visit, tried to warn her on the short walk what *wounded* meant. Dirty bandages round his face, Albert called for his mother to make Jane leave, but his mother did not hear. Jane made tea. Albert ignored Mr. Francis, instead picking off his bandages, unwinding them so they fell to the floor. When Jane returned with the tea things, as he knew she would, he faced her. Somewhat. His eyes remained, glaring, but his nose had been shredded away, his ears destroyed. Burns? Bone? Wavy blond hair. He screamed it, coming at her: *Happy now? Happy you helped a forgotten God-wrought beast?* Later, Christopher Francis wept. Jane had run home, confessing the scene only to Robert, who'd then gone delicately to their father. Captain Wright nodded at Robert's confused and evasive sentences and advised his son to leave Furneaux bide, as one would a dangerous animal.

Robert shook his head. He'd not meant to make his sister cry. Jane certainly knew more about the War than Robert did; at fifteen, she'd faced Albert Furneaux. And though Robert would never admit this to her, he could see no reason at all why she should not have the vote.

21. WOUND STRIPE 1
in which Albert Furneaux goes over the top.

July 6, 1916

A constantly shifting bargain in that hospital bed: trade the pain for seeing home, or trade living to see home for an end to the pain? Morphia insufficient, atropine a trap, and nothing could blunt the smells: carbolic acid, pus, bleach, excrement, sweat, soap. The nurses pried off dressings. Experimental treatment – debridement and saline lavage, normally reserved for gut wounds.

Dream:

—Name?

—Albert Furneaux.

—Age?
—Nineteen.
—Religion?
—Methodist.
—Home?
—Port au Mal.
—Bayman come to town?
—I can fight. What more do you need? Sir.
—Report to the sergeant. Next.
Minnie. Whiz-bang. Rats. Men.
Matron:

—Private Furneaux. Newfoundlander, are you? I doubt you remember me, but I pulled one of your teeth when you were ten in Port au Mal. Now. We'll be changing the dressing over your eyes and nose today. The doctor has said you may open your eyes today, if you wish, if the scabs permit. But we need to help you restrain yourself.

Those words hurt, too – what you said of a wounded animal, a lashing beast, and why Albert had once shot a broken-legged pony, the tormented whinny echoing a shred longer off the rocks than the shot, why he'd once brained a sick dog. Yet men twitched, too, barrage complete, or suspended. Men bucked and writhed, frothed and bled, staggered on rotting feet, drowned in mud. Captain Sturge, tidy and bright, young man from St. John's, going to law school at war's end, and an officer. Albert had thought an officer like that deserved a clean death, one to the heart or the head. Dignified and quick. What fell at Albert's feet: bleeding parody of a man, parody seasoned with sadism and chance. Albert Furneaux had never heard the word *sadism*, but that night he accused God of it, of wanton cruelty, his unsteady lamentation leading him to something yet more terrible: God's distance. Cruelty organized and drilled and excused by chain of command and the unanswerable need to make random violent deaths mean something. Captain Sturge fell. Struck backwards by tiny hands, bullets through the chest and neck, one just under the rim of his helmet. Violated flesh pried apart so blood and brain might flow through cloth, over leather, Captain John Sturge, aged twenty-four, offended, angry that this bullet had found him, then this one, then this one. If he'd banged his rotting toes or snatched bread from a rat, he'd wear the same face, say the same word: *Bugger.* A crammed lifetime, smelling of schoolhouse woodsmoke, salt air and lavender powder. *Bugger.* That was what fell at Albert Furneaux's feet, once more, and Albert stepped over it, for the order had been given to advance.

Nurses:

—Private Furneaux?

—Capelin.

—Hush, Private.

—Over the top. Nothing more than capelin. Signalling.

—Ssh. Your eyelids are healing.

He must have flung his arms over his eyes – forearms as burnt at his face – but his spared eyelids bore only scratches. Harrow of noise: someone had called his name. Nonsense, of course. God himself couldn't hear a prayer lost in the Somme obscenity. Mothers couldn't hear their sons.

—You may open your eyes.

Scabs resisted, and daylight hurt.

Albert looked at the wall. A beautiful wall. Tomorrow he'd loathe it, but right then the sight of the wall prompted him to drop his strict plan to burn the clapboard Methodist church in Port au Mal.

Matron held a drink to his lips and instructed him in a voice that would brook no nonsense to swallow deeply. —A little experiment of my own. Chloral hydrate.

Albert's mind slipped out, like an ice pan into night, and Matron accomplished lavage that day without the patient's screams.

22. THIS IS A TEST OF THE EMERGENCY BROADCAST SYSTEM 1
in which Nichole Wright and Marc Dwyer, aged twelve, sneak into the Janeway Children's Hospital to visit Claire Furey.

May 16, 2008

In September 1983, a few weeks after the Soviets shot down KAL-007 so it fell like fire from the sky, I took Marc Dwyer to see Claire at the Janeway Children's Hospital. We were all twelve, just starting grade seven in Junior Form at St. Brigid's Academy. Marc and Claire loved each other but didn't seem to know it yet. Just good friends, yeah yeah yeah, two artists drawing and painting side by side for hours in happy silence, but good friends can love each other, can't they? Safely?

Claire and I had been trying on our school uniforms a few nights before, wrapping the ties around our foreheads, around our waists, anywhere but our necks. I showed her how to strut, cock and pout like a model, made her laugh so hard she nearly wet herself. But she'd been pale that night, didn't eat supper, her half of the pizza gone cold and dull in the cardboard box. Second day of school, September 9th, when we got our pictures taken, she seemed a bit better, but then she fainted after the photography, clutching her stomach. Tears filled the sudden lines on her face; she scowled so hard she might be sneering. When the red lights of the ambulance bounced off classroom windows, many people, their concern blunted by custom, assumed that Tracy the epileptic girl just took a seizure. But no: Claire Furey, crying out on a stretcher, eyes clenched shut ... and those rule-strangled pricks of paramedics wouldn't let me ride with her – me, her best friend, damn it – no, I had to stay in school. Like I could study or sleep or even breathe with Claire in mysterious agony. Maybe I'd get the same germ soon; after all, I'd used her lip gloss. Mom couldn't tell me anything, because Claire's mother wouldn't tell her anything, other than *Claire is resting and having some tests*.

Not good enough.

So the next day I made my plans to haul my big fleece sweatshirt over my St. Brigid's uniform, catch a different Citibus and go to the Janeway. I could get back to school later, or maybe I'd stay with Claire until two o'clock and then just get a bus home, plead period cramps to Dad and get a note. Mom always checked the calendar, but Dad just grimaced, held up his hand, and scribbled a sick note.

I was congratulating myself on my strategy at recess time when Marc Dwyer tapped me on the shoulder and angrily told me he cared about Claire, too.

I gave him a little shove. —What's your problem, Dwyer?

—You. Not telling me how Claire is doing. Keeping it all to yourself, right secretive.

—I don't know how Claire is doing, all right? I wouldn't keep something like that from you.

Marc never got over the day I bumped him off a seesaw the summer between grade one and grade two. He cried and screamed all the way out of Bannerman Park back to Circular Road. Next morning he knocked at my front door, broken arm in a sling, asking for his stack of comic books back. Sullen, he wouldn't say why.

This time, though, his eyes were sad, not angry. And worried. And darkringed, God, like he'd beaten off bad dreams.

I shoved him. —You idiot. I'm not keeping secrets from you.

That night, while I watched a re-run of *Star Trek* on one of the American cable channels, thinking Uhura was the most beautiful woman I had ever seen and maybe I should get my ears pierced, Claire called.

—Nicks?

Her voice sounded like pulled taffy. She gave my nickname two syllables.

—Claire?

Then she was crying, slowly, almost as though it was a struggle.

—Nicks, come and see me. But don't tell. Swear to God, you won't tell. Gross. Some dirty old man is sizing me up.

—Where are you?

—The lobby. Sneaked out to the pay phones. All I got is my babydoll pyjamas. It's so hot in here. Please, don't tell.

Behind her voice, a loudspeakered announcement by some syrupy T-Rex of a nurse: —Patient Claire Furey, please return to your room in D-wing? Patient Claire Furey, please return to your room in D-wing.

Claire wailed. —Now the whole hospital knows! Nicks, please come see me. Oh, God.

The pay phone beeped rapidly; her ten cents of time had gone. The stupid operator butted in. —If you wish to continue your call, please deposit another coin. Do you wish to continue your call?

The line clicked, dial tone hummed: no more Claire. I waited another ten minutes, then threw some book or another into my school bag, ran downstairs, kissed Dad on the forehead – he was watching the VONB-TV *Evening News Hour*, and that Englishman anchor, Almayer Foxe, smiled as he reported on a high school beauty pageant. I told Dad I had a study session with Marc Dwyer, so I'd just be down at his house, and yes, Marc's parents were home.

Dad nodded. —I'm glad you're friends with Marc again. He comes from a nice family.

A few minutes later I knocked on Marc's back door. Knocked again. His bedroom light shone, silhouetting him as he bent over his drafting desk. I looked for a light rock to toss at his window, but I always threw too hard. So I pounded on the back door with my fist instead.

Marc finally came down. —Sorry, my parents aren't home. You can't come in.

I pushed past him. —Perfect. Now listen up, Dwyer. Tomorrow morning, when we catch the bus for school, we're gonna walk the extra block so we're out of sight, then catch the route ten. Not the fifteen. Got that? Route ten takes us to the Janeway.

—We're gonna see Claire? Were you talking to her?

—Just for a minute. I think it would be good for her if you came, too. Up for it?

Marc blinked then, in that distracted way he and Claire both got, so I figured I'd interrupted his artwork. —Yeah. Yeah. Meet you at the bus stop one block up tomorrow morning.

—Cool. And for the love of God, cover up your uniform.

—Right. Wait. You mean, go during the school day?

—Very good, Einstein.

Marc whispered then, even though we were alone. —But I've never pipped off before.

I whispered back. —Consider it a rite of passage. Go back to your drawing.

—How'd you know I'm drawing?

—Because even though you're looking straight at me, you don't see me. Claire gets the same way.

I left the Dwyers' house – for all I know, Marc still stood slack-jawed in the kitchen when his parents got back, but they were probably used to that – and looked for somewhere quiet to do my homework. Some history questions, some math, breeze through that in fifteen or twenty minutes. Never needed to study. School and university came easy, way too easy. I sat under my favourite tree in Bannerman Park, and as the fog came in, and the rest of the park, the streets, every other human, disappeared, I felt a bit peaceful. Then a dog barked, and my history book fell off my lap, and I remembered people, the hundreds surrounding Bannerman Park, Marc Dwyer hating me for breaking his arm and for being Claire's best friend, my grandfather Wright prosing on about the Janeway and the huge improvements in medical care in Newfoundland since 1949, Claire sneaking to the pay phone, *Please come see me, please don't tell.*

Do you wish to continue your call?

So the morning of September 15th, 1983, Marc Dwyer and Nichole Wright, star students of St. Brigid's Academy – Fine Education in the Jesuit Tradition, Mass Negotiable – for the first time in their academic careers, pipped off. I don't know why we'd never done so before. Easy. Bus driver on the route ten didn't ask us anything, despite Marc looking as guilty as a psychopath blinded on the road to Damascus. I figured I might as well finish my history homework, something about colonies and spheres of influence. Marc just chewed his nails and twice lost his grip on his portfolio.

I hated the Janeway. I get odd feelings off some places, like I can pick up vibrations or secret signals or something. The clapboard church in Port au Mal – I knew the second I glanced at it that something demonic squat in there, some contagious melancholy that curled in your guts and threaded up your spine, sometimes quiet, never banished. When I lived in Ontario, I took a drive through some mill towns along the Rideau Canal: Manotick, Almonte, Reddenborough. The Jim Mitchell case had just broken, and I ended up in this back road actually called The Back Road. Route 7-something on the map, but no one called it that. Mitchell enjoyed abducting and tormenting adolescent boys, usually keeping them over a few days. Then he'd let them go, catch and release. I didn't like the Back Road, and I really didn't like Maclean House, all set up with 1930s and 1940s memorabilia, war posters, tinned ham and the like. Reddenburn House, supposedly haunted, felt fine. But Maclean House and the Back Road – anyway, as Mitchell's trial continued, men testified how Mitchell picked them all up on the Back Road, and some really old lady confirmed that Mitchell once rented a room in Maclean House. This unnerved but hardly surprised me. I just pick up on this shit, like it's a scent in the air. I remember being a youngster in the back seat of the car, riding along Torbay Road and suddenly dreading St. Raphael's – cringing as we drove past – long before I even knew what St. Raphael's meant.

The Back Road: solo aberrance.

St. Raphael's: tolerated aberrance.

The Janeway: hope and healing and utterly misguided if not sadistic treatment, all at once. Do no harm.

Maybe suffering leaves a stain.

Swallow *that* without malt whisky.

Battleship grey paint flaking away from darker grey bricks beneath, the Dr. Charles A. Janeway Children's Hospital stood like Moloch on a hilltop, paws on either side, maw open beneath the maroon Helvetica lettering of its name. This monument to hygiene, wartime and fear – utilitarian, sharplined – stood as a late gift to us poor and truly downtrodden of Newfoundland. Built by the Americans, like the rest of Fort Pepperell, the Janeway had passed to the Newfoundland government in the 1960s, not long after the American military reduced its presence on the island. When the Soviets invaded Afghanistan in 1979, American soldiers returned to Pepperell, occupants once again. New paint on the old checkpoints. Clipboards and lists. Amber lights. All so quiet when we got off the bus, diesel exhaust thinning out into salty air and the whiff of the dump. White sky. Unseen gulls cried.

Marc dropped his portfolio again. —We're not supposed to be here. Maybe Claire's in the Janeway school today. Maybe she's asleep. When does the next bus come? We can always say we got on the wrong bus by mistake. We can –

—You still have that St. Christopher's medal your Nan gave you last birthday?

—Yeah.

—Then we'll be fine.

But even I faltered at the entrance. Shit once, shit twice: two freaking khaki-fatigued *guards*. Both well over six feet and two hundred pounds. Both armed. One wearing a camera. The other carrying a clipboard. Accents foreign and familiar as television.

—Sign in, please.

The chain attaching the pen to the clipboard clanked. No mere connected line of spheres as you might see in a bank, the chain's links were thick, black and heavy enough to skew a signature.

I signed in, dotting my "*I*"s with sunbursts, like always, like a fool. Ever a time for fake name ... but lie to those guys, guys with guns? In my novel, *Once I Stood*, when I wrote about the soldiers guarding the Janeway, I made the character based on me mouthy and hard, way smarter than the grunts, quoting Christopher Marlowe at them, for fuck's sake. Even I didn't believe in her on the page, but my God, I wanted to.

Gone pale as the clouds, Marc scribbled spikes. His voice squeaked. —Is this new?

The camera soldier snapped our photo and brightened up the fog. I winked out, for just a second, all dark until the soldier answered Marc.

—Your feet are treading on United States Army property. All visitors will sign in and will be recorded.

—Are you going to call our parents?

Clipboard winked. —Once you step inside the Janeway, you are back on Newfoundland soil and not in my jurisdiction. But this parking lot and entranceway still belong to Uncle Sam.

I tugged on Marc's arm and then smiled at Clipboard. —Gee whillickers, we didn't know that. Thanks, officer.

—I'm a private, ma'am.

I smiled again, took Marc's clammy hand like we were boyfriend and girlfriend, and hauled him inside. The heat and stink inside, after that fog, almost hurt.

Marc jerked his hand away. —Why did you smile at them like that?

—Like what?

—Right slutty.

—I am not slutty!

The triage nurse glanced up from her work. A toddler with pigtails and an oozing ear watched *Sesame Street* and paid no heed, but her mother frowned at me like I'd just revealed myself to be the Whore of Babylon. Which is pretty much how I felt, with Marc calling me slutty. I could have kicked him.

Marc shook his head. —Those two soldiers sized you up.

—We got in, didn't we?

—Just don't do it again, okay?

—All I did was smile. Now, do you want to go see Claire or not?

Marc blushed. Red on his high cheekbones, blue-green eyes into relief, black hair, scandalously long by St. Brigid's Academy standards – yes, small wonder Claire loved him. I could have, too.

The triage nurse spoke to us over Cookie Monster's happy snarfs.

—Can I help you?

I smiled again. I'm wickedly charming and polite when I decide to be. —Just visiting, thanks. We know where to go.

Marc patted my head as I led him up a corridor. —See, that time you smiled right nicely. Wasn't slutty at all.

—Will you let go of the slut thing?

—Stop shoving me, then.

I turned away from him and found what I needed: a floor plan. Because I remembered D-wing well enough, just not how to get there.

Marc looked over my shoulder. —So where is she?

—Dwyer, before we go any further, I need a promise from you.

—I already swore I wouldn't tell we were pipping off.

—More than that. The ward Claire's in. You tell a soul, you even whisper it at night to your teddy bear, and I will kill you.

—Haven't got a teddy bear.

—Claire's on D-Wing.

—So?

—D-Wing. With the nut jobs.

—*Why?*

We turned a corner, and the odours of feces and disinfectant strengthened. The blasting heat did not help. VOIC played through various radios – God knew where the speakers hid – and Neal O'Dea introduced the slate of topics for discussion on *Free Line*.

Quiet stink.

Even Marc had the sense to whisper here. —But why? She's got a bad stomach.

I remembered a pneumatic tube junction once hovered over the nurses' desk in D-wing, obscuring their upper bodies and faces – only their hands visible, opening tubes, unrolling messages, sending out other tubes ... and their voices, polite and cold: *Now, Nichole, let's get you all cleaned up down there.*

Light greenish blue, like a dead version of Marc's eyes, the nurses' desk looked more like a bar to me then. I glimpsed it again years later during the demolition, exposed to the open air, and almost strode up to it to ask the ghosts for a malt whisky and a Demerol chaser, stat.

No nurses behind the desk. Must be in a meeting. A pile of black binders – patient charts. Head-smacking happy thrill, this blatant chance to steal.

Took me maybe five seconds to find Claire's chart. And her room number. And her diagnosis. I crammed the binder into my book bag and hauled Marc along.

Alive. Never felt so alive again as that moment of stealing Claire's chart and dragging Marc Dwyer to see her. Every choice packed with meaning and result.

At the foot of Claire's bed, though, I nearly shut down. Marc and I both tried not to stare, but the girl in the bed across from Claire ... no, I must write this scene ... arms lashed to the bed rails in what looked like gauntlets, or narrow corsets, eyes dull and fixed on a poster of a smiley face ... soiled diaper.

Finally tearing his gaze from the restrained girl, Marc clicked his tongue when he saw Claire. —She looks right old.

Claire lay on her right side, curled up, pale face ruined by her pain-scowl. Should have been laugh lines.

I jiggled her ankles. —Furey-girl, wake up.

—I'm awake.

But she said it with her eyes shut.

—Prove it. Who's here?

—You, Nicks.

—Someone else.

Claire got one eye open and dragged herself into some version of sitting up.

—Marc.

I stepped back and let Marc go on by her side. Then I took out her binder and tried to decipher doctors' tracks.

Epigastric pain LUQ.

Marked tenderness. Rebound tenderness.

Palpable mass LUQ?

Bloodwork normal. X-ray normal.

Provision dx: somatoform pain. Patient is child of a single mother. Resultant anger and stress becomes referred and greatly exaggerated abdominal pain. Nurses note some vomiting.

Patient agitated, unwilling to consider psychological explanation. Insists severe pain felt, particularly after eating.

Orders: Valium 5mg IM Q4-6, NPO x 48 hours. Gravol IM Q4 as needed x 48 hours. Reassess.

I tore this top sheet out, folded it carefully and stuck it in my pencil case. How dare they call Claire a faker? Her pain so obvious – she wouldn't eat pizza on the weekend, for God's sake, and Claire would live on pizza if her mother allowed. If the paramedics had let me ride in the ambulance with her, all this crap could be straightened out by now.

Claire cried as she explained to Marc how the nurses gave her needles just above her bum, how she had no privacy, how it all hurt. Then she stopped in mid-sentence and pointed to Marc's portfolio. —Working on anything new?

—KAL-007.

I thought Marc meant James Bond first, but Claire, as usual, flew far ahead of me. —That was on VOIC again this morning. The nurses play the radio really loud sometimes.

Marc flipped through his portfolio. —Not done yet, right rough.

I only saw a plane. —Didn't you draw any people in it?

Marc rolled his eyes so that I felt like I had a forty IQ. —The human being is implicit in the line of sight.

I sneered, mocked him. —Implicit in the line of sight.

Claire reached out to touch the sketch. —You drew it from the Russian pilot's perspective.

—Soviet pilot, technically. He may not be Russian, right? Might be Latvian or Estonian or something.

I interrupted this sweet little geography lesson by dropping Claire's chart onto her bed. —Claire, you seen this?

Claire's eyes filled up again. —They think I'm lying. Honest to God, Nicks, it really hurts.

—I know. These doctors are idiots. I stole the page –

Howling. Stretched out 'til the note broke and the noise fell but then rose again, insistent, steady and penetratingly loud, falling away as though aimed elsewhere, but God, rising again. A fucking air raid siren. Marc's voice crackled out, and I tried yelling but could only grimace and cover my ears. Claire sat quite still, tracing the Soviet pilot's line of sight with her finger. The girl in the other bed moaned. Sudden audible patches of an announcement on the PA, sneaking under the siren: American soldiers ... Fort Pepperell ... testing readiness ... readiness ... patients remain ... rooms ... evacuation procedure number six ... American soldiers of Fort Pepperell ... readiness ...

Brisk footsteps in the corridors. No closets. No long blankets on the beds to hide us beneath. And wrong bus or not, the clocks read well after nine. No denying being on the pip now, nor the serious danger of being caught.

Claire tried to turn to face the door. —Run. Run!

The girl in the other bed copied Claire, as best she could. —Un. Un!

Footsteps getting closer, approaching the nursing desk, passing the desk, approaching the room. Marc grabbed my hand, and we darted into the little bathroom, damned certain not to turn on the light or shut the door. Marc got himself right behind the door; I jumped up to sit on the sink.

Dear God, the wastebasket held soiled diapers.

And that demented howling, all the worse for being mechanized and predictable – a train reared up on the tracks, whistle like an elephant's trumpeting before it surrendered to inevitable gravity and stomped you –

—Un!

Footsteps, padded footsteps: I could see those feet as clearly as I'd once seen nurses' hands under the pneumatic tubes: white pillowy shoes, leather with rubber soles and wide laces, *all cleaned up down there* ... cold water seeped into my grey flannel skirt.

—Unroom. Room. Un.

The nurse spoke now, much more gently than I expected. —Sara, shh now, I'm sorry about the noise. Just relax, my love, and look at your happy picture.

She talked differently to Claire.

—It's a drill. It'll be over soon.

Subtext: don't you dare complain, you rotten little malingerer.

Try ignoring cold wars when you're squat into a dirty bathroom in the dark with someone your best friend might be in love with, someone you yourself want to kiss, worried sick and indignant over said best friend, smelling some crazy girl's diaper and trying hard *not* to remember your own visit to D-wing, all while pipping off school, hiding from a nurse, and getting dirty water and God knows what else soaked into your grey flannel skirt. Russians shooting civilian planes out of the sky, Americans guarding a parking lot, Doomsday Clock set at two minutes to midnight, nuclear annihilation inevitable as a school bell ...

Marc would choose that moment to get the hiccups.

Familiar rhythm to it.

I swung my legs, lip-synching the ba-bop-bop chorus to Duran Duran's "Planet Earth." A few minutes later, I skipped merrily down the corridor, Marc behind me for a minute or two, singing "Planet Earth" out loud now like my soul depended on breaking through the air raid siren. Nurses closed patients' doors, and one even questioned me. That's when I ran – stupid, because the minute you run, you look guilty. That's how I got in D-wing in the first place, running. Guilty. Siren still howling, up and down, in and out, that noise nourishing and destroying me, run run run, switch songs, "Waiting for the Night Boat," yeah, zombies and nurses, and me no bigger than an agate stone darting down stairwells to an uninhabited basement – oh look, pneumatic tubes in the ceiling – coming to a sweaty stop before a door marked *Shelter.*

Lacking *Drink Me* but pretty sure the pursuing nurse screamed *Off with her head*, I figured *Shelter* would have to do.

Do you think I could explain to the soldiers and doctors in the bomb shelter under the Janeway, the very stern-looking soldiers and doctors practicing their evacuation procedure? The day after the Russian military shot down a civilian plane? Assuming it was civilian ...

Cots. Crates. White labels, red crosses. An entire wall, at least ten feet tall, lined with drawers and cabinets. Caged electric bulbs. In one corner, a really big mousetrap. And a small transistor radio, receiving VOIC.

VOIC World Atomic Time is brought to you by ...

We could hardly hear the siren.

Golden Pheasant Tea, the best tea for the best day and every day, and Port of Call, Water Street. Make it your next Port of Call.

I fell to my knees and bawled my face off.

Cried again when Mom picked me and Marc up, took us home. Didn't care about being grounded. Just wanted to explain that Claire did not fake and did not lie and most definitely had not gone crazy. She just needed me there with her to explain everything, so she could get the right treatment. Just needed the damn doctors to *listen.*

Claire's Poppy Best visited her that evening. Shorty afterwards, the hospital moved Claire to a private room on the medicine floor and offered her some pain meds. The doctors promised thorough testing and speedy diagnosis. Testing, yes. Diagnosis: viral?

Viral.

23. "UP TO HER KNEES IN GRAVEL"
in which Gabriel Furey hips his partner.

Dec. 26, 1978

—Gabriel, it's not true.

—You slut!

—You'll have the neighbours banging on the walls in a minute.

—Fuck the neighbours! You –

—You'll wake up Claire.

Gabriel sighed, took a drink, took a breath. —Mike Morgan says he saw you leave Bob's place.

—Yes now, and Mike's a fine sober judge of character. Surprised he can see past the bottle cap.

—Not man enough for ya, am I?

—For God's sake, Gabe, zip your pants back up.

—Can't face it? Love for you, that is.

—Shrivelled up in the short and curlies, yeah, that's love. Like you and that slut over to the Sand Bank the other night. You even know her name?

—Dory.

—Dory?

—Dory Matchstick or something, I dunno.

—Dorinda Masterson. Yes, I know all about her, trying to tell me about my women's rights and equality and all the rest of it, and then she's out trawling for my man. How much have you had to drink tonight?

—Bob now, I s'pose he shaves his sac, do he, the pretentious cunt? Or is he right fast, like the Six Million Dollar Man?

—Gabe, so help me, if you wake up Claire – you're gonna trip. God, there's no talking to you when you're drunk. Sit down until – my hair!

—Now you listen to me.

—Let go of my hair.

—Don't be bawling like that. You're gonna wake up Claire.

—Gabe, let go.

—Are you sleeping with Bob?

—You're hurting me.

—Proper thing. Mike says –

—Gabe, please. Shh.

—You're not getting off that easy. Don't be at that. Stop it. I said stop, ya cunt! No fucking blow job's gonna cover your sins. There. On the floor with the dirt. With the earwigs and the carpenters. Where you belong. Not even wearing shoes, how can I be hurting ya? Mess. Fucking mess. Callie. What am I after doing to ya? Callie, honey, can you sit up? Let me get some ice. Sweet Jesus, girl, I'm sorry, I'm sorry, come here I help you to the table. Talk to me. Callie, just talk to me. Tell me it's all right. Cal. Don't you dare give me that fucking cold silence now – Callie. Talk to me. Hate me. Kick me. Spit on me. I don't care, just talk to me – no. Don't. Don't go. I'm begging you, Callie, I am on my fucking knees here, don't stay quiet. Cal, ducky, don't leave me like this ...

24. MYOPIA SKY 2
in which Richard Fahey barges in on Robert Wright.

July 12, 1954

—It's eleven minutes after nine. I'll presume Mr. Wright's in Engineering?

— Sir? Sir, please, you can't go in there.

Richard Fahey ignored the VOIC receptionist, a new girl from east end St. John's, and strode towards Engineering, down in the basement. The little Chapel Street rowhouse barely contained VOIC these days, but Fahey knew the way.

Various VOIC staff stared at Fahey as he headed for the stairs, not quite certain they saw him – Richard Fahey, former partner, now arch-competitor of Mr. Wright, walking through the hallways of VOIC Radio in his starched shirt and signature bright red tie as though he belonged there.

Descending steps too shallow to accommodate a man's foot, ducking the pull-chains of several ceiling lights, Richard got to the cold basement. The unsteady softwood floor had been hastily laid over rocks and dirt. Equipment hummed, gave off some heat. Richard had warned Robert for years that one flood in that basement would bankrupt him.

The coal chute banged. Shaggy darkness brushed past Richard: Orion, Robert's Newfoundland dog, given free run of the station and stinking as ever, nails scratching on the stairs, old coal dust falling gently from his coat. The dog always went directly to Robert. So Richard followed Orion, who acknowledged him with a chuff as he lay down in front of Robert's shut office door.

Richard almost knocked. Old habit.

Hand on the doorknob, Richard overheard two voices, almost identical – Robert Wright and his younger brother, William.

—You took those photos?

—Robert, the entire photo club took some.

—Photo club, indeed. And where is the young lady now? Still tied up?

—She was no lady, Robert, I can assure you. Quite willing. She wants to be an actress.

—So you don't deny it?

Silence.

—William, is this your Society of Adepts' community service? Dirty pictures? Tell me this: how old is that girl?

—Old enough to –

Richard stepped over the dog and opened the door.

Both Wright men's eyes narrowed behind new horn-rimmed glasses.

Robert's mouth tightened as he struggled for courtesy. —Mr. Fahey.

—Mr. Wright.

Some of the black hairs on Robert's arms fell onto his rolled and loose white shirtsleeves, and his waistcoat sagged, surprising Richard. *Tailored clothes bagging off him like that? He's lost weight.*

Robert looked down at his dark desk. —William, I need to get to work.

—You won't help me?

Robert regarded his brother with contempt and some slight derangement. *Too far, William, and by God, you'll not haul me overboard with you.*

—Get out.

Richard shut his eyes until William left. Then he sat in the rightmost of the two chairs before Robert's desk.

Robert now sat with his shoulders well back, arse forward, hands folded on his belly, as though he planned to daydream. He addressed the ceiling. —You've got gall, showing up here like this. I expect there's a damned good reason. What do you need?

Irritated by truth, Richard snorted. —I might have gall, but you're the one thinking a lot of himself.

Robert studied the wood panelling on the wall this time, his voice steady in repetition, ignoring Richard's protest. —What do you need?

—Rose.

At least no one's taking pictures of her. —Not again, Fahey.

Richard spoke to the calendar, unable to look anywhere else. Robert Wright's neat black Xs marked the spent days. —Out overnight this time. They've torn up Riordan's Back. They're afraid she's in the woods this time. You know what the woods between Riordan's Back and Port au Mal are like. The ponds.

Robert squinted at Richard with exasperation and concern.

Richard smiled a bit and shrugged. —I don't know what they're going to do with her. Least it wasn't all that cold last night.

He could think of nothing else to say.

—Fahey, why didn't you come to me before now?

—I just found out!

Richard's accent thickened when he yelled. He quieted himself.

—I just found out, b'y.

Wright's voice retained precision and those stylized vowels he tried to pluck from the BBC. —What was she wearing? Think, man. What was she wearing?

Richard let his mouth fall open, and he shrugged.

Robert scowled. —We shall put a stop to this.

Richard nodded. He could not look at Robert.

Standing up now, Robert glanced at his appointment book, unlocked his desk drawer and removed a small black velvet bag. —We must embarrass your brother. Nothing drastic, nothing blatant. That's not how it's done. Just enough to let him know that we know precisely why she runs away. *Newsbird* is in Torbay. You'll stay here and write the news story. I'll call it in. Full alerts. Lost child. Television and radio, your station and mine. Everyone with a wireless, and those happy few with televisions, will know Rose Fahey of Riordan's Back is lost. And by God, Richard, soon enough they'll also know she was found safe. How – how can you still call that man your brother?

Richard followed, prisoner first to his brother Harold's will, now to Robert Wright's. Strong men, both of them, and Richard Fahey could stand up to neither. In the control room now, Mr. Wright explained the need to leave Mr. Fahey in charge; the faces staring at Richard now: familiar, just older. Old Captain Wright's ship's bell still sat by the mic to ring in the newscasts. The smells comforted Fahey: floor and wood polish, hair oil and leather shoes, the metallic underarm sweat of men. Richard followed Robert to the lobby; Robert instructed the receptionist to call the office of Prime Minister Best and make apologies. Velvet bag in one hand, Studebaker keys in the other, Robert turned back to Richard, nodded quickly, and left. Richard Fahey knew he should return to his own station, knew he should leave the VOIC building, never mind Robert's pompous orders, but, having interrupted Robert Wright and set him to a task, he was duty-bound to wait for Robert Wright's return and any telling-off that may result.

A light wind lifted Robert's hair as he stashed the velvet bag in the Studebaker's trunk. His new glasses slid down his nose again, and he pushed them back up. Robert had gone wandering in the woods between Riordan's Back and Port au Mal, twice getting quite lost. At eight, he nearly fell into one of the sudden ponds, trees dense until a quick slope to deep water. The second time he'd have fallen in, except his pants snagged on a tree root. He still had the scar. He'd since flown over those woods many times; he knew those ponds. He also knew his doctor's orders from a visit back in June: —You are not to fly, and you are not to drive. I cannot make it any clearer than that.

Why did I have to see the body?

'Twas coming ashore.

Robert drove to the airfield. His sweaty hands smelled of Orion's shaggy coat.

25. SITE 1
in which Thomas Wright loses his father.

July 12, 1954

—He went *where*?

Richard Fahey's mouth open and shut like that of a caught fish. Suddenly, he could not make a sound before Thomas Wright.

Thomas flushed dark red. —Dr. Cart grounded him weeks ago. He's not even supposed to be driving, the pigheaded fool! Who told him to take his plane up?

But Thomas did not wait for an answer. Instead he ran back out to the parking lot, determined to chase down his father, get him out of the sky – hell, drive to Harbour Grace, if need be.

It needed be.

The sun burnt the land. Thomas remembered the sun, glare on the windshield, glare through the ripples of road dust that looked now like waves of sand in some forgotten desert. His Studebaker, identical to his father's, rumbled in third, protesting as the right front wheel dipped into a pothole wide enough to be named and fished. Dirt roads. Better than no roads. The front of the car banged again; the road had washed out here earlier in the spring, some torrent of runoff cutting deep, leaving a hard bump. Dust rose, and Thomas knew he should gear down, take it to second and drive sensibly, but he'd come two hours already, and a Wright did not turn back.

A moose calf and cow emerged from the trees. Thomas saw them in time and braked, stalling, cursing. The calf took its time, looking from one end of the dirt road to the other, seeing destination nowhere. The cow waited on the other side, gesturing once with her head. The calf shat. Thomas took his hands from the wheel and stick and raised them to heaven. Then the calf turned round and plodded up to Thomas's open window. The calf's neck, a promise of strength ... Thomas saw now the calf was male, and he imagined it dark and huge, majestically antlered, dead at his feet. The calf snuffled. The cow waited. Harbour Grace at least an hour's drive away, and then a boat to Port au Mal ... Thomas rammed his fists into the dash.

—Move, you goddamned steak on legs. Go on, before I run you down!

The cow backed away a step, but the calf merely snuffled some more. Then he dropped his head, as though tired, on the Studebaker's roof.

Hunting. Organized hunting, that's what they needed, every man licensed to hunt moose for meat, cull the herd, cull the herd. Too many moose, an infestation – no, a plague of moose, maggoty with moose. Not even indigenous. Some fool had imported them from the Miramichi, tasked a farmer to round up bulls and cows and herd them onto a boat so they might sail to Newfoundland and there breed and delight hunters. Thomas shut his eyes and tried to tell himself he smelled moose steak frying, not this filthy beast leaning on his car. He would bring this up with Prime Minister Jack Best. If they couldn't shoot them all, they should round them up and send them back, send them back where they came from, yes, back to the bloody Miramichi, the Great Newfoundland Moose Repatriation Act of 1954. Sweat pricked out on Thomas now; his heart thudded and he gasped when the moose calf dropped his head on the roof twice more. Thomas glanced up for dents. Then the cow called, irritated as any mother, and the calf departed with a final expulsion of leafy gas.

Thomas whispered it. —God damn you.

Tears smudged his glasses. He must get to Port au Mal, a place he'd only visited in summers, loathing it. Thomas wanted his Aunt Jane. Sensible Aunt Jane, always saying the right thing, sometimes saying nothing at all.

Damned fool.

Thomas drove. Ange O'Dea met him in Harbour Grace, then took him the rest of the way to Port au Mal on his fishing boat, the wind forcing air into their noses and eking out tears. Thomas climbed the Jackmans' stage, nodding to his cousins, who nodded back, and he shook the hand of Neal

O'Dea. Overhead, obscured by fog, *Newsbird* growled, and Thomas stared up, trying to find it, making himself dizzy. Then Thomas followed Ange, while Neal and John O'Dea took a Newfoundland bitch to keep searching for Rose Fahey. Only then did Thomas notice he wore a suit and dress shoes, hardly the clothes for a hike in the woods.

A flare lit the fog, and *Newsbird*'s engine stuttered and cut.

26. CONTINUITY 3
commercial break

CLIENT: PORT OF CALL

SPONSORSHIP: 7:45a news, Monday, Wednesday, Friday
Noon Hour Gun News, Tuesday and Thursday
Tips for Housewives, 4:15p, Monday to Friday

READ DATES: June 20, 1956 'til further notice

SALESMAN: Ralph Abbott

WRITER: Thomas Wright

READER: By the clock.

It has long been a tradition in St. John's to expect the finer things, a tradition no one questions. You can expect and find the finer things where this tradition is strong, at Port of Call on Water Street. Established in 1929 by Mr. Harold Canning, Port of Call remains the favoured port of call for those who can appreciate life's finer offerings. And when the finer things are not just expected but easily found, then one knows the tradition is sound. You will bask in this tradition at Port of Call on Water Street, where Mr. Harold Canning still works on the sales floor. Port of Call, Water Street: make it your next port of call.

27. UP THE POND 1 – "HUNGER AND NIGHT AND THE STARS" in which Dan McGrew nearly drowns.

July 1941

Muskeg deceives. Short grasses grow on top, hues varied, sudden and subtle as steeping tea, and water tables, embraced by sphagnum to lie flat or cling to a hill, peek out as tiny rivers. Grasses shift, and the pines taunt and dare with each croned branch: *I can survive here; can't you?* Grasses fade, autumn blaze obscuring muck. Deep muck. Muskeg swallows: dead plants and trees, animals, equipment, people. The railway line here in northern Ontario had been difficult to lay. Sometimes in spring, before the workmen knew, the muskeg melted, and the sinking of tools might be silent and quick, the sinking of heavy gear maddening and slow, depending on water tables and mud, on the glint-reasoned whims of God.

Nine-year-old Dan McGrew positioned himself on a map of Ontario. South, way down south, not far west of Ottawa: Reddenborough. Nearly two hundred forty miles northwest of Reddenborough: the McGrew cabin. Dan turned a new page in his scribbler and sketched a map of Canada, avoiding the mistake that irritated Mr. Howe, the teacher who travelled the area by railway car. *Stop Canada at the eastern border of Quebec. Ignore Labrador, for she belongs to Newfoundland. Underneath, for the Maritimes, drag your pencil round Cape Breton, then stop.* Dan happily omitted the hard-to-draw Newfoundland, though he dreamt one night of odd grey and purple cliffs close enough to touch from Cape Breton, if only he could reach the distance. Then he fell off Cape Breton and woke up.

Bored with geography homework, Dan turned to mathematics. Mr. Howe had set him algebra more suited to high school; Dan sketched out quadratic equations as though writing poetry in another language. Graphing them, he discovered perfections. Too soon, far too soon, he covered up the algebra. He'd not see Mr. Howe for two months or more; he must ration out this beauty until the train and the teacher came back. English composition then. *Write a 500-word essay on a man who matters to you. Use descriptive and expository techniques.*

Dan groaned. He loathed composition.

My father, Clayton Angus McGrew, matters the mostest to me.

Dan drew a line through his awkward superlative.

My father, Clayton Angus McGrew, matters very much. He is serving overseas with the Princess Pats. He is a sergeant. He is an artillery expert. His ancestors came to Canada from Scotland in 1827.

So much for exposition.

My father is five feet five inches tall. His shoulders are broad. I do not know how much he weighs. He is a miner and works very hard. He is also a good Catholic. That is what my mother says. There is no church here, no mass and no confession, but he is still a good Catholic. My mother is a midwife.

Dan crossed out his mother, but then wrote her back in, giving her a new paragraph.

My mother is a midwife. She likes to tell me the same old stories when I ask. The same old stories I like to hear are MacLean's Daughter, which is scary, and The Cremation of Sam McGee. That poem is good on winter nights. And I like to hear about the lady who was known as Lou.

Dan hesitated, then barged ahead. No point ducking the truth, as Clayton McGrew often said.

I am named for a Robert Service poem, but I will not be shot. My mother says if she ever had another son, she would find a way to call him Sam McGee. If she had a girl, she would find a way to call her Lorna Doone. Sometimes my mother is very sad.

Two hundred and three words. Dan sighed. Not even halfway there.

History some incomprehensible babble about the Hudson's Bay Company – Dan ignored it. French conjugations – little effort and less accuracy. Dan returned to his composition.

My mother is visiting ~~Mrs St Mrs Sticow~~ a Russian miners' wife. She is overdue, whatever that means.

Fourteen more words, not counting the mangled name.

My Dad used to come kiss me goodnight before he washed his face. His lips were rough. His eyes were like wet holes in dust. I miss him.

Twenty-eight.

Dad knows how everything works. All he had to do is look at something, and he can tell you how it works. He is a shaft-sinker. He was a shaft-sinker. He will be a shaft-sinker.

Ink on his fingertips, Dan smudged the paper as he counted his words. Thirty-five more.

I hope the war is over soon. I was really proud when my Dad first left, but the first Christmas he was not here was awful. My mother is tired all the time. Hardly anyone can pay her for being a midwife. Some people can't even speak English. Mum says she ~~can't~~ cannot ask payment of people who don't speak English yet. Sometimes they give her food, and she carries it back over the railway track. Mum walks the railway track. I am proud she named me for a Robert Service poem. Robert Service is a good poet. Mum says there are poems out there that do not rhyme, but I ~~don't~~ do not care. Poetry that rhymes and tells a story is good poetry. I can recite many poems. Robert Service. Keets and Shelley. Tenneseeson.

Hmm. Expository and descriptive. Maybe time to ask a rhetorical question?

How can it be a poem if it does not rhyme?

Then he wrote, not meaning to:

Where is Mum?

At sunrise, Dan took the track. He carried no water, no food, for he expected at any moment to meet his mother. Haze and muskeg shimmered.

The Russian miner's wife answered the door, waddling and carrying an infant to her chest while a toddler peeked round her skirt. She kissed Dan's forehead several times, stood back a bit and looked at him sadly. Thirsty, Dan wanted to ask the Russian woman for a drink, but she closed her door.

Maybe an hour later, Dan reached the next clutch of cabins, very near the mine, mostly bachelors' homes, mostly empty. The salted language Clayton McGrew had wished to keep from his wife and child tumbled freely from one man's mouth, happy cursing, a wicked indulgence of hard consonants and arcing rhythm – thrilling. The joyful noisemaker, unwashed for months and unshaven for years, leaned back his head and laughed at the sun.

—Motherfucking Satan bedamned splintered Christ on the cross bleeding on the God damned gaping crowd below, eh. Too many motherfucking trees. Too much God damned sky.

Then he glanced quickly over his shoulder, startled. His eyes darkened, shrunk somehow.

—Hey. You're Clay McGrew's boy.

—Yes, sir.

—What in the name of all-fired jumping fuck are you doing up here?

—Looking for my mother.

The bearded man turned to face Dan properly. His sweat-rotted thin flannel shirt strained over his muscles, and his entire upper body seemed too large for his tight and narrow hips, for his delicate legs. Emotions scrawled themselves across his face: happiness, arrogance, certainty, fear.

—The midwife, eh?

—Yes, sir.

—I saw her.

The bearded man turned around now, bending forward at the shoulders, managing to loom at his height of five foot two. —I saw her. Walking up the track.

Muskeg surrendered to rock on either side of the rails.

Dan looked up the track, looked back down the track. Blackflies settled in his ears.

The bearded man got angry. —Go find your mother. Stay on the track, eh. Muskeg'll get ya. Too much God damned sky.

He said it as a warning. Then he leaned down and picked up a stone – the stone pelted Dan's shoulder.

—Go. Go on. Find your Mommy. Go go go.

Grateful for the tears drowning the blackflies on his face, Dan turned and ran.

At sunset – so thirsty – Dan sighted a cabin far off from the track. Testing the ground with his foot, finding it solid, he left the rail line and weaved past an old pine, eyes half shut, bruised shoulder throbbing. *Rest, drink, ask for* – too far. Dan slipped into muskeg, up to his hips before he understood soft ground. Sphagnum wrapped his waist, then his ribs, and cool rot flooded his shoes. No time to pray, no time to breathe, and a tree root glanced his face. Feet brushing something small and round, Dan grabbed the tree root: right hand left hand, desperate pull and begging the sogged wood not to break; it bent, goading him to the surface. Coughing, vomiting, crying, dirty water streaming from his nose, from the top of his head, Dan huddled on hard ground. Feet arrived, then hands, and someone male dragged him, taking him under the arms, this pressure tickling, and Dan lost eleven days to fever, vomiting, diarrhoea and recovery. Visions of muskeg, of the cursing miner, a blackfly swastika, Hitler's face, spent out with loon calls and wolves ....

Mr. Howe correcting Dan's homework as Dan sipped weak tea, Mr. Howe told him Mr. McKinnon, the man who now sheltered them, had expected Dan's mother, but she had never arrived. Dan should entertain no false hope. A family, said Mr Howe, shaking his head in delighted wonder at Dan's algebra, a family in Reddenborough needed a strong young man to help on the farm. —Food and lodging, Daniel. And in September, you could go to school.

—But how will my father find us?

Mr. Howe sighed. *My father is five feet five inches tall.* —Daniel, this is difficult. I think you know what I must tell you.

Dan giggled. —You're lying.

Mr. Howe gently shook his head. —In times of war –

Dan's voice deepened, cracked. —You're lying. Too much God damned lies. Too many motherf – you're lying.

Mr. McKinnon had returned and stood now in Dan's doorway, his face obscured by the shadows of being inside.

Dan begged. —You're lying.

Both men shook their heads.

—Why can't you be lying?

28. LOGGER 1
in which VOIC Radio broadcasts live from a model plane exhibition.

July 11, 1970

VOIC's Johnny Hepcat – Jim Reid when he was at home – and Tim Stratton had parked the VOIC Chevy K5 Blazer on the shore of Quidi Vidi Lake in St. John's. They sat back, prepared to waste a sunny Saturday afternoon obviously meant for cleaning the barbecue or tidying up the shed in fine male company. Few dozen cold ones wouldn't hurt, either. The missus'd be hanging out the wash or tilling the flowerbed; the youngsters would go hither and yon on their bikes, baseball cards flapping against the spokes – Jim had spotted an entire colony of banana seats on his front lawn that morning, then a matching colony of kids swigging Kool-Aid in the kitchen – and braver souls might even drag out the lawn chairs and catch a few scarce rays. Truly glorious. More to the point, Sunday called for rain.

But VOIC's Johnny Hepcat and Tim Stratton had a remote. Not just any remote. A car dealership – normal. Carpet or paint store – dull but normal. Grocery store – bit effeminate, but normal. No, today's remote broadcast, live and right here on 570 VOIC: a radio-controlled model plane enthusiasts' club. Thomas Wright's son Lewis belonged to this club, which may have explained why VOIC's finest found themselves trapped in a hot Chevy K5 Blazer reporting on the progress of little buzzy things with wings.

Jim glanced round at the ground-pilots – each one edgy, suppressed aggression bubbling up. Most of these young men had never scored a goal, never hit a home run. Jim guessed a few had been kissed but had likely been charged for it. Today would be different. Today meant defiance of damning social expectation, of snotty girls, stunned jocks and gravity. Today, their custom-built model planes would fly.

Johnny Hepcat here for 570 VOIC, live on the shores of Quidi Vidi. Now, I know what you're thinking – it's not Regatta time yet. No, today is the final round of the – what are they, Tim?

The Newfoundland Model Plane Club.

The Newfoundland Model Plane Club, and they're down here today with remote-control planes they've built themselves. You got to come see this. We're talking Newfoundland aviation history here, folks, from biplanes to jets, all kinds of different planes down here at Quidi Vidi. This is Johnny Hepcat –

and Tim Stratton –

broadcasting live from the Newfoundland Model Plane Club Exhibition at Quidi Vidi Lake, right here and only on 570 VOIC.

Jim clicked off the VHF and took a swig from Tim's Thermos.

—Lamb's again?

—Don't like it? Bring your own.

—One of us has got to be fit. Not having you get another DUI in the station rig. Jesus Murphy, I thought Ben'd skin you. I don't know how he kept that from Mr. Wright.

Tim swallowed some more. —Young Lewis found out. He told Mister. Gutless little prick. I'm back on probation.

—Not like Mr. Wright can fire you with the ratings we get. Luh, little Sopwith Camel. That the one Snoopy's supposed to fly?

—Promised the wife I'd clean out the garage today. Every time I touches her, all she says is, 'You got that garage done yet?'

I'm Johnny Hepcat, broadcasting live here on 570 VOIC from the shores of Quidi Vidi for the Newfoundland Model Plane Club Exhibition. We've already seen three model planes make their rounds – these are remote control planes, and they have to follow the same route as the Regatta rowing teams, and – uh oh, looks like one's after falling into the water. What a disappointment. But no odds, folks, it's a beautiful Saturday, and there's loads more model plane action coming yet. This is Johnny Hepcat in the VOIC Chevy K5 Blazer for 570 VOIC.

And we're back here on 570 VOIC for more model plane action at the - did that thing just crash?

This is Johnny Hepcat at Quidi Vidi for the - oh, that's too bad - for the Newfoundland Model Plane Club Exhibition ...

Broadcasting live here in 570 VOIC - another one down.

Tim tucked his Thermos under the seat. —Dan McGrew's coming over.

Jim watched VOIC's chief engineer negotiate crowd and mud, dressed, despite the summer heat, in a three-piece brown suit, beige shirt and brown tie.

Dan smiled gently and leaned against the driver's door. —Planes aren't having much luck today. Lamb's, Stratton? When are you going to move on to a good sensible Scotch? Smells much better.

Lewis Wright's model Hercules circled the route perfectly. The judges called out a score that placed Lewis in the top three.

Jim leaned back as Tim passed the Thermos over him to Dan. —Gotta go on the air now, b'ys.

A model Cessna took off. Jim opened the VHF and started his report. The Cessna abruptly crashed into the lake, broke apart and sank.

Dan pursed his lips. —Hmm. That wasn't supposed to happen.

Jim gave his report and signed off. —Only another fifteen minutes of this. What a waste of a Saturday afternoon. Sure, half the planes crash.

Dan reached in and took the VHF, elbowing Jim in the belly. —Excuse me.

Final round. The three top scorers, including Lewis Wright, would now have to pilot their planes on a random course designed by the judges.

The first plane ascended; Dan opened the VHF as if to go on the air.

The plane fell.

Tim barked out laughter.

Confused, Jim pointed to VHF and empty sky. —Dan, do you mean to tell me –

Dan said nothing, but tucked the VHF into his jacket pocket. He hummed quietly.

Then, when the second finalist launched his plane, he opened the VHF again.

The plane fell.

Dan passed the VHF back to Jim. —Interference. Every time you went on the air, you blocked the remote controls. VOIC crashed those planes.

The announcer in VOIC Control had meantime gone to an unscheduled commercial break to cover Jim's absence.

Lewis Wright, the only competitor left, had technically won by elimination, but the judges insisted he pilot his plane one last time. Tim Stratton nodded at this, but said nothing. Lewis accepted the ruling, and shortly his model Hercules buzzed over the Blazer and then nicely rounded the boathouse.

The control room called. *—Jim? Ya there or what? I need a report.*

Jim glanced down at the VHF in some fear.

—Jim, pick up, willya? Mr. Wright's in the building today, and he's after making me check off each report. He knows there's one left.

Jim now looked to Dan. The engineer silently admired Lewis's flight path.

—Jim, Mr. Wright's coming down the hall. For the love of Christ, call in. Commercial island ends in five seconds. Four. Three.

Two more yards, one more …

The plane fell.

This is Tim Stratton down here with Johnny Hepcat in the VOIC Chevy K5 Blazer at the Newfoundland Model Plane Club Exhibition …

Scattered on impact. Floated briefly.

And if you weren't down here at Quidi Vidi this afternoon, then you missed a fine time. One of the best Saturday afternoons I've had in a while. Broadcasting live from the end of the Newfoundland Model Plane Club Exhibition, I'm Tim Stratton, right here on 570 VOIC.

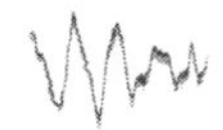

29. STRIGES
in which Gabriel Furey sees things in an old light.

February 13, 1979

Fishy. Sharper tang of stale urine. Hands up and down his ribcage, his face, his hips – sweat – could this time be the peace time? Depended on Brother Stephens' own demons. Caress, abandon or thrash? Twice Gabriel got the buckle end, once across the face, the same mouth that had

– groan escaping past his teeth, Callie chasing Claire out of the kitchen, *Daddy has a headache* – and Christ, Christ, mercy and grace, where the hell – knees on the floor, still the old tiles of the kitchen on Chapel Street, yet the taste, the ache in the jaw, *You've such a little mouth, Gabriel Furey, for one who never shuts up.* Sweat, cold. Tears, hot. Through the coming focus, the return to being artist and father, Gabriel saw Claire, haughty in her fear as she peeked round the kitchen doorway – Gabriel saw Claire as Brother Stephens had seen Gabriel. Brave new – that screaming, him? Christ, he'd frighten Claire, neighbours would call the cops. Possession. How to explain possession. Explain how Brother Stephens shot his bitter salt seed down Gabriel's throat and then gestated deep in Gabriel's heart until he grew like vines to infest Gabriel's hands that now dug into the tiles so they'd not reach for his daughter. Begging Callie: *Take her out. Money in my jacket. Just get her out!* Run. Only option. Run, and drag Brother Stephens with him, pry him and his infestation the hell away from Claire.

30. "HOW DRY A CINDER"
in which Robert Wright and Jack Best discover Colleen Best dead in her home.

March 30, 1942

Sweet Jesus.

Robert Wright turned from the kitchen, from the stink of it all. Behind him, Jack Best waited as if on a precipice, waited for the final word: jump or step back.

Robert shook his head. The man's wife –

Jack surprised him. —She hasn't been right since Tessa died. Not right at all.

Neither have you, Jack. —We should leave the house. The gas.

—Let's move her.

—What?

Jack took a breath, forcing the gas into his lungs. Newfangled gas stove, and Colleen had to have one. Nausea came. —We've got to move her. I'm not having the constables find her like that.

—Jack, she –

Jack had already gotten to the kitchen. —We'll get her on the fainting couch. Make it look like she fell asleep and left the gas on and died that way.

—We can't – you – hang on, Jack, you can't do it alone.

They carried the shockingly heavy but not yet stiff body of Colleen Best to the fainting couch, where she liked to read in the afternoons. Beneath the gas, Robert smelled blood; a doctor would later discover a haemorrhaging that suggested miscarriage.

Jack found a note on his dresser, told no one – failures and regrets, where it could be deciphered.

The constables shortly arrived at the house of Mr. and Mrs. Jack Best. VOIC ran no story here. The newspaper obituary read *died suddenly.* No one else spoke of the matter, in public.

31. UNSENT 1
in which Claire Furey writes a letter to her father.

Dec. 12, 1981

Dear Dad,

Do you like the stationery? It smells like strawberries. Pop bought it for me. He thinks a young lady should have nice stationery. He got me the red pen too. It's got a pink feather on it. I can now go a few days at a time before I remember you. It's getting better. I started a new school. It's the private one you didn't want me to go to. I'm sorry. I like it there. Lots of art time. I think Pop's paying for it. I got a new friend called Nichole Wright. We're best friends. She does my hair and everything. Mom and me moved to a new apartment. Guess what? I take the bus. Not a school bus, but the real Citibus, route 4, all by myself. This is really stupid. Why can't you send us your address? I hate you sometimes!

Love,
Claire

32. "SCATTERED AND SMALL" 1
in which Robert and William Wright lose their father.

October 12, 1947

Captain Tobias Wright kept himself company by reciting favourite hymns. Troublesome enough to have the old skipper out on the low shore in the fog, but he also stood naked, save for his left sock, and would not be persuaded to stay indoors.

Up in the back yard of the old house, Robert and William studied their father's back. Spine curving between broad shoulders, white hair in tufts …

—Pray to God. Pray to God. Heartless, indifferent, grey sky gone black like the water in winter. Salt desert! God!

Robert trembled.

William took Robert's arm. —He threw Dr. Jessop off the Jackmans' stage.

—Yes now, Jessop, bigger quack than a pond full of ducks.

—Only a matter of time before Father harms someone. Likely Mother.

Tobias pointed at a wave. —Not cleft for me, are ya! Foul. Foul.

The fog wet Robert's glasses. —Is he singing?

—No tune here. Either side of him, now.

—He only drank half. I told Jessop he'd taste it. William, if he falls in –

—All we could do.

Tobias Wright turned around, face slack. —Eye-strings break in death. William is a monster, all darkness stuck together, but you'll never live to be my age, Robert. Children's children!

Then the old man tottered.

William ran easily towards their father, but Robert's heart pounded, as it had the day he nearly drowned off the low shore. A hidden bottle clinked against his keys in his coat pocket: chloral hydrate, prescribed to Tobias Wright. *Knock him out,* Dr. Jessop had said. *We must be humane, before he hurts someone.*

Tobias stared so sadly, heavy with lucid knowledge. —Resurrection of the flesh. But not for you.

William tackled his father. Knocked on his back, Tobias tore at his son's waistcoat, grasped a rock and raised it towards William's head. Blood heavy, Tobias dropped the rock.

William straddled him. —Chloral hydrate's taking effect.

Tobias tried once more to raise his head before going quiet and still.

Gulls screeched like galing children.

Only now did Dr. Jessop approach. He'd been hiding behind the house. Injecting Captain Wright with another sedative, he gave brisk orders to get him secured to a stretcher so they might load the Captain in the ambulance for the long and bumpy drive to St. John's, never mind the dangerous climb from the shore.

To St. John's. Not to *The Hospital for Mental and Nervous Diseases* – never say that out loud. Just *St. John's*.

Hope, watching from her sister's window several houses away, wept.

—Over and done. Over and done.

Too much sorrow and shame in even remembering ... Tobias Wright's illness became a forbidden topic, like Ellen's consumption and her long stay in the San. His children would never visit. Good as dead. Just a matter of waiting now until his body came ashore.

He would die in a straitjacket and diaper, screaming.

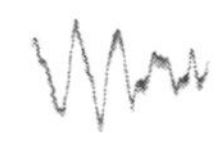

33. OHM 1
in which Robert Wright watches a storm through snow.

July 9, 1954

—What have you got there, Father?

Robert gently laid the heavy box on the dining room table, not yet cleared from Etta's afternoon card party. Twenty-three-year-old Thomas shifted lipsticked cups of leftover ginger ale – did he smell rum? – and a smudged tally sheet, giving his father more room.

—This is the window through which we can see the future, if Richard Fahey is to be believed.

—Not giving in, are you, Father?

—Very funny.

—Old radio man like you –

—All the more reason I must become conversant with this new medium. Not that we're in anyone's broadcasting range yet.

Robert and Thomas both smiled and pushed their heavy glasses up their noses at the same moment. Then Robert crammed a handful of Bridge Mixture into his mouth, chewed, cocked his head to one side and studied the unmarked box. —I swear, if I get to the grave with all my teeth, it won't be with any credit to your mother. Get that candy out of my reach, would you? Now we'll get this television out. Mind the cups. Plug it in over there.

—Tidy little thing. Marconi, good brand.

—Seventeen-inch bundle of wires and lights. Thomas, look. You can see static. Snow. Interference, emptiness – you can actually *see* it.

—I see the men behind it.

—Indeed, you do not. I told you, no one's broadcasting television here. The signal is hollow, like –

I refer to that record, Mr. Chairman ... to the news story on that.

Thomas laughed as the sound and visual came together. —Old radio man like you shouldn't have such doubts.

Robert took his glasses off, stuck them on top of his head, and leaned so close to the screen that his eyelashes touched it. —And a young radio man should show more respect. They're American – I think we've picked up the McCarthy hearings. Fritz Littlejohn said he'd cover it, gavel to gavel. Fiddle a bit with the – got it.

Senator McCarthy, I did not know, Senator – Senator, sometimes you say – may I have your attention?

I'm listening ...

May I have your attention?

Thomas peered over his father's shoulder. —He looks hung over.

I can listen with one ear and talk with –

No, this time, sir, I want you to listen with both. Senator McCarthy. I think until this moment –

Good. Just a minute. Jim, Jim, will you get the news story to the effect that this man belonged to the – to this Communist front organization.

—Hung over like a snake shedding its skin.
—This is better than ship-to-shore.
—Pass over the Bridge Mixture.

Jim, will you get the citation, one of the citations showing that this was the legal arm of the Communist Party, and the length of time that he belonged –

—Dear God.
—Do not take the Lord's name under my roof, Thomas.
—Sorry, sir.
—Dear God, that man looks like he might get apoplexy.

Until this moment, Senator, I think I never really gauged your cruelty or your recklessness ...

—Fading, damn. Get it back, get it back! Thomas, help me. Gently, just turn it slowly, slowly in case we miss the signal. Come back, come on ...

Little did I dream you could be so reckless and so cruel to do an injury to that lad.

Robert struggled to speak round another mouthful of candy. —More going on here than we know. But it is still an old story. I can't pick McCarthy out.
—Camera's back on the other man.
—Must be Welsh.

It is, I regret to say, equally true that I fear he shall always bear a scar needlessly inflicted by you. If it were in my power to forgive you for your reckless cruelty, I would do so. I like to think I am a gentle man, but your forgiveness will have to come from someone other than me.

Robert chuckled. —Well said, sir.

Let us not assassinate this lad further, Senator.

Let's, let's –

You've done enough. Have you no sense of decency, sir, at long last? Have you left no sense of decency?

Thomas shook his head. —McCarthy makes one ugly Icarus.

—Icarus might at least be excused by youth. Not again. Damn that signal.

For another fifteen minutes, the Wrights took the Lord's name all over the house as they tried adjusting the Marconi, holding it at various heights in the air (*Christ, don't drop it, Thomas, whatever you do*), moved it to other spots in the house, but no more faces ghosted onto the screen. The snow shushed and buzzed until Robert snapped the television off.

Thomas picked through some Bridge Mixture, hoping to get Turkish Delight. Instead he bit into a raisin. He grimaced, swallowed. —So, what does an old radio man like you think of this window to the future?

—Future, my backside. Window to the past, more like. Mr. Welsh might as well have been wearing a toga. The battles never change, Thomas, just the costumes. Mind you, I could have watched that for hours.

He nibbled a final piece of candy and discovered he'd picked Turkish Delight. Thomas and Libby had always fought over Turkish Delight. He gently tossed the candy to Thomas, who caught it in his mouth. They both laughed.

Then Robert leaned awkwardly against the table and studied his son. —Nothing for it, except to try to catch the signal again. Up for it?

—Yes, sir, even if it takes all night.

34. COPE AND DRAG 1

in which Gabriel Furey runs from his past and kills a cockroach.

September 15, 1981

Thanks to his mother being Canadian – or so he'd been told on leaving St. Raphael's – Gabriel Furey could, through a bilious process, obtain Canadian citizenship. The necessary paperwork sat under dust on Gabriel's dinette table in his Ottawa apartment. Not particularly proud of how he'd ticked *Canadian citizen* on his arts grant application forms, he told himself he'd get the citizenship eventually. Besides, he reasoned, looking out the high window of his apartment off Bronson Avenue, he could compete against any Canadian artist.

The fuck?

He wrenched off his hard-soled slipper and hurled it at a cockroach on the living room wall. A sticky crunch, a brown and yellow stain; roach guts dripped between sketched studies for *Sea Angel* and *Louis Riel, MP.* Gabriel put down his whole wheat toast and marmalade and tea, suddenly no longer hungry.

Sea Angel. Nine feet of bronze. Bought by the City of Ottawa and installed on Sparks Street for more money than Gabriel had dared ask. Paid off his materials, paid off the foundry, sent Callie money for Claire … that left three months' rent, or two months' rent and some groceries. Another painful trip to the bank. Withdrawal slips, bankbook, twitching letters and numbers – tellers always helpful, always courteous, but beneath the nail polish and sprayed hair, pitying. Gabriel wanted to scream how he was not illiterate, but then what was he? His signature on bank forms looked like a boy's, a boy just learning cursive. Old nausea before print … he'd fucked up Claire's name. Supposed to be Miranda Elizabeth – or Kevin Thomas, depending. Callie wailing Gabriel's name, Gabriel barging into the delivery room, and that little dickwad Dr. Johnson palpating Callie's belly as if she were a jelly he could go face and eyes into, nurse escorting Gabriel right back out again … baby almost six weeks early, doctor kept losing the baby's heartbeat and saying so, giving Callie irregular updates, *Got the heartbeat, nice and strong, oh, lost it again, no heartbeat,* Gabriel tearing down the hall and not just finding a doctor but ramming him against the wall, a tall man, Gabriel straining to reach his shoulders.

—You a doctor?

—I'm Dr. Noble. Is there a problem?

—My wife's in labour, and that born fuckheaded fool in there keeps losing the baby's heartbeat!

—Dr. Johnson's with her, is he?

—Find the heartbeat, please!

—Let me see what I can do.

Gabriel let him go, amazed later that Dr. Noble said nothing about this rough treatment. As Dr. Noble pushed open the delivery room door and pleasantly addressed his colleague, Callie screamed. Someone said *Crowning,* someone else said *Blue,* and then two nurses flanked Gabriel, advising him they'd called a priest, as Callie requested. Gabriel almost argued that Callie was Protestant, the Prime Minister's daughter for God's sake, but instead surrendered to desire for the stunted comfort of ritual. As he waited, alone now in the hall, he tried to remember if Vatican II had cancelled Limbo, tried to reason the grace in the denial of heaven to upbaptized infants – *Jesus, can ya get any more innocent than unbaptized babies?* A priest flapped by, two long white hairs lately departed from his combover stuck to the back of his robe; nurses followed wheeling a crash cart …

Why the hell am I remembering all this now?

Gabriel took down some of the studies for *Sea Angel* so he could clean up the roach mess.

Resuscitated, the baby would shortly be taken across town to NICU at the Janeway.

—A little girl, Mr. Furey. Do you have a name for her?

The form, little rectangles, meaningless small print. *Child's name. Mother's name.* Tears.

The nurse took the form back. —Is this *Claire*?

—Looks clear to me.

—Just correcting the spelling here. Her name is Claire?

—The mother's name is Callie.

—The baby's name.

—Miranda.

The nurse wrote *Miranda* under *Middle Name*. —Very pretty.

—Can I see her?

—Not just yet.

—I want to see my daughter.

—I'm sorry, Mr. Furey.

—Let me see my wife.

—She's resting right now, while the nurses clean her up.

—When can I see my daughter?

The delivery room doors swung open; an infant in an incubator, so small, wrapped to the chin in a pink blanket, part of one shoulder visible: long blonde down, inches long, almost feathery. Eyes shut. Mouth very small, cheeks sunken, skin pale. Oxygen tubes taped to her nose – *God, they make them that small?* Face wrinkly, ancient, endangered, new. Name card taped to one corner: *Baby Furey, Girl.*

The nurse squeezed Gabriel's arm. —Just over four pounds.

—Is that good?

—For a preemie, that's excellent.

His daughter already distant down the corridor, imprisoned and protected by a clear plastic shell.

Sea Angel a winged female form emerging from water, Claire's face.

Gabriel crumpled the studies. *Louis Riel, MP*: incomplete and late. The project he'd gotten a Canada Council grant for, the project with a buyer lined up, some politician. Life-size bronze of Riel in a heavy coat, chin down, hesitating. Touring Parliament Hill one day, Gabriel had seen the spot where *Riel* should go. The buyer agreed, promised to place the statue there until ordered to remove it and promised to bring a debate on Riel and history to the House. Gabriel had grinned and shrugged. So long as he was left alone to get Riel's chin right, and so long as people would see the art.

Couldn't be as easy as that, of course.

AMPLITUDE

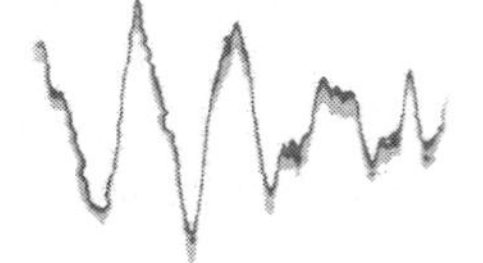

35. UNSENT 2
in which Claire Furey writes a letter to her father.

Dec. 12, 1989

Dear Dad,

Nichole Wright, my best friend, is gone to Canada. She's going to university at Carleton. She called me last night. She's studying this Russian literature course, and she came across this phrase the Soviets used. When an artist was afraid to release a work publicly but wrote it anyway, he called it "one for the desk."

So here's one for the desk.

I hope you're well.

I've got a full time job. I'm working at VOIC Radio. I'm a receptionist. I have to wear a skirt or dress every day. I won't be doing this long, just until I can get my painting going.

Sometimes I dream about you, and you're always cold.

Please, Dad, write or call so I know where you are. You don't have to talk to Mom. Just me.

Love,
Claire

36. CULTURE SHOCK 2
in which Claire Furey runs into her future and keeps quiet about it.

January 10, 1979

Claire Furey was too smart for her own good. Everyone said that. Claire pretended to ignore this judgement, but secretly she revelled in it. At five, she could decipher newspaper articles and draw her own pictures to accompany them. She became particularly fond of illustrating fire after her father left. That morning, Claire waited patiently at a front window of their Chapel Street rowhouse, waited for her mother to come in from the narrow sidewalk where she stared down the steep tail end of some new absence. Claire wiped condensation from the window and peered again. Callie had come inside; the stairs creaked. Claire met her with her newest drawing, a young dragon riding atop its flying mother's back, and offered Callie tea.

Callie nodded, scowling.

Balancing the heavy kettle, Claire felt cold. —Where's Dad?

Callie stabbed at the teabag with her spoon.

Claire figured it out. She really was too smart for her own good. But she had to hear it.

—Mom, where's Dad?

Callie's voice like the kitchen floor: —He left.

Claire glanced down at the dull and cracked linoleum and recalled her father's bare right foot next to his socked left one, the tickling of his chest hair against her cheek as she'd crawled into his lap late one night when his raised voice, matching Callie's, had wakened her. Gabriel took Claire, cuddled her, smoothed her hair, and kept yelling at Callie over the top of Claire's head.

Callie eyed her daughter. —Claire, your nightie barely covers your bum. Go put some clothes on.

Claire put her pencil and sketchpad down. —Can I have Lucky Charms today?

Gabriel would have refused, spewing out a comfortable sermon against the evils of sugar, television and Irish stereotypes. Callie bought the cereal anyway, because Claire worried too much at eight about her weight and ate sparingly.

Callie nodded. —Use the whole milk.

—Don't you care what I eat?

Callie stared at her daughter. —Claire, that is quite enough.

Nearly sick after a third bowl of Lucky Charms, Claire heard her mother run a bath. Claire waited for the bathroom door to lock shut, a tricky enterprise with the old brass doorknob, before sneaking into her parents' dark and messy bedroom.

Gabriel's one suit and one good shirt still hung in the closet. His sweater, jeans and winter coat were gone. Dresser drawers empty, too, no t-shirts, no shorts, no socks.

Crumpled lined paper on Callie's dresser.

More water ran into the tub.

Caillie. I am suffic smuthring under expectashuns. I am afriad of how I see her. Monster, me. Cant sey ti. Cant sculp it. I lov'd you, I truly did. But I got no peese. Ile send$ for her. When I can. Love. Pleese. Gabriel.

Letters danced. Meaning blared.

Claire put her father's letter down. *It's all my fault. I got sick and bothered him when he was sketching.*

Callie splashed loudly in the tub, blew her nose.

Not a word. Not even a frown. Claire gently put the note back and walked quietly to the bathroom door. She listened; quiet crying, yes, oh so quiet so as not to disturb Claire. She would do the same, nary a sound to bother her mother. Least she could do, after driving her father away.

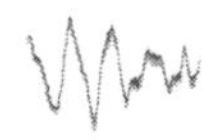

37. ON THE PACKAGE

in which Claire Furey suffers a rancid bastard of a day.

February 17, 1979

—Claire, I don't know where you get these ideas.

She'd been hauled in once more and now stood before Ralph Abbott's wide desk. A few years before, she'd sat in the office directly across from him, huge windows allowing unfettered views of Ralph answering the phone. Writing up something to be typed for a fax. Cutting his toenails. Or best of all, bending over to look for a file in a bottom drawer and so mashing his leopard-print underpants against the thin beige material of his trousers' arse. Yep, connect to the whole world on VOIC.

Come to think of it, the wildcat drawers appeared the same day as the Great Coffee Fiasco, around the time Claire received the title "Sales Secretary" engraved on a brass plaque, a script font curlicued beyond legibility. So far Claire had managed not to mount it on the door; instead she hid it in her office window behind some sales contract binders. The clock read twenty after eight, which meant she must bring Mr. Wright his morning coffee. The big 30-cup urn still bubbled and swished, but twenty after eight meant twenty after eight. So, first measuring two tablespoons of coffee whitener into a VOIC-logoed mug – a white mug, not a grey one – Claire siphoned off a cup of Butler's Choice, Republic Beverages' Finest Coffee. It smelled like fresh tar. She stirred the mess briskly, then trotted to Mr. Wright's office, her steps clacking first on the terrazzo floor, then silent on the thick carpet just outside Sherwood Forest. The small brass plaque on the door read *101*.

The air did seem more humid near Mr. Wright's office, but the nickname Sherwood Forest came from the office's size and unforgettable colouring. Emerald carpet, very plush, displaying footprints. Many, many large plants: ficus, spider, dumbcane. Brown squares and rectangles of different sizes mosaiced the wall, lined off with indentations of dark teal. Leaf-green sheers skirted the floor, while the heavy drapes boasted a pattern of squares within squares, showing beige, brown, yellow, pistachio and puce.

Thomas sat hunched over his large cherrywood desk, making notes with a green felt-tip pen. The padded shoulders of his dark blue blazer made him seem taller and broader than ever. The blazer, like the desk, was cut on sharp 1960s lines, clean and efficient. Before Thomas's desk sat two leather couches, armless and spare, finished in olive leather, matching the olive telephone. Yet Thomas never wore green. Beige, blue, brown, even maroon, but not green. The visual tension then between the shades of his office and the shade of his clothes made his green eyes seem all the greener, little beads of olive edged with grey, eyes that could nail a visitor to an armless couch or communicate secrets the receiver must struggle to decipher.

Nicks will get eyes like that if she's not careful.

—Good morning, Mr. Wright. Here's your coffee.

Thomas said nothing until Claire had nearly shut the door behind her.

—Claire. Who told you not to make enough coffee? Who's after drinking all the coffee?

Lord, what's he after now? —The coffee, Mr. Wright?

—Yes, the coffee. This black stuff I drink every morning. Why is it that several days in a row now I have called out to request another cup, only to be told no coffee remained?

Claire winced. That had happened twice in the last week. She'd been quick to put on more, but the urn needed a good forty minutes to finish a brew.

—Claire, I want you to do something for me.

Those awful eyes ... —Yes, Mr. Wright?

He handed her his green felt-tip pen. —Write me up a list of who drinks all the coffee, and how many cups.

—Yes, Mr. Wright. Will that be all?

—Bring it in to me as soon as you're done. I don't care if I'm on the phone. Just come straight in with that list. And bring me back my pen.

—Yes, Mr. Wright.

—And Claire? Would it hurt you to dress up a little? This is a place of business. Surely you're not allergic to skirts and dresses?

—These are dressy pants, Mr. Wright.

Thomas looked hard at her, perhaps about to argue that pants belonged on men, but he stopped himself.

Back at her desk, Claire eyeballed the stack of paperwork already waiting for her. But it must wait.

Claire observed the urn for the next half hour, confirming typical usage, then made her list.

Ralph Abbott 3 mugs
Matt Wright 4 mugs
Lewis Wright 3 mugs
Nichole Wright 1 mug
Ben Philpott 3 mugs
Mr. Wright 1 mug

Thirty eight-ounce cups of coffee, right there. Claire admired how the green felt-tip made her handwriting seem stronger, then smiled at Mr. Wright's list. Matt and Lewis: sons. Ralph Abbott: brother-in-law. Ben Philpott: trusted general manager. Nichole Wright: cousin. Well now, who would get yelled at for drinking too much coffee?

Claire padded back into Sherwood Forest. Mr Wright kept his back to her, intent on his telephone conversation and the trees outside his window. She placed the pen and list near the telephone, padded back out.

After lunch, Matt Wright, apologetic and fumbling, spoke quietly to Claire.

—Can you make sure no one else drinks from that coffee urn in the mornings? We can't have Skipper upset.

But nowadays that foolishness lay behind Claire. She had proven herself able, resourceful and hard-working enough to be awarded the job of Creative Director; she faced a whole new wad of foolishness.

Ralph repeated himself. —Claire, I don't know where you get these ideas.

Claire did her best to smile. Charm went a long way with Ralph Abbott, but Claire loathed her own hypocrisy even more than she loathed Ralph's particular smell. Claire guessed that Ralph might bathe once a week; otherwise he rinsed what showed with a sour facecloth. Over the five days his cuffs and collar went black. By Friday his office reeked like a cask of vinegar.

Claire shifted her weight to her right leg so that her left hip cocked up slightly against the seam of her skirt. —First quarter's a great time to try something new.

—But I promised the client –

—Just on a demo basis.

One briefly speechless salesman. An awkward moment. Claire noticed the black grime on Ralph's beige telephone receiver, the dust on his sales contract book.

Then Ralph cleared his throat. —Who told you to think of this?

—No one told me. I thought of it myself.

—I've been in sales here at VOIC for over forty years, and never in all my days –

Right hip this time. —Come on, Ralph. You're exaggerating.

—Indeed I'm not, my lady. And in my day office girls did not interrupt.

Office girls?

—In fact, Miss Furey, I happen to have here something you could benefit from.

And from his top desk drawer Ralph took a piece of eight-by-ten paper, typed on an IBM Selectric to judge by the font, probably sometime in the early 1970s. He did not pass it to Claire but merely waved it in front of her.

—The VOIC Decorum Policy. An oldie but goodie. We used to keep this posted in the ladies' restroom.

—Ralph, that's not going to help us make budget.

—And someone's told you what will?

—No one's told me anything, Ralph.

—Perhaps that's why you don't know how things work. Imagine telling one of the salesmen he can't choose a script from the package.

—I didn't say he couldn't choose. I merely suggested –

—He assures me a member of your department laced into him, Claire. And called him a crass name.

Note to self: tell Nichole to refrain from saying 'Only a stunned fucker would prefer a ready-made ad from the package.' —My goodness. He didn't take it personally, did he?

—He most certainly did. He feels he's a respectable family man and a responsible citizen. Your staffperson's words cut him to the quick. He went home sick because of it.

This is the same man who can make the word copywriter *sound worse than* slut. *Very good.*

—I'm sure she never meant –

—We can deal with that when he comes back to work tomorrow. The three of us have an appointment with Ben Philpott about it. Frankly, Claire, we're appalled. You're a model employee. You don't normally forget your place. I am compelled to ask, my dear: just who do you think you are?

Nominally I'm the Creative Director. You know, in charge of the Copy Department? —Ralph, we're wasting time that I could be putting towards this demo. All we're proposing –

—Writing the commercials yourselves. Foolishness. VOIC spends a lot of money on those packages. Didn't you get one this month?

—Yes, we got the binder. It's full of the same old stale garbage it's always full of. Whether you want blank or blank, then blank can help. After all, blank has been in business since –

—It's been good enough for over forty years. Why –

—Because I have a brain in my head, that's why!

Ralph stood up. —Don't you take that tone with me, young lady.

—Young lady? I am thirty-three years old and just as deserving of respect as the salesman who went home sick. When I say the Copy Department can write the commercials ourselves, I mean –

Their voices carried. Matt Wright peeked out his office door. At the other end of the hall, so did Lewis.

—Claire, you have no right –

—I have every right! I can vote, can't I? I can think, too!

Their audience grew to include Ben Philpott and visiting client Wince Blanford.

Ralph went very red in the face. He slammed his fist down on his desk. —You will sit down and fill in the blanks!

—You don't want copywriters. You want glorified typists. Is that all the women are in here?

Suddenly aware of their onlookers, Ralph took a breath and stole some dignity from the past. —You tell me, young lady.

Claire whirled around to leave but stopped short. Ben Philpott blocked the doorway, looking ready to take Claire by the collar of her blouse. Wince Blanford muttered to Matt and Lewis how he'd never stand for a girl at his dealership getting on like that, no, sir.

Then Ben projected his voice so it might be heard in Canada. —Claire Furey. If you're done causing this disturbance, you can go home for the rest of the day. Consider yourself suspended, and make no mistake: this goes in your permanent file. And as you leave this building today, I want you to consider the following and how it will affect the remainder of your career here. When it comes to getting something done, there's the right way, the wrong way, and the VOIC way.

Ben stepped aside.

Claire walked very slowly back towards the Copy Department, eyes filling but no damn way would she shed a tear. Ralph's suddenly merciful voice followed her round the corner. —Perhaps it's just her time of the month.

Claire told Nichole she had developed a migraine and would go home. Nichole, under headphones, smiled and nodded. —Feel better.

You cold ignorant bitch. You and your fucking magic last name – you'd get away with murder in here. And coffee.

In her car, Claire turned up the stereo very loud and then screamed. As the air and racket scraped her throat, little ideas entwined one another in her head, ideas of how to finish her painting.

A few extra hours to paint. Not all bad.

The following morning, Claire found something new in the women's bathroom. Bolted to the wall.

Framed, too.

The VOIC Decorum Policy.

Nichole arrived shortly afterwards and handed Claire a fancy latte.

—You never did say yesterday. Can we write the copy ourselves, or what?

Claire sipped the coffee. Nichole had remembered the cinnamon, the brown sugar.

Best friends, Claire?

Always.

—Show them what you got, Nicks. Go mad.

Dizzy with new freedom, Nichole churned out twice her usual volume of commercials. Claire made certain that Ralph's demo was number one on the list, with a bullet.

The client bought thirteen weeks because of that new commercial.

Claire and Nichole heard no thanks.

38. CONTINUITY 4
memorandum

To: All Staff, 570 VOIC St. John's and 680 VOIG Gander.

Date: March 15, 1967

Re: New VOIC Broadcast Centre

Mr. Wright is pleased to announce that the move to the new VOIC Broadcast Centre on Kenmount Road will begin on April 1st. The Broadcast Centre's proximity to the transmitters on Kenmount Road will only make VOIC more efficient and even better able to deliver top-quality broadcasting to the people of Newfoundland and Labrador. These state-of-the-art facilities will include 45 RPM and 33 1/3 RPM turntables, full newsroom, ample restrooms for male and female staff, and a full engineering section and test centre. All material at the Chapel Street studios will be discarded. At present, the commute from downtown St. John's to Kenmount Road is forty minutes. All staff are instructed to plan accordingly.

39. SITE 2
in which Thomas Wright tries to follow Ange O'Dea's trail marks.

July 12-13, 1954

The boggy woods ruint Thomas Wright' s wingtipped brogues within a few steps. Mud and moss climbed at his ankles, soaked the hem of his tailored trousers. Up ahead, Ange O'Dea seemed to favour one leg but said nothing of it. Blackflies tormented them both: ears, eyes, nostrils, mouths. Near dusk, Ange suggested retreat for the night; Thomas expected one of the old stories of the fairies and sneered. Darkness settled, and Ange made trail marks, little cuts in the trees they passed.

Broken branches.

Newsbird had landed on her belly. Cracked wings, smashed wheels, shattered windscreen. Robert Wright, still belted in, seemed unmarked – no, no, scant hope burnt off. His bare eyes, open but dull, stared nowhere. A thin line of blood had dried at the right corner of his scowling mouth, and his grey skin had long gone cold.

Ange never told anyone of Thomas's terrible scream. Others heard it; they, too, said nothing.

Later, unsure how he got out of the woods and into the old Wright house – Aunt Jane waiting for him – Thomas drank while Ange, Neal and John retrieved Robert's body. Thomas imagined them hesitating a moment, struggling for balance: *Handsomely, b'ys, handsomely.*

Tiny bathroom, draughty and low; voyage by car and by boat; stench of a moose; blatant truth of a wrecked plane: Thomas threw up.

Various women now accompanied Jane, cooking, cleaning, murmuring. Thomas sat on one of the old handmade armchairs, not quite in the world, and his father's body lay on an old sheet. Elias Simms had not yet finished the casket. A strange woman had strewn lupins and clover about, but Aunt Jane had washed Robert's body, removing his final privacies, sponging a thin chest, rinsing muscular legs, combing his hair. Internal bleeding, belly gone purple, blue and grey like the rocks? Visitors came, but Thomas would remember no faces. Neal O'Dea kept Thomas's glass full of rum, and Thomas gulped it, never mind his usual derision for it as the drink of old ladies and baymen – *Screech, what kind of a name for a drink is that?* Then Thomas recalled his promise to telegraph back to VOIC, tell Richard Fahey and Uncle William that the lost child had been found, but when he stood to go to the post office – he'd borrow Ginge's boat and get to Harbour Grace on his own, Ginge wouldn't mind – the floor tilted and the noise of chatter swelled. Thomas sat down again; the telegram would wait. Right then he didn't give a sweet damn about the lost child, only in that she'd been his father's final errand. The little fool, getting lost in the woods like that, dragging the likes of Robert Wright to seek her out. Thomas drank some more, and it seemed to him he'd become the chair, near as solid, as rigid, and no one looked at him. *Mr. Wright* this and *Robert* that and *I minds the time when*, but no one looked at Thomas. Battles coming: the station, the station, he must take the helm at the station, *God damn it, not yet!* Thomas later recalled dreamily insulting Ange O'Dea, informing the elder to call him not *Thomas* but *Mr. Wright*, and Neal O'Dea had been appalled, but Ange once more said nothing, and Robert Wright shrunk overnight. The next morning in dull dawn his remains looked at once frail and heavy. Black hair so perfectly black, white hair over the ears so very white, face deprived of eyeglasses and now vulnerable, drawn and sad ... Thomas glanced over his shoulder, hearing someone at the back kitchen door, then glanced back: his father's face, soft and slack with death. The door opened quietly, and Thomas got set to yell at this intruder, so early, so brazen, but right then his head hurt too much, and he backed into a shadow to avoid the slicing light.

Rose Fahey stayed by the cold stove a few moments. Thomas wondered why she waited; then he realized her eyes must adjust to the dark. She stepped in, carrying her shoes in her left hand, bare feet quiet, and crossed slowly to Robert Wright, not seeing Thomas in a shadow. Rose smelled the rum, smelled the old flowers, and out of uncertainty and nervousness, she giggled. Thomas nearly roared; he would have frightened her, he knew, likely made her cry, but she cried already as she lightly touched Mr. Wright's left shoulder and then darted away. Turning her back to the dead, to the hidden watcher, Rose crossed herself, stamped her foot and whispered. —I hate you, God!

She slipped back outside, and when Thomas peeked out between the musty curtains, Rose had already disappeared into the woods.

Throat sore, Thomas wiped his face again. How would he tell his mother?

The corpse of his father sighed; just air, just escaping air.

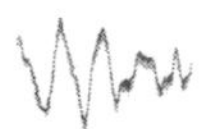

40. SILVERN VOICES 2
in which Thomas Wright instructs VOIC announcers Neal O'Dea and Ben Philpott to watch their language, and Dan McGrew builds a wondrous machine.

July 12, 1969

Only the control rooms enjoyed immunity to the intercom at VOIC. Announcements pierced each office, washroom and doorway, and even the great outdoors. Engineer Dan McGrew, eating lunch on fine summer days beneath the transmitter a quarter-mile up the rocky hill that made up half of VOIC Valley, often heard thinned-out calls for co-workers. Dan himself wore a pager on his hip. He'd earned the privilege to be paged only when the station went off the air.

However, on this summer day, Dan McGrew, Neal O'Dea and Ben Philpott were being called to report to Room 101.

Dan disliked both the passivity of receiving a page and the ignorant irony of referring to Mr. Thomas Wright's office as Room 101. Then again, *Sherwood Forest* wasn't much better. Neal and Ben, who had also read Orwell's *1984*, grinned each time the main secretary spoke the phrase *Room 101* over the intercom, but most employees paled, sweated and gasped like any political prisoner summoned to a final, intimate tyranny.

Mr. Wright, Dan had discovered, also knew *1984* and did nothing to discourage the use of *Room 101.* —You see, Dan, Big Brother's big mistake was never appearing in public and never walking the corridors where his people worked. You've got to be seen when you're in charge like that, but be seen sporadically.

Dan had nodded, mocking Wright once again with his straight face, his earnest voice. —The right way, the wrong way, and the VOIC way, sir?

—Precisely. You can't have cult of personality without the personality.

Folding up his paper bag and brushing fir and spruce needles from his backside, Dan eased himself back down the hill. His name again, echoing off the doorports, wisping up past the concrete, past the flat roof, in emotionless female sing-song: *Dan McGrew, Room 101, please, Dan McGrew.*

Dan threw his mushy apple to one side, wondering if it might take root amongst the rocks and conifers. Maybe, but it would never bear fruit; you needed two apple trees for that.

Now the pager on his hip cheeped. Dan took it from its holster. The noisy pager weighed more than a rock twice its size.

—McGrew.

—Dan, Mister wants you in Room 101.

The breeze lifted Dan's thinning combover. —Kindly remind Mr. Wright that I'm subject to the laws of physics and cannot, despite his repeated requests, travel backwards in time. I'll be there shortly.

Dan felt a bit guilty after that. Really shouldn't blame the secretaries, but still ... He gritted his teeth as he keyed open the staff entrance at the rear of the building to the tune of *Dan McGrew, Room 101, please, Dan McGrew.*

Women's high heels clicked over the terrazzo floor in the sales corridor as Dan marched to his doom. Four women worked at VOIC, three secretaries and one accounting clerk. Thomas Wright liked to brag how foul language was but rarely heard at VOIC these days, in consideration of the ladies present. Whether Thomas Wright was lying or completely mad, Dan could not decide. Foul language had neither increased nor decreased. It belonged in radio, a sane response to broken equipment, failed contracts, forced overtime, rotten pay, spliced tape, BRATNL bullies, self-made demigods in sales and on the air, feuds, backstabbing, the random terror of Room 101 and the gag of the public voice. How did the VOIC Christmas jingle go, *From everyone behind this microphone, to you and your loved ones in your home ...*

Thomas waited behind his wide desk. A bald older man, shorter but just as dapper, sat beside Thomas: his uncle, William Wright. His green eyes sank under bushy brows and a heavy forehead like Thomas's, but William's eyes were rounder and much more assured. William did not dart or glance like Thomas. William stared. His eyes would glisten sometimes, as though licked by little tongues. Often he smirked, believing his face neutral. His lips, almost too full, looked soft. He had often been mistaken for his brother, Robert, but most people had learned to look the Wright in the eye before presuming to know his identity. Robert's eyes had frequently shown fatigue, exasperation and excitement. William's eyes hid his thoughts.

Seated on the armless leather couches and tensed against either slipping off the cushions or rubbing them awkwardly and producing a fart noise, Ben Philpott and Neal O'Dea glanced at Dan. They had avoided the couch with the deep seat and broken springs, leaving Dan to negotiate the prickly fear of being swallowed by the furniture.

Thomas leaned forward on his desk. —We need to tackle the voices. Fahey's got VONB-TV, so we need to tackle the voices.

No one spoke in the little pause Thomas allowed.

—And by tackle the voices, I mean make them better. We at VOIC are the beacon of communication here in Newfoundland, and I mean for us to set an example.

If William noticed how high and heavily accented his nephew's voice was, he did not show it.

—And by set an example, I mean we're going to have all our announcers talk properly. My Aunt Jane kept a list for me one week of all the grammatical errors Johnny Hepcat and Tim made in the morning show. Two pages she filled out. When I tell Johnny this, he looks to me and says, 'So I needs to get me grammar fixed?' I tell him, 'No, you do not need to 'get me grammar' fixed.' Then Johnny says, 'So I don't bother fixing me grammar then?' And I says to him, 'Who told you not to do that?' This is the calibre we're dealing with here, Ben, so you can wipe that smile right off your face.

—Yes, Mr. Wright.

Neal raised his hand. —Mr. Wright, sir, is there a phonetic standard you have in mind?

Thomas glanced at William, who nodded. Then Thomas answered.

—The Boston states. I don't mean all that *ayuh* from Maine. I mean good, clear English without a trace of an accent. Like we hear coming at us in the dark.

Dan glanced sharply at Ben this time, but Ben said nothing. How many nights had he and Ben spent tuning for broadcasts from elsewhere, mocking others' accents?

Neal cleared his throat. —Mr. Wright, does anyone among us speak acceptably?

—You do, when you're in front of a microphone. Young Kyle out there in the Newsroom is not too bad. Ben's almost perfect. Where did you learn to speak, Ben?

—Like everyone else in this room, at my mother's knee. When I decided I wanted to get into radio, I started visiting an Australian war bride who settled here. She was a widow by then. She'd been a schoolteacher. She broke my vowels and put them back together again. Then, of course, Pat Finch and all the air checks. Pat used to take my air check reels, fast forward and stop somewhere at random, then play a sequence and rip it to shreds. Then he'd send me back into the booth with Kipling and Tennyson and Browning, make me read those poems for hours. Some mornings I still wake up with those poems tumbling in my head. *I'll get a drink in hell from Gunga Din.*

Thomas rolled his eyes. —I despair when I hear Pat Finch. God almighty, everyone in our listening audience has got a Pat Finch impression. 'A liquor store on Topsail Road got robbed overnight. Details are scarce, now. In a related story, yout' were caught relieving theirselves on the Courthouse steps.'

Dan did not raise his hand. —Pat Finch would say 'themselves,' Mr. Wright.

Neal thought of how he changed his voice – or did he let it slip? – when home around the bay, and looked at the green carpet. How had he come to this, tensing his arse against an olive leather couch in a room of proper versus accented? His radio voice, while ostensibly neutral, or at least close to some received standard, still wove, still looped up and down, rhythms and tone irrepressible. —Mr. Wright, if I could ask –

William cleared his throat. Thomas shut his eyes – William's voice so much like Robert's. Breathy Port au Mal vowels. Very crisp consonants.

Something vaguely BBC. All from the chest. —Gentlemen. It's as simple as this. If VOIC is going to survive, it has to adapt. This is 1969, and VOIC still sounds like it's broadcasting from the 1940s. Except for those two on the morning show. I don't know what they sound like, except the man on the street, and that's not good enough. Regardless of your individual egos and any hurt feelings, you have to work to make VOIC here in St. John's the example which the other stations in the network, including Gander and Burin, strive to emulate. And think: a whole new generation of children, listening to VOIC, raised on it at breakfast with their porridge and bacon, will hear proper speaking. And they will emulate it. Within twenty-five years, the accents will be gone. Proper speech will spread exponentially, like a benevolent virus. And we'll show the people of this republic how we can do anything as well as Canadians or Americans, if not better. From now on, it will be VOIC's Happy Five.

Thomas held up a chart he'd drawn on a piece of legal paper, in green felt-tip pen. —Johnny Hepcat and Tim Stratton on morning drive. Neal's got *Free Line* from nine to noon. *Free Line* will be picked up by the whole network. An essential part of the VOIC identity, just not part of the Happy Five. Can't be, with the quality of some of those callers. Ben does noon to two. Charlie's got afternoon drive, and Billy Bongo's got evenings. Charlie and Billy will share Saturdays. Sundays will stay all religious programming.

Neal studied the chart – no change from the current programming. Perhaps the happy face made from the loop of the numeral 5 meant something. —We five, we happy five?

Thomas flipped the sheet face-down on his desk. —There you go. The spoken word is like anything else: there's the right way, the wrong way, and the VOIC way.

No one spoke.

Thomas got behind his desk as if to work. He pretended surprise. —Are you still here? Don't you have work to do? The Happy Five? Is anybody on the air? Are we still broadcasting? Go! Dan, stay behind a minute.

Dan waited until Ben and Neal had left. —Yes, Mr. Wright?

—Can you put together some kind of filter on the output to smooth out the accents?

Trapped by those two sets of green eyes, Dan gave the safest answer. —I don't know, sir. I'll find out.

—Let me know by the end of the day.

Dan nodded and managed not to laugh until he escaped Sherwood Forest. Then he obscured the window to his office with the smoke of half a pack of Export As over the next hour, feet on his desk, while he puzzled out the engineering requirements of an AM broadcast accent-fixer-upper.

Meantime, Thomas received the congratulations of his uncle.

—Yes, sir, Thomas, I can sleep well knowing my money will be well spent now. Fear of God in your staff, too, fear of God. Can't get anything done otherwise.

Towering over William but beholden to him, Thomas showed his uncle great courtesy, faking pleasure. He'd accomplished nothing. Saved VOIC, yes, given it direction forward, earned his uncle's favour ... and an arid heart. He needed a nap. All that mattered was the nap he needed. No, not a nap – he would visit Aunt Jane.

Later, Dan McGrew approached Sherwood Forest, stepping carefully in the previous footprints that already sullied the hallway carpet. —Mr. Wright, if you'd like to come to the control room.

Charlie cued up another few records and wheeled his chair out of the way so Thomas could view the new technology. Another Volume Unit monitor, needle flat and dormant over in the green, sat near the regular one, which now, as the song climbed to crescendo, maxed on the green and twitched for the red.

Dan put his hands behind his back. —So you can see how the VU moves for regular broadcast. Now, in a moment Charlie will go on the air and introduce the next song. Watch the new VU.

As Charlie spoke, the needle of the new VU wavered well within the green. Then Charlie, fingers on the new knob, poised, introduced Anne Murray as H'Anne Morry. The new VU needle slammed into the red. Charlie cleared his throat, then said the singer's name as Anne Murray. Well within the green. Charlie started the record.

—So you see, Mr. Wright, while it does not automatically correct any mistakes, it does allow us to keep track of any errors. When it goes into the red, we've deviated. I am confident that in a few weeks we won't even need it anymore.

Thomas squinted at the new VU. Then he turned and walked out of the control room and back to his office.

Charlie looked to Dan. —Do you think he knows that's complete horse-shit? That I made the needle go by myself?

—And if he does? What can he say? Can't have the needle in the red. Distortion.

Smoke wafted out of the back of the new VU. Charlie cocked his head. —I thought you said that wasn't plugged in to anything.

Sparks danced. Something blew. The monitor window shattered within its frame.

Dan pursed his lips. —Oh. That wasn't supposed to happen. If anyone's looking for me, I'll be down at the Duke of Duckworth drinking a large scotch. Good day.

As he left the control room, a station ID played, assuring Dan he could connect to the whole world on VOIC.

Thomas sat in his office until dark, listening intently to each talk set.

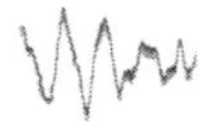

41. "SCATTERED AND SMALL" 2
in which Thomas Wright visits his Aunt Jane and tries to explain something he does not understand.

July 12, 1969

—Did you know Republic Beverages wants to bring back Golden Pheasant Tea?

Thomas rolled his eyes. His Aunt Jane, like all women in his estimation, could get on with the most trivial foolishness when he had something important to say. Jane's only real failing, true, but still maddening when compared to how sensible and intelligent she could be. Even a touch radical, wearing trousers in the 40s and 50s. Thomas suspected Jane tinted her hair coffee brown.

Jane, pleased to be in the kitchen and avoiding the imagery flickering in numb presentation on the television, on all three of the American cable stations – denuded jungle, sky fire – asked Thomas to turn the TV off.

More foolishness. Vietnam, part of what bothered him. Now, without the distracting mask of television, he must struggle to explain.

As the images entropied down to a dot and disappeared, olive green asserting dominance, Jane switched on a small lamp. She'd call her nephew depressed, if he'd permit such a word and all its weakness. A scar of melancholy ran down his mind as though burnt there by an electrical surge. When Etta first brought Thomas, Marie and Libby to Newfoundland from Boston in 1936, the five-year-old Thomas stayed silent for two weeks. Years later, Jane recognized that young Thomas was confused by the sudden existence of Robert Wright, of Father, when Thomas had believed Robert to be just some distant colony. Once in Newfoundland,

Thomas no longer knew whom to love: kind Uncle Richard, or moody Robert Wright.

Jane adjusted the lampshade. —First promise Jack Best made, he kept: electrified the country.

—Turn it off.

Annoyed with his tone, she refused. —While we're waiting for the kettle to boil, Thomas, why don't you tell me what's bothering you?

Where to start? Newfoundland's diplomatic snarl with Portugal, the brazen overfishing by foreign fleets – not boats, fleets – the overfishing by Newfoundlanders themselves, the dangerous promise of offshore oil – God, how to pierce the ocean floor and suck out oil? The three American bases in Labrador, low level flights frightening caribou, reports of malnourished Eskimos, the cave-in at Buchans, the eerie phrase *radon daughters* at St. Lawrence – who were radon daughters anyway, a subatomic Regan and Goneril? – the competition between VOIC radio and VONB television and how dare Richard Fahey ... Add to that all the American money, the selling of hydroelectricity to New York State, American cable television, mushroom clouds and napalm, and a sudden shyness, crippling him at work – shocking, how he could not speak some days – rendering him at ease only in his office. He couldn't afford to care about these people, must remain *Mr. Wright*, must run a business, at all times run a business, fear of God like William said, because the moment you cared, it all came crashing down, balsa wood and canvas from the sky.

Thomas finally spoke. —Distance.

—The kettle's done. I'll be right back.

—Why the hell didn't we join Canada when he had the chance? Jesus Christ, Jane, what good is Responsible when we've sold ourselves piece by piece to the Americans? They'll be after our fresh water yet, just you wait. Clawed open by mines, woods clearcut for paper, ocean bottom prodded for oil: what, are we just one vast resource, a prize? Yes, the ugly girl at the dance everyone despises, even though she can't help how she looks. The ugly girl everyone takes a go at because there's no need to respect her. Laugh while screwing. The ugly girl no one knew could bear the most children. We've whored out our country.

Jane studied Thomas's profile as he turned away: his abundant brown hair, his sideburns framing an oval face, his tall frame in a tight beige suit and Chelsea boots. He looked nothing like Robert. And yet. Jane poured, added sugar. —You're working too hard, Thomas.

He sipped the tea, almost laughing at the delicate old china in his big hands. —I dreamt about Libby last night. Do you remember the time I was getting ready for a date, and she'd dumped out all my aftershave and filled the bottle with salt water? My wife used to laugh so hard at that.

Jane laughed herself, wincing: Thomas still could not name his dead wife.

Thomas put down his cup; he hadn't finished the tea. —Aunt Jane, I'm sorry, but I've got to get back to the station.

She shook her head. —You're so much like your father.

Thomas stood up, bracing against a thrill in his knees, as if he might fall. Jane's word, so much what he needed, yet so intimate ...

He left without saying anything else.

Her full pot of tea going cold, Jane flicked on the radio – *Connect to the whole world on VOIC!* – but then surrendered instead to the television. Voices, no accent, neutral and dull and the desired norm. Jane went to her bedroom then to read, but she kept the television on for the sake of canned laughter and noise.

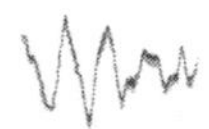

42. UP THE POND 2
in which Dan McGrew drives a bus into a lake but does not drown.

August 1941-August 1967

Orphaned, Dan McGrew lived out the war on the MacCreith farm in Reddenborough, a small town partway between Ottawa and Kingston. The MacCreiths treated him well, well enough for a hired hand. He fell in love with an English war guest, wise and skinny Lucy Upshall, whose brittle East End London vowels yanked Dan so hard he sometimes needed to sit down. Dan also made friends with Johnnie Townshend, another war guest. Harder shelter for Johnnie. He never explained, never complained – Canada so blooming big, he didn't dare – laughing off his black eyes, his bruised ribs, confessing the pain of it only to Dan. No one asked questions, because common sense dictated some of these Cockney youngsters needed sense beaten into them. Nobody else's business anyway. So it remained, until one Friday. Johnnie had not been to school all week. Normally parents or guardians sent a note explaining why they needed a child at home – farm work, perhaps. Lucy and Dan went to visit Johnnie at the very ordinary Lothian farm. Mrs. Lothian, apologizing she hadn't any cake, told them Johnnie had fallen from the loft and cracked his head, and no, they couldn't see him because he was resting. The doctor that night dined with the MacReiths, so Dan asked him about Johnnie; the doctor knew nothing of the accident and left his dinner unfinished. Johnnie had cracked his head, yes, and then not woken up; very stupid of the Lothians not to call him earlier, a bit worrisome, but then Johnnie died, and so did the entire matter. A hasty burial: 1943.

Straight-ahead streets, stratified social classes, and Lucy Upshall fell in love with Dan McGrew. They learned how to smoke together, Dan lighting two cigarettes at once, or more often, they puffed on the same cigarette, and Lucy stretched out legs far too long for the skirts she'd come over with, telling Dan of Westminster Abbey and London Tower, St. Paul's Cathedral and the East End's narrow streets. As the news from England worsened, Lucy really did show a stiff upper lip, reminding everyone of the Great Fire and how it consumed five-sixths of London, yet here London stood. Word reached her of her mother's death, then her father's; her hostess plaited Lucy's hair as Vera Lynn sang "Kiss Me Goodnight, Sergeant Major" on the wireless, and Lucy wept hard, desolate as a hidden scree.

V-E Day rippled the staid surface of Reddenborough. Mr. McLean played "Rule Britannia" on the Anglican church organ, respectable Reddenborough ladies drank gin, and Dan McGrew, fifteen, proposed marriage to Lucy Upshall, sixteen. She said yes. Promised him, held his temples and kissed his face. —Yes, once we're older, you'll come over to England, and we'll get married.

Lucy left for home. Men returned to Reddenborough, Dan meeting one of them on the Back Road: a short man, limping, his face still boyish but wizened, gnawed upon, duffle on his shoulder, RCAF jacket open. He wished Dan good day. Lucy wrote Dan three letters, each from a different address, one smelling of fried fish. After March of 1948, Dan never heard from her again, and while this loss galled him, he told himself loss must be expected. Ever after, he hated hearing Vera Lynn.

One day, when he'd gotten as tall as he ever would, Dan took the train to Ottawa. The MacCreiths had paid Dan, and apart from buying cigarettes, he'd saved it all. The rail line crossed muskeg – a slow trip. In Ottawa, Dan recognized much from photographs and kept being surprised that the Rideau Canal, Parliament Hill and the Chateau Laurier existed, like he did, in colour. The Chateau Laurier, witchy with limestone, turrets and a green copper roof, loomed. Here, men of power smoked cigars discussed and decided railways, the good of the nation, and white men's burdens. Here, even now, diplomats from England splayed out possible futures for the failed Dominion called Newfoundland; the diplomats from Canada ached to escape. Here, even now, toilet paper stocked every bathroom. And on the very top of it all: CBC Radio.

None of this concerned Dan McGrew, although he would shortly come to appreciate the toilet paper. Dan's risky ambition reached farther than politics. Dan wanted communication. Nothing less. And at that moment, he offered up his knowledge, pride and health, hurling a quick prayer at the sky before striding into the opulent Laurier as though he belonged there and daring himself to take the lift.

The engineer who happened to be at the CBC reception desk listened politely, then with interest, as Dan McGrew announced his usefulness. Quizzed, Dan could explain the differences between amplitude and frequency modulation with a brief digression to old spark-gap transmission. Telling himself the studio could at least use an errand boy, the engineer invited the young man in. —Come with me, dangerous Dan McGrew.

Dan became a soundman, a producer, an announcer, briefly and under protest even a copywriter, and finally, assistant engineer. He stayed with the CBC studios in Ottawa until 1967, when, as part of a Confederation Centenary project, he got to drive a bus to Cape Breton so he might conduct interviews there. He picked up an American draft-dodger in Montréal, nineteen-year-old Phil Banfield – Phil spoke reasonable French, better than Dan – and Dan decided to weave Phil into his documentary, never naming him, of course.

Phil laughed. —What'll you call me, the Unknown Soldier?

The bus broke down in Cape Breton's edge. Dan McGrew gazed on the ocean, wind blowing strings of his uncut hair in his face and lifting his thick beard. Phil studied the map, telling Dan where Marconi had built his towers, and they walked to the house where Marconi had stayed. Then Dan recalled his purpose and set about looking for locals to interview.

Miners. Like his father.

Phil Banfield had never seen an ocean. He spent hours sitting on different rocks, studying the water, sketching moods.

Dan emerged from an interview on a Sunday afternoon in early June. He must soon turn back to Ottawa, where he could cut and splice all this tape into something sensible in time for July 1st, if he could ever get the bus fixed. Baffled with good malt whisky, Dan sought out Phil. *Stupid American.* Dan strode and swayed to the shore. He'd warned, the locals had warned: don't get too close to the water. And Dan knew, just as he'd known about his mother, and just as he'd recognized with Lucy Upshall:

left behind. Later, children discovered Phil's sketch pad submerged and tormented by the surf, so it might be days before Phil's body came ashore. Dan's knees weakened, and he stumbled backwards a few steps. This wasn't supposed to happen. And ignorance: Dan did not even know which state Phil came from, and he had no way of contacting the Banfield family, if Banfield was even Phil's real name.

Dan waited out the month, his documentary undone, until finally, a needed part arrived for the bus, arrived from Newfoundland of all places. The infrequent ferry departed after one night's layover, Dan on board. He had no passport, but Customs at Port aux Basques accepted his Canadian birth certificate. Then Dan drove the bus across the island. He'd dreamt those cliffs, dreamt the sound of wind screaming through Wreckhouse. The road, graded but unpaved until Gander, twisted. Dan caught a cold that turned into bronchitis – his lungs maddeningly delicate after muskeg – and a doctor at the cottage hospital in Markland treated him, promising to bill the Ontario government. Dan stayed in Markland a week, never calling himself a patient. On his final day in Markland, Dan repaired the hospital refrigerator. A nurse kissed him; she'd been storing vaccines at room temperature, worrying.

Some hours later, he arrived in St. John's exhausted and driving badly, desperate for a cigarette and seeking out Signal Hill but taking more wrong turns than ever in his life, blaming St. John's itself and its long and twisty roads that changed names every few blocks. Then the brakes failed. Dan threw the map from the steering wheel as the bus hurtled towards Quidi Vidi Lake. Dan leaned on the horn. Several men in yellow satin jackets with pink, white and green epaulettes heaved themselves out of the way. And the tired old bus came to rest in the soft bottom of Quidi Vidi Lake, having t-boned a banner which now floated languidly, red letters on a yellow background: *570 VOIC your official Regatta station.*

Dan blinked.

In the rear-view mirror, Dan watched the men in yellow jackets. They had gathered back together, shaken but uninjured and, of all things, laughing. They clapped one another on the shoulder, as though feeling for broken bones, and the blond one with broad shoulders and a moustache walked with jolly purpose to the bus door. He peered inside, relieved to find the driver alive and unbloodied. Then he spoke, his baritone just the right side of pretentious – very professional, highly trained, most precise consonants.

—Hello, I'm Ben Philpott.

Dan opened the bus door. This Ben Philpott stood up past his ankles in water.

—Come all the way from Canada, have you? I saw the Ontario plate on the back of the bus. Take a wrong turn?

—Yes.

—Would you like to come off the bus now, get your bearings?

—Yes.

—Just a little water there when we come out, about halfway up to your knees.

—Yes.

Ben stood in the cool water while Dan stayed just inside the door, peering round the Quidi Vidi shore. Then Dan took a step, and another, and then slipped, falling face-first into the water.

Ben pulled him up, grinning. *—And I'll get a swig in hell from Gunga Din.* Here, here, don't fight me, let's just get you to shore, cough it up, just cough out the water, it's only water, it won't hurt you. Jim and Tim will help us here. Jim! Tim! Come give the gentleman a hand. Now then, this is Jim Reid on your right, he's brand new to us at VOIC, still a teenager, wants to go on the air as Johnny Hepcat, and this man on your left is Tim Stratton, our traffic reporter, out and about in the VOIC Chevy C/K Suburban and the VOIC speedboat.

—I'm Dan McGrew.

Jim and Tim exchanged dubious looks but kept quiet as Ben recited the opening of Service's poem from easy memory.

They got Dan to shore, where he sat down – collapsed, really – then joined Ben for another stanza. All this while Dan stared at the arse-end of the CBC's bus. Somewhere a radio played, station identification: *Connect to the whole world on VOIC.*

Then Jim Reid waved wildly from the side of the Suburban. —Potts, I got Mr. Wright here on the VHF. He wants to talk to you.

—Excuse me a moment, Dan.

Dan followed Ben, needing to stand near someone. His shoes squished.

Jim held out the VHF as though it burnt him. —Ben b'y, he's jumping mad. Been trying to raise us for the last ten minutes, he says.

Ben pulled an impassive face and took the VHF. —Ben Philpott here.

—Ben? What in the name of God is going on down there? I'm here in the control room with Charlie. In the control room, Ben, not sitting behind my desk using the telephone like a civilized man, but in the control room barking into the VHF because you haven't got that phone line for the Regatta set up down there yet, have you?

—No, sir, not yet. But we're working on it.

—You've been down there since seven o'clock this morning. What is taking so long?

Tim Stratton hiccupped. A faint scent of rum floated amongst them all.

Ben closed his channel, and disgust shaded his voice the way quick clouds on a windy day dull the sun. —I don't know how he expects to run a fucking radio network without a God damned engineer.

—Ben? Am I talking to myself?

Ben clicked back on. —We're experiencing some technical difficulties, Mr. Wright. Of course, we miss Micky O'Keefe's expertise. But we really need an engineer down here.

—Micky O'Keefe is in the hospital, and we both know he's not coming out. So get that phone line hooked up, or we can't do the Regatta broadcast. And if we can't do the Regatta broadcast, then we might as well all meet at the Dole Office Monday morning.

—We could do it on VHF.

—Didn't you hear me? I said get that phone line hooked up.

—Mr. Wright, I really need either someone from BrightSun, or an engineer of our own. For safety and –

Dan put a damp hand on Ben's arm. —Do you need an engineer?

Thomas Wright heard the strange voice. *—Ben, who's that?*

—Dan McGrew, sir. He just arrived from Canada. Came down to the lake to see what we were doing.

—Magoo?

Dan leaned down over the VHF in Ben's hand. —McGrew, sir. I'm an engineer with the CBC. I'm sorry, but I just drove a bus into the lake and ruined your banner. It's a lovely banner, sir. I think we can salvage it.

Silence. Jim and Tim visibly cringed. Ben's mouth narrowed to a thin line.

—Who told you to drive a bus into the lake!

—It was an accident, sir.

—You're an engineer? Experience? The CBC?

—Yes, but –

—Family man? Anyone to move down here?

—No –

—Equivalent of ten thousand Canadian a year, six months probation, and I retain the option to fire you if your references aren't any good. Or if you can't get us back on the air when we go down.

—But, I –

—Dan, is it, Dan McGrew? Dan, can you set up a phone line? Get us ready for a day-long remote? Get a backup phone line while you're at it?

— Well, yes, sir, but I –

—Then stop wasting my time and set it up. I want us fully operational by five o'clock today, or you'll all be up in Canada kissing arse at the CBC. Is that understood?

Ben nodded. —Yes, sir.

Dan clicked – or rather squished – his heels, making Ben chortle.

—Loud and clear, sir.

Suddenly Thomas Wright became aware of an undesirable silence.

—Charlie. We've got dead air. Put on a record. I don't care which one. Put on rock music if you have to. Yes, that one, who is it?

Ben put the VHF in its cradle and shook Dan's hand. —Welcome aboard.

VOIC broadcast "Magic Bus."

Tim Stratton tipped his flask. Jim Reid studied the floating banner and the exit instructions on the back of the bus printed in French and English. Dan blinked.

Ben thought a moment before breaking the silence with advice. —Just remember, it's always 'Mr. Wright,' and you'll do fine. And don't laugh at the VOIC *Spot the Moose* program.

Jim nodded. — That's right. Mister hates moose. I'm sure he'd shoot them from his car if he knew which end of a gun was what.

Ben toed the party line. —*Spot the Moose* is a valuable public service provided by VOIC. Whenever our listeners spot a moose, we ask them to call the station toll free and report it. We then broadcast the sighting, all in the interest of public safety.

Jim winked. —Course, it ain't much use on the highway, nary a public telephone for miles. Takes your chances on the highway, where all the moose are anyway.

Ben turned his back on Jim. —Dan, you're about to learn that there are three ways of doing anything: the right way, the wrong way, and the VOIC way. Let's get that bus out of the lake.

Dan patted his pockets, then looked at Ben in startled appeal. —I've lost my keys. Oh. This wasn't supposed to happen.

43. A MESS OF POTTAGE
in which Jack Best gives some reasons.

March 30, 1949

I speak to you tonight as a Newfoundlander. I speak to you tonight as a man who knows who he is. I speak to you who are intelligent men and women, more than able to decide for yourselves what your future should be. I speak to you as a rich man's son who has bloodied himself sealing, who spewed in the scuppers, who lost two fingers tangled in a net. I will not insult you. I will not speak for you. I will not pretend you are too stunned to staunch a cut. For there are no men and women – none – who are as capable, who are as tough, as the men and women of Newfoundland.

I meet you tonight at a crossroads. Not too many crossroads here in Newfoundland. Cowpaths veering off in old directions, worn down since Devon and Dorset accents first sounded here, since Irish joined them. Church paths beaten to existence by love and faith, Irish and English alike. Our decision now is broader than Irish or English, higher than Catholic or Protestant. Our decision tonight is not the Orangemen's Parade, when only the Protestants come out of their houses. Tonight is like the party that follows the Orangemen's Parade, when Protestant and Catholic, men and women, come out to the dance and come together. I wish we were at a dance now. I wish we were gathered round wireless sets to hear music resounding. Tonight you have the heavy duty of listening to me, and I have no pretty voice. I am no natural talker. Tonight we know who we are – a people on the edge of change we may not even feel for twenty or thirty years, when it's too late to stop the bleeding, clean the gouge. Tonight we must decide who and what we are going to be.

Our choices are stark. Once we had three choices: join the United States, join Canada, or remain Newfoundland. Well, you spoke clearly on the first referendum. We will not be Americans. The remaining vote was divided between Confederation with Canada and our own Responsible Government.

What exactly do Confederation and Responsible Government mean? Really mean, in plain speaking?

Confederation with Canada means Newfoundland becomes a province. We become a part of something much larger. Just a part. Now I'll be honest. Confederation has its advantages. Every choice has its advantage, and I'd be a lying hypocrite if I did not acknowledge them. Why would we choose Canada? Wealth. The old age pension, that baby bonus: both are great securities. God knows Newfoundland has suffered. God knows Newfoundlanders starved in the Depression, starved day by day until our legs collapsed for rickets and beriberi, until our children hacked consumptive lungs in pieces upon the sheets and died. And now, the old folks, they deserve a comfort. Who among you cannot think of an elder who has worked and suffered and now deserves a comfort? Skipper John Sturge maybe, or Aunt Mary Kelloway. Miss Cleary, the schoolteacher who sacrificed any chance of marriage and children of her own to teach yours. Your own mother, flour settling in the hollows beneath her eyes. Your own father, fashioning the lath of a killick, rheumatism, mending a net. Our elders deserve a comfort, deserve the ease of knowing there's money coming every month, deserve to put down their work and rest. And our women, yes, our women, your work so often taken for granted or ignored outright. Rearing children and running a house, all the while weighted with expecting another – this is no time for false delicacy. This is the time for truth. Men, I speak to you now: does not your wife, who works likely even harder than you, deserve the comfort of knowing there's a little money coming in?

These are the advantages of Confederation. Money. New roads and schools. A baby bonus and an old age pension. This decision is no easy decision. But now, as you're considering the comfort of coin, I ask you – I must ask you – What will we give in return? What will we lose to pay for these comforts? Because nothing in this world is free. Nothing. Living in Newfoundland has taught us that. Taught us that each bite of food, each piece of cloth on our backs, is the direct result of one thing, and one thing only: work. There is no shame in worn clothing. There is no shame in dirt roads. There is no shame in a houseful of children who are clean and loved and looked after as best as they can be. There is no shame in being the Newfoundland we are today. None.

So I ask you: what are we trading for that baby bonus? That old age pension? That paved road?

What are we giving away?

Responsible Government, what does that mean? It means a chance to start fresh. I will not bore you with a history lesson. I will not stir old angers with the stories of Richard Squires. I will say we can do better than that. We all know we can do better. I can say England has forgiven our debts. Small mercy there, as we were the only colony not forgiven our war debts from the Great War. England forgave Canada. England forgave Australia. Did England forgive Newfoundland, her oldest colony, her steady source of fish caught, gutted, split and dried, her steady source of men for the Great War? No. I am forced to wonder just how much England wants us anymore. I am forced to wonder if England did not mortally insult us with the Commission of Government in the thirties because she wanted to shut us up. Because we embarrassed her. England's oldest colony. Year after year, decade after decade, suffering cold and salt water to fish for England. And she is shunting us aside. Foisting us on a Dominion that no more wants us than a rich family sitting down for Sunday dinner would welcome a poor relation past the front porch. So much has been decided for us. From the very first our ancestors were not permitted to settle here. We were carted back and forth across the Atlantic for the season, counted and stowed like gear. When England graciously permitted us to settle, she shackled our hands: we could only sell fish where she said. And we were loyal to England. Loyal to the Crown. A Crown far away. And the fog's come in.

Birthright is a slippery word. I am not sure what it means. I am not sure what it is. But I am afraid that if we vote to join Canada, we shall lose our birthright. And I do not wish to lose something I don't yet understand. I don't want to drop a sapling overboard.

I am not going to tell you how to vote. I am asking you to vote so you might look at yourself reflected in the bucket of water you draw the morning after the vote. I am asking you to vote so the sapling might take root and become a tree.

My name is Jack Best. Thank you for listening.

44. STAUNCH A CUT 1
in which Jack Best reflects on reasons.

April 2, 1949

Close. Always known it would be close, but this close? Migraine aura descending in black zig-zags and a red circle, Jack Best folded his handkerchief and replaced it in his pocket. Stomach jigging for days, *my worthy opponent* – oh, worthy. Scrapped with his mouth, talked like a gift, convincing, and even many who did not like him liked what he said. But the repeater had won it. Sore convinced of that, Jack could still never thank Robert Wright for building a VOIC repeater near Harbour Grace, because Wright had done it as a newsman, present all sides of the story, fair and equitable. But but but – broadcasting the debates outside St. John's, Jack Best's simple speech carried beyond Water Street warehouses to at least some of Conception Bay, the mess of pottage speech, one he got asked to deliver again and again, the one that drew everyone out of their houses in winter, cramming into schoolhouses, snow melting at their feet, slippery, sturdy dreams of doing better for the children: fifty-one to forty-nine, dead people voting on both sides; fifty-one to forty-nine, recount after recount; fifty-one to forty-nine in favour of Responsible Government. In Notre Dame a woman so thin, mother of six, asking Jack Best as he climbed back aboard *Newsbird* with Robert Wright, *How, Mr. Best, am I supposed to put birthright on the table?*

Nonsense of dates: Canada would have invited Newfoundland on April 1st. Such foolery was apparently lost on the Canadians. Jack's worthy opponent insisted the decision be called just before midnight March 31st to save face. Jack turned on his radio: another newscast, interminable over the last few weeks. Jack took comfort now in Wright's precise and trained voice, with its influence of Nova Scotia and Boston. Even so, identifiable vowels remained, the Harbour Grace *ah*, the Port au Mal *e*, almost aspirated. Best felt suddenly ashamed of his own pride in manner of speech. Accent, like birth, was so much an accident. Much could be made of it, and much of it could be hidden, warped or mocked, but an accident it remained. Robert Wright now discussed the potential futures of communications in Newfoundland and Labrador, reminding listeners in his pedantic and occasionally patronizing manner that the country must now grow beyond the fishery, continue fishing, yes, but explore forestry, mining, even the arts: *A travelling nurse who used to visit my hometown insisted Newfoundland needed nothing more than book learning, a good meal and a tonic in spring. Spring is here. Time to take the tonic, lean on the booklearning and thereby ensure years of good meals. For the VOIC Signal News, I'm Robert Wright. The VOIC Signal News is a presentation of Port of Call on Water Street. Port of Call, ladies and gents clothing, tailored and ready-to-wear. Make it your Port of Call today.*

Jack Best nodded. Wright would take to the grave the truth of his vote. Today Robert Wright simply took stock of reality and bent himself to it. Jack opened a notebook: ideas and dreams. A university. A world-class museum and art gallery. A headquarters for the Newfoundland Rangers. A proper teachers' college. On another page, proposals from American military officers: an air base on the west coast; a naval base on the Great Northern Peninsula and another on the Burin; wilderness training in Labrador – all after proper compensation, after helping the country build its public works. Jack hated the phrase *public works* and could not say it without lisping. American money: mines, forestry, open up the interior, and once people settled the interior, they'd need roads. And who would build the roads? Vistas of work, years of steady employment, never again the dole. Never again a population so riddled by debt that children couldn't stay awake in school for being hungry – if they had a school. Head throbbing now, pounding, punishing him for lack of sleep. Migraines. Doctors. Specialists. Answers. Never again the diseases of malnutrition, bones betrayed by rickets, lungs devoured by TB. Never again a little girl dead of septicaemia.

45. WOUND STRIPE 2
in which Albert Furneaux receives the very best of care.

October 1916

Dark, isn't it? I'm over here, behind the glow of the batteries. Who's a good Tommy, then? You are, Private. Good enough to have been sent here to Boghall Hospital. Back to Blighty, you'd call it. Let's snatch that silly card pinned to your tunic. Shell-shock, indeed, why, there is no such thing. Merely failure of nerve, Private. I am here to give you back your manhood. Do you understand? Your record states you have not spoken since July. I tell you, Private, you can speak at any moment you wish to speak. I am a doctor. I know these things. None of your jerking about and sign language here. Private Furneaux, neither of us leaves this room until I deem you are cured. Is that clear? My nurses strapped you into that chair so we might force the random energy which feeds your spasms back into your voice. Electricity is the quickest way. I shall apply these plates here, to your throat, until you get past your failure of nerve and speak. Right. That's knocked you back. Let's prop your chair back up. Speak. Speak. I shall go easier this time, but I expect a result. Speak. Vowel sounds, please. Neither of us leaves this room until you are cured. You may speak at any time you wish. Your silence merely exposes your failure of nerve. Speak. Speak!

46. DIOGENES SYNDROME 2
in which William Wright considers treacheries.

1977, feedback looping

Treachery. Voted out and pensioned off, useless before my time, am I? Sleazy pups. Young crowd should know better. Baymen winning seats, half of them not fit. Descendants of underfed, illiterate, runty fishermen – wouldn't know if politics is good to eat. Pure stupidity, ousting the deputy ministers. Sacrifice the ministers, yes, purge the old guard, but for the love and honour of God, the deputy ministers – we're the only ones who get things done. Institutional knowledge. Rubbing fat into the fat pig's arse. Reform and a new crowd, a new way. Talk all ye like, but how will ye manage it? Slowly, by inches, not with the one bloated scratched-up slab of legislation. Young crowd, arrogant, got to argue every step of the way. Like arguing with my son about Nichole's lies. Child's dangerous with imagination, could ruin a man with one sentence. Gone crying to her mother because I showed her bad pictures. Nichole couldn't say when I showed them to her. Good laxative's all that child needs. Lying, trouble-making little slut, dares to be so pretty – ruin me! After me explaining how to forget – forget even all the surprise of white light burnt past your eye-strings straight on through the back of the skull ... just choose not to look. Shine no light. Everything will be all right then. Everything will be fine. So special to me, Nichole is. More crib death each generation, like Nature gropes at correction. Special, Nichole. Why it hurts to much. Treachery.

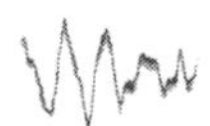

47. BAPTISMA PYRO
in which Nichole Wright catches fire.

May 17, 2008

When Hangashore Printing put out my novel *Once I Stood* in 1990, they devised a Merit Run. In total, they would print fifteen hundred copies, ridiculous for a first book by some no-name who held the semi-colon bound fast in iron chains and couldn't wait to show you, and for a press with no distribution outside Newfoundland. The merit part? Once the first five hundred copies sold on a deferred royalty scale, Hangashore would print the remaining thousand and then pay a royalty of fifty percent, less editing and production fees. Or I could choose a seven percent royalty on the selling price of each copy sold. Defer, b'y, defer me for the Merit Run. Hangashore's editor, who has long since died of drink, hardly made a mark on my manuscript. Hot shit, clearly. And me just nineteen, brilliant as Marie-Claire Blais, nineteen with my first book out. Finally all coming together, late nights wearing down pencils, gritty dawns, filled scribblers. Bring it on.

Eighty-two copies sold.

To the district libraries on the Local Interest Plan.

My family, ignorant by design of the secret identity of "Cassandra Vocum," purchased none. I'd have told them once the first good review appeared, then once any review appeared. They still don't know.

Once the libraries digitized their card catalogues, tracking those eighty-two copies got easy. Way too easy. I stole seventy-eight. Who knew that Pithy Bight, Barn Bay and the abandoned Laceton possessed their own little libraries? I only drove through Laceton. Gulls followed me, perhaps hoping I carried food. The Laceton Library sat attached to the tiny post office, both buildings in the shadow of some seven-foot statue, probably bronze, or maybe iron – Claire would know, damn it – once painted black like an anchor, now dull and rustpocked. The statue faced the post office – strained shoulders, bent knees, swirling blackness, weighted. A fisherman hauling his catch aboard. All fine and wonderful, hurrah for heritage and art wrestled from history. Except the damn statue stopped at the neck. Headless.

So I didn't bother with the Laceton Library. Or the ones up in Labrador in Goose Bay and Komatik. Computer noted my book had never been borrowed up there. In Buchans I'm listed as *Water Damaged.* Buchans flooded in the winter of 2002, and the creeping ice and slush submerged bottom shelves. Once I drowned.

Seventy-eight library copies. My own five freebies. The storehoused remainders, purchased shortly before Hangashore's bankruptcy auction, mouse-chewed and reeking of piss. Let's see, what else? A rented hatchback. Lighter fluid. Matches. Middle Cove Beach, of course. Sooty cliffs, dark trees, treacherous rocks and salt water, all the colours of gulls – throw in a few gulls while we're at it, some kids in hoodies asking what *capelin weather* means, brown and green bottles, and the odd dog. Every

July the literary crowd – the real writers – held a small press festival on this beach, bonfire and microphones in some smoky *Fuck you* to Major Publishers. No better place.

Fuck you, Cassandra Vocum.

Fuck you, William Wright.

I kept my fire going for hours, all through the darkness, not that I quite know when I started. Sparks jumped into my hair. I stripped off my denim and fleece down to my tank top and boy-cut panties – black, if you must know, both pieces. Legs needed a shave. Beyond sleep and waking. Utterly no desire to sleep, just to burn my books.

Near sunrise, fogged-out as the starlight was, I hauled my clothes back on and poured water over the remains of my fire. I'd gotten cold. Further up the beach, perhaps last night, someone else had burnt birch. The remaining junk lay blackened and scaled. I said it to the moving white sky: *Hey! You want me to be birch? Cloven pine and snotty var too easy, burn too fast? One good split and I'm exposed?*

Alone. Good thing.

Took the birch junk with me, let it soot-stain my clothes.

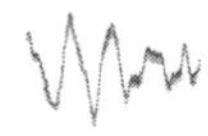

48. DANGLING MODIFIER
in which Rose Fahey attends a wake.

October 12, 1967

—Never thought Alice Fahey'd have a closed casket, her so careful about her looks. Not vain or nothing, just careful.

—You never heard? Hung herself.

—Sacred heart. Not true.

—True. With the gossip, can you blame her?

—I blames Rose. Spreading them dirty stories –

—She'll hear you.

—Proper thing. Someone needs to tell her the damage she done, saying that horrible stuff about her own father. I remember Rose throwing herself at Larry Jackman when we were in school. Troublemaking slut then, troublemaking slut now. I hope she never forgets how today feels. Look, they got cherry cake set out.

49. A SECOND AFTERNOON'S PLEASANT DISCOURSE in which Ange O'Dea and Commissioner Grant-Mainwaring's wife dig up some rocks.

April 1-3, 1938

Maybe an hour's walk from Whitbourne, four men cleared a field for farms, or so they'd been tasked. Complications of this particular operation of the Commission of Government's Land Settlement Scheme included snow, bog, a rising river, a bounty of rocks, and a Commissioner's wife.

The lady in question pricked across the path, quite irritated – snow and slush got down her boots, perhaps. Behind her, walking much more slowly and with some pain, Commissioner Michael Grant-Mainwaring seemed taller than ever, despite his stoop. When he reached up to adjust his blackrimmed spectacles, his hand shook.

Mrs. Grant-Mainwaring, perhaps forty-five, stood with her hands on her hips and glared at the Newfoundlanders with the decrepit entitlement of a memsahib.

—You there.

Ange had been leaning on his spade, sweaty, cold now that he had stopped digging. The Commissioner's wife could have been addressing them all at once, but only Ange had the guts and folly to answer.

—Yes, Miss?

—How long have you men been working to till this field?

—Three weeks, Miss.

—You will address me as Mrs. Grant-Mainwaring.

She had missed the respect implicit in *Miss*, but Ange said nothing.

—What is your name, Newfoundlander?

—Angel O'Dea, Missus.

Michael Grant-Mainwaring, breathless, looked up. Ange nodded to him, very subtly.

Mrs. Grant-Mainwaring slowly shook her head. —A more blasphemous name I've not ever heard.

Rupert Ginge spat. —Then you've never met young Lucifer Barnes? Or Christopher Drownes? What of Satan O'Toole?

The Commissioner found his voice. —Gentlemen. Could you tell us the progress you've made.

Rupert and the other two men, like Ange, all fathers of thin children, had travelled by train to prepare a new community for farming. The community, already named Elizabethland, would produce potatoes, carrots, turnip and, if the settlers proved themselves resourceful enough, apples. Once the men sowed the first crops and built suitable little cottages, they might borrow the equivalent of a year's dole and send for wives and children.

Above all, the Newfoundlander might learn of work beyond fish. Elizabeth Grant-Mainwaring fully supported this excellent plan. She'd even risked her digestion one night by enduring a heated debate over Land Resettlement and Newfoundland character with no less a personage than Lord Amulree himself. The good lord's 1933 report hinted that Newfoundlanders stood at once far too stubborn and far too dependent – *Like a suckling babe who has grown teeth and opinions,* another civil servant had remarked over dessert – but Elizabeth Grant-Mainwaring defied Amulree with her terribly modern mind. She thought, nay, insisted that the Newfoundlander, like the Irishman and the bullock, might be brought to better pasture and docile productivity if only properly guided, if only shown the way. To shocked gasps and one rebellious cry of *Hear, hear,* Elizabeth sat down again and asked who would like more rum sauce.

Being the Newfoundlander's champion at table, she dealt harshly with him in person. —Satan O'Toole, indeed. And how do you expect your wife and children to live here come May when you've not even tilled the field, let alone started the houses? Answer me that.

Ange politely passed his spade to her. —Besides the snow, there be one or two rocks in the soil.

Mrs. Grant-Mainwaring snatched the spade. Her husband closed his eyes and bowed his head, in some sort of domestic agony, Ange thought.

—Mr. O'Dea. Have you no moral energy at all? Stand aside, please.

She knew how to dig. In both England and India, her flower gardens had won prizes. Within a few moments, she had broken the cold soil and spaded the dirt to one side. Then she dug again.

Metal scraping rock makes a disagreeable noise. Here it clanged in everyone's teeth and no doubt added to the Commissioner's headache. Some more scraping, of dentistry perhaps, some grunting more suited to obstetrics – and then Mrs. Grant-Mainwaring dropped to one side a rock that weighed at least twenty pounds.

Themes and variations for another quarter hour. Ange got very cold but kept quiet and still. So did the other men. And the Commissioner.

Elizabeth Grant-Mainwaring did not give up. She merely stopped – a crucial distinction. Ignorant of geology, of the glacial debris scattered all over this scraped island, of the acidic soil on the Avalon Peninsula, of habitually late last frost, ignorant of all these and of the need to ask, she planted Ange's spade, walked swiftly back towards and then past her husband. Then she stopped, turned to face the working men, the stubborn snow, and the likely failure of apples. She shouted over the noise of the rising river. —If this community should fail, I shall hold each one of you responsible.

Two nights later, the river burst its banks and flooded much of Elizabethland. The men struggled to Whitbourne in cold darkness; none died of pneumonia, though Ange stayed sick for weeks. The water did not recede. Soon even the maps abandoned flooded Elizabethland, and it took the personal intervention of Commissioner Grant-Mainwaring to ensure the men got paid for their work. A Land Committee worked out the wages; each man received an extra week's dole. When this memorandum landed on Grant-Mainwaring's desk for his signature, he recoiled in his chair, disgusted. *Yes indeed, the Commission will receive a blistering letter from me, call my secretary in ...* Then his chair tipped. The fall against the fireplace cracked his skull. He died, loyal servant to the Empire, angry, pained and quite conscious of the indignity of his position, mouth ashy.

50. SEMISUBMERSIBLE
in which journalist Rose Fahey returns to Newfoundland to write about an oil rig disaster.

February 15-17, 1982, and later

—Rose, did you lose anyone?

Rose Fahey glared over her shoulder at her editor, fingers chattering still with the keys of her typewriter. —Why do you ask?

—Because you're from there, eh.

—Canadian citizen since 1980.

Rose's eyes returned to her rapidly filling page. Peace came from words on paper, from letters and sentences, paragraphs, and best of all, artificial byline: final control. Peace came from blackening white silence.

Today she blackened the silence at her desk in the office of a national Canadian news magazine. Deliberately underdressed in faded Levis, a white shirt with a rounded collar, and a red sweater, Rose flicked her hair out of her eyes. Telling people she was from Newfoundland usually meant enduring a round of Newfie jokes, stonefaced – all meant in fun, no offense eh, but did you hear the one – and she thought it curious how ethnic jokes often followed a period of immigration. Polack, Paki, Russki, Newfie – white Canadians so needy and fragile that every newcomer threatened their very identity? Rose considered it the afternoon she received her Canadian citizenship.

Her editor tried again. —Just where New*found*land is such a small place –

—Newfound*land*. Newfound*land*. Is that so hard?

—But all the reports on the radio, they say New*found*land.

Had to be a mistake, *had* to be. The enormous *Sea Sentry* could not sink.

Cold took Rose, cold distant from Toronto's snow and slush and still air. Salt water cold. The cold beyond freezing. Cold merciful enough to stun before it killed – not before it terrified.

—Rose, will you go?

—You only want to send me because I'm from there.

—I want to send you because you're one of the best we've got. And because you're from there. Flight's at two-forty.

In her head, Rose outlined her article and rehearsed her speech to get past nurses. —I still know people at the main hospital in St. John's. That's where the guys'd be brought. How many survivors?

—Rose, wait.

—Throw me a line here. How many survivors?

—Not official yet. Looks like none.

—And a deep grave surely.

—Rose?

—I'll go.

—Can you have it filed by Wednesday?

She ripped her story from the typewriter platen. —Take this, willya? Apparently I have a plane to catch.

Rose Fahey filed the same story as everyone else, her stomach tight with too much tea and memories of seasickness: a winter storm. Winds over a hundred miles per hour, swells over sixty feet, a hundred feet – the proofreader could convert to metric – failed separation of platform from rig, salt-shorted relays and ten degree list, fifteen degree list, men missing survival suits, men missing lifeboats when they jumped, the supply ship lowering her own inflatable lifeboat that simply blew out of reach, the supply ship crew fishing with long hooks for stranded men, heaving searchlights, dark hours not eased by dawn.

Rose attended three services, St. John's, Burin, Port au Mal, unwillingly memorizing the hymn "For Those in Peril on the Sea." A memory of Robert Wright's copy of Melville, cenotaphs in a whaleman's chapel. Gut-knowledge: the startling delicacy of dories, frigates, whalers, iron ore freighters, semisubmersible oil rigs. Compassion spread so thin it broke, like a fiddle string played too hard, like a rescue line in a North Atlantic storm. Gut-knowledge heavy, but not heavy enough to drown ... service in Port au Mal, Methodist churchbell tolling once for each man, tolling eighty-four times, then tolling thirty-eight more for the age of Port au Mal's Larry Jackman, whose wife – widow – Anna kept an arm round her son, Chris. He stood stricken, angry at the adults who dared to shuffle in sadness as though the story could possibly be true, as though *Sea Sentry* really had sunk in the night. When Chris spoke to people who wanted to shake his hand, his voice cracked: *I got a Wayne Gretzky hockey card. You wanna see it? I was saving it to show my Dad, but I'm after showing everyone today.*

Rose did not write about lurching through school with Larry Jackman, reeling and waltzing with him at the Orangemen's Lodge and defying anyone to utter the letters *RC*, and wishing Larry would grope her arse in the shadows at the walls. One night Larry whispered in her ear *Come outside, we has a talk.* Something about salt water and stars, and Rose argued something else about necessary departures, and Larry sighed. They'd so easily lost touch. Rose knew writing face-on about Larry Jackman, about connections, would have made the better article. It just hurt too much. Now: time for facts. Time to write it clear and clean, to write it, as she often told herself, like a man. For the first time, she did not use a pseudonym but signed her byline *R. Fahey.*

Years later, she woke from a hard dream of the *Sea Sentry* – sharp list, hidden stars, unanswered pleas. The dream recurred even after she wrote and published a piece in the *Globe and Mail* on Larry Jackman. The dream's nights ebbed out sleepless. Larry's ghost stuck, a salt water stain.

51. QUEEN'S ENGLISH 2
in which Almayer Foxe settles a former colony and claims it for his own.

February 1982

Leaving me? But your portfolio. Just yesterday I spoke to the agency in London ... of course you're model material, my dear. I should know. All those photos, my camera loving you, oh yes, I am most adept at photography of beautiful women. Lying – my dear girl, I would not lie about the modelling agency, on my honour as an Englishman ... Can't say I've heard of the Adepts and their photography club. Those hard shots are simply to show your diversity, your courage. The London agency would never demand ... A bit drastic. Please do not force my hand. Not at all. If you wish to go to the police, no one's stopping you. However, I do have my own reputation to consider as a newsman and something of a celebrity, and I should particularly dislike having to show your portfolio to your husband. Or your daughters. Shh, I assure you I'd do no such thing unless forced. Do we understand each other? Promise, well, promises don't come free. Seal my lips. One last session, to remember you by once I destroy the other negatives. If you scream once more ... over here, be easier if you didn't twist so much ... really, it's not as though this is new to you. Do not make me strike you again. I smudged your lipstick. Errands to run. I'll take the photos later. More authenticity if you've been left alone first, I think. Don't look at me like that. You who came here of your own free will to threaten me.

52. CONTINUITY 5
memorandum

Thomas Wright, President, CEO and Owner
VOIC Radio Network
Connect to the whole world with VOIC

November 6, 2001

To Mr. C. Feltham
President, Broadcast Regulators Association in Telecommunications of Newfoundland and Labrador (BRATNL)

Clement,

I hope this letter finds you well and in tune with the upcoming Christmas season.

I am writing to inform you that the BRATNL receptionist, Nichole L. Wright, is urgently needed here at VOIC. You will recall how highly I recommended her to you as a BRATNL employee. I need her back to fill a gap in the VOIC Copy Department. As you know, fourth quarter is our busiest time. I need Nichole to report for VOIC no later than November 13th. I will of course compensate you by recommending another girl to act as receptionist at the BRATNL offices. Please do me the courtesy of informing Nichole of these developments as soon as you can.

With fond best wishes for the holidays,

Thomas Wright, BRATNL President Ex Officio

53. MYOPIA SKY 3
in which Robert Wright nearly loses his glasses.

July 12, 1954

Robert Wright hated to hurry. First William today, then Richard, now Rose. Dear God, that troublesome child ... her troublesome home. The Faheys' kitchen: electric eggbeater, ice box, empty rum bottles, Golden Pheasant tea tins. The Faheys' new house, paid for by Richard: clapboard siding, indoor plumbing, electricity, that new insulation, even a telephone jack. A room for Rose. A pity Richard hadn't thought of a locking door for that room – such corruption ...

Robert shook himself and concentrated, smelling now the sunwarmed leather seat, the canvas harness, fuel, and fresh air.

—Contact.

The propeller did not catch; the groundman tried again.

—Contact.

The groundman ducked, almost bowed; the engine blubbed three times and still did not catch. He patted the Tiger Moth's nose, coaxing.

—Come on, sweetheart, come on.

Robert rolled his eyes. His left arm and shoulder ached, as though he'd tried to start the propeller. —Heave it out of you. Reach this time.

The groundman's arms raised high on the blade, he bowed down, and this time *Contact* sounded like profanity. The engine caught, and the Tiger Moth shuddered and purred. The groundman waved clearance to Mr. Wright, and Mr. Wright waved back. Taxiing now, Robert let *Newsbird* build her energy, and then he guided her to the runway. This sweet last moment for *No*, for turning around, still groundbound, and claim some technical difficulty, some obscure flaw. Robert heard Dr. Cart's voice again: *I'd say you're distinctly unwell. You are not to drive, and you are not to fly.* Robert snorted. Today he'd not even bothered with a maintenance check. He'd given *Newsbird* a careful check on Saturday – it had been rather like one baboon picking fleas and ticks off another – and this was only Monday morning. Paused now at the runway's start, Robert checked his gauges and ran over the map in his mind. And without conscious thought, he accelerated, and without recognition, he grinned.

Newsbird climbed fast on favourable winds. Robert quickly left Torbay and St. John's behind; he made note of Octagon Pond in Paradise, of the low and lovely beach in Topsail; he crossed Conception Bay, reluctant to waste time following land, and the water glittered in its dull purple. Carbonear, Harbour Grace, Bay Roberts; Robert lowered *Newsbird* so he might better see what hid within the trees. His heavy glasses irritated his nose; he pushed them a bit, wishing again he might return to the more delicate frames he'd worn before – he could fit goggles over those. The heavy hornrims slid again as he glanced down at the ground. A tricky flight ahead of him.

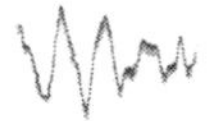

54. SAVED
in which journalist Rose Fahey interviews former Christian Brother Michael Stephens.

March 17, 1991

—Is it recording now?

—Yes.

—And you won't record my name?

—No.

—Very good then.

—March 17, 1991 at 2 pm. This is Rose Fahey with a special report for CBC Radio. Last week, the Roman Catholic Church officially closed St. Raphael's Home for Boys, an orphanage which existed in the east end of St. John's since 1898. Run first by the Jesuits, and then by the Christian Brothers, St. Raphael's has become synonymous with systematic abuse of boys. The abuse has been verbal, physical, psychological and, in many cases, sexual. Many of the former St. Raphael's boys, now grown men, struggle to keep marriages together, to hold down jobs. Two years ago, the first St. Raphael's boy, Peter Kielly, came forward with his story, one of vicious beatings and forced sexual acts, a story at first difficult to believe. However, Kielly was only the start. Many men followed, and soon the everyday horrors than had been life in St. Raphael's were common knowledge. Then, a flood of allegations against individual priests. The Catholic Church in Newfoundland and Labrador, it seemed, was rotting from the inside out. In all of this, we have heard from the boys and men, occasionally girls and women, who were abused. Today, we are going to hear from an alleged perpetrator, a former Christian Brother who claims he worked in St. Raphael's through the 1960s and 70s. Now living in a Canadian city, this former Brother is not facing charges. Nor is he under investigation. He approached the CBC independently. Listeners are warned: what follows may be graphic and disturbing. When were you at St. Raphael's?

—Oh, it was all so long ago. The 1960s and 70s, as you said.

—What was your position?

—I was a teacher.

—Did you have any authority over the boys?

—Of course. All the teachers lived at St. Raphael's, like the boys. We supervised their education, their diets, their health and hygiene.

—Did you –

—Speak up.

—What did you … do?

—My duty. It began as my duty. Then beauty interfered.

—Beauty.

—The beauty of watching. Oh, don't you look all the questioning innocent. And a woman of your age. The beauty of watching is the other side of the thrill of being watched. That you know. I see it in your eyes, and now you can't keep my gaze. There you are, back again. You have nice eyes. Hazel, is that the colour?

—It doesn't matter.

—Your lashes are sparse. A thing about the boys, their lashes. The occasional redhead with red lashes, so delicate and rare against the white skin. But it was dark boys. Yes. One in particular, G–sorry, no names here. He had the name of an archangel, and eyes to match. Deep brown eyes, all confused, and later, all afire. Dark lashes.

—What did you do?

—Saved him. For something special. The other boys I would simply watch, but this one with rough voice, all destruction when it broke, all glory when he sang. Tenor. We got him singing the old Irish songs. Coached him to relax his jaw, open his mouth wide, control his breathing. And then …

—Go on.

—He … serviced me.

—Do you mean, with his hand?

—Mouth.

—You compelled a teenage boy to perform oral sex on you?

—Yes.

—And this doesn't bother you now?

—The past is past.

—Did this happen a lot?

—Once or twice a month, at first. It stopped once he turned sixteen. He was getting too tall. But that precious time, between the first hair and enough strength to fight back, all that precious time, he was my special favourite.

—Why?

—He was beautiful.

—I mean, why did you do it? Had you perhaps suffered similar abuse yourself?

—Beneath the crucifixion, how can any one of us claim to have suffered?

—These boys were entrusted to you. If you can't accept that you violated the boys, then perhaps you can explain why you violated your promise.

—Because the boys were there. Should I open a window?

—You're telling me all this freely when I could take this recording straight to the police.

—Go ahead. Then Newfoundland would have to extradite me. By the time it came to trial, I might even be dead. I'm in my seventies now.

—Why did you contact the CBC?

—In the interests of balanced journalism. I thought it was time I spoke.

—I'm cutting it here. For CBC Radio, I'm Rose –

—Who did it to you?

—Did what?

—You didn't come to me smelling sweet and pure, Miss Fahey. There's something about the eyes. Ruin. Wary sadness.

—The interview is over.

—I see right through you. Don't worry yourself. You're far too old.

—Shut up.

—Right through you. When will the interview be broadcast?

55. SLEEP ARCHITECTURE 2
in which different people face the night.

March 17, 1991

After his interview with the Rose woman from the CBC, Michael Stephens ran a bath. Chills took. Nearly eighty now, shorter now by two, three inches, but his broad chest and arms, tufted with white hair, they'd not deserted him. Still some fight, some delight in him yet.

He shuffled naked across his dark living room to look out his window. Interrupted tableaux, silent movies in colour; he loved Ottawa, loved highrises and those dim corridors with a dozen or more doors on either side, mysteries and potential. All those strangers. Some even with children. And he the kindly old man, helping with groceries, holding the elevators, learning the first names of the prettier boys.

Ugly Peter Kielly telling his story of St. Raphael's – laughable. Peter scored grade three on Michael's private system, one better beaten and bruised than caressed. Jealous he didn't get more of Brudder's favour, like that alpha plus dark little angel Gabriel Furey. Michael didn't get hard anymore – vascular trouble that also caused cold hands and feet – but after remembering Gabriel, he certainly felt the stabbing heat of desire. Age. Such a bitter punishment, the best behind him now. Time enough for a cup of tea before bed, perhaps watch the news.

Rose dabbed vitamin E ointment onto the worst of her scratches. She'd pressed too hard on her loofah in the shower, recognizing that only when her old teabag scars bled. Teabags. Pour the boiling water, spoon out the bag, cram it against your arm – relief, relief, pressure and – hee hee – stopcock. Shower insufficient. *You're a dirty little girl, Rose, dirty little girl.* She plugged in her kettle.

Callie Best broke and buttered a slice of bread and passed it to her father. Jack had been discussing the tricky balance of statutory holidays, how he hadn't dared nix St. Patrick's and St. George's Days after removing the schools from the control of the churches, and from there had gone on to the apocalyptic revelations of St. Raphael's. He then spoke with some true understanding of how, well, *fucked up* these grown-up St. Raphael's boys must now be, flashbacks, drug abuse, severe issues with attachment and rejection, and Callie nodded and said Gabriel's name as she poured tea.

Gabriel Furey dreamt not of his old striges, but of a skeletal bird – himself, winged, bones gone hollow and light enough for flight, but he was stuck to the bed on his back, sniffing for the predator. Sweat broke. Slick, he writhed now, legs together and slippery, scrotum elephantine, penis lost. *Come on, Furey, just put your hands down there, or roll over on your stomach.*

Instead, he cocked his pelvis off the mattress. *Just hurry up, be done with it.* And his testicles pained, each one like a bruised polyp on a stalk, sweat sweat sweat, and he could break the spell if he cried like a gull, because half the time gulls sounded like youngsters, so he permitted himself something between a screech and squawk. He whispered. Damned spell unbroken. Sweat. His entire self disappeared within the gull's eye.

Gabriel heaved himself out of bed. Sac normal, balls fine, just the Jesus sweat. Not even eleven o'clock. Still the whole night to go. Gabriel made some tea, ran a hot bath.

Ribs prominent, nipples very pink against his black chest hair, Gabriel hurried into the tub. Steam, soap.

A carving.

Dig it out with a blade. Soapstone. Man in a bath, water all dark, talking to a seagull.

56. COPE AND DRAG 2
in which Claire Furey, Creative Director, decides on her future at VOIC.

September 15, 2003

—So it's as simple as that, is it, Claire?

Ben Philpott looked older than his sixty-four years. He'd rolled up his shirtsleeves, yanked his tie askew, and he'd been just about to wish Claire a happy birthday. Instead, he sat very still, eyes bulging – rabbit buttons on peeled onions, thready veins, rheumy shine.

Intent on Ben as a possible portrait subject – *Manager Nearer Apoplexy Than Retirement* – Claire kept his gaze. Pencils on cream. 2H, 4H – get that tension, the wrinkles, a million short strokes, and behind, in heavy 4B or even charcoal, the gold-gilted dark wood, the gold spelling out *Communication.* And the antique poster reading *Communication Saves Lives.*

—You're just going to quit? I know you paint for a hobby, Claire, and you made a bit of a splash with that mural in 1993, but what about your pension? How are you going to retire on pretty pictures?

—I'm only 33.

—I was on my second marriage and paying alimony at 33.

Claire canned her smarting reply to that.

—I know we've had our differences, but think about this, Claire. Smart young people start saving for retirement in their 20s, if not earlier. How much is this grant worth? It can't be much.

Grant amounts had been broadcast that morning on VOIC, and printed in the two main newspapers as well, but Claire decided at that moment that Ben had no business knowing. —The question to ask me, Ben, is how much is my time worth? The last time I worked uninterrupted on an art project was Easter break in ninth grade. After that, I always had a job. Have you ever been woken up after only a few hours sleep?

—Every time there's a snow storm past two in the morning, Kyle George calls me, then I make the decision on the storm plan, how to get all the announcers in. Then I have to go out and snowblow the driveway.

—How do you feel after that?

—Pretty damn grumpy, some days.

—Try it every day. Because that's how I feel. A few hours' work in the early morning, then I come in here for eight or nine hours and snowblow commercials.

—No one owes you a living, Claire.

—No. But the republic arts council has given me money to work, uninterrupted, on a new project. And I'm taking it.

—In fourth quarter? Our busiest time of the year? You know very well how much overtime Copy and Production will need to put in, even with you here.

By now, Ben's eyes could bore holes through concrete. Claire's eyes stung with tears. Ben drummed his fingers and glanced at his closed office door. Various people passed his office windows, glancing at Claire and Ben each slouched down in their chairs.

Then Claire unsettled Ben with her smile – serene. Resigned, even.

Ben picked up a paperclip from a 1960s VOIC ashtray. —Claire, you're our head copywriter. Our Creative Director. You and Nichole Wright do the work of five people over there. That's quite an accomplishment. You need to think long and hard about this grant. Do you really think you'll have something to show for it?

The paperclip, now straight, pricked at Ben's fingers.

Still smiling, voice soft, Claire stood up. —Thank you for all your encouragement, Ben. Perhaps if I could arrange of a leave of absence –

—Perhaps we might re-consider this later next summer, if we can find someone to replace you.

Claire glanced at her pale reflection in Ben's office window.

Ben spoke over her. —I hope I've given you something to think about, young lady.

—I quit.

Her tears ran freely as she turned her back on Ben and reached for the doorknob. No chance of returning to VOIC now, or of even getting references. Barely had her high school – she'd be lucky to find a job pouring coffee, or maybe, if she worked really hard, answering phones, because no way in frozen hell could she live on her painting alone. Couldn't dare. *Just a girl from Newfoundland. Just not good enough.*

Ben's oddly quiet voice reached her. —Why?

Her mother studying Claire's sketch, stroking her fever-sweaty hair: *That's really good, honey. You get that from your father.*

—Claire?

—Faith.

57. UNSENT 3
in which Claire Furey writes a letter to her father.

July 12, 2004

Dear Dad,

I've never wished I had your address so much. I've been invited to exhibit at the Far Flung International Arts Festival out in Eastern Bay. I'm one of the "New Lights." I got a grant last fall, and now I've got a triptych ready and a few smaller pieces. I'm scared shitless. And really happy.

How are you? Please take care.

Love,
Claire

58. UNCOMMON KINDNESS 1
in which Claire Furey attends the Far Flung Arts Festival and meets her audience.

August 7, 2004

Fifty? Seventy? White hair, doesn't colour it, but her skin's so smooth ...

Whatever her age, she squinted at Claire Furey's International Far Flung Arts Festival name tag. —Is this your first time at Far Flung, dear?

—Yes. It's quite an honour to be invited.

—Red tag, so you're a painter. My goodness, look at this big thing. Did you paint this all by yourself?

—Yes, all by myself.

—Is this a trio?

Claire smiled, at once protective and careless of her exhibit. —More of a triptych.

The older lady studied the three connected paintings. —Rather dark, aren't they?

—It's a study of St. Raphael's.

The woman seemed to be swallowing something bitter and cold: three-day-old tea, perhaps. —But you would have gone to St. Uriel's. The Sisters didn't – you must have –

—I didn't grow up in an orphanage.

—You what?

The cool wind off the bay did not reach the stifling church hall, and Claire wished she'd pinned her hair up. —I didn't grow up in an orphanage. I –

—Then what gives you the right?

—Pardon me?

Low and clear and hard: —You have no right. This is not authentic. Not your experience. This is not art.

Replies blasted through Claire's head, flashing and jagged: compassion, study, empathy. But none of this came out, only two little words.

—I'm sorry.

The woman seemed about to reply, but said nothing. Sadness, anger, approval and sudden doubt played across her face. Then she moved on to the next exhibit, voice syrupy.

Claire dug her nails into the palms of her hands and bit the inside of her bottom lip until it bled. *Sorry? What the hell do I have to be sorry for? Come on, Furey, find some guts.*

Another woman approached Claire and her painting. This woman's hair – expensively cut and coloured. Money.

—Hello. What's this called?

—*Archangel's Fury.*

—A large triptych. Very ambitious. Been painting long?

—Most of my life.

This woman studied the centre panel now, with its colours of fire and a child clinging to a caduceus, possibly crucified on it. —How much are you asking?

The modest price considered Claire's youth and thin reputation but not her time, not even the three weeks she'd gone without tea while painting the left panel. She'd drunk boiled water, counting coins for bread, apples and cheese, remembering the advice given in Alden Nowlan's *Various Persons Named Kevin O'Brien*: bread for energy, cheese for protein, apples for regularity. Even then, she'd collapsed. She'd allowed her mother to buy her soap, toothpaste and tampons, insisting she needed nothing else. Then she'd run out of toilet paper. Newsprint sufficed, but one night she dreamt that the ink transferred to her delicate skin, that her labia carried print.

—Fifteen hundred.

The woman's eyes opened wide. —One thousand five hundred dollars?

Say you'll take it. Say it's a steal. Say it speaks to you. Say fucking anything. Please.

Now the woman shook her head at the younger generation and their sense of entitlement. —It's too expensive, dear. You're just starting out.

Claire let out a long breath. *Fuck you. Fuck you with a rusty harpoon, you cold-hearted, patronizing sow.*

Grateful that food and drink came free to participating artists, Claire crossed the hall to the snack table. She swallowed down some nausea at the sight of the pastries; she'd been hoping for fruit. Sweaty people navigated round the old tables and chairs and filled the church hall. A general arts festival, Far Flung welcomed all genres but emphasized two different disciplines each year. This time round the visual and literary arts could strut. One Canadian and one American writer had been invited and would read later that evening; throughout the day, Newfoundland and Labrador writers would read. No big-name visual artists had come, sparking scandal. Had the Far Flung Committee failed somehow? Pissed off local talent with their relentless search for a Canadian or American to headline? Or pissed off a Canadian or American with the truth of flight times?

A poet, his voice calm and a little high, addressed the crowd from a podium. Claire sipped barky tea from a small foam cup, wishing she'd made it herself. The poet read something about Chapel Street. Claire wanted to listen but also needed some air. The two women who had viewed her triptych now chattered loudly enough to disturb others. Claire kept still. Leaving the room now would disturb the poet even more; his exasperated glances over his book at the insistent talkers had no effect. Claire wished she stood closer to the women, so she might trip and oops, accidentally spill her tea on them. That'd given them something to yak about.

Prayer, Furey. Meditation and prayer.

Yeah.

God grant me patience, and please hurry.

Chapel Street. The way the light played off the harbour some nights and suddenly the front room seemed underwater; God, she'd pretend to swim round that living room, graceful as a mermaid could be with a sticky face and pigtails, wiggling over the white couch with rust-coloured flowers on it. Did the poet live there now? In that house?

I am suffic smuthring under expectashuns. I am afriad of how I see her. Monster, me. Cant sey ti. Cant sculp it.

How dare she paint about St. Raphael's?

Furey's fury.

Love. Pleese. Gabriel.

Applause as the poet finished. The two women kept talking as the poet introduced a new writer working on his first novel, a young blond guy with a three-day beard and eyes like blue ice in springtime. He wore a black t-shirt with a white fish skeleton painted on it in what looked Liquid Paper.

Claire remembered to applaud the new novelist, tried to smile. *Another writer, great. God, they have it easy. Get your book published and you can't buy a box of Smarties at the corner store without seeing it on a rack. Meantime all my work's hidden in the studio. Can't sell one single fucking painting.*

Brief panic flew across Fish Skeleton's face, but he snatched ferocity out of the air, cocked his pelvis and described his work as the odd bit autobiographical. Then he narrated a comic scene of guy choosing a dildo in a Toronto sex shop while his girlfriend tries to talk him into a penis gag.

Claire winced, then laughed at Fish Skeleton's dialogue, stomach tight. His voice certainly carried. —And I says, 'You expects me to put that in my mouth? Just to show I loves ya? Girl, are you cracked?'

Daddy, what's wrong? Your headache? Mom, quick, I think Dad's sick again.

The two older women had finally stopped talking. They'd gone a bit pale.

Your father grew up in St. Raphael's, Claire. Do you know what that means?

Binges. Gabriel would disappear, then come home three or four days later, bearded and red-eyed yet somehow able to stand up straight. *I'm sorry,* he'd say over and over to Callie, *sorry.* But that note on the dresser: *I lov'd you, I truly did.* When did he stop? For God's sake, *why* did he stop? How can you just stop loving someone?

—'Next thing I knows, *she's* the one strapping on the Thunderin' Cyclops ...'

And that note, truly meant for Callie?

Gabriel would sing, voice beautiful but loud: *There was a wild colonial boy* ... Neighbours pounded the walls. Callie shut the bedroom door, let him sing.

—'And I sings to her then, 'Swing low, sweet chariot' ...

Claire sang when near tears. She'd taught the trick to Nichole years ago. Sing louder than the feelings, and the tears won't come.

—'Tears comes to me eyes then, because I likes the risk, and I likes me skin, but suddenly I'm feelin' right small.'

Jack Duggan was his name ... something like hiccuping.

And then the chatting women, all scowls now, got penned in. Claire wanted to sidle between then, offer a small plate of snowballs and lemon squares, politely enquire which offended them more, Fish Skeleton's descriptions, his gusto, or his singing a bit of hymn in the church hall. Getting elbowed, Claire ended up stepping into the church kitchen. The women followed her, Coloured Hair squawking in some desperation to escape the sexy young man – young enough to be her son – and the Thundering Cyclops.

Then Coloured Hair, eyes glittery, took Claire's arm. —Furey. Now, which Furey owns you?

—Oh, no one owns me.

Now the white-haired woman snapped her fingers. —I knew it. You're something to Gabriel Furey. That tone of voice, and your yellow eyes –

Yellow?

Coloured Hair nodded, as though all existential concerns now made sense, and as though Gabriel Furey was her favourite dessert. —Mm-mm, the stories we used to hear about him. Brilliant artist, though. We all said so, didn't we?

They waited, apparently expecting Claire to say *Thank you*. She said nothing.

White Hair smirked, for just a second. —Trying too hard to be Daddy's girl? Lay off the bottle, my honey. Bad for the complexion.

—I haven't seen my father for twenty-five years. And I don't drink.

Claire said this just as Fish Skeleton got another spasm of laughter, something about lubrication and tonsils. The women did not hear her.

Coloured Hair turned to White Hair. —Had some temper on him, Gabe did.

White Hair patted Claire's arm. —Yes, my dear. But he's a treasure, a national treasure. He must be a big influence on you.

—I've never seen any of my father's work.

They heard that.

—Never?

Claire shrugged, voice cool, deeply bothered. —His two bronze sculptures are in Ottawa. He did something in copper and gold up in Kirkland Lake. I think there's a piece out in BC. His mother was Canadian, so he got citizenship. But I've never seen his work. It's all up in Canada.

—You must at least be grateful to be a Furey.

—Excuse me?

—Your father's genes. Such a gift.

—Yes now, my father's genes. His genes painted this. He just magically poured pixie dust on my head, squirted out grace and talent for me when he came and knocked up my mother. The only reason my paintings exist is because I'm Gabriel Furey's daughter, is that it? Back door, easy way in, and the only reason I got invited out here is because my last name's Furey. *I* painted it! Me! I frigging starved to finish that triptych! And Gabriel Furey's got nothing to do with it.

White Hair and Coloured Hair looked at Claire coldly. Then Coloured Hair licked her lips. —You certainly have your father's temper.

Claire barged past the women, escaped the thick air of the hall and Fish Skeleton's raucous standing ovation. *I'm a fraud. A total fucking fraud. I don't belong out here. Should have stayed at VOIC. Where do I get off thinking I can do this? How the hell am I gonna pay the rent next month? Already two months behind. I've got to move back in with Mom now at the age of thirty-three. I can't do this. I can't do this. He's going to sell every God damned copy of his book this afternoon, just you watch. God, I'm going to throw up. Deep breath in, deep breath out. Okay. Settle down, Furey. Nicks would just say you're jealous.*

Of Fish Skeleton.

And Dad.

She'd be right.

Thinking this, Claire almost collided with another woman, this one at first thirty-ish with her bobbed blonde hair and neutral make-up. As she inhaled on her cigarette, her face settled into sucklines, making her look a well-moisturized fifty. Her companion might have been twenty-five, and he had that lean and hungry look grad students in English get when they think they're winning a power game.

The young man had just asked the smoking woman – his mother, perhaps? – if she thought the ambiguity was deliberate.

Smoke wafted. —Ambiguity? For Christ's sake, Dylan, it's irony. Like the fuzzy dice in my SUV. The kid's being crucified. And Raphael's supposed to be a healer.

Claire gasped. So did Dylan. The smoking woman turned to face Claire.

—I've been looking for you.

Buy it buy it buy it buy it, you almost get it, though there's as much irony in that painting as there is in my bra... fifteen hundred: two hundred for the light bill, hundred for the phone, eight hundred for some of the back rent, and hell, two hundred for groceries. Save some. I can make two hundred go far, apples, bread and cheese, peanut butter and tuna fish, macaroni ...

The woman held out her hand. —Dr. Dorinda Masterson. I'm with the university.

Buy it buy it buy it ...

—I wanted to ask you –

Fifteen hundred, but if you want to take it today, I'd consider fourteen hundred. I don't need clothes – wait, winter boots. Thirteen hundred if it's cash.

—Why do you have those three paintings connected together? It's an elementary mistake, one I can't really blame you for making, because I'm sure you were excited to come out here. I mean, you'd have to work hard to make them coherent enough to be a real triptych.

You –

Dr. Masterson ground her cigarette under her heel. —You look pale. You're not one of those girls who starves herself, are you? You don't look that stupid.

—I'm just tired.

—All the excitement of being out at Far Flung with real artists, yes, I'll bet it takes a toll on you.

Every drop of venom left Claire at that moment. Her legs gave way, and she held on to the side of the church.

—Dylan, help her.

Dylan stood further from Claire than Dr. Masterson, and by the time he reached the church wall, Claire had fallen to her knees. Dylan hauled her up easily, and Claire leaned hard on him, suddenly wondering whose fishy body odour she smelled. Dr. Masterson asked which bed and breakfast Claire was staying at and declared she and Dylan would drive her there, that it would only take them five or ten minutes out of their way. Her voice dared Dylan or Claire to disagree.

Describing the ride to Nichole later from her bed at the Levitz Hospital in Gander, even Claire didn't quite believe it. —Only a five-minute drive, but they had me in that car forever. They completely missed the little dirt road my B&B was on, and blared on out towards the highway.

—That's where you say Hello, kidnapped artist back here. Or jump out.

Dylan drove. Dr. Masterson talked, occasionally asking Dylan for confirmation.

—Brave in the same way playing dress-up is brave, wouldn't you think, Dylan?

—Guaranteed. Anxiety of influence, with some Bakthinian –

—All first works are autobiographical in some way. Write what you know. Paint what you know. Dance what you know. Tarted-up diaries passing as art. Don't worry, Claire. You'll grow out of it. Dylan, how would you deconstruct the painting from an anarcho-Marxist perspective?

Dylan deconstructed. Claire caught something about levels of irony implied in the gaze and the reciprocal relationship between painter, viewer and child, and the postmodern flames' comments on the absurdity of hell.

Gabriel, singing: *You are a plundering son.*

Dr. Masterson then picked Dylan's analysis apart for him. Undeterred by the tatters thrown in his lap, Dylan nodded when Dr. Masterson asked for another analysis, this one through Foucault's philosophy of punishment.

—Panopticonically speaking ...

Claire suddenly recalled a shred of some play Nichole had made her read, Christopher Marlowe, *Massacre at Paris*, the Guise encountering Remus the scholar, inventor of the flow chart and Grendel-seeding father in his way of future literary theory. The Guise's satisfying order: *Stab him.*

—... the implied voyeurism begs the question: is the viewer innocent or guilty? By standing by and studying the pain, is the viewer complicit in it?

Claire met Dylan's glance in the rear view mirror. —That almost made sense.

Frig, that old bag was right. My eyes are yellow.

But Dr. Masterson's voice obscured Claire's. —Oh, for God's sake, Dylan, don't come all Susan Sontag on me now. You need to think –

Claire groaned. —Let me out.

—But Dr. Masterson, the responsibility of viewing –

—Responsibility? It's undergraduate folly to even entertain the notion that art is somehow connected with society. Next you'll lapse back into talking about the human condition.

—Claire Furey's painting –

—Is immature. That does not mean your response to it needs to be.

—Her painting is forcing us to consider St. Raphael's –

—It's just a painting. Just like that poem today was just a poem, the novel just a novel. Disconnected texts. Existing as far apart as the stars, and long burnt out by the time they reach us. What are we doing out here?

They'd come to the highway. The sign offered Clarenville or Gander. Left or right. Then Dr. Masterson turned around. —My God. You're still in the back. Why didn't you say anything? Are you – Christ, don't faint. I don't think I could handle it –

Infected bile smells and tastes like rancid mushrooms. It's quite green, sort of a kelly-olive shade, a striking canvas for little blood clots. Such inflammation in the bile ducts creates some pressure on the stomach – projectile vomiting. Claire's ambitious expulsion missed the purple fuzzy dice and but splattered nicely on the windshield. Then Claire moaned, amazed at the sudden sickly pain under her right ribs, at her rattling teeth, at Dr. Masterson's cold hand on her forehead.

—Shit. Dylan, get the paper towels and wet wipes out of the back. Oh, hurry up. Claire, can you hear me? Claire?

Admittedly rather far away from Dr. Masterson, Far Flung and the rest of reality just then, Claire only wanted to sleep. But that damn pain, over on the left now, too, boring out her back –

—Claire. It's about half an hour to the hospital in Gander if we drive fast. The road's not paved until we're in the town limits. Can you handle the bumps? I'm calling ahead. What should I tell them?

Claire rattled off the drill. —History of biliary colic. Cholecystecomy in 1999. Obstructive jaundice in 2000, idiopathic. Suspected history of acute pancreatitis. And no CT scans – I'm allergic to IV contrast, anaphylaxis – *God*, that hurts! Five previous admissions for this. Pain's at seven out of ten, God, not now, please.

—Shh. Claire, we'll get you to the hospital. Dylan, just mop up the worst, we can do the wet wiping on the way – Claire, stay with me. Don't you *dare* faint. Dylan, drive, for God's sake. Do I have to do everything? Claire, you – Claire?

59. BY ELECTION
in which Jack Best pleads for a door held ajar.

October 12-13, 1949

Spit flew as Jack spoke. —What do you mean, *No*?

Gerald Canning, son of merchant Harold Canning, good friend of Prime Minister Jack Best, trusted advisor and, co-incidentally, Minister of Resources, did not often see Best like this: eyes deep and dark, kinky hair now sticking out, chin jutting.

Gerald sighed and put his palm to the back of his neck. —I'm telling you, Jack, you have to put this to a parliamentary vote, and you'll be voted down.

—They've come all the way from Europe, from – they damn near died. All of them. And we're going to turn them away?

—You want to be voted down on your first motion? Jack, see sense, now. What are we going to do with refugees in Newfoundland?

—They're not refugees. They're doctors, lawyers, architects, writers, painters, God knows what else, and they're willing to settle wherever we ask. *Wherever* we ask. We could have a doctor in nearly every outport. Or Labrador. Gerald, doctors in Labrador, think about it.

—Doctors, sure, but we can't pick and choose.

—The rest of them would bring something, too, business acumen if nothing else. We need people to come here. We lost the best part of a generation back in the Great War, and we're still not over it. Why the hell would we turn them away?

Gerald studied the deep maroon carpet where the desk feet rested, studied Jack's ornate desk, carved and curved and polished. —You know why.

—We'll just turn away bloody boatloads of people without a home, boatloads of people who could make this a better place, because of semantics? This is 1949. The Commission of Government turned away a boatload back in 1946. I thought we were better than the Commission.

—It's more than semantics, Jack. Jesus, b'y, these people deny Christ.

—No, they don't. They're just still waiting. They're a patient people, and we could learn a lot from them. And, God damn it, if Protestants and Catholics can live together here – we're not blowing each other up, like Ireland – why not Jews? Who's the idiot –

—Jack, listen to me.

—You said that in '46.

—That decision got made by someone else. Boat didn't even make landfall.

—Where'd they go?

—I don't know. Canada, maybe?

—Showers and ovens. Doors held ajar in storms.

—Shut up, Jack. You already got your pound of flesh out of me. But you have to put this to a vote. That's the best advice I can give you. No, the best advice I can give you is just say no to them now and be done with it. And you know you can't just invite them in on your say-so. I know that's what you're thinking there, Jack, but you do that, and you might as well raise your three-fingered hand in the Nazi salute.

—Now, come on –

—You are not an emperor. Put it to the vote.

Jack blew out a long curse. Parliamentary democracy could be a pain in the arse. And now he had a speech to write.

Thank you, Mr. Speaker.

Anchored in St. John's Harbour is the steamer *Mikhail*.

This cargo ship was never designed to hold the one hundred and six people on board.

Thirty-eight men, not including the crew, fifty-two women, sixteen children. These people are leaving Europe, leaving a land of much political instability, and looking to make a new home in a land of peace. These people have chosen Newfoundland and Labrador.

The passengers on the *Mikhail* have asked for refuge. We have a long history in Newfoundland and Labrador of opening our doors. If someone bangs on your door at night in the middle of a howling gale, do you not open it? If a man pleads, do we not hear? Yes, these people are Jews. These people are leaving behind destruction and fear we cannot imagine. These people have asked to settle here. Here, in Newfoundland and Labrador. Before any man voices religious objection, let me ask him to picture himself standing on the shore, squinting at the water at night, trying to make a prayer real and have a coastal boat chance along to his little community because a child's taken a fever. Or his wife is confined and having a troublesome birth. This is no time for delicacy. This is a time for truth. We are a poor country. A poor society. We have a rich culture, but a poor society. And what is it I mean by "poor society?" I mean we need people. We need to settle the interior, build and staff more schools, revivify business. And we need more doctors.

I shall now put the question to each man individually. This will be a free vote. You must not feel obligated to vote along what you perceive to be a party line. I doubt the Loyal Opposition has a unified policy on this matter. I know Government does not.

Therefore, I ask the Speaker we declare the matter of whether to accept the refugees open to debate, to be followed by a free vote.

—Jack, b'y, come on, did you really think it would go any other way?

Jack Best turned from his office window, from his view of Bannerman Park.

—Yes, Gerald. Yes, I did. That's why I tried.

—Have you slept yet? We were up thirty-four hours.

—I went home and washed, but it's going to be a while before I get any sleep.

—Wasn't a total loss for them. My father brought half his store on board, so at least they got to purchase some goods, new clothes and whatnot.

Make it your next Port of Call. Jack saw a black zig-zag line float across his left field of vision: migraine aura, a warning clear as a foghorn.

Gerald smiled in the sympathetic manner of a mother with a worn-out child.

—Come on, b'y, sit down at least. I'll tell your secretary to get some tea. You getting a headache?

Jack did sit down, weary the moment his arse touched the chair. He rubbed his forehead. —Tell her to make it a pot. Strong. And make sure it's Golden Pheasant.

Soon, Jack and Gerald sipped tea and talked quietly of the seal hunt and the Canadian hockey broadcast they'd picked up a few clear nights ago – of anything but the denied *Mikhail* – until Jack's secretary knocked on the door to announce the two o'clock appointment. Gerald took his feet off Jack's desk and rolled his sleeves back down.

Jack blinked his dry eyes several times. More zig-zags, and the red circle that started so small but swelled in throbs until it consumed him.

—Two o'clock?

Gerald shrugged on his jacket. —The electrical engineer, von Something. Von Haldorf. William Wright got him.

Jack could not stand up. Stunned and tired, tie askew, he watched Gerald fasten his cufflinks, watched golden curilicues spin madly. The red circle grew. —Von Haldorf?

Gerald checked his hair in the small mirror behind the office door.

—That's him. Fix your collar and tie, there, Jack.

William Wright, aggressively eager junior clerk in the Department of Resources, entered with a tall man, maybe forty-five, balding but not yet grey, in excellent physical condition. In fact, the tall man engaged in regular calisthenics, hiked, snowshoed, skied and swam, and would become one of the first people seen in Newfoundland to be running for his health: Herr Doktor Johann von Haldorf.

Delight threaded William Wright's face – a foul delight, Jack felt. Jack usually found William Wright obsequious where his brother Robert was merely courteous. Gerald spoke highly of William: *Best thing about young Wright is that if I ask something, it's done right away. Doesn't matter what.* Jack thought then, much as he thought now, that it is impossible to hold in complete respect a man who does your dirty work with no protest.

Gerald nodded to William, who actually smirked, and then William spoke, his deep voice elegant and gently touched with the Port au Mal accent, much like his brother's.

—Mr. Prime Minister, Mr. Canning. May I present Herr Doktor von Haldorf.

Jack held out his hand. —Herr Doktor von Haldorf, I'm Prime Minister Best. Welcome to Newfoundland and Labrador.

—I expected you at the waterfront. Do you normally leave foreign dignitaries to lackeys and junior civil servants?

William paled as though he'd been kicked in the gut. Jack bowed his head, straining for diplomacy.

Gerald rescued him. —The House was in session for nearly two days.

Jack looked up. —We had a debate.

—Debate. Ah. You need electrical engineers here. That is why you invited me.

Gerald nodded. —Yes, Herr Doktor. We have many communities not yet –

—I worked for Westinghouse, Edison, General Electric. I designed the electrical grid for Benford, North Carolina. You know it?

Gerald and Jack shook their heads. William had backed up to the door and seemed to disappear.

—Benford uses electricity more efficiently, and more cheaply, than any other town its size in the US.

Jack nodded. —Impressive. You said you worked for Westinghouse and General Electric?

Von Haldorf pointed to a light bulb in the lamp on Jack's desk.

—And Edison. I have done much research on your country. One of your campaign promises, Mr. Best, was to electrify Newfoundland and Labrador.

Jack couldn't help being pleased that von Haldorf pronounced *Newfoundland* correctly. The red circle had a yellow centre now.

Von Haldorf smiled – a charming smile, avuncular, as though he must first tease Gerald and Jack before giving them candy. —And how many electrical engineers do you have?

Gerald answered immediately. —None.

Jack could have kicked him. Crooked black lines swooped.

—So, do I stay, or do I get back on the boat and go on to Canada? You'll find my salary demands very reasonable.

Jack thickened his brogue. —Must have been some lot of demand for a man as smart as you during the war.

Von Haldorf studied the Prime Minister a little harder. —Mr. Best, don't waste our time playing the stunned fish. If you want to know more about me, just ask me. I hide nothing.

Jack chuckled, despite himself.

Von Haldorf continued. —I was with Westinghouse until 1939, when I went back home. My boss understood, and America was neutral. In Germany I designed electrical grids and communications arrays.

Jack knew a thousand reasons why he should, as a man of state with a country to electrify, not ask. But he asked regardless. —What did you do during the war?

Still, fright swooping down from many directions, von Haldorf spoke quietly but clearly. —I flew for Luftwaffe.

No denying the migraine now.

I'm about to offer a job to a former Nazi pilot. Jesus, have mercy on my soul.

—I admire your honesty, Doctor von Haldorf. Some men might be less upfront, less bold about their history.

—I did what I did. Germany became difficult. Choice became complicated. And you need electrical engineers.

Jack closed his eyes. Maybe when he opened them, von Haldorf would be gone.

Von Haldorf stubbornly persisted in existing. —How do your people light their houses? Kerosene? Seal oil?

Gerald tried to change tack. —How is your room at the Hotel Newfoundland?

—Adequate.

—You must be tired. I know your ship only docked this morning. Mr. Wright, will you take Herr Doktor von Haldorf back to the Hotel? We can reconvene tomorrow morning at ten.

William Wright, who'd kept still and quiet as a coat rack, stepped forward smartly. —Yes, sir, Mr. Canning. Herr Doktor, may I take your bag?

When Gerald returned after escorting von Haldorf out, he rolled his eyes at how ill Jack looked. —Jack, for the love of God, go home and get some sleep.

—I don't want him.

—We need him. We promised to electrify by '51.

Pound, pound, pound. —I don't want him. Soon as I can stand up, I'm going home. When I come back tomorrow, I'll expect you to have made the right decision. You're Minister of Resources. This is your portfolio. He's your decision.

—Who will rid me of this turbulent Nazi? William Wright found him.

—On your orders.

—That's right, Jack. I am so convinced that von Haldorf's the right man, the man we need, that I sent a junior clerk over to Germany to meet him. Two weeks of sailing, I'll have you know, then a week in Berlin, or what's left of it, then two weeks of sailing back. All on our tab. All an investment in our bright, bright future.

Unsteady, Jack held open the office door, signalling an end to debate.

—Jack, you –

Gerald stopped. The staff might hear.

—I hope you're feeling better soon, sir.

Saying nothing, Jack closed the door.

As Gerald left the Prime Minister's Office, Jack's secretary whispered over her typewriter. —Mr. Canning. You have a paperclip stuck to the seat of your pants.

Alone in his office, Jack wished he could pray, but his head hurt too much.

60. A TRAVELOGUE
in which William Wright tells Robert about a recent voyage.

October 13, 1949

Robert Wright contentedly cooked supper, hamburgers in one pan and cut potatoes in the other. Both he and the children had developed a taste for American food, and duplicating at home the taste of a hamburger and fries at the Fort Pepperell Commissary had become one of Robert's more trivial quests in life. So far he'd had no luck with authenticity, but the attempts were always tasty.

Etta sat in the living room, feet up on a hassock, reading a Boston newspaper, resting before going out to the Friday night meeting of the Ladies Auxiliary Moral Work Brigade.

Libby, the youngest, slid into the kitchen from her running start from the living room. Thirteen and goofy, she hugged Robert round the waist and ran to slide into the living room. Then she snatched a magazine from her sister Marie, who complained in her predictable manner, and who, at seventeen, should have been above chasing a younger sister and uttering threats like Boadicea. Then they both tripped in the long legs of Thomas, who, while clearing his throat, oops, accidentally stretched his legs at the wrong moment. Etta looked over the top of her newspaper; Robert stepped back from the stove and glanced through the kitchen doorway; the girls lay in a heap on the floor, Libby's underwear showing.

Thomas looked over the tops of his glasses. —Savages belong outside. Now are you two going to behave, or not?

Marie picked herself up and went upstairs to her room, cold dignity trailing behind her. Libby sat on the floor at Thomas's feet. —You gonna make me, Mister Man who's all nervous about his big date tonight?

—Go on with you, Libby. You're not worth the time to smack.

—Mister Man's got a date, Mister Man's got a date –

Etta rolled her eyes. —Elizabeth Anna Wright, behave yourself.

Then she heard a voice at the back door by the kitchen, and she rolled her eyes again: William Wright's tentative *Hello*, tentative only in disguise, for he knew everyone was home. Was there no peace?

Robert greeted his brother as he turned a patty. —William. Come in. You had supper?

William looked rumpled and drawn but somehow pleased. —I've been nursing von Haldorf all day.

—So you won't want sauerkraut on your hamburger. Thank you for the tip, by the way. We did a little news story on von Haldorf this morning.

William nodded. —The Minister really wanted him, so I do what I can.

—Even leak to the media?

—Only to you. Why in the name of God are you doing the cooking?

—I like cooking.

William shook his head as at a great mystery. —Women's work.

—Don't let Libby hear you say that.

—Hamburgers are German.

—Mm-hmm.

—And the streets were clean.

—Oh, yes.

The hamburgers sizzled, at a delicate stage, but then William could have struck an iceberg and not been distracted from his speech.

—The streets were clean, and clocks chimed the hour. Now buildings were bombed, to be sure, but they've got the rubble cleaned up. Somehow.

—Did you go to Germany for Gerald Canning?

William nodded. Then he turned on the radio, the six o'clock newscast obscuring his storytelling. Finally, he came to stand near the stove, a few inches from Robert's ear.

—This goes no further, Robert. Between you, me, and the fencepost.

Robert nodded.

—Canning called me at home three weeks ago. Said he needed a favour. Said the request as good as came from Best himself. That got my attention, I can assure you.

Robert didn't doubt it. Even use of the superlative in common speech caused William to straighten his shoulders.

—So I invite Canning in, and we have a drink, and he wastes no time. 'Will,' he says to me, 'Will, I need you to go to Germany.'

'Germany,' says I. 'Germany? What do you need done over in Germany?'

Then Canning picks up his briefcase. 'I need you to meet with a Dr. Johann von Haldorf, electrical engineer, and convince him to come to Newfoundland. I've already been in correspondence with him, but he needs the personal touch.'

Well now, I know as well as anyone we need electrical engineers, but a German? So I says to Canning, 'You want me to go to Germany and sweet-talk an engineer?'

Canning nods, then passes me his briefcase. 'And I need you to give him this.'

'You want me to woo him with a briefcase,' says I.

'Open it,' says Canning.

The bloody thing was locked. Heavy, too. 'I can't,' says I.

Then Canning takes out his business card, or half of one anyway, and he says, 'No one can. You'll know it's the real von Haldorf you're talking to when he gives you the other half of this card. Then you can give him the briefcase. He'll have the key, and he'll open it in front of you.'

That's when I noticed Stephen in the doorway, holding his teddy bear and rubbing one eye with his fist. He's only three, but he doesn't need to be hearing stuff like this. So I pick up Stephen there, and he's so warm just then, Robert, I felt like I'd never truly known he existed until that moment. So I says to Canning, 'You take your suitcase and your filthy money and you get the hell out of my house.' Canning won't move. So I yell at him some more, and he finally leaves, not taking the briefcase with him. So I throw that out the door after him, and it makes this funny *whump* when it lands, and he picks it up and goes home.

—You kicked Gerald Canning out of your house?

That part of the story surprised Robert most of all.

William sounded as though he'd been accused of lying. —Yes. Kicked him out, him and his briefcase. No good. First thing Monday morning, Canning struts into my office, hands me shipping passes to Germany and then chains the briefcase to my wrist.

—What?

—Don't you laugh. Honest to God, just like in the pictures, a handcuff on the briefcase. I couldn't believe it. And Canning says, 'Remember, he'll have the other half of this business card. Keep this half in your wallet so you can match it when you see him. Now call your wife and tell her you have to go.' So I go to Germany. Long crossing stuck in my room, let me tell you. And like I said, the streets were clean, cleaner than they are here. And I meet von Haldorf in an office, and sure enough, he shows me the other half of the business card, and he unlocks the cuff – good thing, too, for the chafing.

Robert glanced at his brother's left hand – two scabs healing on his pointy wristbones.

William continued. —And then von Haldorf opens the briefcase, and looks inside it a long time, and then he says to me, 'You count it.' That way I'm part of it all, see, can't ever claim innocence? Cunning bastard. So I count it.

—Count what?

William stared up at Robert as though at an exasperating mule. —The money.

Oh, my God. —Whose currency?

—American.

Libby called out. —Dad, are those hamburgers ready yet?

William looked so terribly serious. —I'm not going to tell you how much.

Small mercies. —Why did you tell me any of it? I'm a newsman.

—You're my brother. I had to tell someone. Jesus, Robert, don't you dare start investigating this. I'll be ruint.

You're ruint already. —William, what in the name of God were you thinking?

—I had no choice. Canning told me to do it.

Robert looked full on his brother now, spatula upraised. —Never again. Do you understand? Never again. Pawns are the first to die.

Libby slid into the kitchen. —Hi, Uncle William. Staying for supper?

—No. No, thank you. I'd best be getting on.

William's voice quivered just a little too much. He put his hat and shoes back on, nodding to Marie and Thomas as they came into the kitchen, calling out a hello to Etta, who ignored him. Then he murmured to his brother. —I am more than a pawn.

And he left.

Marie raised her eyebrows, thick Wright brows her mother had just taught her to tweeze. —What's wrong with Uncle William?

Libby sprinkled salt on the fries. —Is he mad because he lost at chess?

Robert smiled as he handed Thomas a plate. —William doesn't know how to play chess. Neither do I.

Thomas pushed his glasses up his nose. —It's a dangerous game.

Robert wondered how much Thomas had heard.

Libby just laughed, giggle after giggle.

61. LOGGER 2
in which Jack Best calls in to VOIC's *Free Line.*

MARCH 4, 1975

... and the young people today, Neal, honest to God, I don't know what to be saying.

We were discussing garbage collection, caller.

But it's the young crowd –

The topic is garbage collection.

Now you're interrupting me, too?

I just want you to get to your point.

My point is, we're going to hell –

I'm going to have to cut you off there, caller. We have network commitments, and we're already overdue for a commercial break. You're listening to *Free Line*, right here and only on the VOIC Radio Network. And we'll be right back after the break. Call in with your thoughts today on garbage collection, 273-5211, or out of town, 1-800-570-VOIC.

Neal took off his headphones and rubbed his forehead. Only an hour in to the program. Only Tuesday.

In the facing control room, eighteen-year-old Kevin White waved his hands, signalling he needed to talk. Neal put his headphones back on.

—Neal, got your next caller lined up.

—Tell him to go to hell with that last caller and the young crowd.

—I think you'll want to talk to him.

... make it your next Port of Call.

—I don't want to talk to another living soul for the next month.

If you're needing a new car, go see Wince ...

—Go 'way, Neal. You'd talk to rocks.

Neal smiled. He'd done so, in the mines.

...Wince Blanford Chrysler looks after you.

—I'll bite, Kevvie. Who is it?

Whether it's to wake yourself up or calm yourself down, Golden Pheasant Tea ...

—Jack Best. You know, the Prime Minister fellah.

Neal sat up straight. —How much time left to the break?

—Forty-eight seconds.

—Patch him through. Mr. Best, are you there?

—Hello, Neal.

—Welcome to *Free Line*, Mr. Best. We'll be going to air shortly. Shouldn't you be in the House this morning?

Golden Pheasant, best tea for the best day, and for every day.

And we're back here on *Free Line* on the VOIC Radio Network. I'm Neal O'Dea. On the line this morning I have the Prime Minister of Newfoundland and Labrador, Jack Best. Good morning, Mr. Best.

Good morning, Neal.

I must admit, Mr. Best, that while it's always a privilege to host you on the airwaves, today it is also a surprise. Isn't the House in session this morning?

I suppose.

You suppose? Mr. Best, as Prime Minister –

I haven't entered Republic Building this morning. I spent some time on the bench outside, but then I got cold and walked across the street to Renouf's General Store and put money in the pay phone.

You're talking to us from a pay phone? Correct me if I'm wrong, sir, but don't you have a telephone in your office?

I already told you I haven't entered Republic Building today.

Of course. So, Mr. Best, is there a comment you'd care to make this morning? Is – that blasted operator.

If you wish to continue your call, please deposit another coin. Do you wish to continue your call? Do you wish to continue your call?

Mr. Best, are you there?

I'm here. Neal, I'm taking a rest from politics. Neal?

This is rather sudden, Mr. Best. You've led us – led Newfoundland and Labrador – I know you've suffered some ill health recently. Is this the reason?

No.

Mr. Best, is your cabinet aware of –

No.

Is there a succession plan?

We're a parliamentary democracy, Neal. Hold an election.

But Mr. Best, you can't just –

If you wish to continue your call, please deposit another coin.

Mr. Best, are you there?

Do you wish to continue your call?

Mr. Best?

The other party has terminated the call.

Ladies and gentlemen, we need to verify that phone call, but right now it sounds like the Prime Minister has just resigned over the air. We'll go to a commercial break and have more on this story when we get back. 273-5211, or if you're calling long distance, 1-800-570-VOIC.

Every housewife knows that value and selection –

—Kev, was that genuine?

—I dunno. Came from a pay phone, I can tell you that. Newsroom's gone cracked. I know there are young bucks stirring up the House, trying to force Best out, but can he just leave like that?

In the hallway, Thomas Wright jabbed a finger at a retreating Ben Philpott, speaking loudly enough to be heard past the control room's sound tiles. —Who told you the Prime Minister just resigned?

—He did, sir. Just then, on the air.

Thomas glanced at Neal, and Neal nodded. Then Thomas looked to the Newsroom, where all eight reporters now spoke intently into phones, hauled on their yellow VOIC coats and prepared tape recorders. Satisfied, Thomas abruptly turned and strode back to Sherwood Forest.

Kevin pointed to the logger reel. —Got another four commercials ready to play while I take this over to Production and get them to cart that bit off. If I'm not back before the break ends, just talk to the audience.

If you're needing a new car ...

—What am I going to say to them?

—Just reassure them.

And we're back here on *Free Line* on 570 VOIC. If you missed it, we just heard from Jack Best – and the VOIC Newsroom has just confirmed this – we just heard from Prime Minister Jack Best, who announced he is stepping away from politics. VOIC reporter Pat Finch is standing by. Pat?

As Neal just said, Jack Best, Prime Minister of Newfoundland and Labrador, has just announced his resignation on the *Free Line* show. Details are scarce, now, but you can rest assured that VOIC will bring you the news first. I repeat, Prime Minister Jack Best has just announced on the *Free Line* show that he's stepping down. In a related story ...

62. THREE DOTS 2, in which Robert Wright listens to a live remote broadcast.

Dec. 12, 1942

—Happy birthday all over again, Daddy.

Robert looked up from his accounts receivable, where he scratched entries beneath dim candlelight. Then he drew out his pocket watch to show Libby the luminous numbers. —It's gone half past ten. You should be in bed.

Atlas, Robert's massive Newfoundland dog, had seen Libby safely escorted to the kitchen and now returned to his spot near the bottom of the stairs. His nails clicked softly.

Libby rubbed her eyes with a fist and sneered at the blackout curtain.

—I'm not tired. When will the war be over?

Robert pushed aside his paperwork and invited Libby to his lap.

—You'll catch a chill.

Libby leaned against Robert's waistcoat, the buttons tickling her face.

—How old are you?

—Forty-one.

—So you were born in 1901?

—That's right. December 12th, 1901, the same day Marconi received the signal.

—And I'm six. So when will the war be over?

—I don't know, sweetheart.

—Whatcha listening to?

—VOIC.

—I know that. What show?

—*Dance Hall.* Mr. Ryall and Mr. Leddo are down at the Knights of Columbus Hostel tonight, on remote.

Libby rubbed her eyes again. —Remote what?

Robert put his left arm round her shoulders, preparing to carry her back up to bed.

—Mr. Ryall and Mr. Leddo have microphones at the hostel so everyone else can hear the party. The beauty of radio –

—Is everyone dancing?

—Yes, everyone's dancing.

—Are they having a good time?

—I'm sure they are.

—When will the war be over?

Robert sighed. —Elizabeth Anna Wright, I have work to do, and you should be in bed.

Etta called gently from the top of the stairs. —Libby, are you bothering your father?

Libby and Robert answered together. —No.

Libby whispered her next question. —Did you like your cake?

—Where on earth did you find a tinned date loaf?

—Thomas found it at Mahon's three months ago, tucked way, way in the back. Mr. Mahon, the tall one, said he couldn't have it, but when Thomas told them our last name, the other Mr. Mahon, the one who smells funny, he said we could take it.

Smells funny, indeed. But Robert did not have the strength to explain to Libby just then how Kipling Mahon's brothers tethered the drunkard Kip just short of the gutter.

—Do you know the Mahons are named for famous writers? The oldest brother is Conan Doyle Mahon. The middle brother is Kipling Mahon. And the youngest is Stevenson Mahon.

—Kipling? Like *Rikki Tikki Taavi*?

—The very same.

Robert held Libby a while longer, stark counterpoint in the kitchen with a sleepy girl on his lap to the raucous party coming through the radio. When Libby's breathing came deep and steady, Robert gently stood. He felt weak a moment, and his pulse raced; he took a deep breath, held it, then made his way to the stairs.

At the top, Etta took Libby and tucked her in. In the neighbouring bed, Marie snored.

Etta touched her husband's shoulders. —Did you have a good birthday?

—Cake in wartime. I felt very loved.

—Coming to bed?

—No, I still have a few hours' work to do.

Etta sighed, very quietly, and if Robert chose, he could miss it.

—Good night, Robert.

Robert did not answer.

—I said 'Goodnight,' Robert.

—Dear God.

From the kitchen, wafting like thin smoke through the quiet house, came wrong noise: VOIC broadcast screams.

Robert leapt down the stairs, slipped on the rug at the bottom, tripped over Atlas, stumbled into the kitchen. Etta ran behind him. He turned the radio up very loud: over the remote signal, women screamed, men yelled *Fire,* Geoff Leddo – was it Geoff? – cursed near the open mic, then screamed himself: *Get out! Get out! Fire!*

—Call the station.

Robert jammed his hat on his head, tied his coat shut without buttoning it, shoved his feet into galoshes.

—Call the station, and tell them I said to cut. Go to dead air. Just cut that signal!

Prepared to run from Forest Road to Chapel Street, Robert darted into the path of a taxi cab, headlights off for the blackout. The driver slammed his brakes and then opened the door, recognizing Mr. Robert Wright.

—VOIC on Chapel Street, sir?

Robert nodded. A stretchy nightmare, yes, yet the taxi cab and the cold and his rattling teeth ...

Blackout. Wartime. Boarded windows, locked doors. Robert leaned against a wall in master control, listening with the others working that night, listening and helpless. Listened in fear. Duty.

The numbers and hands on Robert's pocket watch glowed, time clear even in this cold darkness.

To the public, dead air.

To themselves, cracks, bangs, screams consumed by a hiss and roar, until the flames took the mic, killing the connection with a *bzht,* the noise very like spark-gap transmission.

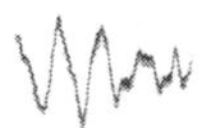

63. SKIP
in which young Lewis and Matthew Wright tamper with signal to noise.

July 12, 1969, to start

East wind threw hard rain against the windows, against the roof of Thomas Wright's house in St. John's. The attic's darkness and dim dust made worse the shadows of what were normal discards. Lewis Wright disliked the attic, the low roof, the exposed beams and the chaos of crates. Matt loved it. Rainy afternoons meant no one could force them to play outside, meant no mowing the huge lawn either here at home, or, worse, at the broadcast centre on Kenmount Road. Flowerbeds, cut in the shapes of the call letters, blazed with orange blooms from June to October, and lay on a steep little hill, terribly easy to ruin with a heavy mower.

The rain also prevented Lewis from flying his model Hercules, a machine he'd worked on for nearly two years. Lewis slumped in an armchair, only the occasional sigh signalling he hadn't died. Matt smiled. He loved his brother – liked him, too – standing as the only one to tolerate Lewis's dreaminess, as Lewis's only friend. Lewis wasn't slow, Matt knew; Lewis just thought differently. Fear prefaced each step Lewis took: would insects die; would the world judder; would he muddy his shoes? Matt earned straight *A*s; Lewis struggled with each assignment, threw up before each test. Yet Lewis was the true smart one, probably even smarter than the American engineers. Only Matt knew that. Matt also knew that if he broke their brothers' pact and spilled Lewis's secret, then Lewis would be tasked to prove it. That strain might cripple him. So Matt kept to himself Lewis's instant comprehension of how bridges stayed in the air, how heavy planes could ascend, how radio waves could be harnessed, modified and made to carry music and voice.

According to their great-Aunt Jane, people once called those like Lewis *natural*, or *fey*, even thinking the fey had been touched by the hands of God. When Matt asked her, at age eight, if she thought Lewis had been touched by the hands of God, she'd smiled.

—Everything's been touched by the hands of God. Go out in the muck, and get your hands dirty. That's how God made us.

Matt had been impressed. He'd then glanced down on his own hands. —Did God have to clean His nails?

Aunt Jane then offered him candied ginger, which he loathed but ate to please her, and Matt would go home that afternoon haunted by an image of God cleaning His nails with His teeth and spitting out the muck. The little wet piles coalesced; maggots jiggled; flies or airplanes buzzed – something dim ascended. Aunt Jane watched Matt chew ginger. —There's not much wrong with your brother a little care won't help.

Considering the attic, the scents of dust and mould, the heaviness of crates, Lewis figured everything out. Not even figured: saw. He tuned the transistor radio and set it on a crate. Lewis saw things, answers to math problems, motives of adults, moments of collision. He'd once pointed at a butterfly, an astonishing breed he could never identify, orange and black like a monarch but with much larger wings, with blue on the wings like lapis lazuli; Matt had just released it from a jar. Matt had captured it unexpectedly, simply having the old jam jar with him for collecting stones. Late June, soft wind, blue sky, and six stones in the jar – deep sea green, blue, purple, grey. Then he spotted the butterfly. Lewis heard the sharp clink of glass on the paved driveway and watched Matt watch the butterfly. Stones had fallen round the butterfly but apparently not damaged its wings. Sun glinted off the heavy glass, hurting Lewis's eyes, and when Matt glanced up and saw his brother's face, both boys knew Lewis did not have to ask. Matt would let the butterfly go. And he did, carefully lifting the jar, ashamed. Lewis pointed again, jaw going slack and creating an expression that maddened schoolteachers; the same sun that glinted off the jam jar now sparkled off spider silk. Caught, the butterfly struggled, majestic wings sticking to the strands. Lewis strode to the web, tearing strands, getting his hands sticky – he would return that afternoon to a habit of repeatedly washing his hands – but the butterfly, as much afraid of Lewis as of the spider web, struggled harder – futility. A large spider descended rapidly, instincts screaming at this interference and destruction, and it landed on Lewis's right hand. Lewis jerked back, shaking both his hands, smacking where the spider had lit upon him, trying to brush something away. The butterfly kept still now, and the spider pricked its way across the web. Lewis felt tears start and turned away, first catching Matt's gaze. Accusation arced between them: if Matt had not interfered, had left the butterfly alone to fly, they would not have seen this brutal and necessary pageant. Lewis tried to say this out loud, but an undiagnosed stutter, which bothered him only at moments of high emotion and manifested as vowels stuck breathless in his throat, reined him mute. His mouth hung open for *I*. VOIC played through an open window; the Beatles sang "Love Me Do" The song ended cold – station ID, kettle drums and brass sting with just a hint of big band: *VOIC, Voice of International Communication. Connect to the whole world on VOIC.* Then came the top-of-the-hour newscast: *The VOIC 3 O'Clock News, a presentation of Port of Call, ladies and gentlemen's clothing, Water Street. Good afternoon. I'm Ben Philpott.*

Lewis remembered the spider, the newscast and "Love Me Do" as he recognized what the attic meant on July 12, 1969. Ignoring the radio's latest reasonable plea to go see Wince Blanford if he wanted a car, Lewis asked Matt to wait. Lewis knew what Matt would find behind a pile of exceptionally heavy crates, beneath a pile of women's clothes from God knew when. Matt fastened a corset loosely about his chest, swung his hips and paraded about the attic. Lewis watched him a moment, then held up a dress, considered relative heights – both boys were tall like their father, already six foot at thirteen and fifteen – and decided to ask Aunt Jane whose clothes these might be. The rain beat harder. Matt smiled, and Lewis understood that his brother felt safe when rain lashed the house. But that buried crate, Matt's skinny arse stuck out as he excavated secrets, that buried crate and an overheard conversation and their father's pained voice as he argued with engineer Dan McGrew about the hidden potentials of radio waves – better left buried, like the boys' Newfoundland dog Hera, who had died the day of the butterfly, poisoned, it seemed, by someone who held a grudge against the Wrights.

—Lewis, look.

Matt shimmied back out of the closet, and Lewis saw beyond him a crate he'd opened so quietly that Lewis had not heard his brother lay the lid on the floor.

Lewis moaned. —Skipper'll have choice words if he knows we're at this.

—Never mind Skipper. I'll handle him. Come on, this is important. Look.

Matt held a portrait, about ten by thirteen, the paper thick and beautifully woven, almost a painter's canvas. Black and white, of course, taken maybe in the late 1940s or early 1950s. It was a man wearing an old-fashioned suit, grey wool coat and vest over a white starched shirt, the collar fastened not with a button but a small bar, possibly gold. Over the bar came a tie, tightly knotted and just slightly askew to the wearer's right; Lewis knew immediately the tie had been green, dark green, like spruce trees. The man was balding, broad forehead visible, remaining black hair quite thick far back on his head and parted on the right. His hair was not oiled or Brylcreamed but looked freshly washed. Over the ears the man's hair was quite short and gone white. His nose was large and seemed pinched on top by rimless spectacles. The glass lenses shielded thick black eyebrows and deep eyes caught in an expression of concern, squinting slightly, as though the man felt compassion for something going on outside, or something that had happened long ago. Laugh lines seemed to start where the lenses ended and arced down to the edge of his mouth. Full lips, long and clean-shaven face ... Matt tilted the photo to another angle; now impatient pained arrogance surfaced in the subject's face, an expression the boys recognized right away.

Lewis said it. —S-skipper's father.

When he turned to look at Lewis, Matt was pale. —He looks just like me.

—No, you look just like him. You've got more hair, though.

—Why don't we have this on a wall somewhere?

—Skipper doesn't like it.

—Why not? Wait, how do you know?

Lewis shrugged.

Matt stroked the frame. —It's going to get damaged up here. That Egyptian guy up in Ottawa took this. Look at the signature. How come Aunt Jane doesn't have this up on a wall?

Lewis shrugged again.

—This is madness.

Matt gently put the portrait on a broken rocking chair, propping it against the chair back so that their unknown grandfather commanded a view of the room. Lewis squinted slightly. Matt had been almost two when their grandfather died, Lewis not even thought of, the story went. Lewis cringed at the phrase; *not even thought of* made him feel like an accident, a burden. Those eyes: intelligent, kind, distant, as if Robert Wright hesitated before looking too deeply into another man's eyes for fear of what he might find. *Killed your mother being born? What a shame. Tore her apart, the way I heard it. She was told after your brother never to have another child, and then you came along.* Lewis shut his eyes; Matt said something about a heavy box; Lewis opened his eyes, and then his grandfather's portrait flickered understanding. Either that, or Matt's movements interrupted the lamplight.

—Lewis, come on, help me out here.

The wooden crate squealed against the attic floor, and something inside the crate clinked. —Jesus. That's a radio tube. Be careful. Don't move it, don't move it.

Lewis took over, prying off the lid gently, working the crowbar in little thrusts, until he had the lid shuddered loose. The boys gently propped the lid against the wall, then slowly peered in the crate.

Matt scratched his head. —I think this belongs in a museum.

Polished mahogany, dials and wires, glass tubes, a queer little antenna, and a tiny yellowed magazine called *Alternating Current*. The magazine's cover, much smudged with a curlicued black border, looked like the trim on a lady's handkerchief. Irregular and smudgy print within did not invite the eye; in one article the font size increased for three paragraphs and two sentences of a fourth. Issue date: March 1933.

—Put it down, Matt, that's full of mildew.

—This is important.

—No doubt, but it's going to fall apart in your hands.

Matt acquiesced, giving *Alternating Current* to his gentler brother. Lewis laid the magazine by their grandfather's portrait. Then Matt went elbows-deep after dials and glass. —What do you say we lift this out?

—You want it to disintegrate? This is old, Matt, older than Skipper. This is like the gear Mr. McGrew's got at the station.

Matt considered the VOIC chief engineer and his large hands, his three-piece suit and string tie, his enthusiastic genius with old equipment. Many times, Mr. McGrew had amused the boys out in the engineering workshop by spreading out wires and vacuum tubes, knobs and Tesla coils on his workbench. In those memories, rain always fell. —Induction, boys. Which of you can explain induction to me?

Matt would admire a vacuum tube in dim incandescent light, able to parrot back without comprehension Mr. McGrew's lecture; Lewis once caught the engineer in a mistake. Mr. McGrew had been delighted, but at that moment their father came round the corner and heard a son talking back to his necessary and respected engineer. Lewis got duly told off, and for months afterwards said nothing more than 'yes, sir' to Mr. McGrew. Later that year, as a birthday present, Mr. McGrew gave Lewis a book about Tesla, and Lewis appalled his father one evening at a rare supper together, Lewis's words slowed by intimidation and random fears, dragged through water to articulation but said anyway, at some cost.

—It's not just Marconi, Skipper, it's Tesla, too. US Supreme Court overturned Marconi's patent, awarded credit to Tesla. How come we never hear about Tesla?

In Mr. McGrew's workshop, unknown to either Mr. Wright or Matt, Lewis was building a Tesla coil.

Now Lewis studied the apparatus within the crate. —We need to take the sides down. Get the sides of the crate down, then we can lift this onto that table over there. Get the sewing machine down first. Careful. We'll never replace that vacuum tube if you break it. Okay, okay, get your hands under the bottom there, you got it? One, two three –

Lewis couldn't stop grinning; he didn't need the old issue of *Alternating Current.* The only difficulty now – telling Matt just what this equipment was for.

Matt handled the old mic – brown, heavy, and looking like an upside-down set of electric clippers. Lewis blew dust off a radio tube and then picked up the cord. He grinned. Whoever had built the apparatus had presumed that household AC would be a sufficient power source. The thick cord, about twenty feet long and covered in a fine knit of dark brown and dark green, ended in a heavy two-prong plug. Lewis took inventory in his head of extension cords and left the attic without telling Matt why.

Matt felt very alone. The rain beat, the lamp flickered. He avoided the portrait.

Lewis returned with an extension cord. —I got us plugged in to the outlet by your bed.

—Why my bed?

—Because your room is closest to the attic.

—Oh.

Lewis glanced round the attic. —Did you read that article?

—What article?

—In the magazine.

—Lewis, what are you getting on with?

Lewis sighed and opened *Alternating Current* to page eighty-three, passing it to his brother. Lewis had once found the magazine left open to this page, next to an open and nearly empty bottle of Newman's Port and their father's glass. Skipper's snores from the living room couch had surrounded Lewis as he sat in his father's chair and read "Reaching the Dead: Some Further Notes on Edison's Last Work." Long words, difficult typeface, seven-year-old boy. Particular frequencies, unseen waves, who was to say heaven did not lie flat and other-dimensional beneath the ionosphere? And most exciting, the article promised, the dead might transmit back.

Matt put the article down after two paragraphs. —This is madness.

—Hang on, now, I'll get the reel-to-reel.

—Lew-issss ...

But his brother had descended the stairs. Matt tried to read more of the article, to study the diagram of a Tesla coil. Then Lewis returned with their reel to reel, trailing yet more extension cord, sheepish. —Got this one plugged in to Skipper's room. Found that cufflink he lost, too.

Lewis tossed the silver cufflink in the air, caught it and tucked it in his pocket.

—Now then. Matt, you get the reel set up here, while I go at the uh –

—Ghostometer?

Lewis scowled. —Matt, do radio waves exist?

—Yeah.

—Can you see them?

Surrendering – no talking to Lewis once he got worked up – Matt set up the reel-to-reel and checked the connection of the highly sensitive mic Mr. McGrew had given them. Matt started the reel and took the mic.

—Test one, check, check, test one, two, three.

Loud playback, the mic having captured background hiss, every rag of Matt's breath, the rain on the windows, walls and roof, the soft rustle of Lewis's sleeves as he rolled them up.

—Good to go, Lew.

Lewis nodded. He inserted the apparatus plug into the extension cord's receptacle.

Hum and light; two readers glowed, something cracked, and the tiny Tesla coil stood ready.

Matt raised his eyebrows. —Jesus.

Biting his bottom lip, Lewis adjusted knobs. The hum of the apparatus grew louder. —Matt, go stand on that crate over there, and I'll get this wire antenna up to you. We got to get it as high as it can go. Wish we had a kite.

—Might as well wish to send it up with Apollo 11. To the moon, Lewis, to the moon!

Matt grinned, but the joke was lost on his brother. As usual.

He hopped up on a box containing, unknown to the boys, ledger books from the Wrights' store in Port au Mal and a manuscript from the mid-1700s written by a shipwrecked Englishman. —Up here good enough?

Lewis glanced at Matt stroking the rafters. —Have to be. Here.

Matt accepted the wire antenna. —How am I supposed to keep it up here?

A foil wrapper glinted; Lewis chewed the gum quickly, cracking it to leach out the sugar. He gave the wet little wad to Matt. —Doublemint. Here. Put that about an inch from the end of the wire. Now blow on it, dry it out a bit. Good.

Matt got down. —Enough's enough. What is this, really?

—I don't know what they called it. But they tried to communicate.

—You can't talk to dead people.

Lewis studied the VU monitor. —Just an experiment. Do you believe in $e = mc^2$?

—E what?

—Theory of relativity.

—I s'pose.

—And you believe in the DNA helix?

—So? DNA's a fact.

—All that information whirling in on itself, four elements in variation. Like radio waves?

—Lewis, what are you –

Lewis glanced at Matt over his shoulder. —Then what's your problem with distance broadcasting?

The apparatus hummed.

Lewis picked up the mic. —Check, test one, two –

The needles went into the red.

Lewis grinned. —We are on the air.

—To whom?

—Whomever – whoever can receive. CQ, CQ, calling all stations, CQ, this is Lewis Wright. CQ, CQ, calling all stations, CQ, this is Lewis Wright. Please acknowledge, over.

They listened, heard nothing.

—Lewis, do you really think –

—Start the reel recording there, now.

Matt did.

Lewis tried again, his voice a little deeper, a little more sure. —CQ, CQ, calling all stations, CQ, this is Lewis Wright. Please acknowledge. Over.

The apparatus hummed. The reel hissed.

—CQ, CQ, calling all stations, CQ, this is Lewis Wright, please acknowledge. Over.

The rain fell.

—CQ, CQ, calling all stations, CQ, this is Lewis Wright, please acknowledge, over.

They'd filled maybe a third of the six-hour reel when Matt turned it off. Lewis's call had become a chant, and it would echo in Matt's head all night.

—CQ, CQ, calling – hey.

—It's not going to work.

—Turn that back on.

—It's nearly suppertime. Come on, there's cold roast beef down there. I'll make you a sandwich.

—Turn it back on!

Irritated now, Matt did so.

—CQ, CQ, calling all – is that smoke?

The original cord, now hot to the touch, gave off smoke and a scent like scorching rubber. The apparatus hummed more loudly, struggling to draw power, and then with a *bzht*, the electricity died.

Lewis's rammed his fists against the floor. —Damn, damn, damn!

Matt had made for the attic door and now glanced down the stairs.

—No lights at all, b'y. I think we blew a fuse.

Relieved the darkness hid his tears, Lewis considered pragmatics.

—Come on, we should get this back in the crate before Skipper gets home. He'll have a canary if he sees all this. Just lay the crate back together, stick this against the wall. I want to try this again next week.

—Then you'll be on your own.

They got the apparatus tucked away, the portrait of their grandfather on top of it – wrapped in an old dress this time, to protect it – and Lewis took the reel and hid it under his shirt. Their father came home not long after, surprised and amused to find his sons camping out in the back yard, then irritated to find not a single light worked. Thomas Wright called McGrew once he saw the melted fuse box, and McGrew called the electric company. And the fire department – wouldn't hurt to let them have a look at this.

The following Saturday, in Mr. McGrew's workshop, Lewis ignored the Tesla coil and instead placed the reel on a player. For two hours of playback he heard nothing but his own drone, Matt's sighs and last Saturday's rain. Lewis then put on the engineer's best headphones, the ones with the leather ear cushions, and plugged them in to the reel player. He re-wound with the capstan depressed, hearing his own voice made high-speed Mickey Mouse chatter, then a different tone, much quieter, probably Matt complaining. Lewis stopped the tape and listened.

CQ, CQ, calling all stations, CQ, this is Lewis Wright, please acknowledge.

There, there: *Signal rec* ... the voice faded, returned. *Signal received.*

A pleased voice, a proud one: male, higher than Lewis's, trained against the standards of the BBC, but decidedly Newfoundland. *Glasses fell. CQ, CQ, calling all stations.*

Then Lewis spoke over it, loud and clear: *CQ, CQ, calling all stations, CQ, this is Lewis Wright, please acknowledge.*

The faint voice again, in and out like shortwave: *Acknowledged ... hear me? Glasses fell ... hear me?*

Mr. McGrew's hand on his shoulder frightened Lewis so much he shouted and then wept. Tearing the headset from his ears, Lewis bolted from Mr McGrew's workshop and banged his knee on the workbench where his Tesla coil waited. Mr. McGrew shook his head; Lewis Wright so intelligent, yet so highly strung. What on earth would they do with the boy? Curious, he held the right headphone to his ear and listened; Lewis Wright playing radio operator, cute. CQ, just as Mr. McGrew had taught him. Dan McGrew put down the headset and re-wound the reel, then brought it out to Lewis, who sat on knoll behind the station, knees to his chest, staring at the window of an empty corner office.

When Lewis told him how and why the tape had been made, Mr. McGrew said nothing. He'd examined the apparatus for Mr. Wright before and pronounced it broken when he'd known it could operate, though he hadn't dared speculate on whether it would, well, truly work. Sensible engineers named for Robert Service poems do not ask such questions. He set Lewis to mowing the lawn, a chore the boy hated but at that moment needed, then listened to the tape himself. Lewis had picked up someone else's ham broadcast, their transmitter likely much more powerful; the Wright apparatus might have reached a mile. Now, local AM or shortwave? Dan McGrew found himself uttering aloud what he had taught the Wright boys so often. *AM is steady, and when you dip in a valley or rise on a hill, it might fade or strengthen, but it will be there. FM is like a sniper's bullet; it's shot one way, damn the consequences. Buildings stop it. Frequency modulation, really. But amplitude modulation, well now, boys, that's a way to deliver a signal.*

Beneath the noise of the tape: *Signal received. Glasses fell.*

Grim, McGrew took the reel and slid it many times over the bulk eraser. No point in having audio like that lying around.

A few weeks later, on a Saturday night, Lewis found himself alone. Matt had sneaked out on a date with the unsuitably Catholic Barbara Taylor. Mr. Wright, characteristically, had stayed at VOIC most of the day, working on plans for increasing the wattage at the station on the Burin Peninsula. The housekeeper had long gone home. Lewis called for Hera – she used to watch the boys when they played in water, barking if she thought they'd gone out too far – but of course Hera now lay underground, buried near the tree in the back yard, roots entangling her bones. So Lewis spent a good half-hour in an agony of decision, knowing what he wanted to do, knowing what he must do, knowing what he had no choice but to do. Washing his hands several times, biting at loose cuticles, sucking his own blood and washing the skin again, then counting his steps from kitchen door to pantry until he'd perfected his approach, he sought an apple from the pantry. Cursing at the pollution of his hands – he hadn't washed the pantry door before touching it – Lewis forced himself to ignore the scream of dirt and chose an apple. A small Mac, nearly perfect, mostly red with one green patch, the leaf still on the stem, brown, dry and brittle but so clearly a proper leaf, like the illustration for *A* in his favourite book, A is for apple, B is for bear, C is for cat, D is for dog. Simplicity, proper places, expectation: A is for apple, B is for bear. The apple so small in his hands, against his long fingers and crawling with germs: round, long, squiggly, many legs, no legs, splitting, multiplying, colonizing the surface. Dirt.

Eating an apple, Lewis decided, was an act of faith. He bit through the thick peel, into the mushy flesh, gagged a little, then unplugged every single appliance and ascended to the attic.

The power surge had damaged the apparatus, but it still hummed to life, one reader registering, the other dead. The Tesla coil did its impressive work, and Lewis's apple, one perfect bite gone, one perfect leaf left, remained perched before the portrait of his grandfather. The apple's flesh had gone quite brown, the peel withered and sunk at the bite, when Lewis gave up. No voice on the reel to reel. There could never have been a voice. CQ? Jesus. Robert Wright's thick glasses in the portrait, his death in a crumpled Tiger Moth, but not one word this time, not a whisper, and Lewis felt shoved aside. Packing away the apparatus with great care, then nailing the crate shut once, he concluded the only possible conclusion: the message had been meant for Matt. His brother had been the conductor. Even the dead preferred Matt. Perfection in the decay of the apple: Lewis tiptoed round the apple and its entropy. Then he tucked the portrait under his arm and hid it at the back of his bedroom closet.

He'd plugged back in nearly all the appliances when his father got home. Matt was still out – it was past midnight – and Lewis feigned sleep on his bed as father ascended the stairs. Lewis held a book in his right hand, and he seemed to have fallen asleep reading it: *My First Alphabet.* He breathed evenly, feeling the gaze of his father, dreading the angry voice.

Instead, Thomas Wright spoke quietly, sadly.

—Fey Lewis.

Then Thomas tugged the wool Newfoundland tartan blanket up over his son and turned off the light as he left the room.

Lewis dreamt of flight.

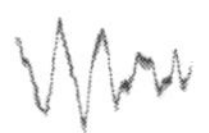

64. "ON DECK AND BELOW" 1 – RANT AND ROAR
in which Lewis Wright remembers his name.

May 1975

The funniest part of the accident: the Americans' disbelief in the brothers' last name. They'd telephoned Matt, once they'd deciphered

Lewis's scrawl in the 'Next of Kin' box. So Matt received surprising news: *Your nephew, Stephen Daedalus – am I pronouncing that right – has been injured at the Gander Flight School, crashed his Cessna 150E onto that little island in Gander Lake*. When both brothers, one through shock, distance and morphine, the other over the phone, convinced the flight trainers that yes, Stephen Daedalus was a false name, and yes, they really were the Wright brothers, Matthew March Jackman Wright and Lewis March Jackman Wright, sons of Thomas Jackman Wright, the Americans got angry. *Boys, we don't like to be fooled with. Comes a time for joshing, and comes a time for serious words. Now who are you, really?* Matt had no choice then but to tell Skipper, but Lewis understood. He'd been conscious at the crash site, an explosion of blood from forehead and nose darkening the windows, enchanting him as patterns of frost might. Both long legs broken – the right in four places – left hand sprained, lips split along several vertical lines, ribs broken on both sides, right shoulder dislocated. The pain propelled him far beyond land, and the dire swiftness of trees blurred beneath his feet. The shock of waking up in bed, the corset of pain, the burning itch of sutures –

In, out ...

in, out

Taking you down again, chest X-rays, skull X-rays, neurologist, surgeon, pins in your legs, and his father ... sometimes on the telephone, sometimes making notes, small transistor tuned to 610 VOIG Gander, the station IDs, music and news formats familiar but off, the comfort of the 1 O'Clock News, when all stations linked up to 570 VOIC in St. John's. Yes, in those moments he'd come home, and after dark once, eyeing the blurry intravenous line, studying the tubing path away from him, this tendril, this growth, winding his sight up the line to the bag, he remembered his name, only then realizing at that moment that, somewhere, he'd forgotten it. He tried to tell his father, but the strange old man with tears on his face frightened him.

65. OHM 2
in which Richard Fahey invites Thomas Wright to listen to a lonely signal.

October 4, 1957

—Thomas, I know we've had our differences, but I thought – there's not many around who'll understand what – the beauty of it – I don't know. My engineer picked this up in his ham shack and recorded it.

Thomas gazed out Richard Fahey's back window. He'd sat here before, in Richard Fahey's front room, but never without Robert. —You and Father would spend hours listening in the dark. Clear nights were best, you'd always say. If we could see Orion, we'd be able to hear from all over, just never in daylight.

—That's why he named the dog Orion. You still get letters at VOIC from people in Wales?

—England, too. Norway, once.

Richard pressed *play*. Static, hiss, and a feeble *beep-beep-beep*.

—Thomas, I don't care that it's Russian. I don't care about the Bomb. *Sputnik* up there's beyond language. Listen to it. Not earthbound and reflected back. It's tearing through the atmosphere to reach us. A satellite, a bloody orbiting satellite, our human reach mechanized, flung at the sky like a prayer at the end of an arrow.

Thomas said nothing.

Beep-beep-beep ...

—Dog up in that, too. Named Laika.

Thomas thought Laika a pretty name but said nothing.

Richard clicked his tongue. —Trapped, though. Probably dead already. *Sputnik*'s going to crack up before it falls. Caught in orbit, gravity, the very thing that's going to degrade it and haul it home, all on fire.

Beep-beep-beep ...

Richard clicked off the reel-to-reel. —Recording goes on for another seven minutes. Trajectory took her out of range then, but she's still up there. You know what that sound is, Thomas? History. Get you a drink?

—I'd best be getting home.

Unable to get warm that night, Thomas slept poorly. He dreamt, as did Richard, of dead Laika and dying *Sputnik*. Seven minutes of static and *beep-beep-beep*, silly and fragile and undeniable; why in the name of God had Fahey wanted to share it with him? Dozing again, hearing *Sputnik*'s signal, Thomas dreamt that each beep birthed a star, that each piece of the satellite could be glimpsed as it fell through the beam of a lighthouse.

66. AN APPOINTMENT in which Robert Wright visits his doctor.

June 25, 1954

Patient's name: Robert Wright, male, aged 53. 5′6″, 142 lb. Reason for visit: chest pain.

—How long has this been happening?

—The pain? Off and on. I hardly noticed it before. More like a squeeze than pain. My pulse will race then.

Dr. George Cart scowled at his notes, then at his patient. Barely thirty, Cart had travelled from North Shields in England, answering Newfoundland's international call for doctors, teachers and architects. He'd settled tidily in St. John's and become the doctor of choice for merchants, businessmen, professors and other doctors, all of whom fancied Dr. Cart's discretion part of a service he rendered them alone. Cart, for his part, found the men in and around St. John's dangerously pigheaded – just like home.

—'Off and on,' you say. When, precisely?

Robert shifted on his chair, doing his best not to squirm. —Whenever I walk quickly. Or run up the stairs. Sometimes when I'm just working at my desk. I know it is happening because my left arm goes numb. The pain's only begun recently. The bad pain, I mean.

—When did you first feel the squeezing and the racing?

—In my thirties.

Dr. Cart glanced up again from his notes. —You've had chest symptoms for almost twenty years, and you're only seeking help now?

—I was afraid it might be TB. But I never coughed.

Cart rolled his eyes and slapped the notes down on his desk. —Even better. Wright, I thought you wanted to go down in history as a great communicator, not Typhoid Mary. Shirt, tie and waistcoat off. Now.

Robert stood, feeling a bit lightheaded, and unfastened his cufflinks.

—Do you always speak to your patients this way?

—Only the stupid ones. Here, is it happening now?

Robert swayed. Anxiety flitted cross his face. A brief punch of nausea, a brief sweat; he remained on his feet. —It hurts a bit.

If a chainsaw could be dubious, it would make the noise Cart did.

—You've gone the colour of your shirt. And unless your wife's been washing you in Javelle water, I'd say you're distinctly unwell.

The cold stethoscope warmed nicely.

—Detecting a noisy murmur, Wright. Could indicate mitral valve prolapse, or may indicate nothing more than its own existence. For all I know, you were born with a heart murmur. But I don't like it. Are you still flying that plane of yours?

—Haven't had her up for a while.

—Keep her down. A man with your eyesight shouldn't be flying anyway. Plain foolishness, licensing a pilot who's myopic and colour-blind.

Robert smiled. His license had been a formality, granted only when William, briefly Assistant Deputy Minister of Transportation, discovered that neither the Commission nor Responsible Government had ever caught Robert flying without one.

—I need to perform more tests on you. In the meantime, you're not to fly and not to drive.

—Unacceptable, Dr. Cart. I must drive.

—You are not to fly, and you are not to drive. I cannot make it any clearer than that.

Fuck the Commission of Government. —I drove here today. May I drive home?

—This once. But no more driving once you are at home. I'm putting you on honour watch, Wright. Do not force me to revoke your licenses. Avoid all exertion. No marital relations. And no climbing those radio towers of yours. I expect to see you the same time next week. I don't mean to pry, and I don't mean to frighten you, but have you got your affairs in order? Seen a lawyer, drawn up a will?

Robert cocked his chin. —Of course.

—Drive safely.

67. ADEPT
in which William Wright introduces Robert to a charitable society and its works.

July 12, 1953

The old squeeze took Robert's chest, as though some clawed hand clutched his heart and lungs. Sweat broke out. Ascending steep Cathedral Street meant fights with gravity in several directions.

Stomping besides him, William breathed and spoke easily. —I can't tell you how pleased I am.

Robert nodded, words impossible. Trying to smile, he turned right and mounted steps. Then he stopped, breathing ragged, eyes blurring on a cement sphere, then rolling upwards to the stained but still grand arch over the doorway. Further up, carved into stone and free of doubt, the sharp square and compasses.

William had not accompanied his brother to the Masonic Temple door. Instead, he stood back by the street, by a little footpath that led somewhere dim. —Robert. Willicott's Lane is down here.

—Not a Masonic meeting?

William rolled his eyes. —Weren't you listening? I said we were former Masons. We've borrowed some of the traditions, picked and chose the best, but the Society of Adepts is quite different altogether.

They walked through Willicott's Lane, Robert working hard to keep up. Then he saw the sign for Feaver's Lane, then – surely not – Willicott's again, then Gower Street.

—William, I need to sit down.

William knocked on a door. An older lady opened the door, old enough to be their mother. She had a strong jaw, blue eyes, copious freckles, calloused knuckles and short nails.

A charwoman? On a Sunday night?

She smiled. —You'll be wanting to go the study. This way.

William did not remove his hat until at the study door. Five other hats rested on pegs. Robert hung his hat, too, then sat down on the bench beneath the pegs. He dabbed his handkerchief over his forehead. He nodded to William when ready, stood up and preceded his brother into the study.

Darkness.

A man on either side took Robert's arms, and someone in front hauled a hood down over his head and knotted it gently under his Adam's apple. Robert gasped, despite the initiation's silliness.

Low lights – kerosene lamps to judge by the smell. Robert still couldn't see or move his arms, that second inconvenience proved to him with unnecessary roughness. His captors shoved forward and down, forcing him to kneel. Robert did so, clicking his tongue as the other two men knelt down with him and took his arms again. Sweat slicked the backs of his knees. No doubt he sweated right through his clothes; no doubt these fools thought they frightened him.

Somewhere in front of Robert, a man spoke, his high nasal lilting merrily despite murky words.

—Brother William, who is this unknown you would foist upon us?

William spoke from behind his kneeling brother. —Oh, Most Great and Excellent Master –

Robert guffawed beneath his hood.

William kicked him. —Oh, Most Great and Excellent Master, I bring with penitence and timid joy an initiate, pending the Society's approval.

—Does the initiate share your penitence?

Robert felt his glasses slide down his nose. Hot air under the hood ... that voice ...

—I said, does the initiate share your penitence?

The man on Robert's left shifted. —Sorry, Dad.

Left-side hauled Robert down further, arms still pinned at his sides, until his forehead nearly touched the floor – appalling strain on his back and thighs.

William spoke. —Yes, Most Great and Excellent Master. See how he demonstrates his penitence.

Then William gently pushed Robert's head down the final half-inch. Fibres from a wool rug penetrated the hood. Now Robert groaned. His thighs felt like they'd snap, and his chest got tight again.

Now the lilting voice chanted, ecclesiastically. —Penitence is truth, and truth is penitence.

William let go Robert's head, and Robert made to get up off his knees, but his guards held him down.

Now Most Great and Excellent walked around Robert in a tightening gyre.

—Penitence, men of goodness and knowledge, men who desire to become adept. True penitence and trembling prayer. Initiate, do you believe in a Supreme Being? Just nod your head. Excellent. Initiate, do you know the end of all things approaches?

Robert kept still for that one. Then he wasted precious air calling his brother's name.

—The initiate will be silent, unless he wishes to be forced into silence.

A desk drawer opened.

William spoke sharply. —There'll be no need of that. I'll not stand for it.

—And who is the Most Great and Excellent Master?

Robert smiled. *There. The short a. This man comes from Port au Mal.*

William acquiesced. —You are.

The desk drawer closed again. —The end of all things is coming, and all of us are damned and must await our call to judgement. Far be it from me to gag a man who wisely chooses silence as he waits.

Now Robert felt alarm. Dizzy with his own carbon dioxide, he dredged up his newsman's voice. Steady, reassuring, authoritative. —Let me up this instant.

His guards did. Robert managed to stand, then patted his throat for the hood's knot.

Most Great and Excellent squeaked. —You're ruining everything.

Robert got the hood off and pushed his glasses back up his nose.

—John Simms. I remember your uncle, George. A more despicable man I never knew.

John Simms stood shorter than Robert, white-haired, blue-eyed. His face looked very soft, as though he'd never shaved. —My Uncle George was a fine, strong man.

Now Robert glanced round the study. The expensive Persian rug, several leather armchairs, books on Rosicrucianism and God knew what else, and an engraving on the wall of a sphere. An eye rested in the sphere, and in the pupil of the eye lay another sphere, and within that sphere another eye ...

John Simms stamped his foot and then pointed to the study door as Uriel might point his sword of expulsion. —William, take your brother out of here, for he has sullied us.

Robert smiled with great courtesy. —I believe you have accomplished that all on your own.

—Never speak of this, Wright.

—I doubt that I could without laughing.

—The Society of Adepts is much larger than you think.

—How many of them do you like to gag?

John turned brick red, with embarrassment or an impending stroke. Robert didn't care. He spat at John's feet, did his best not to look his former guards, presumably John's sons, in the face. Then he glared venom at his brother.

—Charity. You said this was for charity. How much of a fool are you at all, William?

—My charity is for your soul. It's like Father said. We won't live to be his age. You've not attended evening service in years, so you don't know. We have so little time to prepare for judgement, perhaps only as much as a year. I've dreamt it. Over and over.

Robert walked out of the study, grabbed his hat and left the house. He walked slowly, breathing hard, towards his house on Forest Road. He promised himself never to speak to William again, to excise William from his life. But he'd broken that promise before.

68. CONTINUITY 6
memorandum

To: All Female Staff

Re: VOIC Decorum Policy

Date: July 12, 1974

Ladies, please be reminded that the VOIC Decorum Policy remains in effect and must be adhered to at all times.

All telephones will be answered by a pleasant female voice. If you must leave your desk for any reason, please ensure your telephone is forwarded to another girl so the calls may be answered and directed quickly and professionally. It is your responsibility to ensure your voice is pleasing, quiet and perky at all times.

No commercials shall be written to be voiced by a female. Women are spoken to, informed and advised by radio. No woman wants to hear another woman telling her what to buy.

Trousers, pants or slacks are not acceptable wardrobe choices. Skirts or dresses and close-toed shoes must be worn at all times. Bare legs are not permitted. Hemlines must cover the knees.

Short-sleeved blouses are permitted in hot weather. However, after Labour Day, long sleeves are expected.

Cosmetics are encouraged, provided you do not spend an inordinate amount of time re-applying them. Cosmetics are not to be applied anywhere in the Broadcast Centre outside the Ladies' Restroom.

In the event one girl is sick, another girl may be expected to take up her duties in addition to her own at any time. This is to ensure the smooth running of VOIC, particularly the Sales Department.

Conduct outside the Broadcast Centre is expected to mirror conduct within the Broadcast Centre. Remember, at all times you are representing VOIC. You are one of the few, and the proud: you are a VOIC Girl.

Remember that there are three ways of completing a task: the right way, the wrong way, and the VOIC Way. Our continued success depends on you and the VOIC Way.

VOIC DECORUM POLICY IS TO BE FOLLOWED AT ALL TIMES.
NO EXCEPTIONS.

69. GEOGRAPHICAL CURE 2
in which Nichole Wright defies her past.

May 20, 2008

The January morning in 2005, when drifted snow blocked all the windows at VOIC Radio and Maxine Batten warmed up her bagel on the photocopier, I seriously questioned my decision to return to Newfoundland. Not so much a cul-de-sac as another country, cartographically and mentally. Where men were men, women were kept in their place, and fish were forbidden. In one course or another at Carleton University, I'd read that when the colonized sees himself as the colonizer sees him – that is, as inferior, misguided and in dire need of the colonizer's gracious leadership – then that is the moment that colonization is complete. And likely irrevocable. Of course, it's never that simple. Or so I chanted in April 2005, through gritted teeth on the psych remand ward, where I'd slid down the wall to sit on the floor and hug my knees to my chest, baby done got me them Thorazine blues, hurry up, Lithium Lover, do me fine, sanity's cover, set me free from them mind-in-amber, cruel-to-be-kind elixir, IV drippin' Thorazine blues.

I tried explaining it to my shrink, nice guy named Dwayne Miller.

—See, this is the time. Either my belief will shatter for the Ibsen life-lie it is, or it'll be the rope I haul myself out on.

—What belief is that, Nichole?

—I am not my grandfather's personal little colony. I am the woman I choose to be. Despite my history. Because of my history. At the same time. Am I getting through to you?

But I hadn't reached that particular communication whirlpool yet in January 2005. That morning I was still recovering from 2004's fourth quarter and a manic little sojourn back to Ottawa. Fourth quarter 2004 had happened something like this.

CLIENT:	ZAP ELECTRONICS
FEATURE:	Sponsorship: Clocks of Christmas, 570 VOIC St. John's
START:	Nov. 15, 2004 (contract start date: Nov. 12, 2004)
END:	Dec. 24, 2004
LENGTH:	15-ish seconds
SALESMAN:	R. ABBOTT
WRITER:	N. WRIGHT
ANNR:	Whoever's available, for God's sake, just get this on the air. Ralph is billing this from last Friday.

SFX: Westminster chimes and "Jingle Bells" from Banjo and Harpsichord Christmas, side 2 cut 2.

ANNR: The VOIC Clocks of Christmas toll for you, reminding you that there are just six weeks left to shop. That's right, just six weeks left to shop! This timely reminder from Zap Electronics, Topsail Road, now financing plasma TVs! Next Clocks of Christmas tolling update in fifteen minutes, right here on VOIC.

Not so bad, really, until the client wanted to rotate specials. That means recording as many different versions of that countdown spot as it took to get all the specials mentioned. For every single day of the countdown. Yeah, Production could record the body just once and then get the announcer to record the date-drops – just four weeks, just twenty-one days until the end of time – but someone still had to cut and paste all the text and audio together. Still the only copywriter after Claire resigned and Barry Kendall transferred to Production, writing regular and Christmas copy, plus the *Books of Christmas*, for five stations, I felt just a teensy bit overworked. Luckily Claire and I had, without permission, refreshed most of the text in the *Books* last year, so there'd be some variety. When I first heard the term *Books of Christmas*, I thought we might be broadcasting a reading of Dickens, or even Andersen – yes, the Little Matchbox Girl would go down quite well of a Christmas Eve. Books – ha. Ratty binders, some of the sheets captured within old yellow VOIC commercial script forms, thin paper weighted now with years of correction fluids and re-writes for changing sponsor names. Books of scripts: thirty-minute blocks of music to air Christmas Eve and Christmas Day, each half hour brought to you with warm and heartfelt wishes for the season, as you bask in the gentle warmth of the fire, sipping a cup of Nan's best tea and trying not to eviscerate cousin Carl with the wishbone, by Insert Client Here.

So I offered to call the owner of Zap Electronics and tell him just what, where and how often to rotate.

Ralph Abbot, the salesman, smiled. And grew. He managed to get taller somehow, and his voice deeper, whenever he talked down.

—Nichole, I have every confidence in you as both a fine copywriter, and as a Wright. You'll get it done. Oh, forgot to give this to you yesterday afternoon. The client's new sell line. Has to go at the end of each spot.

I read it. —Ralph, you can't be serious.

SFX: Westminster chimes and "Jingle Bells" from <u>Banjo and Harpsichord Christmas</u>, side 2 cut 2.

ANNR: The VOIC Clocks of the Christmas toll for you, reminding you there are just four weeks left to shop. That's right, just four weeks left to shop. How will you do it all? With Zap Electronics, your one-stop shop for all your electronics needs. If it's in stock, they've got it! Next Clock of Christmas tolling update in fifteen minutes, right here on VOIC.

November rotted out with clacking keys, ringing phones, howling fax, too much coffee, doughnuts and pizza; the memory of it tastes like powdered sugar and melted cheese. Memory again, insistent but polite like

Jehovah's Witnesses at the door, recoiling at a magazine cover showing several antique cameras, matte black, silver and bare-bulbed. Old dread – him dead eleven years, dead, buried and a playground for worms – no good could come of this.

December.

ANNR: The VOIC Clocks of Christmas toll for you, reminding you there are just 21 days left …

—You want *what*?

—I *want* you to do as I ask, Nichole. As the client asks. A different special each time the feature airs. Don't forget, my work pays your salary.

Ralph always took offense when a woman questioned him. Claire had mastered the trick of sounding confused while gently guiding Ralph to a smarter decision and allowing him to believe he thought of it. Me, I just struggled not to smack Ralph upside the head. Barry Kendall, interrupted by Ralph's arrival, sat down to watch the show.

I balled up Ralph's copy request form, which he hadn't bothered to fill out correctly. Usually Ralph just cut a client's ad out of the yellow pages and taped it to the sheet. Many of his forms looked like ransom notes. This time, however, Ralph had gotten lost. Apparently Zap Electronics, their only location in west-end St. John's, now wanted to air their commercials on the Burin Peninsula. Then I chucked the form over my shoulder. Before Ralph could vent his outrage, the paper bounced off the window and landed back in my lap. Neither Ralph nor Barry could quite hide his smirk.

Then, God help me, I tried reason. —Ralph, *Clocks* airs four times an hour–

—Three, really, when you look at the top of the hour, though we charge for four. That kind of overlaps –

—And he wants a different special each time? There's no way to make this work.

Barry popped a chocolate-covered espresso bean into his mouth. He'd just been describing the potency of last night's hash and how he needed some edge back. —Just re-write your contract to daypart the buy so an even number of commercials play. Then from 6a to 9a log one special, from 9a to noon another–

Ralph shook his head like a dog that's just tasted something bitter.

—No no no. I can't follow the logging rules. The client wants a different special every fifteen minutes.

Barry leaned back in the chair, hands behind his head. His reddish moustache bristled out. —It'll upset the Conductor.

Ralph suddenly paid attention. After all, Barry had a dick and balls and therefore must know what he's talking about.

The mysterious Conductor Ozymandiaized Ralph almost every time, as he'd look upon its workings and despair. But then, for Ralph, the Conductor existed as pneumatic tubes in the aether. Ralph also feared the fax machine, which transmitted, he thought, on a time zone lag; many times he'd faxed a contract with errors in it and then asked Claire to *Go cancel that out.* Claire would press a few buttons, and Ralph would rest assured she'd aborted transmission. But fax anxiety withered next to the Conductor, for lo, without the Conductor, VOIC could not broadcast. I watched Ralph one day as he loitered in Master Control, every line on his face deep – Master Control, like the smaller booths, once lined with carts and 45s, then carts and LPs, then carts and CDs, now bathed in the dull glow of six different computer monitors. All music, stingers, IDs, commercials, weather drops and even most newscasts waited in digitized storage for not the click of a button but the tick of the internal clock, one no doubt on VOIC Atomic Time. If the commercial and music logs did match up on timing – we called it *filling the hours* – then commercials mightn't play. If commercials didn't play, then VOIC lost money. Strictly timed talk sets could cut an announcer off in mid-word or become dead air if the announcer didn't talk long enough. Dead air, besides making Ben Philpott drop whatever he had in hand and run for Master Control – from the men's room once, unzipped – triggered the Babysitter, an automated backup program that kicked in with a particular set of songs to alert VOIC staff of the problem. Manfred Mann to start, I think, and then "Hey, Jude" by the Beatles to buy some time, then "Sonny's Dream," by Ron Hynes. After Ron, the Babysitter's program would randomly pick songs from the music library until the Conductor signalled its return. Point of pride for Engineering: since they'd installed the Babysitter, Ron never got to finish. Conducted VOIC would be back on the air by the time we found out Sonny's Daddy was a sailor in the first chorus, but everyone in the building would be singing or humming "Sonny's Dream" for the rest of the day. Broadcasting the Two Minutes of Silence on Remembrance Day with the Babysitter got tangly. We actually had to send out sound effects of crashing surf – just turned down the outgoing volume – so the Conductor would perceive intact signal. One year, someone forgot to send out the noise over the Silence, so the Babysitter kicked in, and "Doo Wah Diddy" ghosted over the Silence like the debris hurtling through space in the opening credits of *The Twilight Zone*, or like the signal of another station. Long live the new silence. Naturally, that happened the same year that Ralph Abbot, horrifying everyone, sold a sponsorship of the Two Minutes of Silence to Wince Blanford Chrysler. Thomas Wright had a few things to say about that, but money was money, and commission was commission. So remembrance of the war dead got teed up with the full-sing 30-second Wince Blanford jingle; after all, a product-sell commercial might be in poor taste. An announcer could interrupt the Conductor in extreme situations – to inform VOIC listeners of the fall of Sauron, the Rapture, or of a moose on Kenmount Road. If the network stations outside St. John's had slaved into 570 VOIC, as happened from about 9a-6a, local programming only permissible in the morning shows, then any crash of the Conductor in town could take the rest of the republic with it. Should Ralph overtax the delicacy of the Conductor, then the Conductor would, like Khrushchev, bury him. And his commission, too.

I'd explained all this in several meetings. So had Claire. But no mere unordained female might invoke the power of the Conductor.

Ralph licked his lips, simultaneously knowing and dreading the answer. —What happens when we upset the Conductor?

Barry smiled sweetly. —Bad things.

—Bad things?

This time, Barry whispered. —We go off the air.

Ralph sighed, weighing this life-death-commission conflict. —So there's no way to give the client what I sold him?

—Nope.

Ralph glared at me then, as though I'd just delivered this terrible news, and hauled out his heavy guns. —I'm going to see Ben Philpott. I'll bet he can make it work.

Once the door closed, I took one of Barry's espresso beans. Long night ahead.

—Can it work?

—Yeah. It's just a fuckload of unnecessary farting around. If Ralph filled out his sales contract right, which I doubt, then the Traffic Department could log it, but then we'd have to assign a whole whack of different cart numbers, one for each version of the commercial –

—Still making extra work for Copy and Production.

—And you can guarantee someone up in Traffic won't catch all the different numbers, and the wrong one will play a thousand times –

The phone rang. The ID screen gave one of Ben Philpott's extensions. Ben had two phone lines, 117 and 159. If you got paged to or called from 159, Ben just wanted an update on a project or someone to come join him in a meeting with an irate client to look pretty and take earnest notes. If he used 117, he was seriously pissed off. Ben did not need to use the intercom if he wished to make himself heard, but he did, and the lower tones in his amplified-in-stereo baritone made windows hum. The last time I'd heard *Nichole Wright, one-seventeen please, Nichole Wright, one-seventeen,* my conscience stormed – *Shit, did he find out I left fifteen minutes early last Friday?* – and I'd nearly dropped my cup of coffee.

Barry and I read the caller ID on the phone screen. B PHILPOTT 117.

Ralph would defend his commission to the death. Well, to the death of a copywriter.

I picked up the phone, tempted to answer *Hiya, Potts, how's it hanging*, but instead I rattled out the regulation internal greeting. —Better radio, VOIC, Copy Department, how can I help you?

—Ask not for whom the bell tolls, Nichole.

I laughed, even though Ben sounded far too tired for jokes. I laughed a lot that quarter. —Can I, with my crossbow, shoot the albatross first?

—Just get Ralph's countdown on the air.

The answer flew out my mouth without checking with my brain. A cheerful answer to that commanding male voice, the answer any well-brought-up good girl, especially a parfit gentle Wright, would give. One that ground me further into the dirt. —No problem.

Barry's eyes bulged as he mouthed *No problem?*

Ben cleared his throat. —You're a better man than I am, Gunga Din.

Barry laced into me before I'd even put the receiver down. —No problem? You know that's overtime for both of us!

—We always work overtime in fourth quarter.

—Because a salesman is too lazy to get his own bullshit straight?

—Look, I don't like it either, but the work is here, and we're here to do the work. This is the best job I've ever had, Barry. Best job I'm likely to ever get, too. At least I'm using my talents.

Barry sneered. —At least you know your place. Spineless bitch.

ANNR: The VOIC Clocks of Christmas toll for you, and you have just twenty days left to shop, just twenty days! This reminder from Zap Electronics, Topsail Road, now featuring twenty-four-inch plasma TVs. Zap Electronics. If it's in stock, they've got it!

Instructions: Repeat above, substituting each of the following for "twenty-four-inch plasma TVs." Do this for days nineteen to one.

* twenty-eight inch plasma TVs
* thirty-six inch plasma TVs
* forty-eight inch plasma TVs
* each of the specials in the attached two-page newspaper ad

Yes, the correct sell line is "If it's in stock, they've got it."

And NO, I'm not typing it all up for you. You'll recall I do this feature for seven stations and that no other copywriter's been hired. Hear that wind whistling? It's calling your name in the Copy Department. Your head would look lovely on a pike this time of year. Red and green.

Each of the seven VO-network stations tolled their own *Clocks of Christmas* with their own local sponsors. The AMs each ran their own twice-daily Turkey Draw, too, complete with sponsor sell lines and, for added value within the station, cheating phone calls from listeners.

—Connect to the whole world with VOIC, better radio, Copy Department, how can I help you?

—I needs the list of sponsors for the *Turkey Draw*.

—You do you realize, caller, that the rules of the game state you're supposed to listen for the sponsor names and then call in?

—Can't be bothered with that. Rhyme off that list before I calls in to Mr. Wright's office to complain. I knows him, I do.

Most days I recited the real list, but some days, for some special callers, I made sponsors up. Occasionally I slept well the night after hearing a listener on the air attempt to claim a free turkey by spitting out Quart of Gall on Water Street, or Ballcocks Knockery on Blackmarsh Road, for all your knocking needs, since '69.

I love live radio.

The FM stations, thank God, were far too hip for turkeys. They just ran the *Clocks*, the *Books*, and that stalwart clue-based guessing game, *Feel Up the Vibrating Stocking,* sponsored by Golden Pheasant Tea.

I'd get so much more work done at night. Republic Beverages had just released a line of hyper-caffeinated energy drinks, Cabot's Brew and Sugar-Free Cabot's Brew. This poison looked like fizzing sweet crude. To inspire the best possible commercials, sell lines, drops and jock-talk mentions – these last allegedly ad-libbed – Republic Beverages sent up five cases of

Cabot's Brew to VOIC. I quickly claimed the two cases of sugar-free and then accepted a case of regular as a joke gift from Kevin White, the Ops Manager. Kev enjoyed hiding other peoples' possessions – laptops, business card files, coffee cups, even high-heeled shoes. He really liked stringing out packed lunches. Fresh fruit might be impaled upon a pencil, or tucked in a desk drawer, one bite taken. Sandwiches might be displayed in the Test Centre, red light shining on the plastic wrap. Cigarettes disappeared from packs, little changeling golf pencils left in their place. Once Kev gave me a pair of dangly fishing lures and suggested I might wear them as earrings. The case of energy drinks arrived as a cloaked dare.

—Nichole, you can't drink four of these at once, can ya?

I drank them. Got palpitations and the sweats, but I did gain firsthand experience of this exciting new product, allowing me to write truly edgy-yet-conversational, not-*too*-out-there commercial copy, just like the client wanted. Didn't sleep for three days – added value.

I wrote a series of two-voice commercials, one set on an oil platform, one on a deep-sea trawler, one at a winter boil-up with snowmobiles revving in the background. I only missed some background lass piping *Manly, yes*. Republic Beverages loved the commercials. Orders for Cabot's Brew soon outstripped supply, and choosing it over imported energy drinks became a political no-brainer. Clients started asking for me by name to write their commercials – which, being the only writer in the department, I'd be doing anyway. Still, salespeople charged a premium for the promise of my skills. Not sure where the premium went. Or the other days of December, though I do remember Ben Philpott taking me aside at the staff Christmas party.

—Nichole, are you getting enough sleep?

Laughed again, saluted Potts with my glass of Cabot's Brew. —Sleep? Do I look like I need sleep?

Right there, between the bacon wrapped scallops and the cheesecake, something frayed. Then snapped. Spark-gap flywheel unharnessed; words words words, dervishing round my head and laptop, Christmas dinner with my parents and grandmother Wright, all the old quarrels, raised voices and hidden meanings, Christmas night with Claire and her mother, all so much more sensible, and finally Boxing Day, my day to get the hell off this island, show the passport, fly to Canada – back to Ottawa, where it began, really, this feeling, this delicious polar opposite to sadness. Where the sadness rooted. Scholarship to a Canadian university in 1989, study journalism at Carleton and do something useful, maybe come back to VOIC a fully accredited journalist, though I'd still have to work five times as hard as anyone else, prove myself something more than a poor cousin to Thomas Wright. All planned out. Except I changed my major to English in 1990. Parents none too thrilled, *Not very practical, Nichole,* but they lived so very far away now, and suddenly, in a different country, I felt like I could breathe. No one in Ottawa gave a sweet fuck that my last name was Wright; no one threw expectations at me like a net. After arguing with Mom on the phone about my major, I crossed University Avenue by Dunton Tower to go stare into the Rideau Canal, dead grass and fallen leaves in various states of sinking, and I agreed: hell yes, not practical. *Choose your battles, Nicks*, Claire always said. Second year, third year: choose my theory and pillage my own intellect, be Odysseus and Polyphemos at once, flaming log and eye: semiotics, hermeneutics, deconstruction, feminism, Marxism, new historicism – digging my nails into Shakespeare's shoulders, glancing shyly at Kafka, sucking Marlowe's cock for all the imagery he could squirt, the verse mere jism … bottles. Smirnoff too clear. Sleeman's too noisy. Glenfiddich, oh yes, I had class, right discerning: single malt, drunk and broke. Yet how to fight off the sleep? How to stay drunk and wide awake, taking it all in, splayed out for every rot-toothed edge of beauty in this life while not going mad for the pain of it? Malt to take the edge off, coke to put it back – white lines between the blue lines on looseleaf, thought I was clever – bank card refused, March 1993. Problem. Like the positive pregnancy test. And the abortion. I still dream that I'm begging, over and over, *Get it out, get it out,* then hearing a baby cry in my apartment, trapped in a shoebox somewhere, and if I find the shoebox – sometimes I don't – wasps fly in my face. Taking the Route 7 down Bank Street, browsing first in Prospero's Books, then barging past one lone protestor, a man in his seventies bearing his hand-lettered sign, red paint of course, *Abortion is Murder*, and I nearly screamed at him the way I screamed at God in my worst dreams, until I saw him wipe his running nose, then try to wipe the rain from his thick glasses. Knees hit the floor inside, women on either side of me, all three of us crying – still, no worse than cameras and fingers, *Get it out.* Hard. Walk away, put it behind, find work.

Standing in the nearly empty Rideau Centre, late December, 2004, recalling this, I caught the smell: the café at the bottom of the escalator had burnt the eggs.

There. In the burnt eggs: sadness.

I bustled down the escalator, looking like an inept thief but not caring. Onto Rideau and Sussex by the Elephant and Castle – where the hell had the Terry Fox statue gone? – and up to Sparks Street, stores there as tawdry and tired as those in the mall. The bronze statues, the bear on its hind legs with a salmon, the long-legged dancing figures of *Joy*, and then *Sea Angel*, Gabriel Furey's work, an old woman with shrivelled breasts breaching the water, pre-pubescent face set towards the sky. It looked like Claire when she was eight, nine, grade two, grade three. Not that Claire had ever seen it, and not that I had truly seen it the ten years I'd lived in Ottawa – Christ, what was wrong with me? But that face, the slope of the nose and the fat cheeks: Claire. A homeless man with snot frozen in his greying beard, big brown eyes and brown teeth, also studied *Sea Angel.* Then the man abruptly turned away and asked a passerby for change.

I returned home in early January 2005, flight delayed several times for storms, sitting next to a talkative New Englander most of the way – Van Dyked, annoying as hell, and, it came out after his hands jerked and he spilled Coke all over my legs, afraid of flying. So I listened to him. Told me all about growing up in and around Salem and Boston, and I assured him that St. John's might seem familiar, shame he couldn't have come in the summer. He also had the lightest brown eyes I've ever seen, more of a golden tan. I finally ditched him at the airport, once I saw him get into a cab, got home myself and collapsed into sleep on the couch.

Back to work the next day. Snowdrifts blocked the windows. Yet here I stood, just in time for the new corporate training session. *Training*, God, as though we were all seals who should be grateful to be slapped with fish when we balanced balls our noses. Beat the hakapik of unemployment, I suppose. Maybe.

I had driven to VOIC on my own that morning, negotiating un-ploughed Kenmount Road in my 5-speed Sentra. Second gear, the entire trip. I nearly rear-ended a sand truck. Truth told, I'd have slid right under it, me and my Sentra decapitated, an image which later in the day carried some appeal. I got to the Ladies Room, its door decorated with a luminous VOIC logo sticker, tried to tidy my hair, aimed a sneeze at the VOIC Decorum Policy, then tromped off bootless to a coat rack, forgetting the bootless part and stepping in two different puddles of slush. The wind shoved at the windows and whistled round the glass.

A dim light shone in swipes. Silhouetted against the copier, intent on the truth beneath the lid, Maxine Batten sang a hymn, possibly "Amazing Grace." She warbled something about the earth dissolving like snow.

Maxine had started at VOIC in the early 1960s. Front Desk, Logging, Sales Secretary, Accounting, even filling in as Mr. Wright's private secretary – yes, she'd done it all, at least, as much as a woman could. The first woman copywriter, considered an exciting and risky departure, got hired in 1986; by then, Maxine had already been injured. No doctor could prove what many suspected, that Maxine suffered brain damage when the VOIC Big-I sign exploded. In 1982, VOIC held an art contest, inviting listeners to design a new logo. A grade ten student won, with her offering of what became nicknamed the Yellow Devil. The logo actually spelled the call letters backwards: C, I and O fell from above into the warm embrace of V. Two lightning bolts came out of the V. Initially red on black, the design drew complaints from a few churches, notably the Church of Prevenient Grace and the End of Things in Port au Mal. Satanic, they said, devilish, signs of evil. Thomas Wright, who, as I understood it, had no time for the Church of Prevenient Grace in particular, changed the red to canary yellow and the black to bright red. This Godlier logo became the neon topper for the Big-I, with the call letters changing upwards to pink, white and green all day, and all night. The Big-I itself, a brown and yellow art deco phallus, displayed temperature and time, supported a camera that allowed reports on automotive traffic, and, just in case anyone forgot, showed the call letters, in descending order this time. The Big-I and its topper, the letters on the building and then the four flower beds carved into the front lawn, V,O, I and C ablaze with orange mums each summer, left no doubt of where one stood. However, all good things … on a muggy July afternoon in 1984, the Big-I broke down. Maxine Batten, on the Front Desk that day, fielded the usual assortment of calls – after all, you could depend on VOIC to know everything: *When do the dole cheques get mailed out? Is City Hall open today? When do they pick up the garbage in Mount Pearl? How long is this good weather going to last? What time is it? Because I need to set my watch.* This last question tipped events. The digital clock in the Front Desk's miniature switchboard, connected via some cunning wiring by Dan McGrew on Mr. Wright's orders, had gone blank. Maxine glanced up to peek at the Big-I through the window. No display there, either. The topper still bubbled in pink, white and green, but time-and-temp had definitely gone. Golden Pheasant Tea sponsored weather drops, which included readings from the Big-I; Port of Call sponsored VOIC World Atomic Time-Checks. Big clients. Big money. And no data. Maxine put the caller on hold and darted outside, down over the first lawn, almost losing her high-heeled balance on the second lawn. She cringed, because God knew what might happen if she fell and damaged the VOIC flowerbeds. So Maxine put her hands to the Big-I, almost in supplication, and gazed up.

The lightning bolts shone green. Then lightning struck the Big-I.

Maxine flew backwards a foot or two, more concerned about the grass stains on her skirt and the ruination of her hair in the rain than about the strike. Smoke wisped out her ears, the story goes, and mascara ran down her face.

Ever after, Maxine seemed, well, scattered. Her time on the Front Desk ended after complaints she kept callers on the line too long, discussing cookie recipes and the state of the fishery with them. Accounting – a disaster. Sales Secretary – a longer stay, but in the end, Maxine feared technology even more than Ralph Abbott did, and the day a computer arrived for her, she cried. She continued to work at whatever odd jobs came up, until someone got the brainwave to put her on charity telemarketing. Here she blossomed, selling airtime to tiny businesses in rural Newfoundland and up in Labrador on a twofer plan: for each commercial billed to the client, another would air and be billed to the charity organization VOIC Gives. She kept these clients on the phone forever, talking about everything and occasionally dropping in mention of this fabulous woofer offer, or did she mean twofer? Cruddy jerks like me joked that clients bought just to get off the phone. Kinder souls assured us Maxine's good heart came through the phone. Whatever her secret, she hauled in the money, and could therefore do no wrong.

I hope all this explains why Maxine's photocopying that morning in January 2005 did not surprise me.

—Hoop-de-doo, Nichole. How are ya, my trout?

—Fine. You got in okay this morning?

Maxine turned to face me by way of answer. Burgundy velvet dress, black sheer stockings, black pumps, gold earrings, gold necklace, three gold rings, one diamond ring, one ruby ring, gold watch. —My man got me here. On his way to plough out the Prime Minister's house. He's doing some good with the snowclearing and landscaping business. Sure, I don't need to work. I just come in to get out of the house.

By now several more photocopies had emerged: dark grey, with some sort of black ring in the middle.

Maxine lifted the photocopier lid and patted the bagel beneath. —Not warmed up yet. You want something hot for breakfast on a morning like this, my trout. Can't use the toaster. Keeps catching fire.

—Fire?

—My bagels keep getting stuck, and of course I always forget what I'm up to, and next thing I know black smoke's pouring out the kitchen. Then Engineering gets all upset with me because I'm after tripping brokers.

Finally, an explanation of why the toaster had disappeared.

—You want some of this bagel, Nichole? I see you staring at it.

—Gotta go, Maxine. Commercials to write.

Reflected in the windows of the Copy Department, the glow of the Coke and Pepsi machines made me think of a new box of crayons. Red, blue.

A white binder poked out from beneath Maxine's pile of copy information forms. I brushed her thirty-odd forms aside – lipstick on some of them, Christ, did she kiss her copy info goodbye – and picked up the binder. The cover read, in black Arial font:

C-Thru Servitude.

Finally, the fruit of all those multiple choice quizzes we'd done online the previous October, under a strict time limit.

But *servitude*?

NICOLE WRIGHT

—Name misspelled. Off to a good start.

C-Thru Thinking. A Program to Implement a Common Corporate Language.

—Esperanto for radio?

C-Thru Thinking is divided into three modules for different levels of corporate existence. C-Thru Management. C-Thru Sales. C-Thru Servitude.

—Let me just guess which level I'm at.

C-Thru Servitude Evaluation. Personality Arc for Nihole Wright.

—How many different ways can you misspell my name?

Fault points: 11 of 14. Red zone employee.

The first graph looked like a sketch of flames. Watermarked behind the flames, a pink blob arced gently, presumably some sort of ideal.

Nichole Wright. Gender: Female. Position: General staff, data entry.

—Data entry? I'm a God damned writer!

Nicole Wright is an imaginative person who sees herself as a natural leader and deprived of certain privileges and tokens of respect to which she feels entitled. Nicole is in her heart a Yes Woman, waiting to be told what to do so she might make a show of reacting against it. Nicole avoids confrontation and lets her perceived problems simmer. Nicole shows little initiative, relying instead on guidance from those above. Test scores indicate an average intelligence at work. Nicole is ideally placed in a data entry position, preferably away from the general public. Her volatile personality is a liability. Nicole is compassionate. Nicole would be an inconsistent disciplinarian. Nicole likes to name-drop to advance herself socially. Her eye is on a position of power for its own sake. She is unlikely to handle responsibility well. Nicole is assertive to the point of being aggressive. Her erratic work ethic handicaps her chances of advancement. Nicole craves advancement and recognition. Nicole's work may be exemplary, but she is not inclined to get on well with others.

—I run with chainsaws, too, you fuckers.

My stomach growled. I hadn't eaten before leaving to drive through the storm.

I threw the binder across the room; it hit the door. Tall darkness interrupted the glow of the Pepsi machine – Ben Philpott approaching the Copy Department. Snowflakes melted in his eyebrows and his Russian-style fur hat, and he pronounced my name as though addressing an ingrown toenail.

—Nichole Wright. I just send Barry Kendall to pick you up in the VOIC Hummer. And you're supposed to be waiting for him in your front porch. Just like the storm plan said.

—What storm plan?

—Ralph Abbott gave you –

—Ben, I don't know anything about this storm plan. All I know is that Wolf Broadcasting flew in this presenter from the States for an 8:30 start.

—How did you get here?

—I drove. With my erratic work ethic.

—Your what?

I pointed to the binder splayed behind the door. —Says so right there.

—I will remind you, Nichole, that we are spending a lot of money on the C-Thru program so we can come online with the rest of Wolf Broadcasting. See that you behave accordingly.

—How much money, Potts?

He tromped to a coat rack, snow falling off him.

By nine, roughly half of the VOIC servitudinous workers had gathered in the boardroom for yet another corporate training session, courtesy of the takeover by Wolf Broadcasting. Draught crept in around the newly installed fire exit, and ice lumped the metal windowsills. The one baseboard heater had been cranked to blast, burning the ankles of anyone who tried to stand by that wall, crowding people even more. The rubbery beige walls, textured and ribbed and now brown in several spots from nearly forty years of passage and grime, seemed to be falling inwards but on a different timeline. Bootprints wrecked the vacuum tracks on the deep sapphire carpet. The long drapes, also dark blue with green spirals and orange cubes on them, had been pulled back, exposing the yellowed sheers. Both the drapes and sheers had been bought when the broadcast centre opened in 1967 and not replaced since. Today the once sacrosanct managers' boardroom smelled of damp wool, sweating feet and plastic three-ring binders. Outside, the worsening blizzard spewed hardbiting snow and freezing rain. The rattle and scratch against the windows added to everyone's irritation; most of us had been up way before dawn, shovelling and salting and waiting to hear if we'd be picked up in a station rig or be expected to hack our own way through the storm. This winter's Storm Plan had failed the way light does in a blackout.

Ben Philpott addressed us all. —I recognize that this has been a difficult morning, and that our communications were not clear. But I don't have to remind you that we're all here in radio because we love it. And being a broadcaster carries great responsibility. People out there depend on VOIC. In weather like today's, it's no exaggeration to say our listeners depend on us for their lives. Schools, businesses and even the university are closed, but we here at VOIC will struggle and prevail, ensuring that necessary information is broadcast, and that our listeners are informed of what will no doubt be rapidly changing weather conditions. Now, it is my distinct pleasure to introduce you all to our esteemed visitor …

Here Ben's gaze settled on me, some heavy warning in it.

—C-Thru Thinking representative and presenter Art Dimmsdale.

I choked on my coffee.

—Art comes to us all the way from Massachusetts. He had a difficult flight in last night, and he is here at great expense to the company, because we believe our employees deserve the best. Could you please join me in welcoming Art Dimmsdale of C-Thru Thinking.

A scattered few of us clapped. I slouched down in my seat. Just as well, because the Van Dyke with the fear of flight did not acknowledge me as he entered through the anteroom door. He grinned at us, or rather, he showed us his teeth, took a quick gulp of coffee, and then turned his back.

—So I write these letters on the chart, I C U. Can anyone tell me what that means?

Barry Kendall addressed the ceiling. —Intensive Care Unit.

Art squinted at Barry's name tag. —Good try, Mr. … Sparks?

—Doobie Sparks. It's my on-air name.

—Right. Good try, but that's not the correct answer.

Jim Reid laughed. —B'ys, I feel like I'm playing *Who Hid What Now in the Golden Pheasant Teapot.* Anyone else?

Everyone chuckled, except for Art. Recognizing immediately he'd been excluded from an in-joke, he dropped all pretence of a smile. Within an hour, Art had smoked any laughter to a butt and ground it under his heel. I wondered if re-education camps worked this way, with laughter feared and fatal.

The C-Thru training videos, filmed in the late 1980s, judging by the big hair, houndstooth blazers, padded shoulders and amber-and-black computer monitors, emphasized the sacred importance of servitude. A Screen Minion who looked like an extra from *Dallas* spoke to us with a toothy earnestness.

And we don't mean what you think by the word servitude. We mean something completely different. By see-through servitude, we mean everyone

seeing his or her place in a company's machinery. We mean seeing into another's communication style and adapting to it. We mean seeing past your own communication style as you attempt to understand the task you've been given. We mean ...

I studied Art Dimmsdale as the Screen Minion continued. Did this Arthur, who came from Massachusetts but never once commented on Hawthorne or his own name, ever stand behind a podium at night, alone in a strange hotel, mic turned off and notes before him and only pretend to explain C-Thru Servitude? Did the sky blaze a letter behind him? Two, perhaps? Or three entire words, say: *Fucking balls-up bullshit.*

I said those words out loud, just as everyone broke into pods for another Servitude Groupthink. Only Barry chose to hear me.

Red zone employee. Volatile personality.

I slumped down further. I didn't even doodle, just sat still, even through the bathroom breaks. Later, I hardly noticed how Barry and three other people stood up and laced into the presenter, demanding logic, demanding sense: *If most managers use an Assertive Communication Style and won't tolerate an Assertive Communication Style back from people they don't consider equals, how are we supposed to communicate? Why should we adapt to them, especially if it won't change anything?* Then Ben Philpott's voice o'god sounded like a murmur as he called everyone to order. I kept staring at the pink arc behind my graph, at the different misspellings of my name, and at the character sketch that had sucked out even the will to cry.

The weeks spun out.

Tableaux vivants. Cave paintings. Stereopticon. Bog bodies. Polite descent. Dark mouth behind me, *open wide*, jaw cracking, spit-warm emptiness falling over me, tiredness settling on me like dust, couch to shower to work, work to couch. Skip the shower, so much effort, and for what? Dirty dirty *dirty*. The trouble with memory is its muskeg, its seductive promise of truth, even on shards and fingers – get it out – worst of all I'd loved him. Like I was supposed to, good girl. To love him meant to allow him, to sit back or sit down or turn around or bend over and concentrate on something else and not ask why, at nineteen, fellating a man for the first time, I already knew how it would feel and taste, not ask why, at thirty-two, visiting a dentist, my jaw might be so tense, my molars so worn, not ask why in moments of random fear when I lacked skin and separation between myself and the air – when I'd been the air, and this family member I loved breathed me in, transformed me in his lungs, breathed me out – not ask why I spaced out sometimes and realized it only when my butt cheeks ached from being clenched so tight. Tight, precisely what he'd liked, though only fingers, fingers and photographs. Yes, photographs, first the exciting ones, glossy naked ladies, then the dangerous ones, matte little snapshots, black and white, garish 1970s colour all leaching to tones of red: little boys, little girls. Smooth. Like me. Stand like the glossy ladies. The forbidden became a habit; even other photos taken by innocent adults, I posed – in one, aged five, eager to please, red t-shirt and blue jeans on Topsail Beach: cocked hip, baby teeth. Everything was all right. Not that bad. Just some photos. He hadn't hurt me. Hadn't happened, really, because he loved me. Invited me to go for drives, to explore the storehouse. Yes, loved and special. Anger – ha. Me a shaken bottle of, let's see, Coke? Foamy sweet. Orange Delight? Too sticky. Cream soda, the clear kind, hard bubbles but the cap secure, dome of twitching flesh at my tailbone – hot and salty, never sweet as cream soda, but hey, I'm gifted with imagination. If I could transform my grandfather Wright's semen to cream soda, surely I could transform the whole narrative to fog. I could even stand to one side in my bad dreams now, like the one where I stand with various Wright relatives and watch through the glass of the VOIC test centre as one of Lovecraft's Cthulhu, erection twitching, swiftly raped me, shook me, beat me off the floor, snarled and threw back his head roaring triumph. I saw this being done to me, and my father saw, and Thomas Wright saw, but like them I kept still. Done, the Cthulhu split briefly to green on the left, red on the right, like a VU meter, and the needle slammed far right, struggled, fainted back far into the green. I nodded. Thomas and my father nodded. And we all returned to work in different parts of the building, because everything was all right. Later in the same dream, I studied a portrait of Robert Wright and caught my own reflection in the glass: the same green eyes, one slightly smaller; the same heavy brow, the same style of glasses for fuck's sake, and the same worried squint.

My novel got stuck in a bog, but Claire's big grant – finally, Claire got something good, enough to live on for eight months, maybe a year if I had her over for dinner most nights. Art would result. Something that would heal. Me, I couldn't even manage to fill out a grant application form. So if I was going to write, I had to pry time open, a tangly business when you're nearly disconnected from time, or from any understanding of it. Nuisance memories again – exposed bog people. Cthulhu. Tailbone. Squint. English accent heard for years delivering the news, touching my hand, just happened to be in my favourite bookstore, just happened to turn up at my favourite coffee shop. If I didn't know better, didn't already know I'm hardly worth the effort, I'd say Almayer Foxe stalked me. Not that we spoke in public – VOIC and VONB, speaking? Laughable. Especially a Wright, my God, split the skies and rent the earth now. Gentleman still, solicitous and kind, utterly calf-eyed over me, and I thought he could decipher the tableaux vivants, smell the bog people. Yeah, he understood me. Stroking my hair one evening, holding wine to my lips, he murmured how lost I seemed. *Ignorant of your own beauty, Nichole. Let me show you.* The ease of the inevitable, because Almayer Foxe said he loved me. Am I getting through here? Because he said he loved me. So I posed. Soft. Hard. Brutal. White light knowledge, strobing: I had to find the plane. I could be saved once I found pieces of *Newsbird.*

Hours in the archives broken by flashes and blank spots – finally, a likely source for the remains of the plane, an old man in Port au Mal called Rupert Ginge. His shaky handwriting back to me: he'd picked up *Newsbird,* all the broken pieces of her that he could find, and under the old salvage law he owned those pieces. Neither the government nor the Wright family would finance a reconstruction. No one cared. No one had asked about the pieces in years.

Write commercials, feed Claire supper, visit Almayer, shower, sleep. Write commercials, feed Claire …

—Nichole Wright, one-seventeen, please, Nichole Wright.

—Looking for me, Ben?

—Come in. Close the door. I must admit, Nichole, how shocked I am to need to have this conversation with you. How can a smart young lady like you be utterly unaware of the consequences your personal life might have on your professional life? You have been seen, many times now, coming and going from the house of Almayer Foxe. In case you've forgotten, Almayer Foxe is the general manager of VONB-TN and VROM-FM, our chief competitors.

—I hadn't forgotten.

—You're too young, and too well-brought-up, too good a girl, to know the truth about Almayer Foxe. Nothing's has ever been proved, and no one's laid charges, but the stories …

Ben closed his eyes, dropped his voice.

—Stories of him convincing women who really ought to have known better – housewives, women well-over twenty-five – to pose naked for photos so he could act as their modeling agent. Not just naked, either. I'm talking hardcore porn here.

—It's not hardcore unless it shows a sexual act, Ben.

Eyes wide open. No witty comeback, no scrap of Coleridge or Kipling here.

—I beg your pardon, Nichole, but I could not have heard that correctly.

—I said it's not hardcore unless it shows a sexual act. The only person in those photos is me. And that's between me and the photographer.

—No, it isn't!

Ben slammed his fist on his desk hard enough to make his coffee cup jump.

—Nichole, that man takes more and more photos until he has a fine crop of imagery to blackmail you with. Do you understand? And given your last name –

—Oh, God. For once, just for once, can we leave my last name out of it?

—The chance to blackmail the Wright family? Who wouldn't take that? Believe me, that's mother's milk for a monster like Foxe.

—Did Mr. Wright call you up from Texas and tell you to say this?

Ben blushed. —I am assuming Mr. Wright does not know. I am hoping, for your sake, that very few people do know. Now. Is your car on the parking lot?

Holy fuck, was Potts firing me? My voice shook then, and tears pricked my eyes. Somewhere I took note of that, of how I could still feel. —Yes. Why?

—Because I want you to get in it, go home, and think long and hard about what we've just discussed. Then I really want you to break off any contact with Almayer Foxe.

Dignity after tears so often hollow, but I grabbed for it regardless.

—Or what?

—Nichole, what has happened to you?

Genuine concern in Potts' baggy eyes now, and pity.

Don't you dare pity me.

Signal to noise. —I love him! That's why I let him, all right? I love him. Can you possibly understand?

One of my cracked and worn molars crumbled then, and as I spoke, a piece of my tooth landed on Ben's desk. Tense jaw moving, gnashing now, reluctant from habit to free the slippery necessity of words.

—He loves me! Fuck this shit.

So I quit. Just walked out of VOIC Radio, face wet, eyes red, Ben left looking like a villain, because he was too much of a gentlemen to ever tell anyone else what we'd discussed. Even at that spiked moment, I knew that about Ben, and I loved him for it. But I didn't have time for sense right then, not when I had to focus the immense new energies just released by my words.

Reconstruct, renew. Heal. Get it out. Beautiful forgotten drive out to Port au Mal and Riordan's Back. Wreckage of the plane. Rebuild. Shattered gauge. Splintered wings. RAF yellow dullgrimed, ragged. Transistor tuned to the wavering signal of VOIC. Fray and snap. Fog, too full to see.

Noise. Voice.

70. STATION IDENTIFICATION in which Robert Wright recognizes his enemy.

August 1952

—An understanding?

Richard Fahey smiled, but Robert determined the expression a smirk. The other guests nodded discreetly, and conversation's hum dropped a level. Then a newspaper photographer waved at them both, and Robert grinned on schedule. In the blindness of the flash, he muttered the likely caption to Richard. —Rival St John's businessmen demonstrate courtesy and grace at the 1952 Businessman's Luncheon.

Richard and Robert moved apart as soon they could. Robert spoke clearly and well, a touch too jovial. —So, they let you in, Fahey? This is a hundred dollars a plate, you know.

Richard nodded at the head of The Newfoundland Electrical Company and his chief electrical engineer as they passed. Then he tugged his suit jacket into place. —I paid for a table of ten, Wright. And you?

—It is nobody's concern what I've paid for. The money goes to The Anchorage. That is all that matters.

—I thought we had an understanding.

Robert smiled again, greeting two cabinet ministers. Amazing how easily he could smile when it was such a chore to get out of bed. —About charitable fundraising?

—Robert, do I have to insult you so I might apologize and then shake your hand?

Robert stopped short. —What is it you want?

—I want to shake your hand.

—Do you? I'm surprised you don't want to kiss me.

Richard Fahey almost gasped. —Don't you blaspheme in my hearing, Robert Wright.

Robert considered what he'd just said. As if his words even mattered. Once the listeners got their morning newscasts alongside their oatmeal and tea, Robert could just sit, slouched and mute. Many assumed Mr. Wright mourned his dog; Atlas had darted into the street after a neighbour's daughter and been hit by a car, not before nudging the girl out of the way. The driver had been drunk. Atlas made a dent and then fell onto his side. The driver careened away, tires screeching further on, and the startled child would not budge from Atlas until her mother picked her up. Even then she screamed and kicked. Etta, returning home from a bridge game, discovered the scene and telephoned her husband, insisting the receptionist interrupt Robert's meeting – meeting, oh yes, a dirge of a conversation with William about the Society of Adepts. William had been detailing the Ritual of the Dark Dog, how by staring into a mirror at night he'd come to understand the unmoored sadness of their father. Disgusted, Robert tried not to listen, but each sentence from William sucked out more of Robert's will until he wanted only to sit quietly and permit William to explain himself. Still, he fretted about Atlas, who had not come to the station with him that morning; Robert had left him snoring by the bottom of the stairs. William described how the mirror rippled. Etta called.

Yes, Mr. Wright mourned his dog, but he felt another absence. He'd woken up one morning tired and empty. That was it. Tired and empty. The best part of him had fled, slipped its leash, leaving just a dumbshow-smiling shell of himself. And William.

Richard Fahey now slapped Robert's shoulder and treated him to another big public grin. —Come on, b'y, shake my hand. Wish me well.

Conversation had dropped again, and Robert knew others watched them. He squinted, trying to ignore the audience, the politicians, the VONB television camera. That evening on television, moments of the luncheon would play out over Fahey's commentary as rapid smudges of black and white, and doubtless this would be one of them.

Despite all his better judgement, Robert did not allow the tiny envelope from Richard to fall from his hand and placed it in a pocket as soon as he reasonably might. He sat down to luncheon, cod au gratin, chef's salad and baked Alaska, sat with his brother William and a few more lackeys from the civil service. Conversation touched on the deplorable need for The Anchorage, morals these days, bastards and delinquency, and if my daughter ...

Robert killed the conversation. —Imagine what it must feel like to be one of those young girls.

He kept quiet the rest of the meal, thoughtful, and when he returned to VOIC, he dealt with several small crises and a newscast. The day petered out nicely, Robert idly wondering, as he skimmed easily though engineering and accounting reports, precisely where did children born at The Anchorage go?

Robert came home to a quiet house – Etta out playing bridge again, Thomas, now married, and with a son of his own, Marie at a show with her young man, and Libby no doubt visiting friends one last time before leaving for university. The gentle evening air drew Robert outside. The brilliance of Venus pierced the bruised pink of the sky. His children had grown, children no more. Marie would be married in another eight months, and Robert hoped the strain of commitment might knock some vanity from her. Thomas – unutterably proud of Thomas. And he adored Libby, bright and feisty Elizabeth Anna ...Wright. Not Fahey. Etta's red face on the waterfront ... *No.* Robert had tasked himself to love Libby, raise her, hold nothing against her, and he'd succeeded, mostly by not thinking much about it, mostly by keeping busy. But when had the girls become women; when had Thomas stopped playing with toy cars? When had Etta gone grey? Yes, Etta's first grey hairs grew around the time he hired Micky O'Keefe; Marie's first dance invitation came a few months shy of getting the repeater fixed in Heart's Content; Libby's acceptance to Smith on full scholarship arrived the same day as Richard Fahey's resignation: *Don't worry, Robert, you'll get your money back. Of course I didn't tell you. If you knew I was going to use the money to start a television station, would you have loaned it to me? Von Haldorf is helping, and I've got some Americans interested.*

Robert took his glasses off and shut his eyes, letting the breeze play on his face. The heavy glasses sat upside-down in the grass, attracting curious insects, and one intrepid ant circumnavigated a lens. Robert knew he should eat something, even if it meant going out to a restaurant, but he'd become so tired of eating alone, eating after dusk. He picked up his glasses again, brushing at a tickle on his cheek as he put them on, and the ant fell in a long descent to the ground. Then Robert took the envelope from Fahey out of his pocket, a tiny envelope, one a money-changer might use for sorting American pennies from Canadian pennies and Newfoundland pennies. Folded within: a personal cheque and a small note which read *For Libby's college fees.*

Drawn on Fahey's personal account. The loan from Robert could be suitably traced to a business account, so at least this cheque was not Robert's own money flying back at him.

—How dare you, Fahey?

Bitter acknowledgement at that moment undimmed by time.

—How *dare* you? Do you truly think you might a prostitute out of Libby, too?

He'd likely made one of Etta – no, *no!* Libby did not in the least resemble Richard Fahey. She didn't look Robert, either. And Libby, like Thomas and Marie, knew nothing of these questions assailing Robert. Hardly their concern. Why even discuss it with Etta – what could they possibly discuss when even thinking on it invited madness?

Robert slowly walked back into the house and tucked the envelope into his small oak jewellery box, where he kept cufflinks and the old Ingersoll Radiolite pocket watch. Then he mixed a double rum and Coke. He still nursed it, in the dark at the kitchen table, when Libby and Etta came home.

Libby teased him. —Daddy, you think too much in the dark. Is this my destiny, too, to be found in the dark in my dorm, just sitting and thinking?

Robert laughed and cried suddenly, and hugged her too hard. Libby made to push away but stopped and let him hang on a moment longer, startled at his strength, and at her fragility – such tiny shoulder blades and ribs. He let her go.

Etta wiped her own eyes and then playfully pushed Libby up the stairs.

—We have to finish packing. And we must have a women's talk as well.

Later, in bed, Robert pictured the envelope from Fahey in the oak box, could see it hover and glow, sway like a censer; he chuckled. Etta murmured in her sleep. Robert hushed her, promised himself he would make the family breakfast in the morning even though it meant waking them at 6:30 – he must be at the station by 7:00 – and decided what to do with Fahey's money.

Happy and tearful goodbyes, Libby bristling a bit at Thomas accompanying her to Smith but in truth relieved to have her older brother there for the transition. They sailed from St John's; when they landed, Thomas rented a car and drove Libby the remaining distance.

—This means a lot to me, Thomas. You with a baby boy at home.

—Matt and his mother will be there when I get back. Any idea what you're going to do with your life?

—I want to write books. Tough books, like Conrad. Or Kafka. He said a book must be the axe for the frozen sea within us. I feel this urge, Thomas, like a trapped bird, but I can't write yet. I don't have anything to say. I haven't lived long enough.

Thomas listened to this without passing judgement, noting the beauty of the trees in Massachusetts. —We were born here.

Libby turned in the seat. —Do you think I can do it?

—Write books? S'pose.

—I'm a girl.

—You're a Wright.

—What's that got to do with anything?

—You're just like Dad. And you tore right through school. Set your mind, girl, and you'll do it.

Libby thought about that. Then she became oddly timid. —But do you think I can do it like Conrad? Tough, I mean, like a man. Not like Virginia Woolf, I mean, she's good, but she's so, I don't know, feminine. Frail. One misstep and *To the Lighthouse* would collapse. And *Mrs Dalloway* is so depressing. She just dissipates, like the fog. See, this is part of the problem. Like Virginia Woolf. Free, but hardly tough. Emily Brontë was tough. But then, she was afraid to leave her house and died of consumption. Emily Dickinson wouldn't even show her face. I can't explain it. Do you know what I mean?

—Not a clue. But I can tell you this: you and Aunt Jane are the toughest people I know.

Libby gasped, then lunged over to hug him.

Thomas grinned and shrugged her off, turning on the wipers. —Get off me, ya nut. I'm driving.

Wretched telephone call from Northampton, Thomas nearly hysterical, voice keening high. —I'm sorry. I'm so sorry. The road was so wet. Broke my arm. Libby got thrown.

Someone took the phone from him; a doctor spoke to Etta now, and over his nonsense – he paused to order Thomas sedated – Thomas cried out as long as his voice held. —I'm sorry, I'm sorry.

Reviewing his bank statements in the airplane, how the cheque from Fahey had gone into his account and an equal amount had come out, written over to The Anchorage, Robert Wright the businessman tallied costs in American dollars; Robert Wright the father wept unaware. Etta cried next to him, not that he could hear this over the jet's engines. This hole, this absence, this enormous wound which by rights should not even be his: this pain. Months later, when glimpsing a photo in his office of Thomas, Marie and Libby did not cause tears, Robert recognized his enemy in this world. Not his wife. Not Richard Fahey. Not even thieving God, mysterious, vague and undeniable as a rock in the fog. His enemy – time.

FREQUENCY

71. COPE AND DRAG 3
in which something lost is found, then lost again.

Date: September 15, 2004

To: Deputy Minister, Department of Heritage

Fr: Fabian O'Dea, Banked Acquisitions

Sir:

My question is simple. I have written repeatedly to advise you of the existence of an eight-foot bronze statute entitled *Louis Riel, MP*, recently recovered from Banked Acquisitions Storage Unit 12 after said storage unit burned down. The statue suffered smoke damage but is otherwise intact.

Department records on the acquisition of *Louis Riel, MP*, are difficult to collate. I have discovered that a former New Democrat Member of Parliament had purchased the statue with the intent of installing it in front of the entrance of Main Block. You may recall a short debate about this in the House of Commons. I can find you the relevant Hansard transcripts on request. It was around that time that the Member who had commissioned the work was challenged on some of his spending records. The statue was subsequently donated to the Department of Canadian Heritage.

The artist's name was G. Furey. There is no Social Insurance Number on the acquisition forms for G. Furey. I have contacted the former Member who originally purchased the statue. It was his memory that G. Furey was a man but not a Canadian citizen.

Louis Riel, MP is controversial in its subject matter. The merit of the statue as a piece of art is beyond my ability to judge. The problem is this: if the statue is not put on display, then where, and for how long, should Banked Acquisitions continue to store it?

I look forward to your reply. Please be advised I will be taking vacation next week.

Best regards,

Fabian O'Dea, Chief Inventory Officer
Banked Acquisitions

72. STAUNCH A CUT 2
in which Colleen Best reflects on reasons.

December 12, 1940

I wanted to send for the doctor, but Jessop's a hard man to find, even in Port au Mal. A little voice poked at me, Jack, nudged me, and I'd go up to her room and bathe her forehead, and then I'd look at her feet. One was beautiful, a perfect little foot, but the other wore the abscess, and she was shaking, shaking all over like a bird that's just hit the window. It was a rock, I figure, that sharp rock out in the back garden by the well, I mean, she never should have been playing by the well, water tastes like iron this year, and she cut her foot, and it bled. You know what Tessa was like. She ignored it, went back to picking flowers, seeking fairies. I took her walking with me later, dressed her proper, those little high-button boots you ordered from England, bit too small for her, but I wanted to get the wear out of them, and then after shopping we came home, and your sister came for tea, and Tessa went upstairs and took a nap, and, and Jack, that was last summer, and the nurse never once mentioned the cut on her foot, not once. Tessa walked funny in September, and there in October she was tired all the time. I took her to Dr. Jessop then, and he lanced the abscess on her foot and gave her a tonic, and she screamed all the way home, and Jack – Jack, God is my witness – I thought she was fine. I thought she wanted cuddles and attention and Mama all the time, but Dr. Jessop had lanced the abscess, so she had to be fine. She was four years old, Jack, small youngsters like that get on with foolishness, and I – I thought she had a cold. I wasn't going to send for you in Port au Mal because Tessa had a cold. Then the fever, like I told you, and the trembling and the sweat, and that awful colour her face was, grey like cinders or rotten slush. It took hours. Finally she died in your sister's arms, because I had to find a chamber pot. Dr. Jessop came by, after the fact – I tried sending for him when it was happening, Jack. Twenty past two in the morning. I sent the maid to go get him, but he would not come to the door. When he finally did come to call, he used some foolish big word – septicaemia, yes, that's it, my God, but you know everything, Jack – blood poisoning. He said we had to bury her quickly, the corruption was what killed her, corruption already begun, but Jack, I did not choose a stone. *Theresa Katherine Best*, I told them, *1936-1940, Suffer the Children*, but you would be picking out the stone.

73. ON DECK AND BELOW 2 – MERCHANT PRINCE
in which VOIC News Director Kyle George takes Thomas, Matthew and Lewis Wright moose hunting out of season.

July 12, 1986

Ten after four on Saturday morning. Fog clung to the pond and the trees, hovering maybe two inches off the ground. The barrens five miles off, or even the truck next to the window, never existed. Fog looked white only if you didn't study it too closely. Walk into it, and the fog parted, briefly non-existent, but only where you stood. Particles of water too small to make you actually wet infested the bones with cold. Even the trip to the outhouse could be hazardous, making real Ted Russell's line, often quoted by Ben Philpott: *of pathways cut through fog*. Lewis Wright sat silently at the dented table, ignoring the map of the island on the wall behind him, dotted with the coloured heads of pins. In his lap lay the new .303, identical to Matt's, identical to their father's, and neither Wright knew how to use it.

Lewis tasted the muzzle. Just rehearsing.

Useless. A word to defile a burnt wire, a flooded car wreck, not a man. A word escaping on a breath of fury and shame. Lewis ignored the mockery at work, derision blatant beneath courtesy; he recognized others' impatience with him, denied his own furious sloth, and he did as his father told. Lewis Wright signed papers, executed decisions, tallied numbers; Lewis Wright hid within himself, eyes shut, mouth tight: *Please don't make me come out.* Hidden or not, he felt the sting of his father's words flung at his absence, in the short moment between hallway and Sherwood Forest: *How useless is Lewis at all?* Ten minutes late for the executive meeting because he'd been sketching a Tesla coil. How useless? No, worse than useless, and the knowledge sank into Lewis that morning with the gun warming on his tongue, sank into him like dampness: an accidental murderer. Always in someone's way.

He'd killed his mother, being born.

He'd never heard the whole story, only enough to stain. A conversation between Thomas and Jane, Lewis watching reflections in the French door, Thomas gazing at Jane in some desperate wonder. —Transverse. Caesarean. Women aren't supposed to die in childbirth anymore. Why are people stolen from me, Jane?

Snores. Matt turned in his bed, then Thomas, then VOIC News Director Kyle George, that Saturday morning their host and guide on an illegal hunt. Neither Lewis nor Matt understood this sudden bloodlust in their father. Thomas Wright disliked being in the woods, despised long drives.

—I hate moose.

Thomas's voice, kept low, seeped through the walls. He spoke to Kyle, who was showing him how to load his .303.

—They're a bloody nuisance. Never should have been brought here, look, closed environment, no real predators. Never mind the season. That's just foolishness. We got IFAW up in arms over the damned baby seals, but they got no understanding of population control, and they'll never step in to protect moose because they aren't cute. And we got laws telling us when we can and can't hunt.

Now Thomas came towards the stairs, new boots clumping. Matt called out he was awake; Thomas and Kyle descended. Lewis sighed, slid the muzzle deeper into his mouth.

Brittle jolliness from Thomas. —Kyle, I really appreciate this today. I just, I needed something different. The stations have got me drove. And I've got to be honest with you. I – I get antsy this time of year.

Thomas could not believe he said that out loud. He kept the rest of his racing thoughts to himself. *And I noticed something there last night, in the sunset, when we were out on the deck and the light hit Lewis a certain way: the spit of Father. There he is, gun across his lap.*

—Lewis, sleep well?

—Just fine. You, Skipper?

—Strange bed. Kyle, you sit down, now. Least I can do is make the breakfast. You got eggs here?

As Thomas puttered in the kitchen, Kyle gently took the .303 from Lewis. He flicked the safety back on, then ran his hand up the muzzle and felt warm spit. He said nothing. Could not possibly speak. Thomas cracked eggs, melted butter; Lewis responded where he should, welcomed his brother, so utterly normal. A swampy weight crammed Kyle George's chest, sank into him. Sunlight glared through the dirty east window, the Wrights' flannel shirts hung so crisp and new on their bodies, and Matt's stubble only made him look younger. Kyle would keep an eye to Lewis Wright, and if he could steal a moment, he'd unload Lewis's gun.

No theft, just mystery: Lewis shot a young bull, first antlers, no trophy moose but a kill just the same, clean shot through the heart. Kyle congratulated Lewis Wright as much out of relief as pleasure, and he grinned as Matt and Thomas turned away from the carcass, sick at the gutting, but Lewis knelt and did as Kyle bade. When Thomas's stomach calmed, he glanced at his younger son: again, that ghosting. The intensity of expression, the absorption in the task at hand: Lewis gutting the moose, his father preparing the news.

Kyle George dreaded the drive back to Chamberlains, where his friend would cut and package the carcass, dreaded encountering the police or a wildlife officer. Guaranteed trouble if the Rangers caught them, no matter how hard Kyle might plead the truth: *Honest to Christ, I never thought either one of them would hit anything.* The Wrights surrendered their weapons; Kyle unloaded them, locked them away in their cases, saw the blood grit under his nails, at his cuticles. He glanced once more at Lewis, who got in the back with his brother, timid and detached, perhaps unmoored.

Warm spit. Better a moose than a man.

74. LOGGER 3
in which VOIC's Kyle George reports live from the scene.

February 11, 2005

Jim Reid's voice crackled in Kyle's cell phone. —We got three witnesses now just called the newsroom, say the chopper just kept losing altitude. Can you see it? She's roughly half a mile in the woods.

Kyle had been at work since four that morning, and his recent erratic sleep, not helped by tumblers of rum, seemed to take hold of him. Sleep. Those microsleeps truckers have on long hauls, where the mind cuts out for a mile or so, where the body overrides the will and snatches at rest – thirty seconds, sixty seconds …

—Kyle?

—Got visual contact.

—That's great, Kyle, but we work in radio.

—Still no smoke.

—She's only three miles from the Paradise town limits. Lots of trees to go up if she catches.

Orange roof lights flashing on his VOIC X-Terra, Kyle pulled onto the shoulder where two police cars had parked. Another helicopter approached, loud, low.

—Kyle, just cued the on-the-spot news stinger. You're on in three, two, one ...

This is Kyle George, reporting live from the scene of a helicopter crash near Kenmount Road. The helicopter has gone down in a wooded area. So far, there are no signs of the pilot or passengers, and there is no sign of fire. Constable Squires tells VOIC News that Kenmount Road is closed to traffic in both directions for the next several hours. Rescue operations are currently being hampered by fog and deep snow. For VOIC News, I'm Kyle George.

—Yes, b'y, Kyle, me son. This is why we keep winnin' the Murrows.

This is Kyle George for VOIC News, and I'm near the scene of a helicopter crash near Kenmount Road. You can hear another helicopter in the vicinity. That pilot is looking for the crash site and may have – yes, they've identified the crash site. Kenmount Road remains blocked to traffic. In another hour the light will start to fail. Motorists are reminded to find an alternate route. Live on the scene for VOIC News, I'm Kyle George.

Just a news story. Bad news story, but a news story. Cover the news. Broadcast the news. VOIC, first with the news.

I'm Kyle George for VOIC News, still near the scene of a dramatic helicopter crash earlier this afternoon near Kenmount Road, which remains closed to motorists. I've been speaking with eyewitnesses who describe hearing a helicopter very low in the sky, and then seeing it sink through the fog and seem to glide into the woods. Police are … the snow in the woods is very deep and - stand by. Stand by. They've reached the helicopter. The helicopter is buried up to the rotors in snow but appears mostly intact. No word yet on the status of the pilot or co-pilot. NL Transport did report that two people are on board. Pilot and co-pilot - stand by - and this was a training exercise, but right now motorists are advised to take an alternate route because the crashed helicopter is buried up to its rotors in snow. For VOIC News, I'm Kyle George.

—Kyle, y'all right?

—Tapping like the sailors in the *Kursk*? As if. Drowned out by that other bird.

—Stinger's cued. You good to go? You're live in three, two, one. Kyle?

Dead air.

Commercial, Gosse Milley Rideout Tiller Law Offices.

—Kyle, you there? You hearing me?

Police officers shouting into radios. Rescue helicopter veering out. Sudden light – Kyle surrendering to the same instinct that let him slide into home plate every time – ditch, face into the freezing dirty water, cell phone held up out of the way – debris – metal, fibreglass, branches, flesh – hitting the ground, hitting the water in the ditch.

Commercial, Wince Blanford Chrysler.

—Kyle. What the fuck is going on?

Pattering, really, all those pieces falling in the snow. Sort of a scraping, the ones that landed on Kenmount Road.

Commercial, Port of Call.

—Kyle!

—Yeah?

—Kyle, do you read me?

—Fire.

—Ambulances and fire trucks are already on the way. You all right?

—I can see where the helicopter landed now. Fire. Patch me in.

—Are you all right?

—Patch me in, Jim.

—Three, two, one …

… scene of the helicopter crash near Kenmount Road. There's been some sort of explosion, and we now have a small fire burning in the wooded area. Rescue crews on the way. You can probably hear the sirens in the background now. Details are scarce, but there should be considerable activity here in a few moments. Motorists are reminded to plan an alternate route, as ... debris on Kenmount Road. Closed. Debris. For VOIC News, this is – stand by –

—Kyle? Do you read?
–bzht–

75. THE RELIC
in which Ange and Neal O'Dea attend a fresh grave.

August 4, 1972

The only child who'd made it back for the service at Holy Redeemer Cemetery in Riordan's Back was Neal. Not that Ange expected the entire brood; Jeannie, his third wife, hadn't mothered either one of them. Mary, Mary Ruth Maynard the first wife, mother to … every child except Fabian. Mary died on Liz. Quiet loner Fabian came from Catherine, the second wife. The last postcard from Fabian postmarked from New York State ... But Neal had come. Stunted, wiry Neal, smarter and better read than many at the university. *And how in God's name did you make it as a miner, my son?* Neal suited in dark blue, waiting while Ange, on one knee, murmured to the new grave of Jeannie Bursey Hicks O'Dea, asking her one last time what in the name of Jesus she'd been doing up on that rotten ladder by herself.

Ange stood up slowly, an ache in his hips. *God, I loved her.* Then he smiled at his son, eyes wet. Neal smiled back, nodding.

—Neal b'y, this is getting ridiculous.

76. WOUND STRIPE 3
in which Albert Furneaux and Christopher Francis speak.

1917-1921

Rest cure, Albert. You stay in bed and do nothing with your hands. Not my prisoner – my patient. You're home now. I shall look after you, just as I once taught you school. No need for 'Mr. Francis' now. Call me Christopher. Failure? I will not be grading you. I will only be sitting with you. Well, I'm not good for much else around here. I'm going blind, Albert, though I can still read with some good light. And I'm no use on the water. Now rest.

In love? Me? An impertinent question. Where was I? Coleridge, of course. *Well, you are gone, and here I must remain, this lime-tree bower my prison.*

You asked me last month if I'd ever been in love. Do you remember Nurse Jarwick from England? She would travel around Conception Bay and down to the Southern Shore. I do believe you're right – yes, she did pull your tooth.

Of course I asked her to marry me. Never a finer woman.

Overseas, nurse at the Front. She said she could never marry a Newfoundlander. But she writes to me.

Albert, this handwriting is difficult for me. Could you read it? From Mary – Miss Jarwick? *Great Expectations*, yes, I sent that to her ... read that again. Albert, read that again and swear to me you speak truly. She said yes? *If you would still have me, I would marry a Newfoundlander.*

Influenza?

Such a delicate thing, that sea urchin in your long fingers, Albert. Yes, I've found you out here in the dark. The hour before dawn, you know. I memorized every step to the burying ground before you could walk, so don't – thank you, nice catch. Too old, my eye. I'm forty-one.

—You could fall up here, Christopher.

—So could you. Very nice to hear your voice.

—Not telling you nothing.

—Double negative.

—What?

—I pointed out your vernacular and charming but incorrect use of a double negative. If you were still my pupil, I would set you one hundred lines: *I will not do no double negative.*

—You stunned bastard. It hurts me to laugh. I can't open me mouth enough.

—If you survive the pain of laughing, Albert, I have two other tasks for you. Go to Mrs. Wright and ask for humbugs. Can you do that?

—I'll wear bandages on me face. Wouldn't want to scare the lady. Help me?

—If you wish. But first, help me back down this hill.

Mary, I know you cannot hear me, but even to the dark I need to say I miss you.

77. MYOPIA SKY 4
in which the sky abandons a Tiger Moth, and Ange O'Dea finds a pair of glasses.

July 12-13, 1954

Ange O'Dea ignored the wishes of his sons, Neal and John, and kept walking on his beat-up ankle. The day before, talking Clarence Jackman blind, Ange had stepped in a killick, slipped, shook the killick into the water, where, unattached to a net, it sank. Then Ange had stepped in a lobster trap, breaking it, slipping again. Then, in kicking off the shattered wooden box, insisting sea lice crawled up his leg because of it all, he thwacked his ankle against an anchor. All that happened in the morning, before Riordan's Back and Port au Mal found out Rose Fahey had run off again, in the woods most likely, you knows now, and before everyone learned, at the same moment it seemed, that native son Robert Wright took his plane up to search from the air – you remember Robert as a youngster, half-blind, couldn't tell his colours apart ...

Ankle sore, undeniably, Ange waited in front of his house, fuming with impatience and that useless feeling that so enrages you precisely when you have no strength to release that rage. He couldn't even keep his balance to cut wood, let alone join Neal, John and Artemis. Beside Ange, feeling equally impatient and useless, Wright's son, Thomas.

So he watched the sky. Watched that neat yellow plane round the woods in long ellipses, lower, higher, Wright's dark head peeking over the sides. Ange listened hard for the dog's bark, but, once *Newsbird* veered off, he heard only seagulls and the ocean.

Wright shot a flare when he found Rose. He circled a spot tightly now, the Tiger Moth's engine so loud, then stuttering – the shards of silence drew everyone's eyes up – and in the shadows, somewhere in the trees, *Newsbird* crashed.

Ange ignored his own sons' protests and accompanied them to the stages. Thomas, expensively dressed and every inch the townie, looked around suspiciously. Ange said nothing – what the hell could you say to a man whose father had just crashed his plane? Christ, Christ.

Neal, John and Artemis bore on towards where Wright had shot the flare; Ange led Thomas to the plane, trying to hard not to limp. Stopping once to take a breath, to let the pain subside to a dull roar, Ange found something odd: a heavy pair of black hornrimmed glasses, lenses shattered. Thomas saw very little right then; Ange picked up the glasses, shook out the loose shards, wrapped them in his handkerchief and put them in his pocket. Then he and Thomas continued.

Half an hour into the woods they found the wreckage.

That night, Ange pondered the engine, how it struggled just before the crash. And no fire; had the plane run out of fuel? Wright had lost his glasses; did one of those gauges tell him something he could no longer read? Ange found no comfort in reasons. Not at night, drinking, and certainly not earlier in the day alongside Thomas at the wreckage. No comfort, because discovery tasked Ange to close Robert Wright's eyes.

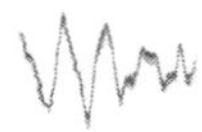

78. A THIRD AFTERNOON'S PLEASANT DISCOURSE in which Ange O'Dea refuses to sit still.

July 5, 1993

—Are you ready, Mr. O'Dea?

—S'pose. Feel a bit foolish in this sweater.

Chris Jackman adjusted his own tie. Twenty-two now, Chris stood as a scrawnier version of his father, fair and blue-eyed, twitchy as a hare near loose dogs. Ange peered at Chris for some memory of Larry's quiet calm.

—It's all about authenticity, Mr. O'Dea. So you got to keep the sweater on. I can get you an electric fan if you like.

—Don't bother with it.

—Okay, Mr. O'Dea. You just sit back. I'll be through with the first crowd in a few minutes.

So, wearing a sweater indoors in July, Ange sat back in a delicate rocking chair, facing a woodstove whose chimney went nowhere. On the wall behind him hung sepia-tinted reprints of photographs of Coaker, Best, and of all people, Commissioner Grant-Mainwaring. A lobster trap blocked the path from the rocking chair to the woodstove, while a line of bright yellow rope strung between two dented stainless steel pillars, donated by a local bank, served as the fourth wall. Ange picked up the prop net. Machine-woven and bright green, almost fluorescent, the net rasped his fingers and could never be bent to accommodate the drews he'd once knit. The meshes looked huge, and the line smelled not of salt water but strange chemicals.

Chris stood smiling in the lobby, welcoming the first guests. His bosses from the Department of Tourism, Culture and Recreation on hand, Chris spoke terribly well, overcompensating on the correct aspirations and sounding more like he had asthma than good diction.

—Welcome, everyone, to the first in what I hope is a series of LHDs across the country. What are LHDs, you ask? Living History Displays. With Living History Displays, we have taken the bold step of not only collecting and professionally curating artefacts from our rich and storied past, but also daring to integrate palpable history itself. Or, in simpler terms, we have contracted local persons to act out and demonstrate bits of our heritage which are already in danger of becoming inaccessible.

Polite applause. Ange decided to look busy with the net. Quickly bored with the hakapik, rusty washing tub and kerosene lamp, the crowd seeped towards Ange.

—And now, our first Living History Display.

Ange rocked slightly in the chair, suddenly anxious to prove himself more than a wax dummy.

—Ange O'Dea is very much a representation of a typical Newfoundland outport man. Good with his hands, very resourceful, and speaks only when he has something to say.

Ange's face got hot. All of his wives had fondly complained of how much he talked. He fingered the net, studied his cuticles.

—Behind Ange are some photographs of notable figures in our history, and you will find photos of these men in many outport homes still.

A woman asked about the man with the glasses. Chris replied with a mostly accurate summary of the Commission of Government's run on the island. Then, something struck him – inspiration perhaps, or dementia.

—The Commission of Government sat in St. John's, of course. Sometimes one or another Commissioner would travel to the outports to observe conditions. But Ange O'Dea here did something special. He went to see a Commissioner. And he walked all the way to St. John's to do it.

No, you fool, I sailed from Riordan's Back to Holyrood, then took the train to St. John's.

The crowd gasped. Appreciation, awe, for the tenacity and strength of a past generation.

Chris continued. —All the way to St. John's and demanded an audience with the Commissioner.

I stole no man's time. Didn't know about appointments.

Applause.

Ange found breathing impossible, as if he had fallen in.

—He got his audience and pled his case. And this, ladies and gentlemen, from a man who cannot read, and cannot write his own name.

Stunted applause, very uncertain.

—Ange O'Dea, his mark.

Ange stood up, vision quite intent on the woodstove chimney. He dropped the net, stepped carefully over the lobster pot and the yellow rope. The crowd stepped back; Chris stayed rooted to his spot.

Several hours later, Chris knocked on Ange's back door, the one by his kitchen.

Ange opened the door but did not step aside to let Chris in.

Chris's blond hair blew around, revealing a developing bald spot. He squinted, chin down, tie gone. He did not speak.

The wind blew mist onto Ange's face. —Chris, my son, you got a lot to learn.

Chris turned around, shoulders hunched. Ange struggled with himself, wanting to invite the younger man in, make him tea, but Chris walked away.

Ange scowled. —Maybe you can walk all the way to St. John's, now.

Chris heard him; his shoulders twitched. But he kept on walking.

Jesus Christ, what the hell's the matter with me? —Chris, wait. Chris, come back. Come in. Please, Chris, don't go off like that.

A door slammed, headlights came on; Chris started his black and silver Dodge Ram. Ange couldn't compete with that racket, but he did stay in his doorway, cold and damp, until Chris's tail-lights disappeared.

79. OHM 3
in which Lewis Wright studies radio towers.

July 12, 1974

From his father's bedroom window, Lewis Wright could see radio towers. Loads of radio towers about, most of them VOIC's. Red and white poles, very thin-looking until you actually got near one – deceptive.

Mr. McGrew once told Lewis a story about VONB-TV and ice.

—One of their towers had gotten coated with ice during an April storm. This often happened. I worry about it every winter myself. It was a particularly heavy storm that year, and the tower in question was in danger of falling down, weighted by several inches of ice on one side. So what did these fellows do? Got out their .303s and tried to shoot off the ice. Their chief engineer became so thoroughly disgusted he actually called me at home to tell me about it. He needed to talk to someone who'd understand, you see.

The radio towers' lights blinked, sometimes in unison, warning aircraft.

—Another time, another ice storm, everybody lost their power. I mean everybody. VOIC stayed on the air, because we had generators. Our competitors did not. This ice storm lasted three days. We had no way of knowing it would be so long. And the generators got low on fuel. It was ice over snow, and getting dark, and – no, not me, this is the surprising part – your father. He hadn't gone home for forty-eight hours by that time. He kept an electric razor in his desk for just such an emergency. Good thing we had those generators, on top of the hill as they were. Snowmobile wasn't getting up there. If you didn't slip on the ice, you went through it and up to your hips. Hard climb, that was. He doesn't know I followed him. Frightened to death he'd get hurt. But it was your father who got to the generators, gassed them up, kept us on the air.

Ten o'clock at night, and Thomas had yet to come home from work. Lewis watched the warning lights go briefly together, then chaotic. It must mean something. Lewis had tried to explain that to Matt but failed. All of it. It must mean something.

80. THREE DOTS 3
in which Thomas and Lewis Wright explore signal to noise.

Dec. 12, 2003

—Dad, what have you got here?

Thomas looked up from an old crate – inside which glass clinked – tempted to open it, to study once again the old issue of *Alternating Current*, but then he would be tasked to explain the magazine and the apparatus to Lewis. —Junk. Old junk. I don't know why in the name of God I'm keeping it all these years.

Thomas had woken that morning from a sickening dream of needing the bathroom in the old Wright house in Port au Mal, but the bathroom, indeed the entire house, was at sea, pitching, and in the dream Thomas kept falling asleep, only to wake to his full bladder and the harsh tossing of the bathroom floor. A moment later, seawater invaded. Sitting up, Thomas had felt a quick presence, a gentle touch of his father's large hand on his own forearm, and for maybe three seconds Thomas dreamt again: his father's body in the old front room, and the warning drone of nosedive – sound effect kindly supplied by movies. Thomas forced himself from bed, almost crying, and in his well-appointed St. John's bathroom, with tile walls, hand-held shower, bidet and carpeted floor, he shat out a quantity of waste and whatever virus had invoked fever and gastritis. Now, about twelve hours later, he decided to clean out his attic and called his sons to demand help now, today, this minute, but only Lewis had been home.

Thomas kicked the crate. —Junk.

Lewis slowed his search. He knew precisely what lay in which box, under which sheet, but his father needed soft handling. And a little acting on Lewis's part.

—Dad, whatever happened to the gold coins?

—Your uncle William came out to Torbay with me, said we had to check on Father's car. Father left his car out there, a Studebaker, he was so proud of it, like the plane, washed it every weekend unless we had rain – and we were looking for his things in the car. All he left behind was the registration and a little bag made of black velvet. I didn't know what to make of it, but your Uncle William, he snatched it, and he said: 'He was supposed to take these. Back in 1936. These are my share, seven French and one Portuguese. He never took them.' And your uncle William stared up at me, like I'd offended him, and he looked ready to strike me. Then he said 'Robert told me last week he had something old to give me back.'

Lewis fought down excitement. To offer Uncle William's coins to the rest of the Board of Directors for the new Admiral's Rooms Museum ...

—So where are the coins now?

—In the bank.

Lewis felt like he'd barked his head. —The bank?

—William's wife. God love her, she meant no harm. She took the coins to the bank and deposited them. Came to five hundred dollars. A tidy sum. But nowhere near their true value.

Lewis hardly knew what to say to that. He returned to the trunk, full of ledgers, old clothes belonging to a short woman, and banged his knuckles off something heavy.

—Dad, is this the ship's bell?

—I took that home in '72. We made a master tape of it, carted about a dozen copies. When did we stop using the bell for the newscasts?

—1987. We went to that digital satellite sound effect. When we linked up the west coast and Labrador.

—'Connect to the whole world on VOIC.'

—I liked the old leading light ID, too. How did that go?

—We used that when we were on Chapel Street. 'A leading light of communication in Newfoundland: VOIC Radio.'

Lewis touched the bell's dents, the patches of oxidation. —How old is this?

—Belonged to the Captain. My grandfather.

—What was he like?

Thomas thought for a moment. —Stern. He took Jack Best fishing for six seasons.

—The Prime Minister?

—Mm-hmm. Toughened him up. Best always credited Captain Wright with turning him from a spoiled brat to a man.

Lewis raised his eyebrows. —What did the Captain think of radio?

—He didn't understand it, see. Didn't understand why his son would go up to Labrador and operate the wireless station there. Depressed him. Nothing his sons did was good enough for the Captain. I think that's why Father left home so early. Towards the end the Captain wasn't right in the head. Melancholy, used to weep over distance. 'Distress,' he'd say, and Nan would hush him, 'signal, distress: how awful if someone heard it over too great a distance.' He couldn't stand to be helpless. Died in the Waterford.

—But you've got to send out the signal

Thomas glanced at his son, who rarely raised his voice.

Lewis stuttered a bit. —Y-you've got to send out the s-signal. There might be someone there. Even if you drown, there might be s-someone who heard you first. Same reason you hang on to floating wood long as blood flows.

Fey Lew. Thomas thought it this time not so much with condescension but fear.

Then a painting flashed into his mind: *Raft of the Medusa.*

Lewis opened another box. —I wonder if da Vinci figured out radio.

—Did da Vinci paint that?

—Paint what?

Thomas considered his words.

—Dad, you sure you should be up and around, doing this?

—I'm fine. How the hell could da Vinci figure out radio? Wasn't he in Shakespeare's time?

—He figured out flight.

Thomas moved boxes with no apparent purpose for a while. Lewis did the same.

—Dad, did you ever get it to work?

Weakened by fever, Thomas answered his son. —Yes. Down at Chapel Street. Blew every fuse in the building. Whole row of houses went out. Just like you nearly blew up this house. I thought Dan McGrew was going to resign on me that day.

—You knew?

—I suspected. I know now. So you sent out the signal. Like Ben Philpott keeps saying, alone on the wide, wide sea.

—Three hours' worth.

Thomas grunted – almost laughed. —Three hours. Oh, God. Lewis, did – did you hear anything back?

How to acknowledge what he'd denied for years. —Yes.

Thomas stared at the crate.

Lewis continued. —I didn't hear it myself. I caught it on tape. A voice. It said *Signal received.*

Thomas's lips moved. He cleared this throat; he breathed quickly.

—On tape? You got it on tape? His voice, his voice, my God, I've just wanted to hear his voice, once more, because, I, I never said – he was a good man, Lewis, a good man. Stolen. That stupid little girl. She ruined everything –

Thomas's guts clenched; *not now.*

—Dad, Dan McGrew erased it.

Thomas wanted to cry out. He couldn't.

—I listened to it in Engineering there one Saturday that summer. The summer I finished the Tesla coil. And he frightened me. So did the tape. I ran outside, mowed the lawn, ruined the V that day, remember? Sneaked back in later. The reel lay next to the bulk eraser. And when I played it: nothing.

Rage. Thomas would have welcomed rage. A tantrum would be normal, predictable behaviour, but when Thomas opened his mouth, nothing.

—He meant well, Dad. Best of intentions. Recording like that would scare a priest. Jesus, Dad, stand up, b'y. You need the bathroom? All right, down the stairs, easy now. Don't fall. Dad, Jesus, don't cry. Please. Just whistles, had to be, not signal but noise. It was just a tape. Matt. You want Matt? You want me to call Matt? Yes, yes b'y, Matt looks just like him. I'll get Matt.

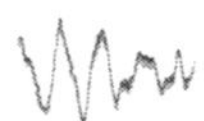

81. HOPE OF THE CONSUMPTIVE
in which Ellen Wright learns the meaning of family.

July 12, 1969

Ellen Wright, people said, had gone quietly, kindly and sweetly dotty. Spared the louder and more masculine madness tainting father and possibly brother, Ellen instead flitted, fussed and generally farted around. She rarely left the old Wright house, except for morning and evening service on Sundays, and some people thought her a closet drinker. She got her groceries delivered, an odd habit in so small a town as Port au Mal, but alcohol did not clink amongst the delicacies. She still answered to *Miss Wright*, still coughed a great deal, suffered dreams of drowning to wake sweat-soaked, and stood thin as a cat stuck outside all winter, nonetheless cured of tuberculosis. The doctors said so. Besides, the City of St. John's had closed the old San.

A lasting side effect of the Sanatorium: Ellen's walled-off heart. Only William had visited her in the 1930s and 40s, his green eyes moist and strange over the white mask covering nose and mouth. Once their father took ill and thoughtlessly added to the family's embarrassment with his hospitalization, William stopped visiting Ellen. Jane stopped sending notes. Robert, well, Robert had never come to see her anyway, and to hear William tell it, resented any reminder that Ellen still existed. Ellen, another inconvenient fragility, another shamesore. If her family did not visit, then she must not be deserving of a visit. This bare reasoning choked Ellen's fever dreams: Robert, especially, just out of earshot, turning away, allowing the dream to morph into a summer afternoon when Ellen heard but never saw the Tiger Moth, and then the engine cut.

Ellen feared silence.

So Ellen chattered, sang, whistled through her days, safe within the walls of the house, from time to time coughing, and from time to time hoping for a visit. Boys dared one another to approach the haunted house. Once a stuttering Girl Guide sold Ellen some cookies, but she never returned. Ellen considered those children family, too.

82. CONTINUITY 7
memorandum

Date: July 18, 2002

Re: Wolf Broadcasting

Mr. Wright takes this opportunity to inform everyone that the VOIC Network is now majority-owned by the Canadian communications company Wolf Broadcasting Limited. Wolf Broadcasting, through a special arrangement with Republic of Newfoundland and Labrador, BRATNL and the CRTC, has extended its already shared programming to encompass day-to-day operations of the VOIC Network. The takeover will be finalized within the next year. The Wrights will pursue other business interests.

Please see your Pension Representative with any questions.

83. UP THE POND 3
in which Ben Philpott suffers a hard bitch of a day.

July 8, 2003

—And therefore it is my intention to implement and oversee the same employment equity standards to the VOIC Radio Service as are in place in the Canadian stations in the Wolf Broadcasting Group.

Ben Philpott sweated through that promise. A few years from retirement, and he sat trapped at the boardroom table with Dr. Dorinda Masterson, a women's studies professor from the University of Toronto, contracted by Canada's Wolf Broadcasting to mesh Wolf's corporate culture with VOIC's. Despite knowing that Dorinda Masterson had been born and raised in Newfoundland and now wished to return, Ben would have preferred to be across the boardroom table from the Inquisition.

Dr. Masterson nodded but hardly smiled. —So you're confirming the report I've read, the report which states that, as of this moment, no equity standards are in place within the VOIC network. None at all.

—As you know, the population of Newfoundland is primarily white English or Irish, and –

—Have you got numbers for Labrador?

—I – I'd need to double-check the census figures, but Labrador has considerably more of an aboriginal population –

—Mr. Philpott, when compared against the Wolf Broadcasting standards, VOIC has some serious catching up to do. Let's start with the obvious. Women.

—We employ several women here at the main VOIC studio, and –

—Every one of them in a secretarial or receptionist role.

—That's not true. Our Continuity Department –

—Oh yes, the token female manager, except she's only a supervisor. The women here must be very good at doing the limbo.

—I beg your pardon?

—The glass ceiling is so low. Tell me about the Continuity Department. You have women writing ad copy?

—Well, no, not writing it per se. We have commercial script packages shipped to us, and we pick out a script and insert the client's name –

—So the women in the continuity department are glorified typists.

Ben frowned. *Where have I heard that before?*

—Mr. Philpott, I am very concerned about the numbers I've encountered here today. I know perfectly well that Newfoundland and Labrador is a sovereign nation and therefore not subject to Canadian equity legislation. But Wolf Broadcasting is. So in a way, while this country is not subject to Canadian laws, VOIC is. Do I make myself clear?

Come near at your peril, Canadian wolf. —Quite clear.

Dr. Masterson shut her notebook computer. French-tipped nails, blonde hair kept in a bob, light makeup – Ben could hear Ralph Abbott's assessment of her already: *Nothing a proper lay wouldn't cure.*

Then Dr. Masterson uttered the words Ben had been dreading. —Why don't you walk me through the building?

Ben started with the portraits lining the hallway to the board room.

—This is Robert Jackman Wright, who, with Richard Fahey, started VOIC Radio in 1936. Mr. Fahey is still alive, incidentally. People from his neck of the woods tend to live a long time. Might be something in the water. The first studio was on Chapel Street, downtown St. John's, until we moved to what was Outer Mongolia at the time, here on Kenmount Road.

—I wonder how a Mongolian would feel, hearing that.

Ben took another in a series of deep breaths. —This is Thomas Wright, Robert Wright's son. He took the helm of VOIC in 1954, after his father died in a plane crash.

Dr. Masterson frowned. —I remember hearing stories about that.

—Up in his Tiger Moth, searching for a lost child. These two young fellows here are Thomas Wright's sons, Matthew and Lewis. They've gone on to help their father in his offshore interests, though they certainly welcomed the Canadian Wolf acquisition.

—Just Wolf.

—Slip of the tongue.

Ben winced again. God knew how many different ways that phrase could be misconstrued.

Dr. Masterson did not disappoint. —Wolf Broadcasting does a workshop with all the male employees called 'Clichés: Hidden Damage.'

—Just the men?

—Just the men. It allows us to open their eyes to the implicit and degrading sexism in words and phrases like *cockpit, bushwhacked* and *rule of thumb*.

—Hoary old clichés, I agree. And here we are at what we like to call the Sales Pit. And we've just made five new hires I don't think you have in your report – all young women, doing much better in the aptitude tests than the men we interviewed, one with a psychology degree, another with a business degree, and –

—All gorgeous, too. But I'm sure that had nothing to do with their being hired.

—Nothing at all.

—Who hired them?

Ben started a novena to Saint Jude. —Ralph Abbott, our sales manager.

—And when can I meet him?

Fuck it. —Right now. Corner office, this way. Ah, Ralph must be just down the hall. I'm sure he'll be back shortly. Have a seat.

Dr. Masterson studied the walls, at the many photos of a tall man who looked like a cross between Elvis Presley, Sylvester Stallone and Boris Karloff posing at various VOIC events. A cell phone, a land line, and a computer had been placed at neat intervals on his otherwise empty desk. In the next office, a young and exceedingly attractive woman wrote out sales contracts from a salesman's hasty notes. Beside her: a kettle, a canister of tea bags, and a twenty-line phone, which at that moment rang. So did Ralph's.

Ben gestured to the woman in the next office, now answering Ralph's line while several more lit up and reflected in her glasses. —Not to worry. Bonnie Joy will answer it. We don't have voicemail here. Every single phone call is answered by a – by a live voice.

Dr. Masterson now glanced at one of three wastebaskets collecting drips of dirty water. She gazed up at the stained ceiling tiles. —I heard you had some leaks this winter.

—The entire roof cracked, ours and nearly every roof more than thirty years old in St. John's. Sounded like a plane crashing. Lots of water damage to carpet and walls too.

A drop of cold and dirty water slithered down the neck of young producer Stephen Driscoll as he passed by the hall. —Christ in the garden, now I'm going to die of pneumonia.

Stephen stuck his head in Bonnie's office. —Bon-bon, my baby, can I have one of those tea bags, Bon-Bonnie the Bag Lady?

Dr. Masterson raised a waxed eyebrow.

Ben tried to smile. —Friendly banter. Consensual. I mean, it's done by mutual consent. Stephen comes there several times a day. I mean – ah, here comes Ralph.

But Ralph Abbott did not hear Ben Philpott at that moment, for Bonnie paged three different salespeople to held calls, and Ralph Abbott wanted a cup of tea. Passing before his assistant's open door, he tilted back his head and mimed drinking tea from an invisible cup. Dr. Masterson went pale, then red, as Bonnie threw down the telephone receiver as though it were suddenly corrosive, jumped back from the desk so hard as to knock papers to the floor, and immediately flicked on the kettle and retrieved a VOIC mug and a teabag.

Meanwhile, Ralph Abbott stopped in his door and did a grotesque double-take at Dr. Masterson. —Now, which part of heaven did you fall from, my darling?

Ben interjected quickly. —Of course, terms of endearment have different shades of meaning in Newfoundland English.

Dr. Masterson introduced herself and offered her hand for Ralph to shake. Ralph kissed it. —My, such soft hands for a woman your age. How do you do it, my dear?

Ben discarded the novena to Saint Jude and moved on to his own obituary.

—Dr. Masterson, perhaps you'd like to see the newsroom.

But Bonnie, bearing fresh tea, blocked their exit. —Here you are, Mr. Abbott.

Ralph studied the tea a moment and chuckled. —Bonnie, my darling, is that the right colour for my tea?

Bonnie glanced at it and gasped. —I took the teabag out too early. Oh, I'm sorry, Mr Abbott. I'll make you a fresh cup straight away.

Ralph basked in his own munificence. —Just pour the water over the tea. I'll steep it myself.

—Oh, that'd be great, Mr. Abbott. I'm really busy, and I can't get anyone in Toronto to e-mail us that audio we need for the Pfizer buy.

Smiling at the now slack-jawed Dr. Masterson, Bonnie sighted Stephen Driscoll again and ran out to the corridor. —Stephen. Did that spot come in yet?

Ralph chuckled again. —I'll never get that tea now. Remember, Ben, when these round bags first came out, and we asked, *Are these for light days?* Miss Masterson, would you like a cup of tea?

—No.

Ralph raised his eyebrows, clearly aghast at this woman's rude behaviour. —If you're here about the sales position, all positions are filled.

—Nothing left under your desk?

Ralph, normally slow at innuendo, caught her meaning immediately and flushed deep red.

Bonnie's voice came to them as she returned to her office, still talking to Stephen.

—Call me the second it comes.

—I never gave you seconds, Bon-bon.

Ben wondered if he could get a discount on his headstone from longtime VOIC client Coffin's Marble Works.

Dr. Masterson took a deep breath. —Mr. Philpott, you mentioned the newsroom?

Ralph waved a hand. —Oh, the newsroom's not hiring. They just got their token Eskimo up in Goose Bay.

Ben pursed his lips and instead imagined Ralph Abbott's obituary: *Passed away suddenly of strangulation at the hands of colleague Ben Philpott ...* —Yes, the award-winning VOIC Newsroom. This way. Mind the wastebaskets. We had a fire in that heater in January. We were just about to get the wall painted when the roof cracked. Stand by.

Ben glanced over his arc of sight: VOIC-FM, 570 VOIC, Newsbooth 1 and 730 VOTC, on-air lights glowing at the same sudden moment as all stations broke for the same newscast. It still made him smile.

—I'll just take you quickly through here. They're in their 3p cast. Here on the wall we have some of the many awards we've won in the last few years, including several Murrows –

—I didn't think Newfoundland was eligible.

—The point is journalistic integrity, not your spot on the map. This is Kyle George, our news director. Kyle, I'd like you to meet Dr. Dorinda Masterson, who's here on behalf of Wolf Broadcasting.

Kyle, his back to them, held up his left hand while his right continued typing, saying the text out loud. —*... and the US Coast Guard offered to extend its patrol of the Grand Banks in exchange for* – God damn it, everybody wants something from us. Sorry to keep you waiting – sorry, I didn't catch your name. No, don't sit there. That chair is broken. Watch out for the bucket. You'd think a thirty litre paper recycling bin would be full of paper, not dirty water.

Dr. Masterson gazed up at this ceiling. The remaining tile, gone brown, flaked. Water trickled.

Kyle grinned. —It's water, water everywhere, but not a drop to drink round here, isn't it, Potts?

Ben corrected him without thinking. —*Nor any drop to drink.* We are, of course, getting the ceiling repaired. We've come through an exceptionally hard winter. Kyle, would you like to tell Dr. Masterson about the newsroom?

Kyle delivered his favourite speech as though giving a forecast for good weather. —Despite the old ceilings, 1960s wood and terrazzo floor, this newsroom is an information nerve centre. We're staffed 24/7, we monitor the American, Canadian and British media, and we've been fully computerized since 1982. We pride ourselves in delivering the news quickly and accurately, and without sensation. I'm a member of the RTNDA, and I can tell you that many Canadian radio stations look to us to see how it's done. I'm sure that's the reasoning behind the Wolf acquisition. You're looking for a leading light.

Water trickled.

Ben dredged up bonhomie. —Shall we visit the rest of the building? Down the hall is VOIC-FM, reaching from St. John's to Gander. 570 VOIC, the mothership, reaches the Avalon Peninsula, of course, and other areas on cable TV. Here we have 730 VOTC, broadcasting to Trinity-Conception. Over here we have our two production studios – there's Stephen Driscoll, you saw him earlier – and this is 630 VOCL, broadcasting into Clarenville and Bonavsita. And of course we have a further outside AM network, with bricks-and-mortar stations in Burin and Corner Brook.

—What about Labrador?

—Serviced by cable and local transmitters, but their signal originates in Corner Brook.

—Very impressive, Mr. Philpott.

—Please, call me Ben.

—I'm Dorinda.

—Down here, Dorinda, is the Continuity Department – mind the buckets – must apologize for the smell. First the sewer backed up, and we got the carpets thoroughly cleaned of course, but then the roof started to leak, and –

Dorinda pointed, too late. —Tile over that desk –

The cyst of foam and dirty water burst, tile exploding into many small pieces, brown water drenching onto a desk, computer, telephone and Nichole Wright.

Dead silence.

Laughter.

Her back to the window, and the general manager and guest, Nichole let loose a knotted string of expletives tied end to end like Grampa Walcott's Pigeon Inlet squid.

Ben made a mental note to speak to her about decorum, once again. —That's Nichole Wright. She studied English. At a Canadian university.

The rest of the tour, apart from stepping round at least thirty wastebaskets seconded to leak-catching, remained uneventful. Ben feared his deodorant might have given out, but at least the stink of the carpet would mask him. This meeting with Dorinda Masterson had eaten up most of the afternoon, and he still had to give a St. John's Regatta Day briefing. Finally, Dorinda asked if she could use the board room to make some notes; Ben acquiesced with enthusiasm. As Dorinda walked away from Ben's office, Dan McGrew walked towards it, grinning despite emaciation, despite having an estimated eight months to live. Regatta Day was his favourite day of the year, a radio-man's Christmas morning, he liked to say. Ben just hoped he wouldn't say it right at that moment. Or maybe God would smile on Ben Philpott and cause Dorinda Masterson to say clichés were a cancer on the language, and then Ben could introduce Dan: *And here's our chief engineer, Dan McGrew, who just happens to be dying of cancer of the oesophagus, metastasised to liver and pancreas. Dan, this is Dr. Dorinda Masterson, who just happens to be a royal pain the arse.*

As Dan passed through Ben's doorway, frail beneath a baggy shirt and ghastly pale beneath his jaundice, and as Dorinda turned back around to ask Ben one more thing, the intercom chimed.

Stephen Driscoll had forgotten about the guest in the building. —Bon-bonnie, my baby, my bon-bon, your Viagra is in. Or up. What's that song you sing, to the *Bonanza* theme? Get it up, get it in, get it out, don't mess my hair-dooooo.

Stephen clicked off. Laughter erupted throughout the building.

Ben turned purple and moaned.

Dorinda had opened her mouth quite decisively, barrage at the ready, but Dan McGrew, stabbed with pain, collapsed onto Ben's floor. Dorinda and Ben knelt at Dan's side. Others passing through the corridor now stopped to stare through Ben's huge office windows. In his production studio around the corner, ignorant of all this, Stephen Driscoll pinged open the intercom once more.

—Bon-bon, come get the Viagra spot. I can't keep this up forever.

Dan, eyes suddenly dull, whimpered. —Oh. This wasn't supposed to happen.

84. THE SMALL ONE
in which Ange O'Dea tells Neal a story.

August 12, 1984

Delicate from the start, Neal, no question you were small, and that worried me. Hardly cried, and that worried me all the more, because 'tis all for lungs in youngsters.

'Twas a year before your mother let me touch her again. Just her shoulders. Don't know how long I held her shoulders.

None of you knew about him.

Your older brother – I know, you always acted as the oldest, looking out for the others, and proper thing – but your older brother … hard, b'y… born two months early. Your mother sicking up the entire time. Kept tea down. She'd long for tea in the Depression, when we couldn't get it, and I knew she was thinking of how much she drank on your brother.

Now, what to be doing when her pains took her I didn't know, so I go trotting off to Annie Legge, whose grandmother taught her all about borning. Annie'd been helping her grandmother one way or another since she was seven, but ours was due to be her first. So I didn't know the half of it, but I was verging on certain that a baby due in November arriving in August … well, no good could come of this.

I was twenty-five when I married your mother. Getting old. Said I'd been waiting for her.

And I'd been waiting for him. I was never one for this preferring of the boys over the girls, but when I saw that child was a boy, Neal, he was suddenly real, the truth of him far more now that a wiggly bump. He weighed under four pounds. Bony, all sharp, and his skin like some chart of rivers. Holding him – we took turns holding him, all wrapped up – keep him warm was all we could do, Annie said. Annie and your mother trying to get the milk in, only a few drops. All he could take. Even then we had to pop his mouth open.

Neal, that child did not cry once. Used to stop breathing, go counts of ten, twelve, fifteen. Little shoulders twitched then, and I'd pick him up, practically lost him in my hand, loosen them blankets, and his little arms jerked straight out, his body wanting the air.

I begged him open his eyes a moment. Just so's I could see the colour. Just so's I could let him know I was there, and he could let me know he was there. Christ, rocking in that kitchen chair, near broke me back, three days on shore, Annie scandalized but keeping quiet, and I'd touch his little face, brush my fingers over his heart, take down the blankets just enough to see that soft angel-down on his shoulders, like a duckling, just please, I prayed, please let him open his eyes.

Blue. Dark.

Kept watch, is all.

B'y, his suck was weak. 'Twas no good. And his breathing, like his little lungs kept sticking together, and cradling him in my hands I was helpless as he was. But he'd seen me, opened his eyes and seen me there, and I had to be content.

The priest only arrived every few weeks. No one expected the baby in August. Child buried ten days, and Father comes. So I tell him the story, because your mother's in no condition, tell him I baptized him as much as I could. Little holy water around. Your mother liked blessing the house with it at night, flicking drops hither and yon. Not one Catholic house burnt down in Riordan's Back, she'd always point out, but the Protestants in Port au Mal lost three in thirty years.

He died sometime while I held him. Your mother was feverish, Annie trying to keep her covered up in bed, me by the stove, heat going mad, and never mind Annie, I had my shirt off. Eventually there I fell asleep. Never meant to. Little one held to my chest. Arms ached for days. Just ... he just stopped breathing, Neal. And I missed the moment. Finally opened the door, got air in the house, and the breeze stirred the down on his shoulders, and your mother gasping in fresh air like she was drinking water, and I went outside first time in three days, wondering at the sun and how it dared shine like that when my little boy was dead.

1927.

Six pounds and bare shoulders like the rest of us when you came along in '29.

Never believed in limbo.

Couldn't.

Tuck that round you, now. No point getting a chill.

85. SILVERN VOICES 3
in which Ange O'Dea tucks Neal into bed.

September 14, 1984

Ange O'Dea couldn't make sense of 1984 and didn't want to. The entire year one frantic tangle of bad news, and the communities that had them kept testing air raid sirens. Nowadays the youngsters practiced herding into the school gym and there kneeling down with their arms over their heads when the sirens wailed, yes, a true advance over the duck-and-cover under individual desks. Earlier in the spring Neal had explained mushroom clouds, détente, Evil Empire and a Korean jet. Despite sitting round the woodstove wearing flannel shirts and sweaters and smelling of spruce and fir, neither man could get warm that night. They'd gone walking in the woods, not too far, in to the stunted clearing where *Newsbird* had crashed. New trees grew, and the damaged ones had continued. A few branches still bore faint smudges of yellow paint. Ange's old trail marks could still be read; Neal's hands got sticky with sap. A few days later, Neal got his diagnosis. Ange prayed to get his nightmare back, the one where Neal slowly drowned, because so long as Ange dreamt that, it couldn't really be happening.

The suffocating truth progressed rapidly, and by June Neal had to give up hosting *Free Line*, throwing the audience into a spin of confusion and concern: who would listen to them now? Two replacement announcers had failed with the show, and now the scared and aggressive audience chewed up a third. Newfoundland and Portugal were locked in another diplomatic snarl, and Portuguese boats brazenly fished within the fifty miles, and what are we gonna do about that, now? The American navy sent a destroyer on exercises after three huge Russian factory freezer trawlers made themselves at home around mile forty-eight, but the Americans did not engage or even contact the Russians. Nukes over fish? Never mind nukes – the fishery itself scared the VOIC audience, scared and depressed most everyone in Newfoundland and Labrador. After nearly five hundred years, to still be dependent on one resource, a resource rapidly scooped up by gill and trawl nets, by foreigners, no question, but also by Newfoundlanders and Labradorians themselves: ugly, stinking trawlers, porting in their mortgaged excess a barren future. *Collapse of the fishery? Sure that's ages away, if it happens at all*, one listener argued. *I s'pose you're against the seal hunt, too? Fishery's been here since before John Cabot, and it'll be there for my grandchildren and their grandchildren. It has to be.*

Ange O'Dea turned off the radio. He glanced out his window to the harbour, sighed, and then busked his upper arms. Neal and John had installed proper insulation years ago. They'd installed central heating, too, baseboards and thermostats, but Ange preferred the woodstove. Now eighty-three, he'd reluctantly – reluctantly, mind – given up cutting his own wood, two years before, and now he accepted the blunt ministrations of grey-haired younger men.

Ange walked to his refrigerator, well-stocked with leftovers from community women, all of them forgetting Ange had foraged nicely after his first and second wives had died and still baked his own bread. A carton of milk – milk, of all things – stood near the edge of the shelf. Ange poured a glass, watching the milk shimmer. Liz had gotten him drinking milk when she'd visited with the grandchildren, arguing and threatening to get them to drink theirs, the kids talking back in a strange accent.

Ange glanced at the table, where, many mornings in the 1930s, he'd split the heel of bread between Neal and John and gone the day with one carrot in his pocket. Not a cent nor a scrap of credit, and the inshore fishery off Port au Mal and Riordan's Back long gone ...

Gravel crunched outside, and a car stopped. Katie Morrigan – Ange just stopped short of calling her Katie O'Keefe, when she'd been married twenty-odd years – did not barmp her horn but instead came to the back kitchen door and poked her head in. —You all ready there, Mr. O'Dea?

Neal O'Dea dreamt of breathing underwater. This dream had visited him many times since he was ten or so, when his father told him the story of Robert Wright finding Don Mallory. In this dream, the cold water warmed quickly, better than sheets and heavy blankets on a winter night. Squid shoved themselves along, whales fluked currents, sun lit the water even when fog hovered on top, and Neal could breathe, as surely as if he had gills. The dream always ended on a note of joy, with Neal staring about at seaweed, squid, sculpins, jellyfish and a most beautiful species of underwater rose, then taking his first deep breath and confirming he could live.

The deep breath set him coughing, and as he struggled to sit up, he opened his eyes and took in his room and the weather outside. Yet still he dreamed, this time of sighting Blue John, an especially large deposit, crystalline trapped within a bit of rock gone frothy and pus-white with the struggle, and Neal knew then that the pine choking Ariel had gone frothy, too. Nausea, not a wave but a steady tide, tugged at him, and he fell, fell at least a mile – maybe half an inch – back onto his upraised bed, and with this impact against the fire rocks off Port au Mal came memory ... pain almost amusing, like the pain of walking into a doorjamb, pain wretched enough to make him wish he was closer to death than this – venial or mortal? His voice pleading for help? *It's morphine, Mr. O'Dea. There's no need to be in pain like this. We want to get you comfortable. My God, that little dose is not going to be enough for him as far along as that.*

—You ever been up on Signal Hill, Mr. O'Dea?

Ange tore himself from a nap. —Where?

Katie pointed eastward as they passed the road to Topsail Beach, maybe twenty minutes now from St. John's. —Signal Hill, where Marconi and all that happened. They got this nice plaque now, right on the spot, the very spot, where he heard the signal.

—Neal loves talking about that. The letter *S* in Morse code, three dots.

—I tell you, Mr. O'Dea, I was up there one day last winter, probably gone into town to do my Christmas shopping, a Monday morning, I believe, round about lunch time, and I went up there and sat by the plaque and just stared out for a while, thinking about all the big stuff, 'til I got too cold.

Ange said nothing.

Katie took a looping on-ramp to get on Kenmount Road, and though Ange felt it rude to stare, he did gaze at the VOIC building as they passed ... gazed at the flat and still futuristic roof, the walls of cut maroon slate and orange, green and black square tiles arranged within many white ones, to some order? Meaning?

Inside VOIC, amongst the many bursts of noise, Thomas Wright leant forward on his huge and shiny desk, telling off Dan McGrew while Ben Philpott held his peace.

—Dan, when I pass your office, all I see is a mess of manuals and mail and dirty old ashtrays.

Thomas leaned back, gesturing to his own desk.

—See this, Dan? Neat and tidy. A cluttered desk is the sign of a cluttered mind.

—And an empty desk, sir?

But Ben's sudden coughing fit muted Dan's question. Thomas Wright got genuinely concerned; it disconcerted even him when men turned purple in his office.

—Ben, Ben, are you all right?

Neal felt the oxygen mask coming over his face, smelled the stink of it, the distant brimstone, and grunted gratitude.

On the hospital parking lot, Katie asked Ange if he knew where to go.

Annoyed, Ange clicked his tongue. —Palliative care, second floor. One flight of stairs up, and I turn left, and Neal's room is the second last from the end on the left.

—So I'll just come up and get you when I'm finished running messages? Oh, hang on. Here, I tried fitting this in a Soper's bag, but it's too big. Tell Neal my mother just finished it. It's an afghan. For his legs. You get cold in the hospital.

Ange had to swallow hard before he could speak. —Thanks, girl.

Closing the car door harder than necessary, he turned to go. Katie kept an eye to him, making certain he ducked into the proper stairwell.

Neal slept.

Ange just kept himself from touching Neal's oxygen mask – gelatinous look to it, a dull sheen like a beached jellyfish. Ange could think of nothing more repellent than a jellyfish over a man's nose and mouth, and he shut his eyes. Then he remembered the afghan.

A nurse entered the room —Good morning, Mr. O'Dea. Some hard.

Ange lay the afghan over Neal, admiring the many colours. —He's my oldest. He in much pain there today?

—I got his morphine dose increased. No need to be in that kind of pain. Good to be out of pain, hey, b'y?

—It's good.

Ange tried to dredge up comparisons for Neal's breathing. Numerous colds, two pneumonias: no. The sound of squamous cell carcinoma in a remaining lung, now what did that sound like? Water sucked down a pinhole of a drain? Retreat of a tidal bore? Ah. TB. Consumption, moist racket of lung fraying out – Ange saw Neal's eyes open.

—Neal, you there?

Neal nodded. Then he slept again.

Ange knew the routine now, knew his own limitations, and after another forty minutes of sitting in the hard plastic visitor's chair, he got up and took the stairs, with some difficulty, down to the cafeteria. Elevators frightened Ange, but he did not admit it. VOIC played in the cafeteria, ship's bell ringing for the noon newscast.

The VOIC 12 o'clock news is a presentation of Soper's Supermarkets. Soper's Supermarkets, with locations in St. John's, Harbour Grace, Marystown, Buchans, Gander and Corner Brook. If it's on your grocery list, you'll find it at Soper's.

Doctors and nurses, patients and visitors, swarmed to the various counters, lined up noisily to order lunch. Chatter and money, IV poles and slippers, radio: the noise pressed on Ange as he blew on his tea, as he wished he'd remembered the really nice lunch he'd packed and left sitting on his counter top, right next to the refrigerator, so he wouldn't forget it.

At the table next to him, two young doctors discussed radon daughters. —Oh, man, the whole St. Lawrence thing, it's sad, all these guys coming in with lung cancer. Radon gas. They had no idea how much there was. We've got a fluorspar squamous up there in Palliative, the guy from VOIC.

—What the hell do you mine fluorspar for?

The doctor finished his can of cold Coke. —Freon. You ready?

Ange stood in the gift shop for a while, hands in his pockets, studying the front covers of magazines. When he returned to Palliative, Neal had woken up. He waved and smiled at Ange, waiting until his father got next to his bed before asking him, on a scarce long breath, where the afghan had come from.

—Sadie O'Keefe. Katie Morrigan's mother.

—God love – her.

—Don't go talking, now, Neal, save your breath.

—Man's – hello – own father.

Ange noticed that the nurses hadn't shaved Neal that morning – Neal's stubble grey? Then the patients' lunch trays came, dismaying Ange: bright orange vegetable soup with perfect tiny cubes of carrot.

—Tinned soup? What in the name of God do they give you to eat in here? Small wonder you're dying.

Neal got blue lips laughing at this.

—Settle down there now. You strong enough to spoon that up this afternoon?

Ange knew Neal wasn't, but the question had to be asked. He waited for Neal's headshake. —Here. Let me.

—No – nurse – minute.

—B'y, both you and that soup will be stone cold before the nurse gets in here. You got to eat your soup while it's hot. Otherwise it does you no good.

—No – feed – can't.

—I can, and I will.

—Dad – slow.

—I'll go slow. Take our time.

A spoonful of soup, a few breaths from the mask, a spoonful of soup, cold long before it would be gone, and after maybe a third of it, Neal fell back asleep.

Ange turned on the little television, watched a cop show, a game show, a soap opera.

Neal's teeth chattered long before he woke up. Ange tugged the afghan closer to Neal's chest, then rummaged in the linen closet for more blankets, unaware that Neal could not bear to feel weight on his chest. Then he found the old blue jersey Jeannie Hicks had knit in 1965, and he placed that over Neal's feet.

Around four, Katie poked her head in the door. —All set?

Ange massaged his stiff knees. —Not long now. I hope.

Katie swallowed. She hated bringing Mr. O'Dea to Palliative Care, hated picking him up. She'd not known Neal at all growing up, though she had raised hell with Liz a few times. She hated everything about this, and she startled Ange by hugging him.

Ange got stern. —No need to be getting on like that. He's not dead yet.

Later, Neal spoke in the dark. —Maybe – soup – strong. Sit up?

Uncertain, the young nurse supported Neal to the chair. He often breathed better there, and it would give her a chance to change his sheets. Neal sat down, clutching Sadie O'Keefe's afghan to his thin legs. After five, six, seven breaths, he hissed another word. —Sweater?

Ange spoke in the dark. —I don't get in here enough.

Katie had dropped him at the Basilica in Harbour Grace, and she waited outside, would wait for hours if Mr. O'Dea asked her. Ange lit candles, and suddenly his own dead – three wives, first son, mother, even Robert Wright – felt closer and more real than Katie Morrigan. Then he smelled pine sap and felt Neal's hand on his shoulder. Shaking his head, scowling, Ange walked out of the church and back to Katie's car. She drove him home, but Ange did not go inside his house, instead walking along the beach a while, sitting off some distance from teenagers who'd lit a fire, until young Chris Jackman from Port au Mal waved him over and offered him a beer, and the cursing stopped. Ange drank, listening to Chris's plans: high school, law school, loads of money, all in easy reach somehow.

Ange's telephone was ringing when he got back to the house – probably Liz checking up on Neal, but then she could call the hospital herself. No. Ange knew before he said hello.

—Mr. O'Dea? This is Nurse Fowlow at the General. I'm sorry. Your son has died.

—Thank you, I'll be in tomorrow.

Ange sat in near the cold woodstove alone, breathing in the scents of hardened spruce and fir sap.

86. PETTY PACE
in which aggressive pilgrims colonize Claire Furey.

March 31, 2005

Yellow sheets.

Because the bile duct was a small portal, the cancer loved its new home. Brilliant yellow tides might carry impatient adolescents further on, while cells left behind sang an explorer's hymn to both the voyagers and to themselves, to their commitment to settle and grow. Such room, such space: a hive-mind artistry, an instinct or a plan, no one knew which – this cancer grew in sheets. Not fungal lumps, holey like a toxic mushroom; not tendrils, as some invasion stories went, though the explorers might pray to seed tendrils. The enormous and perhaps impossible voyage to the brain, blind immigration from the bile duct, so crowded now that the sheets fluttered, independent cells cracking loose as ever. Even the liver, no shame there. Up, up, undeniable attraction, not so much moths to light as individuals to mythologies inherited and new: others like us beyond currents of lymph and blood, beyond the organ called skin. Another body near, its orbit like a comet or a moon, influential but disordered in the brain. Mystery shrugged off for mission: over-reaching, perhaps, for ragged cholangiocarcinoma cells, but how else might they know unless they risked failure? Terra incognita. Spheres of influence, stern governorship: here. I claim this land in the name of –

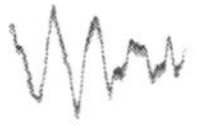

87. SLEEP ARCHITECTURE 3
in which three different people lay down to sleep.

March 31, 2005

God, B'y, will you hurry up and take me?

Rain fell.

So did Ange.

April 2, 2005

Tired as if she'd bled for a week, Jane Wright woke up on the clean white sheets of her bed in the Estuary Home. Nearly fifty years before, she'd welcomed menopause and release from her draining courses. Dr. Cart had diagnosed fibroids as the cause of her heavy bleeding. Jane had smiled. Harmless growths then, not disuse; another doctor had informed her that not bearing children would damage her womb, block her lymphatic system, set her up for breast cancer. She'd called him a misogynist, then gamely encouraged him, as she did her students, to look up the word in the dictionary if he did not know the meaning. Breast cancer in 1973, one breast, her uterus and ovaries departing with it. Radiation then, descents into the basement of the old Grace Hospital where it seemed someone had overcooked a roast of beef. Burnt flesh. Jane had learned. And Jane had lived.

Down the hall, delirious Leon Furey coughed his weak cough and called for someone named Gabriel. In February, influenza A had ripped through Estuary, prompting a ban on visitors. The nurses and staff wore masks, and Jane had never felt so much a burden. Her lungs filled, one lung collapsed, and the nights sprawled into a meaningless parody of themselves. When she thought she'd slept hours, the clock said only ten minutes had passed. When she shut her eyes for a moment, the sun rose. The tedious drip of the IV marked the nights, and the nurses fussed over the skin on Jane's hands, normally delicate and soft, now baggy with dehydration.

And Leon called. —Gabriel, come back.

Yet by the end of March, Jane could walk outside again. She walked slowly, her stride diminished. When her grand-nephew Matt came to visit on April 1st, he walked with her off the Estuary grounds, this ten-minute stroll taking an hour. Jane said little, working not to pant. Then, not wanting to surrender his great-aunt just yet, Matt offered to take her for a drive, maybe downtown? They'd parked in front of the harbour, Matt reading out the names of ships in port, three tourism schooners and a container ship: *Komatik*, *Lady Diana, Lucy* and the Canadian *Bagger.*

—Did you ever see pictures of the coastal boats, Matthew? The medical boats?

—Didn't they used to come in with X-ray machines?

—Everybody had to line up and go down into the boat and have a chest X-ray. Sometimes they took you away on the spot; sometimes you had to wait until the next coastal boat came and got you.

—TB, wasn't it?

—Ellen was terrified, and our father acted as though his family should be exempt. He even threatened the doctor. William finally got hard sense through Father's head, asking if he wanted the whole bay infected. Ellen had to go. Father didn't speak to William for three weeks. Ellen didn't get out of the San for twelve years.

—You want to get out here for a walk?

—No, the wind's too cold. Maybe further up by Rawlins Cross. There's been a flap about the mural that young Furey woman started last fall, and I want to look at it. Some twit of an editor wants her to pay back her grant because he thinks the mural isn't good enough.

Matt grinned. —Calling back his investment, is he?

—It's not his money. There it is. Obviously the mural is not finished yet. I might have known. An editor who permits sentence fragments, dangling modifiers and homonyms in his newspaper is in no place to judge.

Hmphing some more, Jane caught her reflection in the passenger side mirror. Dark hairs on her upper lip, thick black brows, white hair styled in the apparently mandatory short curls of an old lady. She'd ignored her hairstyle for years, considering it a waste of her time and intellect. But at that moment she wondered when she'd gotten so old. *A hundred and two. I feel every moment of it today.*

—Stop at a drug store, please, Matthew. I need to pick up a few things. And stop looking at me as though I am a tedious old fool. This will be you, some day. Perhaps, with medical advances, you'll live to be a hundred and ten.

Jane bought tweezers, depilatory cream, cotton swabs and hand lotion. At night, as her roommate slept, she plucked her brows, ripping out hairs in clutches, tears on her cheeks. Her eyes watered further at the sulphurous Nair.

A nurse knocked on the bathroom door. —Mrs. Wright, do you need a sleeping pill?

Jane had given up explaining it was 'Miss.' Just as all teachers had been 'Miss,' even long after it was acceptable for married women to keep their jobs, so all women over sixty were 'Mrs.' She opened the door. —No, dear, I'm fine.

—You look different. Surprised. Wide awake. You expecting someone?

Jane smiled. —Leave me some secrets.

—I'm just glad you're feeling better.

Jane sat on her bed. The flu should have killed her. Just as the breast cancer should have killed her. Thomas pre-arranged her funeral back in

1973. Jane drew the curtain round her bed, knowing the nurse would draw it back again once she'd gone to sleep. The smoothness of her upper lip sparked a memory of the stubbled roughness of Albert Furneaux's jaw ... the muscles of his arms hard and defined beneath his shirt, even the burns in his face ... Jane kissed those, softly as she could, and then she kissed him hard, and Albert let her, and she begged for sweet heat and friction, and tension released itself in throbs. Later she dreamt of Albert, his face obscured by sunlight, asking to take her arm so they might walk out together.

At shift change, the nurses discovered Miss Wright had died in her sleep.

November 17, 2003

Muskeg trapped the snowmobile, but Dan must reach the VOIC tower, the older one on Groves Road, except in Dan's dream this tower morphed into the big one up on Kenmount Hill, or one of the two towers in Clarenville, or one of VONB's towers on the Southside Hills, always in winter. Complicating his perceptions: steam and snow on his glasses, wind on his cheeks, salt water's stench up his nose, which, even cold, reminded Dan of the smell of blood. And muskeg. He must climb the tower. Bright orange survival suit, snowmobile vanished, snow over his hips – he'd never climb the tower at this rate. VOIC off the air now over an hour, Thomas Wright no doubt banging his desk with his fist: *Get Dan. Get Dan.* Then the weather changed. As the nurse hung a fresh bag of fluids on Dan's IV pole, freezing rain hit – slap cut bite, any cheek he turned – and the tower glistened, red and white beneath crusted ice, a starved lighthouse, and even as he climbed the tower in the sleet, he knew full well the danger, the folly, but Dan had promised to make the repair, and more to the point, he needed to reach Lucy Upshall. Manipulate the sky wave, reach Lucy in England, but what would he say? *Truly, Lucy, you are the only girl I ever loved.* Ridiculous, but true. Behind the freezing rain, dusk settled. The signal weakened.

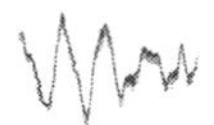

88. CQ 2
in which a signal bounces back to Earth, specifically, into Ben Philpott's office.

April 4, 2005

—Thank you for seeing me, Mr. Philpott.

Ben took three piles of urgent paperwork from his desk and placed them on his credenza. His e-mail chimed twice with incoming messages, and both telephones lines glowed with waiting voice-mail. *Crazy old bat. Don't know what you're doing, waiting in the lobby half the day. Some of us work for a living.* —Not at all.

The Englishwoman glanced round Ben's office, at the bronze sculpture of a helmsman, at the old poster from the 1930s, framed now: *Communication saves lives,* at the small figurine of Winston Churchill sitting astride a bulldog, at the map of the world. Delicate bones had shattered two years before when she slipped and fell on her hip; the hip replacement gave her a slightly skewed walk, like that of a sailor disguising his stride. She wore a light pink blouse, pink lipstick, a grey cardigan, navy blue pants and big plastic glasses, also pink. Outside Ben's many-windowed fishbowl of an office, people walked quickly about, carrying papers, arguing, joking: announcers, writers, salespeople, news reporters, producers; people dressed in tailored suits, flowing skirts and sandals, high boots and short skirts, jeans and sneakers.

—A busy place, Mr. Philpott.

—The VOIC Radio Service is the leading light of communications in this country. And we're part of Wolf Broadcasting these days, but we show the Canadians how it's done.

—I can pick you up in Wales.

Ben blinked. He'd been reading Melville at nights, and he briefly saw Moby Dick's spout as AM transmission, his hump as spark. —I'm sorry, I didn't catch your name just then.

—Mrs. Wicks. I can pick up VOIC online, too. I'd thought the web would be merely a motorway littered with pornography, or a corrupt Library of Alexandria. But I can listen. Digital, yes, but AM is exciting. The fluid signal. I – I can't really explain it. I'm sorry. You must be wondering why I've come. I visited Iceland not long ago, where the water tastes so clean. When you run the tap, it smells of sulphur, but the water, the water – icebergs must be the redemptions of hell. It's been a long flight, please, bear with me, to explain this. In my hotel room one night, in Iceland, I couldn't sleep, and the sky got so dark, and the air got so cold. No proper sunrise, you see, just a dull glow on the horizon. I turned on the wireless. And I caught the VOIC signal. I thought it was Irish radio first, but then I heard something different. In and out. Ebb and flow. But never lost. Not until that glow.

Ben nodded. —It happens all the time with AM broadcast. The waves hit the sky, and –

—A few months later, I was at Poldhu.

—Really? I've long meant to visit –

—The towers are long gone, but there is a little plaque. And rocks. And salt water.

—Mrs. Wicks, do you –

Her lips trembled; it might have been Parkinson's. —I had heard that an old friend of mine worked for VOIC Radio in Newfoundland.

Oh, God.

—A Canadian. I billeted in his town during the war. We were teenagers, and I was so far from home, and so was he, in a way. We fell in love, and we were going to get married. I allowed only Dan to see me cry. Then the war ended. And I went back to England, and my life, my life just happened to me. I tried writing to him again in the late 60s, but I got no answer. He's named for a Robert Service poem, you know.

—'Were you ever out in the Great Alone, when the moon was awful clear, And the icy mountains hemmed you in with a silence you almost could hear.'

—Yes, that's it. I heard not long ago from someone retired from the CBC, visiting Wales, that Dan McGrew went to Newfoundland and is the VOIC engineer. Mr. Philpott, I am so sorry for intruding on you like this today, but I have come a long way. Directory assistance had no telephone number for Dan. Please, can you call him here now?

—You came from England to see Dan McGrew?

Mrs. Lucy Upshall Wicks giggled. —Silly, yes. But life is so short. I've got some savings, oh, I've wasted so much, God, what's slipped away, I must – your eyes.

Ben had a hunch what the music meant. —Mrs. Wicks, I am so sorry, but –

Lucy did not need to be told. —When?

People glanced at Ben through the windows, hurriedly glanced away; Ben would not relish explaining the tears on his face. Damn it, he'd explain nothing. —November 2003.

—A year and a half ago?

—Cancer.

—Had he married?

—No.

Lucy clicked open her purse and pushed aside her lipstick and passport to retrieve tissues. —Oh. I see. While I was in Iceland.

Neither spoke for a long moment. Lucy studied the map, the breadth of the Atlantic. Ben studied the credenza, the telephone. His e-mail chimed.

—Mrs. Wicks, have you heard of the Duke of Duckworth? No? Dan's favourite pub. Let me take you there. I could use a drink today myself.

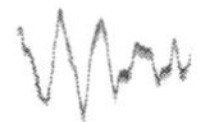

89. DIOGENES SYNDROME 3
in which William Wright considers light in dark places.

July 12, 1982

Not a shed. Common men settle for a shed. Storehouse, like a second bungalow, except the land behind slopes away to the shore of the pond. So. Basements. Divided. Big enough for boats. Yacht club rents the property each summer so wealthy adolescents might learn how to sail. All of them old enough to be put to work. Foul in the mouth, language the likes I haven't heard since I left politics. Dangerous parents. Ignore but never discard. Frayed ropes, lost screws, obsolete gears, all come in handy one day, just wait and see. Glossy magazines fallen between the gaps – old mattresses piled. Kitchen sinks. Windows grimier each year, summer sun painful, white glare. No one can see in, no matter how close they come squinting at the windows. Blind unless I open the doors. Boxes of mouldering schoolbooks, early 1900s. Very old family hygiene manual, seventh edition published 1898, *Light in Dark Places*. Thirty chapters, eight of them addressing masturbation in children. Memorized, chapter and verse, "Tell the Boys," "Taint of Self," "Save the Girls." Salesman I am now, salvage and gear. Helped an American movie crew once, got them parts for a whale. Never would have even spit on them had I known how the movie would show Newfoundlanders, just bearded bloody savages stamping and howling round a whale strung up by her flukes, savages slitting her open, cheering as her foetus slopped to the deck. Like whaling was ever tidy. Or fishing. Mother wore whalebone stays. Wonder who's got them? Never discard. I believed in my father. A good man, a proper man. End of things, readiness is all. Nichole visits me here. Perfect setting, a common man might think, grimy windows and burnt-out bulbs. No. Demons and masturbation. Some days she's afraid of me. Some days she clings. Almost like she wants it, my little moth. My other boathouse, across the water, where seventy years ago a horse sank through rotten ice, still harnessed to a sled full of cut wood, where lily pads grow. Still see the horse's bones, should you know where to look. Just wait. Surprise is cathartic. Readiness is all – as if she doesn't know.

90. GEOGRAPHICAL CURE 3
in which Ange O'Dea helps a woman stand up, despite familiar wreckage.

March 31, 2005

Because he remembered Captain Tobias Wright shouting at the stars, Ange O'Dea smiled gently when the woman huddled in Rupert Ginge's unlit outbuilding whimpered. Ange could almost smell the day Robert and William Wright tackled their raving father as he studied the woman's green eyes and heavy forehead. She didn't look like a thief. Ange couldn't tell at first if he saw any *thing*, let alone anyone, as dusk took the place. But there, broken scraps of yellow – Christ, Robert Wright's neat little Tiger Moth, what did he call her – *Newsbird.* Unwilling, Ange recalled finding Robert after the 1954 crash, recalled closing Robert's eyes – odd shade of green, Thomas had them, too – colour-blind Robert calling green yellow, finding the drowned man when no one else could see him … this woman's eyes, feverish? Stranger. Ange had never seen her before, but the expression on her face now – concerned exasperation, squinting, rimless glasses: Robert Wright ghosted across her face. *What the hell did I have to see the body for?* Because of that, Ange ignored the grinding pain in his knees, thanked God for his recent hip replacement, and offered the woman his hand.

She didn't take it. Instead she pushed aside grimed bits of *Newsbird* and stood up. She blinked, sniffed, adjusted her glasses. —Hi.

—I'm Ange O'Dea. Who owns you?

Her face stiffened. She seemed to gag. Then she clicked her tongue.

—My name's Nichole Wright.

Might have known.

Old habits of speech and deference rose up. —What are you doing in all this mess, Miss Wright?

—Putting it back together. That's how you make art, you know. Out of debris. Sometimes out of nothing.

—You find?

—What time is it?

—Getting dark, so 'tis more than likely after seven. Rupert Ginge know you're in here?

—He told me to come look at the pieces. He left the door open.

—That your Sentra parked out to the Chinese restaurant?

—I walked from there.

—Very good.

—They do a great General Tso's chicken.

—'Tis not bad. I like the mu-shu pork meself.

—It's all about the Cthulhu.

Ange took in her build – easily tall as him, a good five foot eight, and broad across the shoulders. She walked like a man, too, though precisely how she did that Ange could not explain. The leaning forward as though going into a headwind, perhaps. Or the long stride. He had a job keeping up to her.

—The Cthulhu, hey. My son, Neal, told me about them. Some fella named Lovecraft? Monsters who fell from the sky?

—Like perverted angels.

Ange had trouble deciphering Nichole's rapid speech after that, catching something about wasps and a shoebox, then *He was going to give the gold back to his brother, never did use it*, but he had no trouble at all deciding this new Miss Wright was not fit to drive. *Now, what in the name of Jesus am I going to do with her?* People in the old days said family madness tore through earlier and harder each successive generation – nature trying to correct bad stock? The Captain had been drugged. No sign of that madness in Robert, though he died at fifty-three, so who could really tell? William seemed fine. Thomas acted at once obnoxious and charitable, all harried noblesse oblige, but hardly mad …

—In the Test Centre, Mr. O'Dea. Am I getting through to you? The Cthulhu prowling in the VOIC Test Centre.

Ange nodded. —No good can come of that.

—No, b'y, no good 'tall.

Ange glanced around at the houses of Riordan's Back. Not too many had their lights on; not too many were still lived in. Young crowd kept going off to Alberta, getting their visas fast-tracked. Parents kept moving to St. John's. Old ones going into homes. Dying.

Then Nichole sat down on a black and red boulder called the Devil's Couch to face the fog that had the bay socked in.—Nice view. God, I've missed this.

More rapid chatter, some of it standard English, some of it Newfoundland dialect.

—Starting to rain, Miss Wright. We'd best be getting on now. Can I use your phone there?

She took her phone from the holder without breaking her long sentence. Ange smiled his thanks and, making several mistakes with his thick fingers, eventually pushed in Rupert Ginge's telephone number.

It took a few minutes to get Rupert to pick up, another moment get Rupert to understand that Ange O'Dea, who never used the telephone, now spoke from the other end, and what felt like half an hour for Rupert to understand that the young woman who'd wanted to view pieces of *Newsbird* now lay supine on the Devil's Couch and might very well be in need of a doctor. The local ambulance service, which also ran a marriage chapel and funeral home, sent a hearse, because both ambulances were taken. When the hearse arrived, Nichole seemed unsurprised, certainly unconcerned. Ange wondered if he should ride into town with her, he being the one who found her after all, but Nichole was lucid enough to tell the terribly calm paramedics her name and address, the date, and the Prime Minister's name. They asked her if she'd like to see a doctor.

Silhouetted against the hearse, Nichole turned to Ange, briefly desperate, then smiling beautifully.

—What do you think, Mr. O'Dea?

Purple light from the hearse revolved onto the Devil's Couch, each particle of fog, and Ange's white hair. The tide hushed; the beach rocks rattled.

—Girl, I think there's no sense sitting in saved wreckage.

Nichole looked so disappointed. —But I'm trying to make art.

—Wouldn't hurt to talk to a doctor, Miss Wright.

—When I told my grandfather Wright I wanted to use Ms., he told me there were three kinds of women: Miss, Missus and Missed. It's Ms. Wright to you.

Chin high, eyes hard, Nichole climbed into the back of the hearse and asked where she should sit. The paramedics explained they had to strap her onto the stretcher in the back, and she clicked her tongue. The paramedic in the back nodded to Ange and shut the hearse doors.

Seagulls circled over a streetlight, underbellies brilliant.

Ange got himself home, aching damnably in the hips and knees. He put the kettle on, then stood in his doorway, door held ajar, hard-denying but then facing the absence in the house next door. His son John's house. Ange's daughter-in-law Rebecca had gone into town to get John settled on the Alzheimer's ward of Estuary Home. Stubborn winter made the air bitter with its struggle, and the fog hid the stars. How did this all this come about? Him living to see three wives and two sons dead and buried? How in hell could his son John at seventy-two be mouth-deep in senility, while Ange at a hundred and four still walked, heard, saw, remembered? Beaten back, defeated at this moment by not the length of his life but its truth, Ange looked now to the cliff of the bay – Riordan's Back separated from the Port au Mal side only by two stone's throws and unforgiving deep water. Then Ange recalled a day in 1920, William Wright on the Protestant side of the bay, Clary Fitzgerald on the Catholic side, there at the narrowest pinch, losing on their first toss and the treacherous wind an American football. It washed up eventually, ruint. *What I wouldn't give now for Mr. Francis. He could make sense of this.* Yes, Christopher Francis could reason out the needs: misplaced suffering, sturdy health, an accidental interview with a Commissioner, dirt roads and wires, a nearsighted rich boy building a radio station and learning to fly, a favourite son dead twenty-one years, even a lost Portuguese sailor – Sicilian. Except Christopher died in the 1940s.

Tired, Ange sat on the doorjamb. Cold penetrated clothing and skin, and he thought he might pray, but he'd no idea what to pray for. John's recovery – not likely – or John's peace? No more nights like his first in the Estuary – there would be many – his howls stripped of words but not of meaning, experienced nurses soothing: *You are home, John.* In the privacy of the break room, the nurses briefly cried. Over Ange's head, wires hummed. Riordan's Back and Port au Mal still so quiet, and the water, immense and calm, ... As Ange shut his eyes he remembered the framed photos on his front room wall of the three oil platforms, drilled into the ocean floor this time – no fifteen-percent list, flood and dark cold death – burning gas jets streaking briefly towards the sky, standards of defiance. No one had chosen to come to Riordan's Back or Port au Mal to live for thirty years, until some of the real estate crowd started marketing the area as a refuge with a short commute to town. Lots were selling, and already two houses were up, dead copies of each other. Maybe that was why Ange felt so gutted and sad when he discovered Nichole Wright slouched in the old wreckage of the Tiger Moth. Or maybe it was because he felt forgotten.

God, B'y, will Ya hurry up and take me?

Rain fell.

91. QUEEN'S ENGLISH 3
in which the settlement of Almayer Foxe fails.

April 2, 2005

—All these years, Rose, I thought you despised me.

—I just hardly knew what to say to you. Just watched you from afar.

—You make it sound like courtly love.

—In a way, yes.

Almayer Foxe sprinkled soy sauce onto Rose Fahey's breasts. She writhed.

—Keep still, Rose. I don't want to get soy sauce on the couch.

Consumed a moment by Foxe's agile tongue on her left nipple, Rose smiled.

—Thought I'd be too old for you.

—I've wanted to gentle you for years. Coax you.

Right nipple.

—I'm so glad you were with Uncle Richard when he fell.

Fingers on her neck, just below her ears. —Poor man. Like a second father to me.

Rose studied Almayer's face – tears.

Then Almayer stood up and turned away to get his digital camera.

—And that he lost his power of speech is just ...

Not totally lost. He'd spoken to Rose last night, in pieces. —Eezsh bad, Roshe. Izhal hamrah. Throwed me. Hand lease. Coal. Hrite. Hlew hor ou.

—Flew for me?

Robert Wright. And Richard had seen Robert Wright's grand-niece in Foxe's digital camera.

Arms bound behind her, Rose writhed again. —This is starting to hurt.

—Hold that pose. Okay, turn your head. Now draw your knees up. That little-girl-sad face is perfect. What are those marks on your arms?

—I used to scald myself with teabags.

—Chin up ... I can't wait another minute. In the name of her most gracious majesty ... here, let me get you loose. Come back.

—Just getting the camera. I'm dying to see.

—Hit the review button. I need a minute.

—You went pretty easy on me.

—Gentling, my dear.

—This woman here – how'd you get her to look so scared?

—Took a bit of work to get her in that position. Little tiny mouth, too. I threatened to show her family the other pictures if she didn't pose for that one. She tried to run, so I grabbed her before she could leave. She loved it.

—Little boys shouldn't grab.

—Little girls shouldn't play with fire. I wonder if all the Wrights are as mad as she. Ever heard her speak? Terribly fast. She didn't seem to realize what I was doing at first, kept breaking away in her head. What's the word for that?

—Dissociation. Sometimes you can get there on your own. I always needed the teabags.

—You're not leaving yet.

—I need some air. Nice night for a walk.

—You'll catch a chill. All you're wearing is those two cuffs – style suits you admirably.

Rose got near the front door. He hadn't even left her boots in the front porch.

—Come back now, Rose, and give me the camera.

She smiled, so sweetly. —He flew for me.

And she ran outside. Slush and ice numbed her bare feet, but she did not drop the camera. Most other houses on Rennie's Mill Road stood locked and unlit; respectable St. John's had gone to bed. Stumbling, Rose thudded against her car, then remembered the key lay in her coat pocket. A few seconds' lead – Almayer no doubt putting on clothes first – behind her already. Sidewalk still blocked with snow, road somewhat cleared ... headlights. Rose ran towards them, and the car screeched to a stop. Rose got in the passenger door, wet and dirty and still gripping that camera.

—He had me tied up in there. Please. Christ. Christ.

Ben Philpott, fresh from dropping his teenaged son at a party, reached into the back seat for his winter emergency blanket, swerved around the man now running down the street, dropped the blanket onto this strange naked woman with wrinkled scars on her arms, and accelerated. His car fishtailed, and he glanced in the rear view mirror: Almayer Foxe, wearing only pants and boots, running back into his house.

Fucking predator. Monster. No explaining people like you.

—Should I take you to the hospital?

—Police station.

—But –

—I wouldn't be any less naked at the hospital.

Ben noticed the camera in her hand and smiled. —I see.

Rose's teeth chattered, and she stroked a burn scar. She recognized this man's voice but couldn't place it. *You don't know the half of it.*

92. CULTURE SHOCK 3
in which Claire Furey runs into her past.

April 1, 2005

Claire Furey just wanted a quiet place away from her work to think, so when her codeine-addled nightwalk took her not only to the ragged eastern arse of George Street but to a new, dark little hole called The New Caribou Hut, she got annoyed. The spot had been God-knew-how-many dingy different pubs, but no one had ever changed the curtains, which, now grey with dust, hid desiccated insect carcasses. Claire knew she should be at home, or at farthest, Nichole's. But then Nicks had called her from the psych ward – mostly coherent – so Nichole's place lay out of reach. Sweat broke out, and Claire felt exposed as the wind cooled her newly vulnerable scalp. She'd cut off her waist-length hair into a pixie style, exposing rather a lot of grey. The hair waited in a shoebox, though for what, Claire did not yet know.

Codeine voyaged through her, falling with purpose like a tiny spider. Claire's doctors wanted her to take something stronger, but Claire refused.

—Demerol's useless, the Fentanyl patch knocks me silly, Percocet makes me itch, and my apartment's been broken into twice in the last year, so I don't dare have Oxycontin around. What's worked for me in the past? Got me totally pain-free, you mean? Epidural morphine. But there's no way I'm letting you admit me to hospital just so someone can thread a wire into my spine or jab Demerol and Gravol in my arse. I have a mural to finish. I need a clear head.

Tylenol 4s, five hundred milligrams of acetaminophen, sixty milligrams of codeine, about as effective when the pain got bad as a handful of Smarties.

Nichole had laughed. —Too funny, Furey-girl. Finally doctors believe the pain you're in and want to give you good drugs, but you won't take them.

Craving movement and air on her face, she'd walked too far, strayed defiantly, and now she'd gotten stuck. While stoned. She swayed, needing to lie down almost as much as she needed to breathe. She'd not eaten solids that day either, as eating only made the pain worse. Just a sit-down, cup of coffee, then maybe splurge on a bus ride home She crossed the threshold and walked unsteadily into The New Caribou Hut.

Oh, this is a mistake. She caught her strange reflection in the dull mirror behind the bar, glanced at the burnt-bottomed coffee pot and asked for tea instead. Surprised, she watched the barkeep scald a small teapot first before dropping in a round bag of Golden Pheasant and then pouring in properly boiling water from a kettle. Deciding to stay at the bar, Claire turned to look around as she waited for the tea to steep. A dun of smoke and dark wood tables sucked any struggling light. Even the ashtrays were dark, as though a glassblower had exhaled strong tea. Claire coughed. Players, Humphrey Gilberts and Export As: cigarette embers glowed as men inhaled, dimly lighting their faces, that brief forced fire reflecting in the lenses of their glasses. One man wore tortoise shell hornrims, very similar to Claire's; he'd noticed her, the tallish woman at the bar with a denim jacket and black hoodie hauled on over a white Aran Isles sweater, tiny silver hoops in her ears, short-short hair and well, look at that, tortoise shell hornrims and dark brown eyes.

—Claire?

Jesus, no. Can't be. God, please make it not be him.

—Claire Miranda Furey.

—Dad?

Gabriel stood shorter than Claire recalled. His hair, long and mostly white, hadn't thinned much. He wore a beard now too, which really threw Claire off, the beard being much darker with only the odd white hair. Around his neck he wore a Saint Christopher's medal. Faded jeans and yellow shirt tight, Gabriel himself looked starved down and delicate. The old eye-fire, sometimes creation, sometimes anger – Furey's fury – showed itself, torn and dulled. His smile exposed long teeth and brown gums.

—Sit down, ducky.

Stunned and helpless, stolen by a strange current, Claire sat at her father's table.

Gabriel signalled for another drink, nodded to Claire's little pot of tea.

—That all you're having?

—I don't drink.

Gabriel accepted a rum and Coke and paid for it with a Canadian five dollar bill, folded very small. —Good girl. Exchange is nearly par.

Where the fuck have you been?

Claire, my ducky, how do I tell you why?

—When did you get in, Dad?

—Last night. Came down the St. Lawrence from Montreal. Worked my passage to Rimouski, was going to stay there, but like the fool, I got back on board. Hardly what I wanted, but then there are journeys where you got no choice. Only found out after we were bound for St. John's.

Gabriel took deep swallows of his drink.

—You're looking good, Claire. Bit butch, maybe.

Why the fuck did I just say that to her?

—I just cut my hair.

Why the fuck did I just say that to him?

—Short hair's how I knew you. The picture, right?

Gabriel dug out his wallet, a thin and frayed thing too worn to hold money. Behind his expired Newfoundland and Labrador driver's license, next to provincial health cards from Ontario and Quebec, a tiny photo-booth shot in startling colour of Claire at seven, hair short and shaggy and parted on the left, sitting on darkhaired Gabriel's lap as he smiled over her shoulder.

—We got that done the day I took you out for school clothes and a haircut. Remember picking out that green turtleneck? You danced all over Port of Call holding that, pretending you were a leprechaun.

Claire poured tea. —Did I?

Gabriel put the photo away. —Truth of the matter is, leprechauns are grumpy old men. That whole happy little people thing is all Walt Disney. *Darby O'Gillis and the Little People.* And they cast a Scotsman.

Silence.

I can't believe I'm just sitting here, looking at him. I just want to look at him. Should be hating him. Sit in his lap and smell his sweat and the Export As ...

Christ in the garden, might have known. Hiding in here drinking all day in case I saw her on the street, good girl like her'd never come in here ... can't even fucking spell my name, never could, but ... little girl, angel-down in the incubator, had to protect you, would have run all the way to hell or up the Jesus cross to protect you ... how do I tell ya?

Gabriel lit a cigarette. —Understand you're painting. Best kind. How's your work going?

—Got a commission for another mural.

—Saw that one down by the old railway station, picked out your signature. You design that one up on Duckworth?

—Yeah. Sold a few paintings just before Christmas, too.

—Heard some missus from here on CBC talking about you, painting called *Archangel's Fury*? Who bought that?

—Dorinda Masterson. University professor. She helped me out last year when I got sick.

Gabriel's words came sharp and quick. —Whaddya mean, sick?

—Ascending cholangitis that time. Infection in my bile ducts. Threw up all over her SUV, and then she got me into the Levitz out there in Gander.

—Are you okay now? Answer me, Claire.

—Waiting for results.

Claire poured the last of her tea. Gabriel finished his drink.

—I like your work, ducky. Very distinct.

Daddy.

—Thanks.

—Always knew you had a gift.

—I get that from you.

—Indeed you don't. Coincidence, is all.

Claire took a long look at her teacup as Gabriel asked about Callie. Anger rose with steam. So did the pain.

—You walked out on us. How dare you ask me how Mom is? *I* know how Mom is, because I didn't leave her!

—Claire –

—How dare you even be here tonight? What the fuck do you think – you can just catch a boat when it suits you and waltz back across my line of sight? Do you think I can drop all those empty years and just love you again?

Gabriel breathed deeply and gazed at the other patrons, all men in their fifties and sixties, shoulders rounded in some private defeat, each, save Gabriel, alone.

Jesus, girl.

—You left.

—Take this napkin, and dry your face – hey!

Hot tea dribbled down his beard, onto his shirt. Hissing, wincing, Gabriel kept still and allowed the tea to burn.

—Ducky, I sent your mother money whenever I could. Always sent money for art supplies for you for Christmas. Used to eat only breakfast, every day from the first of November to the postal deadline in December.

Claire recalled her mother sobbing into the phone one Christmas Eve about a disconnection notice. *They can't really cut my power in December, can they? I sent them the twenty bucks from Gabriel again this year, but it's not – no, he's not bound to give us child support. He never married me.*

—Didn't you get them art supplies from me?

Claire saw no reason to lie for sweetness. —No.

—Jesus Christ, Callie never –

—She used the money to pay the bills so we didn't get thrown out on our arses in the snow. I don't know how many times we had the phone cut off. And she'd never ask Pop –

—Callie had a job when I left.

—Callie had a young girl in school. By herself. She couldn't work full-time.

—Jack Best's daughter went on the dole? Didn't your grandfather help you out? I know he disowned Callie for staying with me, but you –

—They made some peace, but she wasn't going to let him do everything.

—She's pretty stubborn.

—After Chapel Street, we got this basement apartment on Topsail Road, couldn't sneeze without the people upstairs banging on the floor to make us be quiet, gorgeous big house upstairs, big back yard, too, but we weren't allowed to use it. Mom used to have her dole cheque mailed to a post office box in the drugstore, so no one'd know, and she paid the rent and the light bill one month and the rent and the phone bill the next month out of that. Pop bought the groceries and paid for my art lessons. I didn't figure that part out until I was fifteen, when Mom went in for her hysterectomy.

Gabriel took off his glasses and rubbed his eyes. —I'm sorry.

—Are you, now?

—Don't be like that. We'll talk about art, hey? Stuff of the soul. Cheers, ducky.

Claire shook her head at Gabriel, very much as Callie had often done. The codeine grew legs and a heavy belly, then leapt through her, trailing silken euphoria – sweet numbness.

—All right, Dad. Art. What are you working on?

—Fuck all. I haven't sculpted in ten years. Where the hell is some homeless guy going to get bronze? And you've got to have beauty in you. Come on, Claire. Can you see the beauty when you look at me?

Claire said nothing.

Gabriel lit another cigarette. —Did some clay. Used to sweep up at one of them make-your-own-pottery studios in Montreal. Went in after hours and made these funny-looking coffee mugs with Agonizing Christ on them, 3D crucifixion, sticking out like on the Pope's staff. I pricked out Christ's ribs with a toothpick and sold the mugs on my own. Got fired when they figured out how much clay was after going missing.

—Did you do it for love?

—Do what?

—The crucifixion mugs.

—I did it for enough pocket change to buy a drink.

—But why crucifixion coffee mugs? I mean, something drove you to –

—I don't fucking know. Jesus, girl, if I knew why I did half the shit I've done –

—But you hated the Church. You tried to get me exempted from religion class. You – you're crying.

Gabriel brushed at his eyes. —I'm worried about the Pope.

—What?

He shouted it; men turned. —The Jesus Pope. He came here in 1984. Do you remember? Blessed the fleet out in Flatrock. Fat lot of good it did them. And he said Mass at Pleasantville. I was there, you know.

—You were here in 1984?

—Came by the house on Chapel Street, but buddy said you must have moved.

—At Mass at Pleasantville?

—Yeah.

—Mom and I were there. Me arguing with her the whole time, weren't we nothing, me exempted from religion class, you and Mom never married, bla bla bla, but then Mom said even if we weren't Catholic, we had to go.

—You were there, and I missed you?

—She kept looking for someone. And I couldn't see anything over other people's shoulders, but I could hear him, and then some guy in front picked me up and put me on his shoulders, I was too old for that, thirteen, but I still looked about eight. I was an ironing board until sixteen, and I got to see him. The Pope. He looked kind and very strong. Then I tried to find whoever Mom seemed to be looking for, but I kept staring at John Paul. I couldn't help it. He was so – so, I don't – was Mom looking for you?

Gabriel signalled for another drink. —I never knew what your mother was looking for.

—A husband. And a father for her child. Remember me?

Every fucking day. —Jesus, if she wanted someone half-sensible, she made a piss-poor choice with me.

—All her fault, is it? You couldn't have changed?

—I'm an artist, Claire. We drag conflict with us.

—Whatever.

—S'true. Can't create without the sensitivity to respond in the first place.

—That's your third rum and Coke since I got here.

—Sensitivity, darling. Can't bear it some days. And bar drinks are weak. Cheers. S'like the Pope says, culture's what's going to propel humanity forwards, not economics. I want to be part of that. I have to be. You, too. You know what I mean, that compulsion. Screws into you at four in the morning when you're trying to sleep, like some voice screaming in your ear, some high frequency signal. You now, you pick up a paintbrush, or even a charcoal stick, or just brush the flats of your fingers over prepped canvas; next time you look up, an hour's gone, and you've just gotten started; then it's dark, and the idiotic interruptions, phone calls, hunger, fatigue, but the work's going well, and something smells a bit off and you realize it's your own sweat, and you've worked through the night again. And you still got to go to your day job. Don't matter. That bliss, that strength taking you, possessing you, and for the love of God, shutting up the past yet sucking the past through some thin little straw and spitting it back out into whatever you're ... Jesus, I'm tired.

—How much have you had tonight?

Gabriel raised his glass and regarded it. —Alas, poor Yorick. I knew him, Horatio. I saw that play.

A man two tables over spoke up. —He warn't sober when he came in.

Gabriel stared hard at Claire now, angry almost, desperate. —It's hunger. The work.

—Ten years?

Embarrassed, Gabriel looked away. —Yes, little miss mural painter, ten fucking years. Useless for a decade. Can't even stand up without – and the Jesus Pope is dying. Holy Mary, Mother of God, please don't make him suffer any more.

He locked eyes with her: impostor fury.

—Course, what do you care about the Pope?

Eighteen years gone, and now you're fucking drunk. —The Pope's a man of peace. Going to the Western Wall and slipping in his note, apologizing for any Vatican complicity in the Holocaust, visiting the mosque in Syria, condemning poverty and genocide –

—I'd like to see his apartments. Living end of luxury, I bet.

The codeine spider crept up its big web, and Claire relished the brief sham of relief from the pain. —He's on fire. I want to be cleansed by that fire.

—Hell you do, girl. Would you be following Christ or John Paul? Cult of personality, is it? Women's highest callings in the Church, my ducky, are motherhood and virginity. Pick one. Squeeze out puppies until you're wrung out at forty, or winnow out in some convent, pelvis sacrificed to the nuns until you have visions like Ita's, Christ fluttering in your face as a dove then come crawling to you as a baby to go sucking on your tit. I can see it now, you lined right up there with the Presentation Sisters, or the Mercy Sisters. Forget 'career,' Claire. Forget your art. Your gifts would not be wanted. I'd like to see you now, handling that no-sex-before-marriage bullshit, you likely a right slut like your mother.

Claire slurred now, jaw heavy. —Like you'd fucking know. You left. And as for the Jesus Pope, I like him better than I like you. He's a fallible and flawed human being, but he's a force of God.

—Force of God?

Gabriel stood up, swaying a little. Other men looked up mildly; Gabriel did not care.

—You want the force of God, Claire? Try Brother's dick in your mouth. Ramming at your tonsils. Hadn't washed for days. There's your kneeling at prayer, my ducky. There's your force of God. Now, do you spit or swallow the force of God?

Claire retched, forced her tea back down.

Gabriel spoke quietly, calmly. —Tell me, Claire, what did the Pope do about that?

—I'm leaving.

Gabriel fell back to his chair in some obscured defeat, his eyes set on Claire's chair but his gaze directed somewhere else.

Claire strode to the door, but the man closest to the entrance reached out of his shaded corner and touched her arm. —You Gabe Furey's girl?

—Take your hand off me.

— Answer me. You Gabe's girl? Those eyes – you got to be. He loves you. He shows that picture in his wallet to everyone he meets.

—So?

—I know he left you and your mother. Do you know where he grew up?

—And that's supposed to excuse him?

—No. Everything he does is his own responsibility. But it might explain him.

Claire stepped away.

—You listen to me, girl. You got to get past your own hurt here. He can't. He needs you. And if you're any kind of daughter at all, you'll at least get him home tonight.

—Excuse me?

The man sank back into his chair by the wall, a mechanical doll winding down.

—Work of the soul. You step out of here now, leave him here, you're just taking revenge.

—I'm going home.

—Taking revenge.

Too angry to speak, to move, Claire stood at threshold of the Hut, hissing out breath past clenched teeth. Refusing to turn round, she called to her father.

—Gabriel.

Someone walked very carefully behind her, dignity put on like old clothes.

Claire offered her arm. —Let's go.

The first three times Gabriel fell, they weren't even off the block. Claire stood taller than her father, but he leaned heavily, a wretched weight, and her codeine spider's web tore. The streetlights glared off the remaining snow, and other patrons, still sober at this early hour, glanced in amused wonder at the man and woman with the same glasses and the same eyes, kedging their common stride like Victorian mourners. Voices called, accents varied from flat Ontario and hammocked New England to the thick vowels of the farther Newfoundland outports, while Conception Bay and St. John's brogues arced and clipped. Gabriel fell a fourth time, a quick tug from Claire saving his glasses from cobblestones at the corner of Water and George.

Breathing hard, Claire asked Gabriel where he was bound.

Gabriel pointed down the short Beck's Cove road to the harbour.

—On board the *Bagger.* Container ship.

Then he let go Claire's arm, pitched across Water Street without looking for traffic, and collapsed on the far corner.

Dodging a car, Claire ran across and knelt by her father but could not wake him. She tugged his arms, shook his shoulders, called his name over and over. Finally, she grabbed a handful of crystalline dirty snow and rubbed it in his face. Gabriel opened his eyes, smiled as though seeing Claire for the first time in years, then shut his eyes again. Claire grabbed another handful of snow and rubbed hard, grinding it around his mouth; beneath her force, old dogshit crumbled. Glancing round for fresh snow and finding none, only snow less polluted, she cleaned Gabriel's face with spring melt and the edge of her sweater.

Gabriel's face bled from ice cuts. He sat up, looked mildly about, then got to his feet. —On board the *Bagger*. Container ship. Straight ahead.

The *Bagger* flew the Canadian maple leaf beneath the Newfoundland tricolour. The man on watch let Gabriel on board but not Claire. —Sorry. No visitors, eh.

—Can you get him to bed?

—Won't be the first time. You get home, eh. Not safe to be out by yourself after dark.

Claire laughed, frightening the watchman and herself.

A hour later, having showered off the scents of cigarettes, oil, dogshit and salt water, pain slicing the remnants of the codeine web, Claire sat naked on her dusty softwood floor and gazed down at a prepped canvas. The hunger gnawed. She knelt over the canvas, studying it, pleased not to have her hair fall in the way, but the canvas grain revealed nothing. Her hands ached; tomorrow her knuckles would be red and hot, but she didn't care. Her faulty electric kettle boiled for the fifth time, but Claire forgot it again; the teabag would stay on the counter all night. Some new strength tingled in her hands, and she knew she had to work, must work, but she lacked the materials. Clay – too easy. Bronze – unattainable. Already commissioned for a mural. *Can you see beauty when you look at me?* She recalled reading of the Pope's mute humiliation on Easter Sunday, of his wordless breaths broadcast by sensitive mic over Saint Peter's Square. *Inspiration's a myth,* Claire had so often said. *Talent's useless without discipline. You can't sit around waiting for the lightning.* Yet – a four by six piece, oils and a thin line to look like pencil, cannula in the throat, high collar, microphone.

Studies. Not John Paul, but Gabriel Furey.

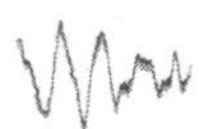

93. UNCOMMON KINDNESS 2
in which Gabriel Furey learns a dance,
and Dorinda Masterson eats some chocolate.

April 2, 2005

The dancer bent her knees slightly, kept her feet still, and bounced. Gabriel copied her posture and nearly tore his thighs apart. The dancer smiled. —Not easy to dance and make respect, eh?

Gabriel kept bouncing. —Not easy in this cold, for sure.

She smiled again. —Cold? This is Harbourside Park. You try Nain. Now you sway, side to side, to the drumbeat.

The drummer kept his rhythm to a resting heartbeat as freezing mist blew into his face. The dancer slowly raised her hands and drew an arc in the air in front of her. —Now I am telling a story about the rising sun.

Gabriel copied her, gracelessly.

—Now I am telling you I had to row my boat –

She broke off giggling. The drummer guffawed.

—Boat, right. Fine tradition, me singing about a boat. My *kayak*. Now I'm telling you I took my kayak over a great distance ...

The drumming resumed. The dancer made a paddling motion as she danced. The drum now high in the air, rhythm deeper, louder, the drummer dancing, too. Gabriel, breathless, had to stop.

— ... and even if you cannot speak my language, I can still tell you my story, if you want to listen. You're sweating.

Gabriel doubled over, hands on his knees, coughing. The drummer leaned down to peer at him. Then he asked Gabriel for a smoke.

Gabriel happily gave them each a cigarette. —You always practice out here?

The dancer shrugged. —When we feel like it. You always try to learn Innu dancing first thing in the morning?

Gabriel watched her smoke the cigarette. The dancer and the drummer might be cousins – black hair, high cheekbones, the same quick smile. *Or maybe I'm just a racist who thinks they all look alike. Jesus, save me.*

The drummer held out his hand. —I'm John. This is Anna, my cousin. You want to stay?

—I can't. But I'll see you again.

Anna and John resumed their rehearsal. Gabriel walked up to Water Street, not certain where he might go next, only that he wanted something hot to drink, and something to beat back his hangover. *Mahon's. Haven't been there in years.*

Dorinda Masterson's painfully sensitive sense of smell could be a nuisance. This morning scents of rotten snow and unclean water, of salt, sewage and seagulls – the harbour – clung to her wool coat. Reader response theory gone olfactory – but worth suffering for fresh bread, spices, coffee and tea, for the scents of Mahon's.

Obscured by glare from the fluorescent lights, old photographs of four Mahons – sons Kipling, Stevenson and Conan Doyle, all bloated and sad, father Kenneth wiry, white-haired and surprised – hung on the dark wooden wall above the glass-doored refrigerator housing exotic sodas, non-alcoholic beer and iced tea. Imported chocolate, cakes, candies and biscuits covered one wall; a deli counter boasting ninety-eight cheeses stood before the other. An espresso machine steamed; a bottle of olive oil tottered; a spider crawled from a box of bananas. The dark floor got darker under dull slush. Old signs mounted near the coffee bar showed the store's changing names: Mahon's to Kelloway's to Indulgentz and back to Mahon's again, permission granted, for a small fee, by a distant cousin of Kenneth, Kipling, Stevenson and Conan Doyle. Once and again Mahon's General Store, the space now adjoined a dining area called The Galley, where people sat at two long tables bolted shipshape to the floor. Bread cooled in the windows of both Galley and Store, steaming the glass.

His hair's gone white.

Dorinda took a breath. Over by the imported chocolate, weighing in his hand a bar of 70% cocoa with chili peppers in it. Beard freshly shaved, cut on his left jaw, moustache thick, eyes dark as molasses behind tortoise shell hornrims – she'd said that to him once, *Lassy eyes*, made him smile – should have died years ago, in a gutter somewhere, in a noose. Instead he dared to stand in Mahon's, battered and scraped, stinking of stale rum, untouchable, beautiful, beyond her – deciding on chocolate.

—Gabriel?

Her voice like a teenager's, frightened and harsh, like the stereotypical libber everyone expected her to be, her asking the boys to dance, spending every scrap of courage and rejected each time.

Dorinda cleared her throat. —Gabriel Furey.

Brown eyes red-rimmed, black-bagged. Voice soft. —Wha'?

—You probably don't remember me.

Gabriel leaned his weight to one side, pelvis arrogant, face sad, as though resigned to a beating. —Remind me.

—Dory Masterson.

—Dory. Unusual name.

—That's what you said the first time we met. The Sandbar, 1978. Used to see you there a few times a week.

—The Sandbar. That wasn't yesterday. Some fellah Marsh owned it. Burnt down in the 80s, didn't it?

—I met your daughter recently.

Gabriel carefully held on to the chocolate. —Claire?

—She's getting a reputation. Her work. I bought one of her paintings.

Gabriel studied Dorinda, trying to puzzle out what she wanted, why she seemed so nice. Dorinda stared back.

Then both Gabriel and Dorinda struggled to recover conversation, words. Odd little noises, protesting too much, thoughts broken to stutters.

Finally, Gabriel managed a sentence. —You're looking good, Dory.

Dorinda bit back the wretched modesty protest of *I'm a size 14. I was a size 8 when we met.* —Thank you.

—Listen, I'm just after getting into town. You got any kind of phone number for Claire?

Dorinda smiled. —I can find it.

Gabriel looked away and questioned a mystery. *She means it. What's she doing being fucking good to me? I'm the devil's own Jesus bagman puked onto the snow. The only one who wants me has got hands like cold rubber and a black robe hissing on the floor like a tail. Damaged goods I am, Dory my darling. Keep your distance before you catch the taint.*

Dorinda's face went academic, controlled. —Chocolate was originally taken with hot peppers as a drink.

—I love dark chocolate. Hardly ever has it. Get a coffee or something?

Dorinda paid for her own, breathed in Gabriel's scent: warm gunmetal, harsh musk, salt water, smoke. Gabriel had put the chocolate back and gotten a tea, then chose a seat in the Galley farthest from the window. Dorinda excused herself and returned a moment later with the chocolate.

Gabriel smiled. Dorinda guessed he didn't smile often, usually hid his dark teeth and gums. Dorinda didn't care. Because Gabriel's smile crumbled his fuck-the-lot-of-ye mask and revealed, however briefly, a truer face: humble, seared, delicate and hard.

Dorinda hurriedly unwrapped the chocolate, broke off several pieces.

Gabriel did not chew the chocolate; he let it melt on his tongue, cocoa and chili peppers penetrating past nicotine damage. A delicate moment, no forced chatter, just being ...

Then Dorinda nearly wrecked it. —You were at St. Raphael's?

Gabriel put his tea down, ran a thumbnail through a cut in the table.

—Bit forward there, Dory.

—Claire's triptych. It's about you.

Gabriel worried a corner of foil. —Wouldn't know.

—The kid on the caduceus. Gabriel, I'm sorry.

—No, it's all open book. Just didn't testify. Pointless.

Dorinda broke off another piece of chocolate; Gabriel accepted it.

—When did you meet Claire?

—At Far Flung last summer. She got sick. She looks like you, lassy eyes and all.

—I remember you now. You were all about going to Toronto. Gonna get your doctorate.

—I came on a bit strong, I know.

—So what are you up to these days, Dr. Dory?

—I'm at the university, freelance sometimes for businesses. Listen, I'm on this Health and the Arts Committee. We're trying to get more arts therapy in to medical treatment protocol. And just more tangible art in the hospitals.

—You want Claire for that. I'm just a crewman on the *Bagger*. Departing this afternoon.

—Claire got the Rawlins Cross commission through the city. An artist of your calibre and experience –

—How much?

—Five thousand.

Gabriel took the last piece of chocolate. He sucked it, let it melt over his teeth, washed it away with tea.

—If I don't report back to the *Bagger* by noon, I'm homeless.

—Wouldn't Claire –

—I can't ask her that. Not – I fucked it up.

—My basement apartment is vacant. Normally I've got a grad student down there, but – if you want. Just pay your own light bill.

Gabriel chewed a fingernail; it smelled of machine grease. —Dory, that's very kind of you, going out of your way like that, but –

—A mural in a hospital. All I'm asking.

Eyes warm, Gabriel leaned in closer to Dorinda, smiled a bit. —Not painting any fucking palm trees or happy faces. I got to be left alone.

—Fifth floor of the General, Gabe, medicine floor: cancer patients, pneumonia, people getting out of ICU, not much sunlight, but – misery, sorrow and the odd recovery. Can you do that?

—You promise to get me Claire's phone number?

—I already –

—Promise?

—Yes.

Gabriel finished his still scalding tea. —Misery, sorrow and the odd recovery. Yeah, I can do that.

94. REPEATER
in which a signal is received, amplified and passed on.

November 18, 2003

The VOIC family is saddened today. Dan McGrew, VOIC's chief engineer since 1967, died last night after a long battle with cancer. Dan McGrew was born in rural Ontario and came to Newfoundland on a strange journey ...

March 2, 2004

The VOIC family is saddened today by the loss of a respected and well-loved newsman.

BITE: "...and Prime Minister Best then spent this afternoon on a park bench in the snow, considering his future. Of his future plans, details are scarce, now."

Pat Finch, a news reporter since 1951, got his start in radio when he was seventeen ...

October 13, 2004

Another old radio voice has gone off the air. Tim Stratton, formerly of VOIC, died yesterday in his home. Stratton had been living alone for some time. After he left broadcasting, Stratton made a brief foray into professional wrestling with the stage name Old Man Strutter. In recent years, Stratton made a living driving a taxi and had announced his candidacy in the upcoming municipal elections in St. John's. Tim Stratton was 75.

February 12, 2005

VOIC is in mourning today for news director Kyle George.

BITE: "This is Kyle George, reporting live from the scene of a helicopter crash near Kenmount Road."

Kyle George died yesterday on the scene of a helicopter crash, doing what he loved best: reporting the news for VOIC. Kyle George was active in the community, volunteering for various Boards of Directors, including the Newfoundland Cancer Society and the Great Newfoundland and Labrador Literacy Project. He was 53.

March 25, 2005

VOIC is in mourning today and feeling hard-hit. Kevin White, longtime announcer, Operations Manager, Republic Music Board liaison and husband to the lucky Kim Parsons-White, lost his battle with liver cancer. He was 48. Kevin White started in radio when he was just a teenager and needed a summer job …

March 31, 2005

…Meantime, calls for a public inquiry into all the Health Board's lab testing for cancer indicators between 2001 and 2005 continue. The calls come in the wake of the revelation that many cancer patients received incorrect test results. Decisions for treatment regimens are based on those lab results. Since 2001, one hundred and forty-two breast and liver cancer patients, mostly men and women in their 30s and 40s, have died. It is unclear if their deaths were hastened by faulty test results. Questions are also being asked about the reliability of laboratory results in general. Acting Health Board Chair Chris Jackman said earlier today that a great wrong has occurred and must be addressed.

BITE: "Good Saturday morning to you. It's the VOIC *Cabin in the Woods Show*, and I'm Stephen Driscoll. Did you hear the one about the doctor and the rabbi?"

VOIC is in shock today. Stephen Driscoll, producer and announcer and host of VOIC's immensely popular *Cabin in the Woods Show* alongside the late Kevin White, died suddenly in his home on Monday. He was thirty. Stephen, who had the gift to make everyone laugh, got his start in radio when he was sixteen, when he walked into the VOIC Broadcast Centre on Kenmount Road and asked to speak to news director Pat Finch. Engineer Dan McGrew and announcer Kevin White were in the lobby at that moment and took a liking to young Driscoll …

95. THIS IS A TEST OF THE EMERGENCY BROADCAST SYSTEM 2
in which Marc Dwyer and Nichole Wright no longer need to sneak into a hospital to visit Claire Furey.

April 5, 2005

—You seem to be coping better than last time, Claire.

—Dialect, right? Pain's after learning me patience.

—Are we controlling your pain?

—Technicolor ceiling. Could you dial it back a bit?

—I notice you didn't touch your breakfast tray this morning.

—Would you? Full fluids, delicious. Runny Cream of Wheat, scrambled egg whites and alleged yogurt. I eat that – I eat anything – and it'll just make the pain worse.

—So we're not controlling your pain. I'm upping your Demerol and Buscopan.

—If it swims like a ducky and quacks like a ducky ... No more Buscopan, please. I can't get out of bed when I'm on that stuff.

—You're not supposed to get out of bed.

—I get bored.

—So you decide to go for a stroll, fall down in the gift shop and make extra work for the orderlies?

—The big guy standing in line behind me? God, he picked me up like I'm no heavier than a pillow. Really gentle. Scars all over one hand.

—I'm on rounds early tomorrow morning. I'll come and see you then.

—So you're not moving me up to Intensive? Good.

—Not today. See how your bloodwork is tomorrow. Get some rest. No drawing, no going for walks. Rest.

—I will.

Claire counted to fifteen after Dr. Penney left before reaching into the bedside cabinet for her sketch pad and pencils. Dizzy, she shut her eyes and lay still a moment. *The mural. Work on the mural, even if just in your head, Furey. Don't just lie here.*

In her sketchbook, Claire had drawn twenty-two studies of Robert Wright from her memory of the portrait at VOIC. Claire kept sketching Wright in imagined profile, in different light, yet over the weekend she'd discarded them, because suddenly the mural did not need Wright – it needed his Tiger Moth. Why not a Cessna? Or a Norseman? Tiger Moths so small and delicate – how had these delicate antiques trained pilots for the Second World War? How cold had it been, flying an open plane? Who trained in them? And how in the name of sweet honourable historical God had Robert Wright ended up with one?

The child had been eleven, the story went, a girl some said, while others insisted no, a boy. Claire had always thought eleven a bit old to get lost, but she'd never really questioned the story. Up in an ancient Tiger Moth – obsessively cared for, yes, frequently flown, sure, but old – up in an ancient Tiger Moth, Wright, vision poor, Robert flew that day not for pleasure, not even for news, but to look for someone lost.

Like her grandfather at the flower service, placing flowers at the base of a child's stone, Tessa Katherine Best, and Claire asking him why.

—Because it's what you do.

Claire opened her eyes: up near the ceiling, Spitfires, Norsemen, Cessnas, Tiger Moths. She smiled, closed her eyes again and pried her concentration back to her mural. There, low over the harbour – the Tiger Moth would go there. It hardly mattered if *Newsbird* had never flown over St. John's harbour; it belonged there in her mural, and people would figure it out eventually.

Claire did not know about the photograph, in shades of fog, taken in 1952: *Newsbird* dangerously low over the harbour, Robert Wright observing a longshoreman's strike. Her ignorance didn't matter, either.

She slept, woke as the pain spiked and the lunch trays arrived. Rolling over, she pressed the call button, ready to ask for more pain meds. The airplanes near the ceiling had vanished.

Pain. Jesus.

But time – there's my enemy.

Soon as this shot kicks in, I'll sit up and sketch the plane.

Nichole's voice.

Come on, Nicks, can't you leave me in peace for ten fucking minutes so I can get some work done?

—Got to get yourself an answering machine, Furey-girl. Your phone was ringing off the hook when I went in for your PJs, but when I got to the phone, whoever it was had gone. Your crazy neighbour said the phone's been ringing twenty, twenty-one times before it stops, almost every hour.

Afternoon light gone, supper trays. Claire peeked under lids: ah, pureed barf masquerading as cream of chicken soup, her favourite.

—Claire?

—Hey, Nicks. Feeling better?

—Released with meds day before yesterday, remember? Just a seventy-two hour remand.

Claire shook her head.

—You've been pretty out of it. Remember this guy?

Nichole beckoned to someone standing in the doorway. A man about her age, tall, bald, carrying a sketchbook.

Nichole bowed and made leg like a courtier in an Elizabethan play.

—May I present to you, Ms. Claire Furey, the long-lost, much-loved and accomplished graphic novelist, Marc Dwyer. Found his website, got a phone number.

Marc took another step towards Claire's bed. —Yellow is really not your colour.

—The soup, or the jaundice? I dreamt about you last night.

—I dreamt about you and Nichole the night before.

—Synchronicity, then?

—String theory, more like, or the Higgs Ocean. God, Claire, this is just too … strange.

—Nah. Reassuring.

Nichole leaned against the wall and signalled Claire she would wait in the hallway.

The fifth floor of the General smelled better than the psych ward, at least, but Nichole shared that observation with no one. Sharing observations right now earned the words *hallucination* and *delusion*; she'd learned quickly after her first twelve hours on the psych ward to shut up. Crazy people in crisis must only say crazy things, the reasoning went, so every time a crazy person spoke, he got more Thorazine. Quiet area, that remand psych ward, save for the squeaking of beds and nurses' shoes.

Old photographs lined the corridor walls: a graduating class of nurses, a women's ward with several dozen beds, patients lipsticked and smiling, one chancellor or another, an iron lung. Doubting the sanitary wisdom of dusty photo frames on a medicine floor, Nicholc glanced at the clock behind the nurses' desk and decided to get some coffee.

In the elevator, she held the door for someone running.

—Marc?

—M for Main Floor, right?

—You were only in there five minutes.

He pressed M. —I don't like hospitals.

The elevator descended.

Nichole punched his arm. —Try being a patient some time. Get back in there. Claire hasn't seen you for so long.

Marc stepped up to the doors, even though they had not yet opened.

Nichole grabbed his arm as he stepped out of the elevator. —Marc, you can't go yet.

Marc shook her off. —I'm supposed to be at ComicCon. Do you know what the airfare to St. John's is like right now? Look, thank you for letting me know, but I really have to get back.

Nichole got both his arms this time. —Claire loves you!

—We were thirteen when I moved away. Let go. Nichole, seriously – let go. Nichole – you're hurting me – my wife – get off – Jesus, get her off me! Get her off!

Penned in by an orderly's arms, Nichole lunged once more, then gave up. A resident knelt down and examined Marc's bloody nose. Noticing scraps of reality – the smells of the coffee shop, the garish pink teddy bears in the gift shop windows, the scars on the orderly's right hand – Nichole snorted at Marc's stuffed-up question.

—What more do you want from me, Nichole?

—No more than you can give!

—I should press charges. Do I need X-rays? Which way to the Emergency Room?

—Marc, take a deep breath ...

—She's had this for years. Doctors used to think she was crazy or faking. Chronic pancreatitis and bile duct cancer, yeah, this sucks. I came as soon as you called. She's dying. I get that. It's sad, and I'm sorry. But I need to get back to my wife.

The orderly loosened his arms around Nichole but did not yet let her go.

Blood dripped from Marc's nose onto his shirt. He nearly whispered it.

—You left me alone in there.

—I have so fucked this up.

Marc stood up.

—Is that the exit?

—Marc, *listen* to me. I won't leave –

—Don't ever call me again. How do I get out of here?

96. MORATORIUM
in which Jack Best delivers his final speech.

February 14, 1992

Television screens on either side of me gone to snow. Mounted police. People – must be thousands. They've got the streets and Bannerman Park blocked. Heave it outta ya, Jack.

I am ashamed of Fisheries Minister Doug Kelsey. Ashamed. How dare he think to broadcast his announcement over television screens when a real man might come out and face the people?

I marched here tonight.

I fished for six seasons with Captain Tobias Wright of Port au Mal, and the salt water saved me. Jackie Best was a spoiled townie merchant's son, mocking the parlourmaid for her Southern Shore accent. Katherine, I wish I could apologize to you now. Jackie Best looked down his bumpy little nose at Captain Tobias Wright the Sunday afternoon in 1913 he came to dinner. Snivelling little coward that I was, I'd gotten out of going to church that morning by pretending to be sick. Now I watched Katherine's lips move as she set the table: dessert fork, fish fork, main fork; dessert spoon, teaspoon, soup spoon. Our front gate was part of a short wrought iron fence, the end of a narrow walking path that morning cleared of slush but still wretchedly wet. Father helped Mother down, while a new man, short but broad, heavy brow and green eyes, helped my sisters. This man was Captain Wright, and he spied me peeking at him through the curtains, and he spat. Then Katherine told me to scoot upstairs and put my collar on.

Captain Wright's first words to me were these: 'The b'y looks healthy to me. No reason not to go to church. Soft. Nails dirty. Details like that can get a man killed.'

Well, you can be sure I tried to snatch my hands back, but Captain Wright held them fast and kept speaking about tests and endurance and baptism by ice. He finally gave me back my hands. Then we sat down to dinner. Of course, myself and my sisters did not speak. Neither did my mother. Captain Wright and my father talked oats and molasses, sleet and men, pelts and ice.

Then my father let fall the blow, saying he despaired of ever making a man of me. Captain Wright said he could see why. Father said he blamed himself for being too soft on me, and Captain Wright placed his two big hands on the table, heavy hands, all spotted and scarred and lined, and he said young Jack would have a choice on the water come spring. He could toughen up, or he could die.

After that, Father and Captain Wright told Bible stories in the parlour. The sad Captain's voice recited: 'Then the Mariners were afraid, and cried every man unto his god, and cast forth the wares that were there in the ship, into the sea ...'

Next spring, the Captain said, 'Just to make it clear, Jack. I've done you a favour, coming to fetch you. Normally my men meet me. Expect no more favours.'

Did John Cabot strain his back hauling baskets aboard? Did Prime Minister Squires ever know the weight of cod? I had to work to keep my grip, but I slipped. We never did understand how, but I lost two fingers that day in the tangle of the ropes. I nearly got dragged to the hold with the catch. Captain Wright caught me, hauled me back, but the state of my fingers, well, bones broken, ligaments torn, skin shredded away. I disappeared behind that pain. Then I tasted rum and felt a strip of sailcloth winding about the fingers, holding them together. I got excused from making fish, and then I took a fever. Captain Wright returned me to St. John's, both of us feeling miserable failures. My fingers had gone black. The doctor then, muttering septicaemia. His laudanum potent but not potent enough. Quick amputation, at least.

And I fished with Captain Wright for the next six seasons.

Tonight, Doug Kelsey wants to tell us the fishery is gone.

Just like Captain Wright is gone.

Look now at my hand. Am I useless?

Are we useless?

To hell with the moratorium.

Our fish could be taken from us. Our seal hunt could be taken from us. In time of war, our young men have been taken from us. In the 1930s, our very right to vote was taken from us. I still don't know what birthright is. And I fear it, too, may have been taken. But I do know this: I have another hand. And I will use it.

Applause so loud out here. Like rain.

Aura?

My head –

97. CONTINUITY 8
COMMERCIAL BREAK

CLIENT: Port of Call

RUN: 28 07 2002-TFN, 1 x 30

SALES: Ralph Abbott

WRITER: N. Wright / on file

INSTRUCTIONS: Re-cut and replace. Please read exactly as written. Client wants "merchants," not "salespeople." — nw

It is a tradition in St. John's to expect the finer things, a tradition some of us may question. But when the finer things are not just expected but easily found, then one knows the tradition is sound. You will bask in this tradition at Port of Call on Water Street, where knowledgeable and experienced merchants are ready to assist you. Port of Call imports the finest from England, from tea to the china cups you serve it in. For the tradition of finer things, visit Port of Call, established in 1929. Port of Call, Water Street: make it your next port of call.

98. THE DEED
in which Nichole Wright signs a form and asks a question.

May 21, 2008

Once home to some merchant family or another, the Grant-Mainwaring Building on Forest Road now sheltered Gosse, Milley, Rideout and Tiller Law Offices. Hidden air conditioning cooled the waiting room – likely once a parlour – and someone had dusted the fake plants. Hydraulic doors, elevators and wheelchair ramps, new crown moulding, original fireplaces, like this sealed one here, tarnished firepoker, painted-over stonework ...

A receptionist clicked rapidly on her laptop.

Woodsmoke. Birch. William Wright's preferred fuel. Sometimes when I caught the scent, in October or in cold late springs, melancholy buried me. Like some complicit spruce shot turpentine at me, weighted me, so I'd fall back into a waiting crack in the birch. God help you with cloven birch, with the papery bark weaving round your mouth. Hard wood, that.

—Miss Wright?

First I nodded, studying my toes, but then I stood up and looked the receptionist in the eye. —*Ms*. Wright, actually.

She bent her knees a bit in a truncated curtsy. Deep laugh lines marked her face beneath the sunlamp tan. —Mr. Gosse insists on the old styles of courtesy in here. Says traditions are traditions for a reason. All the girls are *Miss*. This way please, Miss Wright.

Randall Gosse. A name I'd heard twice growing up, my grandfather once cursing him in a dark room when he thought himself alone, and once begging him for something on the telephone while I ate an apple. My grandfather interrupted his petition with a reminder to me to chew each bite thirty times.

The fireplace in Gosse's office also stood empty and cold. Round patches over the old pneumatic tube pathways had cracked and now flaked. Gosse himself, three days older than the fire rocks at Port au Mal, dry skin crumbling like the plaster seals overhead, sat behind a large desk – solid oak, I guessed, two hundred pounds, fifty of that varnish. Gosse's brown eyes, grotesquely enlarged by the lenses of his spectacles, shone worse than the desk.

He sneezed, blew his nose on a silk hanky. —Excuse me, Miss Wright. Allergies.

—Is it settled?

—My allergies are chronic, I'm afraid. Each spring –

—I mean the land.

The land, you senile zombie, stinking of salt and Ben-Gay, propped up with low-dose Aspirin and your mortgaged soul. Here, try some of my lithium, do you a world of good.

If I were filming Marlowe's *Dr. Faustus*, I'd set old Fausty dragged to hell through that fireplace – mantled with beach rocks and chalk rocks and photos of Sir Richard Squires, Prime Minister Jack Best, Sir Michael Grant-Mainwaring, and Jack Best again in apparent conference with Minister Canning and Deputy Minister William Wright. Take one of those chalk rocks, crack it open, split the rock to reveal that copper-ringed sky, then take that powdery sharp whiteness to the floor and draw a pentagram.

Gosse put his hanky in a pocket. —The good reverend agreed to the price.

—And the time limit?

—I have your cheque right here. He wants to expand the church. Spiritual demand is peaking in these days of alienation, he tells me. I just nod and smile, of course. Three services every Sunday. Morning and afternoon services will be broadcast on a private signal. I understand one may listen in one's car on the parking lot. Drive-in worship, he calls it.

—Still has evening service?

—The reverend says evening is his favourite.

So my useless piece of land, last scrap of the old Wright family fortune, a few acres of rock and bog and one crumbling hearth, worth maybe five grand when it was willed to me, would now be settled by the metastasis of colony: the Church of Prevenient Grace and the End of Things.

Sins of the fathers visited on the grandchildren.

I studied the survey, the map: lines, numbers. I could never have shown someone else the land. I couldn't fucking *find* it. I looked hard for the hearth back there in 2005, but I ended up lounging on some big rock like a couch instead. Don't recall a whole lot of that day – debris of the plane, and that creaking white-haired ... Dr. Miller thought I may have hallucinated the old man, thought my literary mind desired an ancient mariner. I doubt hallucinations could leave outgoing call records on my cell phone.

I turned pages, read clauses. Gosse passed me a pen.

Evening service, unlit.

I signed away the land.

Gosse smiled, somehow. On an uncharted wavelength, his face must have creaked like his chair. —A pang of regret is normal, Miss Wright, especially for a piece of land so long in the family name.

Like I'd ever have built in Port au Mal. Rooted in St. John's now, as snotty a townie as they come, brogue reclaimed – or it reclaimed me – that high and nasal grand way of talking, aspirations and *ing*s intact, *you* not *ya* but the occasional *ye*. Three years of lithium, steady job at the Admiral's Rooms Museums, publicity agent and, just this month, assistant curator for an exhibit of three new paintings by Gabriel Furey and the collected work of the late Claire Furey.

Gabriel might miss the opening. He didn't want to cancel his weekly art class at the Penitentiary, but the Minister of Tourism, Recreation and Culture could not make the opening any other night, and of course with the funding regulations we couldn't open without the Minister on hand. I'd found all this out while lobbying to get the opening date changed, even though Gabriel had told me not to bother – he didn't like crowds. Maddening how he wouldn't let me help him. Just like Claire.

—Miss Wright?

—Ms.

—I'm struck by your resemblance to your grandfather. Your brow, your eyes. I knew William for years. In fact, I drew up the original deed for your land.

I counted to ten, to twenty-five, aching for the Valium in my pocket, but no way in salt-frothing hell would I slip pills under my tongue in front of Randall Gosse.

Gosse cleared his throat. —A late gift from your grandfather, then. From the way he spoke of you, I know he must have been a loving man.

Between Gosse's index finger and thumb, up near his right temple: a cheque for sixty thousand dollars.

I met the lawyer's gaze. —Compensation?

ACKNOWLEDGEMENTS

This book rattled round my head for about eight years. The story of my great-uncle, Joseph L. Butler, crashing his plane while looking for a lost child rattled around a lot longer.

I know – VOIC Radio looks a bit like VOCM Radio. And yeah, I know, some people will wonder – not you, of course, but some people – if the Wrights are a mirror of my Butler relatives, or if Nichole Wright is based on me. Would you believe I made it up?

Deep and warmest thanks, as ever, to my husband, David, our daughters, Madeleine and Alexandra, to the rest of my family for their kind support. It means more than I can say.

Thanks to my various Butler relatives who recognize that this book, while tap-rooted in history, is a work of fiction.

Thanks as well to Killick Press for their patient belief in this project. To Ed Kavanagh, for yet another hard edit, and Leslie Vryenhoek for her sharp eyes and intellect. Jeff Bursey, Gary Butler (no relation) and Richard Cumyn for thoughtful commentary on earlier drafts. Paddy Moore for another deadly-wicked cover. Shelley Andrews. Judy Bowman. Michael Crummey. Amelia Curran. Dorinda Glover (no, not Masterson). Lisa Gushue. Joel Thomas Hynes. Stephanie Kinsella. Ruth Lawrence. John Murphy. George Murray. Jody Sparkes. Lee Thompson. Sara Tilley. Doug Underhill. Kelli Underhill. Shoshanna Wingate. Everyone I ever worked with at VOCM-Radio Newfoundland and Steele Communications.

Hey Rosetta!'s song "open arms" appears on their album *into your lungs (and around into your heart and on through your blood).* Epigraph used with permission.

Amelia Curran's song "Scattered and Small" appears on her album *War Brides.* Epigraph and chapter titles "'Scattered and small' 1" and "'Scattered and small' 2" used with permission.

I am indebted to Michael Eidenmuller, owner of www.americanrhetoric.com, for his transcript of the July 9, 1954 sitting of the Army-McCarthy Hearings. Excerpts used with permission.

I wish Albert Furneaux's treatment in "Wound stripe 2" had no precedent. Historian Ben Shephard's book *A War of Nerves*, Jonathan Cape 2000, details similar – and worse – situations.

The poem read in the background at Far Flung in "Uncommon kindness 1" is "Chapel Street Torque," by Michael Crummey. "Chapel Street Torque" appears in *Salvage*, McLelland and Stewart 2002. I borrowed from that poem in a few other places, too. Additional thanks to Michael for describing, in detail, his former house on Chapel Street.

Unofficial soundtrack: Amelia Curran, *War Brides*; Ani diFranco, *Canon*; Steve Earle, *Washington Square Serenade*; Blair Harvey, *Gutter Be Gutted*; Hey Rosetta!, *into your lungs (and around into your heart and on through your blood)*; Madviolet, *Worry the Jury*; Sinéad O'Connor, *The Lion and the Cobra*; Dolores O'Riordan, *Are You Listening?*